GRIM SORCERY
Deadly Connections

by

B. J. Jones
&
Sofia C. Simões

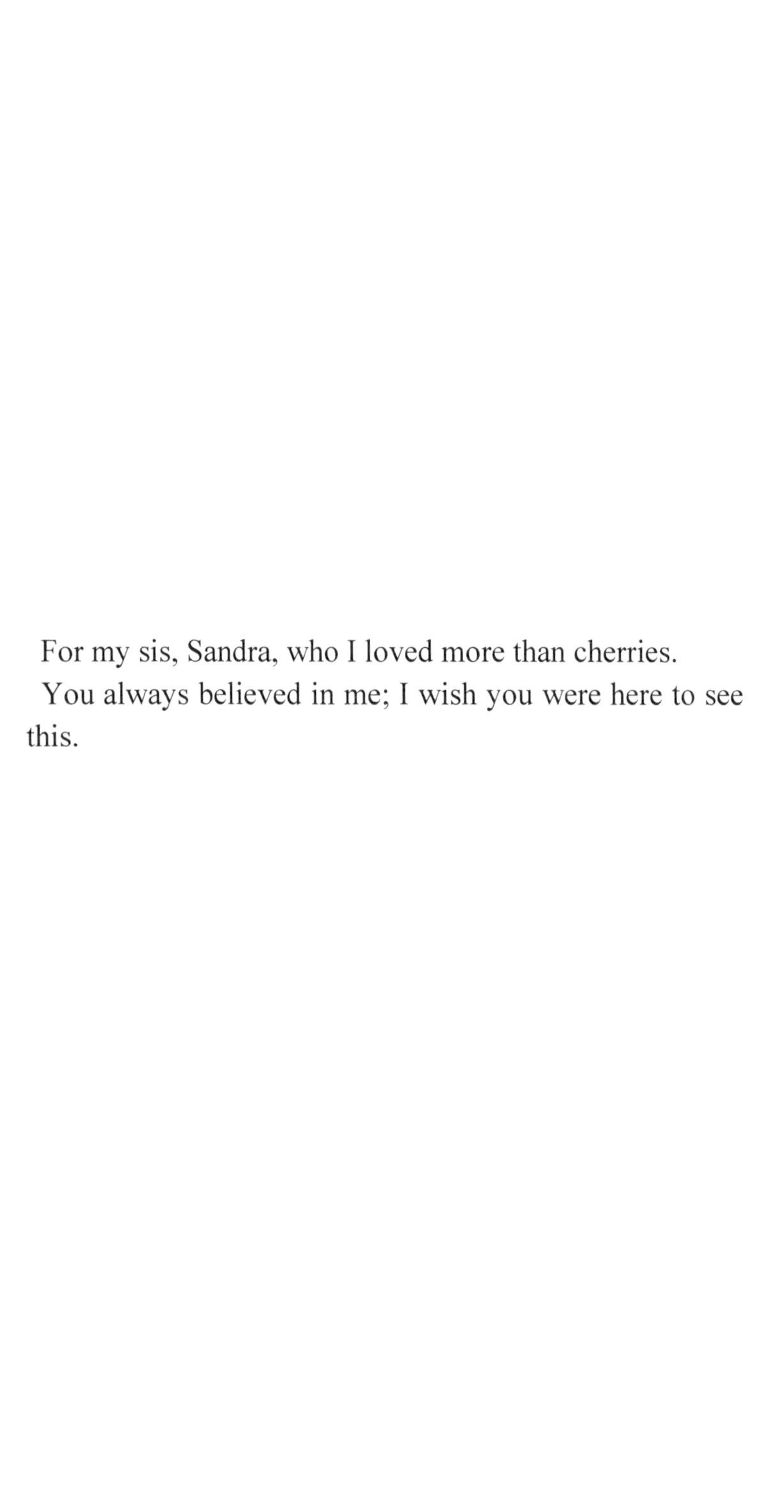

For my sis, Sandra, who I loved more than cherries.
You always believed in me; I wish you were here to see this.

Contact the publisher for more information:
www.queensbrairpress.com
queensbriarpress@gmail.com

ISBN: 979-8-9866658-3-2
Cover Design by: Sofia C. Simões
Editing by: Tara (Between the Lines Editing Services)
Formatting by: Sofia C. Simões

IMPORTANT NOTES
Triggering Warnings

This dark fiction contains various triggering situations, such as graphic violence, graphic language, death and near-death situations, child abuse, torture, blood/gore, and explicit sexual situations.

Liz

I'm a dark sorceress. Sure, I might look like the cute - more like the hot - blonde girl next door. I might even sound cute, until I threaten to eviscerate you for daring to treat me like that girl. I don't have family, friends, or love interests. Not anymore. But that doesn't mean I've forgotten promises made long ago when I did have all of those. One promise made was to keep her safe, and I left her with someone who would do just that, until he couldn't anymore. I need to find out what happened to the soldier who was once something more to me.

I prefer to avoid connecting with other peoples' visions or thoughts. You see, it's not only what the people see, but I also connect to their feelings. Ugh, I hate feelings. I learned long ago that feelings make you weak, and I have been disconnecting from mine ever since. I'm still working on it. I feel the power magic brings, and it feels freaking awesome. Ironically, I started enjoying life after I left the human whose death I now want to avenge. Because of that human, I was accepting—no, asking—to connect to a vision. The human's name was Daniel Costa. So, you know, I don't do this lightly. I needed to see who did this. I wanted to understand why.

Sophie Smith was my childhood best friend. She trusted me then, and she still does, for some twisted reason. She allowed the connection, even though I expected her to fight me. I don't feel strong emotions, but Soph does, deeply. Someone murdered the man Sophie loved, and her visions had shown her every detail. She relived the event every time she touched something of his. I haven't wanted that attachment to anyone since I was a teen. I avoided things like this because these sentiments were a weakness. When we connected, it was not easy on her or me. The moment her feelings crashed into me it was like a sword through my heart. Despair and raw pain wove their way through my chest. I silently cursed Soph for the unwelcome feelings I had to endure to find out what had happened.

Sophie's vision filled me with rage, and I welcomed that emotion like an old friend. The familiar-looking blond witch hit Daniel with a magic blast intended to hurt. I recognized the asshole's voice as well. He demanded that Daniel tell him where to find the witch who bore the curse. He was asking Daniel where to find Sophie.

Tempest Griffin, that freaking bastard! Was it Temp who did this? A force pushed me away before Temp's death curse hit Daniel, but I had seen enough. Sophie had broken the connection. She could not bear to go through it again.

Without noticing, I let out an angry "son-of-a-bitch" before I composed myself. I hated these connections; it was hard to separate my controlled feelings from the chaotic emotions of the other person. It was Temp, that pathetic sample of a witch! I would make him pay, and it would be fun. He killed what was once mine, my human, and I would make him burn for it. Once upon a time, that human,

Daniel, had shown me more compassion than anyone in my entire existence.

Finding Temp would be easy; I could do it since the first time we fucked. All I had to do was create a portal to a who instead of to a where. But that frog was intelligent and powerful. Looking at Sophie, a thought came to me: her powers! This gave me a plan B; if my power was not enough, mine and hers together would make me unstoppable. Well, maybe not invincible, but a freaking badass anyway. I liked plans; I didn't get to be this powerful just by chance. I knew Sophie would agree, she wanted Daniel Costa back, but revenge was the next best thing.

Sophie's powers were foreign to me; they seemed connected to her emotions, and strangely, the grief of the last few days had given her an extra boost. She willingly gave me the extra power. It filled me with an energy I had never felt. It was different from my magic, but it mingled with mine like spice in wine. I had craved that power since I accepted the dark magic inside me. I felt freaking unstoppable, just like I thought I would. I assured her Dan's killer would suffer as I created the portal to his location. I stepped into the darkness of the doorway I'd created, wanting nothing more than to make Temp suffer for making a fool out of me… For taking what was mine.

Temp was hiding in a forest, of course. How original. The energy created by me rolling my eyes, would have been enough to burn the entire forest to the ground. I heard him speaking to someone. His voice was a sound that once brought lust to my core. I mean, a girl has needs. Temp was torturing some poor guy, not that I cared about that. It wasn't something I haven't done before. He wanted to find

Sophie. Good luck with that now that I was there! I walked toward the witch I'd shared my bed–floor, wall, well, everywhere–with, smirking at the thought of killing him slowly. I glanced at the man he was questioning. Red hair, beaten, he was doing a good job holding on to life. Not many people do.

"You lost your touch, frog brain. You can't even make someone tell you the truth," I teased; it was too easy to push Temp. "Pathetic, if you ask me."

"You were always too smart for your own good," Temp answered, smirking. "I expected a little more time after I killed...your little human toy." That wicked smile that once meant we would fuck hard now just brought hate. "Sorry. My bad!"

"You're not getting close to that witch," I said confidently, now close enough to him to see his face clearly. "But it would be fun to watch you try. You will pay for what you've done, asshole!"

Temp grabbed me by my neck and pushed me hard against the nearest tree. My mind held no fear; I was the one with the power here. I was Sorceress Key, and no mere warlock would harm me. Once this had been foreplay, now it was another kind of danger.

"Will I? What are you gonna do about it?" Temp smirked, thinking he was in charge. "Lizzie, Lizzie. You should know by now I always get what I want. And you, dumb little witch, confirmed you know who he is. I will get that friend of yours!"

No one calls me Lizzie! Not since I chose black magic, not since I broke up with the human, Daniel. And no one calls me dumb!

"Adorable. Just adorable how you thought I would allow you to touch me if I couldn't end you right here." I took a deep breath, put my hand up, invoking a lilac flame, and sent it straight to the witch's chest. "That human's name was Daniel, and he was your first mistake. Touching me was your last one!"

The flames licked their way up Temp's body, and he lost his grip on my neck. I smirked while I watched him try to invoke all kinds of incantations and fail with every single one. Who's the dumb witch now? He wasn't getting out of this alive. Insurance meant, never sleep with–or get close to–anyone, unless you could make them vulnerable to your power. Don't ever be the victim! That had been my life motto since I gave up trying to be human.

I stayed to watch him burn. After a moment, I noticed two men there instead of one. The tortured man was still tied to the tree, and someone else was trying to help him. I'd felt a little magic from the tortured man, but it was getting weaker; he was dying. The other man had his back to me, but I could see red hair. I assumed they were related.

Suddenly, the cold air made my skin crawl, and a dark figure materialized near Tempest's body that was laying on the forest floor. Oh, great. The Grim Reaper had decided to show. Was this the piece of shit that took Daniel?

Alton

Have you ever had a nightmare that seemed so realistic that you were sure it happened? In my case, it had. Alias called and asked me to meet him at an office owned by my ex-boyfriend, Pedro. He didn't say why, but I trusted him. He was going through a bad breakup, and I knew Alaric would have no sympathy for him. I owned a small piece of Al's soul, but I got the lion's share of his emotions. It's funny that the guys chose Alaric over me, and I was the one who loved them all. I was a magical clone. I shouldn't even exist, but Sorcerer Alaric Weird doesn't play by anyone's rules but his own. He gave me a part of himself, which is why I can say he loves me, if you ask, though he would deny loving anyone.

If all the "Al" names confuse you, blame Alphonse, our dad. Dad named everyone in the family after himself. This included the children that weren't even his blood and their parents whom Dad rescued from a saucer crash. In case you didn't know, all Weirds, except Dad himself, are aliens. Alena and Alien (his name was a joke that stuck) were the only crash survivors. Dad used his only power (prognostication) to find and hide them from his scientist colleagues. Dad was the 'Al' until Alaric was born; he became the only Al, thanks to Alias's speech impediment, due to his nonretractable vampire fangs. So, you know most of my family's dirty secrets. Well, except the fact that Alias was the one who killed me, and anyone else who dared the love Alaric. He was angry at Al because his girlfriend left him. You might wonder why he didn't just kill Al. Simple, he loved him more than all of us ever could.

DEADLY CONNECTIONS

I still trusted Alias when I stepped out of that elevator and saw what he had done. I might not be a natural person, but in my mind, he was my brother. He killed all the men who loved us. He ripped their hearts out and ate them. It wasn't enough to just drain their blood. Al was a necromancer. He learned it from the Reaper, standing in the corner laughing maniacally. Had I known he planned to kill me, I would never have brought my fiancé along. Alias had a special hell planned for me because I was magically and mentally connected to Al.

Alias drained me to near death, making me watch as he did the same to my pregnant fiancé. We had just had our first neonatal appointment. I was going to be a father. Me! A person who was never born or had a childhood. I was going to be a father of triplets. I watched as Alias drained my love and discarded her like trash. It was a relief when he finished me off. I didn't want to live without her, or them. I was cheated out of life because Alias held a grudge against my maker, Al.

Al saved my soul from being taken by the Reaper. I never signed a contract, but I was created after Al had agreed to become a servant of death. I don't know everything that happened, but I did know Rainn, my girl, shot Alias after he left her for dead. It wasn't that easy to kill a vampire, unfortunately. Al had to finish him off by ripping out his heart. The Reaper offered to raise one of us, but I think I mentioned that Al played by his own rules. He used necromancy to return life to my Rainn and our babies. It was his last act of love for me, and I will always be grateful. He would hate me using the word 'love'. He did everything he could to avoid all emotional ties to anyone, but I knew he felt, he couldn't hide it from me. I had all his memories from the past.

After my death, I lived inside Al's head for months, occasionally taking over when he slept. I was there for appointments, but though I looked the same to Rainn, she knew I was in Al's body. Al didn't love her. If anything, Al despised her. He wanted to bring Alias back; he wanted his big brother. I didn't feel any love for Alias, which should have been how Al felt too.

Alias's soul was taken to the Shadowlands, the home of the Reapers. Al found a way to join Alias in the Shadowlands after many attempts to call him out. You see, it takes three things to return a body to life: a person's heart, a death, and a willing soul. Alias didn't want to return to life. He and Al had been promised a place among the Grims, and he craved that fate. To join Alias, Al's soul had to leave his body; that was where I came in. His body was mine, and he had the freedom to find the asshole that killed me.

I managed to spend two blissful weeks with the woman I loved as we prepared for the birth of our baby girls. Unfortunately, everything was lost on the day of their birth. Finding our father tied to a tree, dying, was the worst. Helping a total stranger kill the Reaper who owned Al's and Alias's souls, meant the two of them joined me. I lost control of the body that wasn't mine, and worse, I was forced to share that body with my killer. I've seen my babies and held them but won't be there for them. Al is in control, and I have no heart, body, or life. I would be better off dead. At least if I was dead, I could get away from the man who killed me.

Alphonse

My name was Alphonse Weird. I'd come from a long line of Wizards and Sorcerers, but I was not either. I was a scientist and a seer. I could see the future. That may sound like an incredible power, but it was a curse. Many centuries ago, a sorcerer cursed one of my ancestors. The curse allowed her to see the past, present, and future. It also drove her insane. The insanity never stopped others from coveting the curse. Our coven wiped out my whole family to stop our line from inheriting the curse of the Wyrds. I knew that sounded weird, but if the name fit. Some people's curse was another's blessing. It was still a curse to me.

I was saved from death by my lack of magic, and my cute face. I was less than two years old when the extermination happened. None of that is significant. I just thought I would tell you how I managed to live before telling you how I died. I'm not a ghost, I am writing this while still breathing, but for me, I watched myself die over and over for years. I knew this story all too well. Visions of the future sounded fun until you watched yourself die.

One thing you learned about the future is that changing it can lead to worse consequences. This began with a bloodline curse, not mine, but someone else's. I hadn't known at the time, that my family's involvement in removing that curse would directly cause my death. This hasn't stopped me, of course, but this time if I had known what I would be getting my family into…

That doesn't matter; we transferred the curse from Sophie Smith to her fiancé, Daniel Costa. He was so crazy in love he would have done anything for that woman, even die. He didn't die from the curse, though. I caused his death; me and my curse.

My day had started so typically, but that was because I wanted it that way. If you could choose what to do on the last day of your life, you'd probably think you would go out and party. I spent the day saying goodbye to my friends and family. Well, I wrote letters to some of them. My children wouldn't understand why I did what I did. Only Al would understand, though I know he will fight his death like he always has.

Tempest Griffin, a high-level mage, nearly powerful enough to be a sorcerer, found me outside the lab as I was leaving work. My eldest son had managed to dampen his fear, but I'd never been able to control any emotion. I was afraid of Temp, but I was more fearful of what would happen if he didn't find me. She couldn't be found. She couldn't be killed. She couldn't be used. Sophie Smith was too dangerous and too precious for them. I couldn't see her future, which meant it wasn't written in stone. She would make her future for herself. I wouldn't be around to help any of them.

I didn't fight Temp when he came at me. He cast a sleep spell on me to keep me from running, but you can't run from the Reaper anyway; he would find you anywhere and any when. I was tied to a tree in the forest when I came to. Temp was standing in front of me, smiling like a cat. I was not a brave man, but I was not stupid, either. I knew what

Temp wanted from me, and I knew if I gave it to him, he would torture me and kill me anyway. I'd spent many months trying to find a way out of this, but sometimes the more you try to change a vision, the more you make it likely to happen. I thought transferring the curse would save Sophie and me. Instead, someone in my coven sold me out. Worse, it had to be someone who knew that I could see the future. That was a concise list. None of that mattered now. I was destined to die and couldn't do anything to prevent that. I could only thwart my killer's plans because today was not his day either.

He started the torture with magic, force magic because he didn't want to ruin his manicure, I assume. Strangely everything I knew about magic I learned from my eldest son, Alaric. The kid had to learn everything on his own because the best I could do was reheat my coffee, which took me decades to learn. I had no talent for spells, and my potion-making was more scientific than magical. Until now, being a magic null had saved my life.

I took the blows from Temp as best as I could. He didn't even bother asking a question until he softened me. It's not easy to shut your mouth when your ribs shatter audibly.

"You know what I want, Seer; tell me where I can find the mage who bears the curse. We know it has been awakened; my clients have felt its presence and the mage who bears it. You would be saving him from a painful death."

He had part of that right. The curse was meant to kill the mage as soon as their magic was awakened. It was a bloodline curse not unlike my own. My curse doesn't kill, but it drove the cursed mad. I was saved from the worst madness by being born a null. Still, seeing the future is enough to drive a person insane.

"You think that a few cracked ribs will make me give you what you want? I know I will die today."

He gut-punched me in answer to my stubbornness. It hurt, but it wasn't so bad that I couldn't hold out a little longer. I had to buy myself some more time. I had seen more than my death, and I couldn't allow Temp or any of his people to get hold of the prize they sought. There were rumors about the curse and the witch who held it. She would be a powerful tool in the wrong hands and a powerful ally in the right ones. The curse was meant to kill her, but she survived to become one of a kind.

"If you tell me now, old man, I will spare you the pain of torture and give you a quick death."

He wouldn't, and he knew that I knew he wouldn't. I had already seen this in my mind. I knew what I had to do and when I had to do it. I'd just never hurt an innocent before. Unlike my sons, I was not a killer. I couldn't even end the life of a spider.

I felt my body heating up like a fever, without chills. The mage was using magic to burn me from the inside. It hurt, but it wouldn't be fatal. I knew I could last for days like this, which wasn't in my vision. The burning made me wish for that quick death, though. I knew I was a coward, but I wanted it to stop. I wanted to rest and didn't want to die like this.

"Tell me the name of the one who holds the curse. I can find him with just a name, then I will finish this, and you will be free from pain. Maybe my boss will give you your life back. He can be very generous for a Reaper."

I knew Temp's boss. My son and stepson were trapped in his realm, or their souls were. He tricked them into signing a contract that gave them power in exchange for their souls. Yeah, I knew Grim; he would break the cardinal rule of Reapers and kill me. I was the last pureblood of a powerful extended line of mages and sorcerers. My children were all half-alien and so were overlooked by the magical community…well, all but Alaric. He put himself out there as the warlock of our clan. They thought he was weak as an alien born from a magic null, but he was more powerful than them. None of that mattered. I could feel my internal organs start to cook. I needed a break and to be alive to deliver a message. In my vision, this had been condensed, so I assumed the torture would be over quickly. The sun hadn't even gone down yet, and I was ready to die rather than endure this heat.

 "Daniel Costa," I gasped. "The one who bears the curse you seek is Daniel Costa." I felt terrible about sending Temp to Dan; he would kill him when he discovered that Dan was just a human. I didn't tell Temp a lie. Dan held the curse, but he was not the mage our enemies sought. I would willingly die to keep the secrets of Sophie Smith from Tempest Griffin.

He opened a portal for himself in front of me and stomped his way through. When it closed behind him, I was alone in the forest, tied to a tree, but at least the burning had stopped. I was thirsty and wished I had enough magic to grab water from the stream I could hear rushing down the mountain.

I passed out; I don't know for how long. When I woke, Temp was there, ready for round two and pissed off. He was pacing back and forth and talking to himself, probably on the phone. My thirst was worse, and I couldn't have told him anything then. Unfortunately, this wasn't the end of me. I would be enduring more torture because he didn't like the truth. Ask me a question, and I will give you the facts, but you must ask the right questions.

Temp was angry, so he didn't bother asking questions. He started throwing force magic at me, hitting me blow after blow with energy enough to cause pain but not death. I lost consciousness again at some point. When I woke, I could hear two people talking. I must have been out a long time; I wasn't feeling pain, which was always a bad sign. I was numb and cold, and I must have lost some blood. The tight ropes were probably the only things keeping me from bleeding to death.

"You lost your touch, frog brain. You can't even make someone tell you the truth," a female voice said. "Pathetic if you ask me," she continued.

"You were always too smart for your own good," Temp answered, smirking. "I expected a little more time after I killed...your little human toy."

"Sorry. My bad!" Liz said with sarcasm.

Elizabeth Key was the first guest to arrive at my party. She was the most important. I could barely hold consciousness but used my strength to stay awake. I had a message to deliver.

"You're not getting close to that witch," Liz said confidently. "But it would be fun to watch you try. You will pay for what you've done!" Temp grabbed her by the neck, pushing her hard against the nearest tree. It almost looked like foreplay between lovers.

"Will I? What are you gonna do about it?" Temp smirked, thinking he was in charge. "Lizzie, Lizzie. You should know by now I always get what I want. And you, dumb little witch, confirmed you know who he is. I will get that friend of yours!"

Liz was fuming, and I'm sure it was because she hated being called Lizzie. I had already seen Temp's death, and that was the comment that caused it. He was too cocky for his own good.

"Adorable. Just adorable how you thought I would allow you to touch me if I couldn't end you right here." Liz took a deep breath, put her hand up, invoking a lilac flame, and sent it straight to Temp's chest.

"That human's name was Daniel, and he was your first mistake. Touching me, was your last one!" The purple flames rose on Temp's body, and he let go of Liz and stumble back. The fire hadn't touched her even though she stood beside it. His death called the second player to the game. He called himself 'Grim,' AKA the Grim Reaper, just because he was boring. Most of them had names they chose for themselves, or ones assigned to them to describe their deeds. Grim brought a cold chill which got Liz's attention. This Grim was Temp's boss and the Grim who held my son and stepson hostage. I wasn't selfless; I wanted Alaric whole again. I needed them both free of the torment. I didn't need a Grim to return from the grave. I had a necromancer for a son.

The Grim ignored Liz and me. He glided to the smoldering body of Tempest Griffin. It was clear from the actions of the Grim that he planned to restore the fallen Temp to life. Liz noticed this too, and she began her attack. She was trying to keep Grim from resurrecting Temp, but she was hurting the Reaper.

15

Liz was too busy to notice the final arrival of my son Alton. He was the magical clone of Alaric, but he was still my son, my blood. He saw me and rushed to my aid. He tried to heal me, but he couldn't, not in the body he was in. Alton had been killed months earlier by my stepson Alias. In Alaric's body, he couldn't heal. Something about taking on dark powers changes a person physically, mentally, and emotionally. Alton was in a rental body since his body had been burned to charcoal. Alaric saved Alton from being reaped, but that act came with a price. Death does not like to be cheated, but I planned to do something worse than cheat.

I tried to say the words to Liz that would make her do more than just knock the Grim away from Temp. He was playing with her, laughing at her. She was getting angry, but not angry enough. I had to use Alton to get my message to her; I could feel my life draining away as Alton worked to free me. We had a connection, Alton and I, that I could never have with Alaric. It wasn't just that my son had never embraced his alien side; he couldn't connect with someone like me. His brain wasn't wired like mine anymore, not since he went dark. Alton was created before Alaric went full dark. He had everything Al had and more. I never said it to him, but he was more son to me than Alaric.

"Alton, tell her to kill the Grim and save Dan; show her!" I said to him in my mind. I sent him the vision of Liz wielding the scythe and slaying the Reaper. She needed only to knock it out of his hand. Alton would use his magic to send it to her. She had the power to do it, and I knew she could wield the scythe; I had seen her do it.

My vision was going black, and it was hard to breathe. The tunnel was darkening, and I couldn't feel anything but cold emptiness. Alton was still trying to heal me, but his body was fighting the magic. He suddenly stopped. I could only assume it was to do as I asked. He would make a mental connection with Liz and show her what I showed him. She would hear my words in her head and see her path. My task here was over; I wouldn't see the outcome of this battle with my own eyes.

I died while Alton was helping Liz with the Grim. I was always told that the last vision I would ever have would be my death, but this vision carried on. It was strange the first few times, watching my body slump and my breath leave. Other ugly things happen when you die, but I won't mention them here.

Liz used the Grim's scythe against him, cutting his head clean from his body. The sight took me away from myself, from my corpse. Alton was on his knees, crying and bleeding. He must have cut himself on whatever he used to cut the ropes.

Liz was glowing with the power of the Grim, but the scythe was fighting her now. It allowed her to use it to kill its master, but it needed death. Living beings could be killed just by touching a Reaper's scythe. Liz knew what to do; I had shown her in the vision. It was the least I could do for him since I had caused his death.

She made a portal and levitated the body of Daniel Costa through the opening. He was already dressed for his funeral; that would never happen now. She held a hand over Dan's chest and spoke some words in Latin. My knowledge of Latin consisted mainly of names for flora and fauna. I never got into the conversational side of it and had no use for the magical side. Whatever Liz said, it caused the body of Daniel Costa to rise and for him to take a deep breath. She placed the scythe on his chest and wrapped his hands over the handle. He sat up, gripping the weapon tightly. His eyes were black as coal, and the veins on his face and neck had turned black too. He didn't look like the young man I remembered. He looked like a nightmare in the shape of Dan. He looked confused, but he held the scythe as if he was born to it…which in a way, he was.

Liz turned to Alton and nodded her head in thanks or respect. He returned the nod, but the fog was so thick I doubted either of them could see. Alton scooped up my body and left the forest. That is where my vision ended. I couldn't tell you what happened to my soul. The things I saw after my death were for my children to know, not you. I may have helped Elizabeth Key get some vengeance and return Dan from the grave, but I didn't do anyone any favors. These events would put a mark on them that wouldn't end until they joined me in actual death. The Grims would hate their newest recruit because he wasn't going to be one to follow the rules. He might follow orders, but he would follow them his way. Reapers can't see the future, not even their own, but I could, and their future is grim. My only regret, in the end, is that I wouldn't get to hold my three granddaughters. They were born the day I died.

Deathripper

The word *summon* invoked a little nervousness, maybe mild anxiety, when I heard it. You were summoned to the principal's office, summoned to the boss's office, called to your superior officer's office, and summoned to court. This summons didn't give me anxiety; it gave me rage. How dare these jokers in their little black bathrobes call me to heel. Okay, so I hadn't been a Grim long. I didn't know that much about the job. I didn't even know my name. I woke to find a sorceress handing me a scythe and telling me I was a Grim Reaper. My scythe wanted to taste Reaper blood, and they had summoned me to a full-course banquet! Do you know the worst part? The freaking thing talked to me! I mean the scythe, of course. It whispered in so many languages that I didn't understand, but mostly it told me it wanted their Reaper blood.

I appeared in the center of a circle in a white room, and a little investigation with my scythe told me that a magic circle was keeping me in place; it made pretty sparks. The fact that they put me in a protective circle told me something even better; they were afraid of me. I was used to having people respect me, or I thought I was used to it. Nothing made sense in my head, but I remembered uniforms and soldiers all obeying my orders. These ragged wannabes wouldn't stand a chance against any soldiers under my command. Probably thousands were surrounding the circle. Less than thirty were seated on a semi-circular dais in front of me. Centered above and behind them was one dude in a less tattered robe. I guess he was the Grand Puba of this cult of death. He had two seats to the right and left of him, and one was empty. Interesting. The booming voice of the one on the highest chair made my knees tremble, but not in fear, more like how you feel at a deafening rock concert. I should have brought some ear protection for that bass.

"Human, you stand before The Omega Council! Kneel before your Superiors…human!"

"Man, this is the twenty-first century, and you don't even rank a salute. You got any stars, stripes, rank bars, or anything that says, 'hey, this dude is your boss'? How do I know that you are my superior? I don't bow to a bunch of assholes in their bathrobes unless I'm in a doJo!"

Yep, I was sure I had been in the military. I don't remember what I did in the military, but I know that these jokers needed better organization to beat me. I wouldn't go into battle with them at my back; they would stab me sooner than any enemy. They all needed a new wardrobe and a shower too. The whole place stank like rotten meat. They all seemed to be confused by my lack of fear. They were whispering at each other, and it sounded like a windstorm. I knew how to take orders and give them, but these jokers didn't know the first thing about discipline.

"Listen, boys and girls, just give me the employee handbook, and I'll study it over coffee. It shouldn't be too difficult. I show up when someone dies, and I use this little shaver to send them on their way to heaven, hell, or wherever…right?"

"Insolence!" the Grand Puba boomed.

"Dude, have you ever thought of being a lead singer for a death metal band? You seriously have the pipes. No microphone needed."

"You will surrender the Deathripper Scythe!"

"Deathripper, I like that," I said to the scythe. He told me it was a good name since we didn't know our own. We were Deathripper, and these assholes should be bowing to us.

"You will surrender the scythe and be judged, usurper!"

"Oh, that is where you are wrong, man. Ripper and I are going to go home, wherever that is. We have not broken any rules, and you have nothing to hold us on. I may be new, but I know my rights."

"End him and take the scythe; we have worthy candidates waiting!"

Ripper let me know that this was where the fun began. The circle dropped with an audible pop. They sent the pawns at me first, young ones like me, with puny little scythes. I cut them down quickly by spinning around with the scythe. No one taught them how to fight; they were gatherers, not hunters. I pretended I was in one of those fighting games, and my weapon was a scythe. Something told me I could do more than just stand in one place and pick them off as they came at me, so I started teleporting all over the place, taking them out one by one until I lost count; the scythe didn't. Every grim killed put a mark on the handle. Cool! My scythe was counting victims.

When I started having fun, they sent me to the penalty box or maybe my home. Ripper seemed to think it was home. He levitated himself to a couple of hooks covered in black velvet. The decor wasn't to my taste, but it was serviceable. It was just a vast library. There was a desk, a chair, and a fireplace that looked like it had never seen a fire. My senses told me that this was it; home. There was no door, no windows, but it wasn't a prison. I knew because I tried popping into the real world. When I thought of the natural world, I appeared at this house on the beach. I didn't know what drew me there, but I was pretty sure I knew who. She was gorgeous in every way, like an angel with black hair and green eyes. She had a deep tan from the sun and wore black, even now, when she slept. There were pills on a nightstand next to her bed. A tissue box and red, swollen eyes told me she had been crying. My heart ached for her, which I thought was interesting. I was dead, but someone hadn't told my body that. I didn't feel hungry or tired, but I could feel the ache of emotion. I wondered if I could feel pain and pleasure. My little soldier told me that he thought we could feel good. Maybe it was just the woman looking sadly beautiful, a weeping angel.

I heard a baby cry, and it drew me to the room across the hall. A small toddler in a crib was rubbing her tiny fists over her eyes. She stopped crying when she saw me. She had dark hair like the woman, but her eyes were a color that looked so familiar. I picked her up and rocked her. She seemed to like me. When her eyes started to close, I slipped her back under the thin blanket and pulled it up under her arms. It was a warm night, but a breeze came in from an open window.

"Why am I not surprised to see you here?" I heard a soft feminine voice ask. She sounded a lot sweeter than I knew she was. Her name was Elizabeth Key, and she was the reason I had the scythe.

"I don't know where 'here' is, or why I came here when I thought of the real world. Why are you here, Sorceress?"

"I am here to see who tripped my wards. If she sees you here, it will only make things worse. You're dead; you need to stay that way." The sorceress was pointing at the angel with tear-swollen eyes. I desperately wanted to know her name.

The Sorceress waved a hand in the air and fucking banished me to the place I assumed was home. It made me feel like some demon or something. It made me angry that everyone could make me go where I didn't want and then forbid me from going where I wanted to go.

I looked at the scythe sleeping on the wall. Ripper didn't need to sleep, but he liked to dream. He was dreaming of killing those in the robes. I could feel his hate for them and the need to taste their blood. I may have been going crazy, but I liked my new friend Ripper. If I were to do this job for eternity, I would have to break a few eggs. Just thinking about that made me hungry for an omelet and coffee. I tried to concentrate on the omelet, and I ended up materializing in front of an IHOP.

I went inside and waited to be seated. There were people all over, but they kept walking past me like I wasn't there. That was starting to piss me off. I walked up to a waitress and cleared my throat to get attention. She didn't even look at me. Instead, she walked through me like I wasn't even there, as if I were a ghost. I could feel my heart beating; the chill of the air conditioner was making the hair on my arms stand erect. I was there, but I wasn't corporeal. I really could have used that handbook. They didn't want me to know what to do, probably because I would do it right. I returned to my cage that wasn't a prison and sulked like a spoiled child. I couldn't get food, so I couldn't get a drink unless I stole one. I had never done anything illegal in my life; I drove without a license once, but that was different.

I started complaining to Ripper, and he twisted to point at the desk. A panel popped out and behind was a drawer. There was a dusty bottle of Jack Daniel's in there. With my drink sorted, I levitated a book off the shelf. The author had filled it with gibberish and a few disturbing pictures. It was worthless to me unless I could run it through Google Translate. I needed a computer or a television, but I doubted I would get internet here. I had a feeling death would be less exciting than my life. Ripper told me not to worry; he had plans to keep us both entertained.

Meanwhile, I didn't think upper management would be happy just hiding me in the basement. It wouldn't take long before the bosses would become brave again and send more pawns. Ripper was excited, but I just wanted to sit and think of that dark-haired angel dressed in white, maybe wearing a white bikini. I felt more alive just thinking about her. I'm pretty sure I wouldn't be me, whoever I am, without her. The Sorceress told me I should stay away, and I knew she's right, but I liked feeling alive. It kind of sucked to be dead.

Al

Have you ever just hopped in the car and taken a drive, not going anywhere, just to end up in the last place you would ever want to be? I was there, Weird Manor, my parent's home in Inverness. The house's name made it sound like we were nobility or something, but my parents bought an old manor house in Scotland and decided to renovate it. My father's ancestors hailed from Scotland and Norway, where I got red hair and a tall, muscular frame. All of the Weirds in our line had red hair like mine. It's my eyes that set me apart from the others. I had lavender eyes, a sign of intense magic, so they told me. It's not like I knew much about my human side other than they were magical beings. My father was an orphan, and no one bothered to tell him about his family.

Alphonse was the last surviving, human Weird. My pointed ears and my analytical mind were from the extraterrestrial side. I was half alien; my mother hailed from a planet orbiting Proxima Centauri. I don't know much about their history either. I only knew that they liked to interfere in the lives of humans, and their favorite pastime was impregnating male humans and forcing them to bear their alien children. It happened more often on this planet than you knew. You'd think that would be enough to make me avoid all of them, but I'd driven to the home of three that sometimes I called my parents. Yeah, I had four parents growing up, which isn't only an alien thing. Polyamory isn't a big deal with them like it seemed on Earth.

Now, you were probably wondering where I drove from. Well, it was a little island in the south pacific you've probably never heard of, and I'm not going to tell you. The people who live there are like me, mostly. Either they are magic users or in the magical closet. You're probably also wondering how my little trip happened. It was magic. Actually, there were gateways all over the earth, natural portals to another realm. It's rare for a nonmagical human to stumble across one, and even uncommon to be able to activate it at the right time. I took five of these gateways from my home to Scotland, but taking a car didn't take much more energy than transporting myself there. I never learned how to make a direct portal like most magic users; maybe one day I'd understand how it was done. Until then, I could use the gates.

I wasn't looking forward to seeing Alien and Alena, my other parents. They had both been deeply in love with my father and were grieving. He wouldn't have wanted them to suffer, but he wasn't there to tell them to stop, and I wouldn't. I had no right to tell them how to feel, even if they tried to tell me how I should feel. Strong emotions were not my thing. I was half logical alien and half mage. The powers I got from dark magic made me a sociopath, sometimes a psychopath. My family thought I was a sociopath, a narcissist, and a general asshole; they were mostly correct.

My father knew exactly when he would die and where. He died to protect his family. I thought it was a waste of death, but what did I know? I wasn't the one who could see the future. Someone in our coven told the wrong people that my father could see the future. No one else knew that he bore the curse, especially not the ones who saved him from death as a baby. The Wyrd curse was something that others envied. Who wouldn't want to know the past without studying or knowing the future before it happens? My version was not as enviable, though many would kill for the power to spy on friends and foes alike.

Around two thousand years ago, my ancestor was cursed by an enemy. The curse allowed her to simultaneously see the past, present, and future. In case you were wondering, yes, it drove her insane. She was also the first known sorceress in the Wyrd family. The curse made her a valuable tool for the Sorceress who cursed her. It gave her visions like the Oracle of Delphi, only without inhaling a deadly gas. Also, unlike the natural seers, my ancestor was forced to procreate. With the first generation, triplets, the curse was split into three aspects of time. The girls were named for the Norns, the fate goddesses of the Nordic tribes. The details aren't as important as you'd think. The curse remained separated through the centuries, popping up randomly in each generation, until they mixed with Alien blood. My brother Len and I were the only Weirds to get the power.

I don't believe in fate, which is ironic, but there was a reason my rambling drive brought me here. Since I was sitting outside a medieval Manor house in a 2021 Tesla Model 3 (midnight silver metallic), I decided to stop creating attention and go inside. My father left a note for us on the day he died. By us, I mean Alton, my magical clone, Alias, my alien/vampire stepbrother, and myself, the family's only sorcerer. He most likely wrote one to all the siblings, even those not his blood. He was never one to show favoritism to one child.

I didn't get much further than the front gate when two red-headed toddlers assaulted me. My twins, or what I would be more apt to call my alien clones. They were mine in DNA only. My alien mother was obsessed with creating magical aliens. I was the first and the best of her experiments, but that didn't stop her from trying. Coraline and Corbin, my twins, loved spending time with the grandparents, and since their stepmother was busy with the triplets, we had agreed that the farm was a better place for them. I picked them up and carried them one in each arm. Cora was a perfect copy of my sister Alie; she looked as human as any toddler. Corbin refused to disguise himself. His skin was blue, a very inhuman color. A former lover of mine carried Corbin and Coraline after my alien mother abducted and impregnated him. Rainn's triplets were the fault of my magical clone, Alton. Something that should never have happened. He was supposed to be an ephemeral creation, and as far as I knew sterile. He was never supposed to fracture my soul and take an equal share.

Usually, when the children were around me, I allowed Alton to take control of my body. It was him they wanted to have hold them and dry their tears. He was the one who had the emotions to deal with family. I probably should explain that on the night my father died, I was not on this earthly plane. I was in the shadow-realm of the Grim Reapers…plural. My stepbrother/ex-husband (don't judge me) was also there in soul and spirit. When Elizabeth Key slayed the Reaper, I returned to my body. Alias followed me, leaving me with three souls in one body. It has gotten a little crowded at times. This made dissociative identity disorder look like biting nails. Not only did my personality change. Alton and I looked similar enough to fool your average person, but Alias and I were never of like minds or looks. When he was in charge, my eyes were green, my hair was brown, and I had a complete set of vampire fangs. Yeah, Alias was a living vampire, but when Rainn Rivers shot him in the head, giving him his first death, he became a vampire.

The twins had no idea that I was not Alton, my magical clone. I wasn't there for a friendly visit, but you could not explain that to toddlers, so I carried them both on my shoulders. I sat them on the worn sofa in the great room and turned to the woman who had walked up behind me, thinking she could surprise me. Polli's blue skin made the drab room seem brighter. Her alien form was much more attractive than her disguise. None of the extraterrestrial parents knew I could feel their alienness. I couldn't communicate with them in their heads, but their thoughts buzz in my head like a mosquito. I barely understood the spoken language, but I didn't need to. This alien woman was my mother, or creator, since my father had given birth to me. She hugged me, which surprised me. We didn't have that kind of relationship. We didn't have any kind of relationship. I was no more to her than the latest science experiment. Polli was grieving, too, in her way. Soon she would return to her home planet that orbited Proxima Centauri. I can't tell you what they call it, but it translates as "earth." Humanoids are highly predictable, regardless of their realm or planet.

"Alaric, you came for the letter?" Polli asked in a monotonous tone.

That she could tell me from the two other souls in my head was interesting since Alton looked and behaved like me. She may have been grieving, but aliens are not as emotional as humans. I didn't have to hide that I was not sad. She was more alien than anyone I had ever met.

"Strange that you always know it's me. And yes, Polli, I came for his letter," I replied while trying to distance myself from her.

She hugged me again. When I was very young, I would have done anything for a hug from her; now, it felt weird. Curiosity will be my downfall one day. I unwrapped her arms from my waist and strode to my father's office without looking back. I didn't hurt her feelings. I got my detachment from her blood and natural sociopathic tendencies. She was just doing what she thought was expected of her as the woman responsible for my birth. My other mother was better at being human.

My father was a scientist in life, but he wasn't powerful in magic; if he had been strong in magic, he would have been exterminated with the rest of his family. Since the Wyrd curse turned into a blessing, our enemies have tried to wipe us out. Some had the idea that the lesser magical Wyrd relatives would inherit the curse when the main family line was gone, but mostly they wanted to take away our advantage. Had they known that they could have taken me with them when they had my father killed, they would be kicking themselves right now. My soul was taken by a Grim, leaving my magical doppelganger in charge of my body. My soul will never be whole again, thanks to an accidental spell. Alton was not the problem, though. Alias is the parasite living inside my head. He has a vendetta against me because I am the cause of his one true love leaving him. It's not safe to love me for more than one reason. Alias will kill anyone who even thinks they love me. Vampires are angry creatures, especially when they are in love.

I sat in the old wooden chair behind the mahogany desk. My father looked to the future in magical and scientific terms, but he'd always loved antiques. The desk was two hundred years old and had been his father's. The letter I was after sat atop the desk calendar with one last notation from three months ago. It just said, 'Goodbye,' nothing more. The envelope was addressed to all three of us. He'd mailed out letters to my siblings, but I had to retrieve my letter because he wanted me here when I read it. I think he wanted me to say goodbye to Polli, but I didn't care about her, and I was sure she wouldn't even remember my name in a few years. Her children meant less to her than the science that created them. It was the only thing I admired about her.

I used the letter opener on the desk to cut the seal on the envelope. Dad had written it on ordinary notebook paper, probably from one of the many spiral notebooks he kept for important or unimportant thoughts. His handwriting could have been better, but it was understandable since he had just witnessed his death before writing it. He tried to explain what it was like once to see the future, but I had just been jealous of his gift. I thought I got the short end of the stick in seer powers; I could see what someone was doing at the moment they were doing it, like watching a live video in my head. It could have been more helpful as far as sight goes. I'd recently discovered that I had power over the present. It may sound strange, but the present doesn't exist. Every second in the future will be in the past before you can nail it down to the present…unless you can freeze time. I was still researching that part of my ability; no one in written history talked about it happening before, but then I didn't usually tell anyone either.

I spread the folded paper out on the desk and read.

Alias, you are not my blood but have always been my son. I know that you and Alien haven't spoken since you learned of your origin, but he loves you as a father should. Forgive us for not telling you the truth. Tom will never understand what has happened to you. He is a creature of another time. Take care of your mother, she will need you more than you know.

Alton, you were there for me at the end, and you will never know the comfort you gave me, son. You are my son, and no matter what happens in the future, you should know that you are a person. Your children will be safe, happy, and powerful. All three.

Alaric, my firstborn, my warlock, you don't deserve the life you will live. The war began with my death; they don't know about your brother, so they will assume you have the power. I never wanted this for you, so I tried to alter your future. Sometimes it works, and sometimes you create the future you fear the most. You will understand this one day, and I am so sorry. You cannot continue alone; you need allies. Don't poke the Grim too much; he was a good man in life, even if he never knew. Still, he is not the ally you need, Sorcerer Weird. I see great things for your future and terrible things, but at your side, you will have an ally that will be indispensable. I know you don't trust anyone; you don't want to feel for anyone, but you need a friend, my son; you have countless enemies. Elizabeth Key, ironically, will be instrumental in securing your place at the top. I won't tell you to trust her; she is like you. I could tell you so much more, but you must judge for yourself. She will be in the blue room tomorrow night. I know you will go because I have seen it, but mostly I know your mind. You are my son, and your scientific curiosity is even greater than mine. It's probably your alien blood. Don't trust your research; she is more than she appears to be. I know it means nothing to you, but I love you. I am sorry I could never show you. I had to make you hard for what was to come, and so did your mother. It's not her fault she was not here for you; it was mine.

The letter ended with no signature; it was dated two days before his death. He was only responsible for four of his children's existence, but I know he wrote a letter to all of them.

I folded the letter and tucked it back into the envelope, then folded the envelope in half and stuck it in my breast pocket. I closed the door of the office as I left. No one would go there again. It was my father's sanctum.

All three remaining alien parents were waiting for me by the front door. I knew what they wanted, but I couldn't shed a tear for him; I wouldn't. Maybe Alton or Alias would when they read the letter, but tears are not me; emotional attachment was not me. I would never grieve my father; I would get revenge, on every person, every creature, responsible for his death. I am what he made me, what they made me. I am a tool for vengeance. It was fine with me; I didn't want the weakness of emotional attachment.

I walked right past my parents and left the house. The fresh air felt good after being in there. I was never good at handling crying, especially my own. My eyes had been dry since I realized that true magical power is dark. They call it black magic like that was supposed to frighten, but I know that nothing in life is black and white. We all live in shades of gray, and some prefer the dark.

Sorceress Elizabeth Key was a lover of the dark. I knew a lot about her, enough to be curious about why my father thought she would be an ally in a war that was just me against the entire magical world. I doubt she even knew that I owed her my existence. She killed the Grim who held me prisoner, but it was a dark and foggy night. My father might be wrong about Liz, but it would be a first for him, and even though I didn't trust anyone alive, I trusted him. Liz was a Sorceress and, as far as I could tell, the only one. She was born with the potential; it was in her blood. Modern mages were very patriarchal. Women were not allowed to rise above men as a rule. Liz was a rulebreaker, and so was I. If there was a written law against Sorcery, we would be outlaws.

My drive home was filled with thoughts of what I would wear to introduce myself to the one person in the magical community who was more of a "bogeyman" than me. She liked to wear black, but I made a better impression in purple. It clashed with my orange hair, making my eyes look violet. Purple eyes were the one thing I knew for sure that Sorceress Key and I had in common. It was considered a mark of great power, but a good witch didn't have great power. A child born with lavender eyes was destined to become, at the very least, a black witch. Sorcery was not white or light power, and less than fifty sorcerers are in this realm now. I suspected that I was going to be responsible for there being fewer of them soon.

DEADLY CONNECTIONS

The problem with getting instructions from a dead future seer is that you didn't know when to show up for the event they told you about. I knew Liz would be at the bar sometime in the night, but with every unknown, I liked to be early to overlook the battlefield. My father had always considered "night" when he got home from work and had dinner. Usually, that was around seven in the evening, so I showed up a little earlier. The bar was filling up with workers trying to drown their sorrows of a workday in whatever alcohol they could afford on their meager salaries. I'd gone through three drinks while waiting and been hit on by five girls and three guys. I let the entire bar watch as I burned all the "digits" written on napkins in my hand without causing damage. Yeah, it was stupid, but it was a small enough "trick" that they would forget about it or work out how they think I did it.

Liz Key entered the bar after the last guy offered to blow me in the alley as if I would bother getting up from the table. He was cute, so I didn't say no, just later. Liz was just as everyone described her; beautiful, unearthly. But I would know if she was anything but human. Some called her 'The Angel of Death,' which seemed to fit her, but she was smaller than I'd imagined. She was dressed all in black, in a leather skirt with a lacey top. She wore knee-high boots with stiletto heels that could be used as a weapon, and for a moment, I wondered if they had. Her hair was a platinum blonde that seemed to have a pink tint to it. It complimented her lavender eyes and added to her otherworld vibe. I could feel her magic and hear it like an old familiar song. I didn't know if everyone else could sense her magic, but they did sense the danger. Anyone in-the-know magically, watched her with the concentration of a rabbit, trying not to get the attention of a wolf.

A man followed Liz to the bar like a dog trying to sniff its owner's ass. He was a warlock, handsome but full of himself. His blonde hair was cut short, military-style, but he was soft around the middle, not fat, just fluffy. I watched as he ordered a piña colada for Liz. She looked at him like she could murder him with a thought. Good, she was just how I'd imagined– shrewd and cocky. A feminist would have shamed the man for presumption; a pushover would drink the over-sweetened concoction without a word. Liz was using the little umbrella to stir the drink, but anyone in the bar could see she had no wish to touch it to her lips. However, her date was not too bright, and I hated brainless idiots. I'd had to deal with too many during my stint as an archeology professor. Worse still, he was stupid with magic. The magical community hated me for not being pure human, but they were breeding themselves out of magic and intelligence. If they didn't watch it, the aliens would take over–or at least this alien. The worst of them called my kind demons. They usually never said it to my face, though. At least not more than once in their lifetime. You don't become a sorcerer by avoiding violence and death.

There was a mirror behind the bar, and it gave me the perfect view of Liz's face. She knew that she was with a stupid man, and she was working him. I had no idea what she was up to, but she would probably be angry when I ruined it for her. She wouldn't be the first magical person I pissed off, but she would be the first sorceress.

The warlock thought he had scored the prize, but he would be taking matters into his own hands tonight, and I didn't have to see the future to know that. Liz didn't have her eyes on the drink, and Stupid thought it was an excellent time to slip something into the glass she would never touch. Do you see what I mean about stupid? I can't abide anyone trying to assault someone sexually. I might have some alien abduction issues, okay?

Liz was already watching me watch her. I figured it was as good a time as any to approach her. I stood and walked up directly behind her. Her date was gibbering in small talk. I hate small talk, and I could tell Liz did too. She didn't turn, but she did eye fuck me in the mirror as if I was dessert. I reached around her, grabbed her drink, and downed it in four swallows. When her date began to protest, I caught the asshole in a Darth Vader-style choke hold and held him there for everyone's entertainment. He flailed his arms and legs around, trying to at least touch a toe on the ground. I tossed him to the floor just before he passed out. Okay, I was showing off a little, but he irritated me. You probably thought I was being chivalrous, but I didn't do anything to protect her. I wanted to eliminate the distraction. Okay, maybe I was showing off more than a little.

The would-be date rapist slowly rose from the floor and conjured a death curse that he sent in my direction. It was an act frowned upon in the magical community, at least in a public place. Humans aren't supposed to know magic was real; it tended to make them murderous, primarily when someone used magic for murder. I brushed his curse off like a crumb on my shirt and turned my back to him. The humans were crowding around him now, some calling him 'Harry' and asking if he was alright. I returned to the bar and Liz, who seemed to be ignoring everything, but I could tell she was hiding a smile. I sat on the stool next to her, facing the crowd, with my elbows on the bar.

"I will give you points for that, but it still does not make me want to jump in bed with you, Sorcerer."

I leaned back against the bar and caught her lavender eyes. Yeah, she knew who I was, just like I knew her. She was more beautiful in person, and her voice was sweeter than I had imagined.

"Beds are for sleeping, Sorceress; I have other plans for you."

That made her turn her whole attention to me, and she laughed. I threw her my most charming smile, which usually turned out to be a sarcastic smirk.

"Honey, you and every living creature in here. What makes you think you're worth my time?"

I turned to the bar for a moment and caught the eye of the bartender. He walked over and waited for me to order. He was cute but too human, even though I had a soft spot for bartenders. That was a story for another time.

"I wanted to see if you were worthy of my time, Sorceress Elizabeth Key," I replied, then I turned my attention to the bartender waiting patiently.

"Can we get a long, slow, comfortable screw against the wall?" I asked, then added, "Make it two."

The drink was something that Liz would only order to be a flirt, but I knew she liked them. How did I know? I could read her mind. I'm an alien, remember? She and I already had a connection, but she didn't know, and it was a secret I wasn't ready to share yet. Alton had opened a link to her the night my father died. (Same brain, same synapses, different soul.)

Liz turned her attention to me, all of me. I knew what she was thinking, and I didn't even have to use alien powers. I've seen myself in the mirror; hell, I've fucked myself as a magical clone. The Rohypnol was already hitting my system pretty hard, but I had a high tolerance for drugs of any type. The drug was doing one of the things that the warlock intended. When you party with a Grim Reaper, you have to get used to ingesting things that would kill an average human. I was feeling very relaxed and flirty.

"Don't get too attached to the package, Sorceress; it's not for you."

I pulled the straw out of my drink and finished it without a breath. The last thing I needed was more alcohol, but I was beyond reasonable thought. Sometimes I answered stupidity with more stupidity, like every male laden with testosterone. Something was off with me, and I couldn't quite figure out what it was.

Liz leaned close and used her thumb to wipe the alcohol off my lip. That light touch felt like kissing a live wire. She had more power than the rumor mill knew, and she wasn't done flirting.

"Are you sure about that?" she asked as she licked the drop of alcohol off her thumb seductively. "Why? You're gay or something?"

I looked away, not because I was embarrassed or ashamed, but because she did something to me with the touch, which wasn't sexual. She sipped at her drink to allow me a moment, which I didn't need, to answer.

"Sorry to disappoint you and every other straight woman in the bar, but yes, I'm gay. And I lie about being sorry."

Her laugh began as a quiet snicker; then she burst out hysterically, with her eyes watering.

"The hottest flirting I've done in a long while, and it's with a gay man?"

That was a surprise. I was used to women walking away from me when I told them I was gay.

"I'm an equal opportunity flirter but I reserve the fun stuff for men."

"That is unfortunate—for all women," she replied. This time she took an actual drink of alcohol.

"So, what pleasure do you seek in my company, Sorcerer?"

I froze in the moment—I do that sometimes when I have no idea what to do in a situation. It was the one thing I did that had nothing to do with my magical abilities and everything to do with a bloodline curse. No one alive knew that I could do this. I still didn't understand why I was able, but it gave me time to think. Why would I just meet a woman on the advice of my dead father? I hated that I was acting like a jealous boyfriend, especially when my actions made no sense. Alias's mind would work this way, but I would know if he controlled my thoughts. I would be staring at her neck, for one thing. Why did I attack her date? Something was wrong with me, and she was the cause. Being near her made me feel like I was touching an electrical fence. I paced back and forth like a lion in a cage. I knew this woman, or I thought I knew her, and she wasn't the type to become my ally, much less my friend. She was dangerous, unpredictable, and sometimes deadly, not just to lovers and family. So why?

My alien abilities were a little invasive, but I needed to connect to Liz's thoughts. I wasn't above using the ability to see what was on her mind. She was sitting on a kitchen counter, wearing almost nothing. I went to her and kissed her roughly; she leaned into the kiss and grabbed my– The clarity of the vision shook me a little. She didn't even know that I knew; it was her fantasy, nothing more.

I sat back on the stool and let time resume. Liz blinked like she had noticed something. She was waiting for my answer. Her mind was closed to mine now, so no more visions of straight sex. She shouldn't have been able to leak anything through the time bubble, but she was a powerful sorceress, probably more potent since her chance encounters with the Weird clan and a particular Grim Reaper. I figured the direct approach was best.

"What do you do for fun, Sorceress? Besides dating brain-dead warlocks?" I was starting to shake from the alcohol and drugs. I never took things so personally or cared enough about others to do something so risky. Liz wouldn't have tasted the drink anyway. I'm sure she noticed Harry spiking it. He wasn't one for subtlety.

She slid a small flask from her bra and waved it toward me. I didn't move; I had enough drugs and alcohol. I'd misjudged the determination of Mister Stupid's sex drive. He probably spiked it with something guaranteed to take out a powerful sorceress.

"You will feel better if you take this. Then we can get to what you want to ask me," she said as she shook the flask in my face.

Liz figured out why I was hesitating, and she took a small sip from the flask. She wasn't trying to poison me further, and it would be rude to refuse–she wasn't Fae. I took the flask from her and knocked it back while she watched.

"The answer to your question, Sorcerer, is sex and magic, and I bet you, of all people, can guess which is more important to me."

I knew because magic and power were what we lived for. I was already feeling better and a little cocky, which is normal too. I didn't know what was in her potion, but it was beyond my alchemy skills.

"Have you ever set yourself against another sorcerer? Challenged someone who you couldn't wipe out like a business? I won't offer sex, but a little magic dueling is always fun…especially when you have a challenging opponent. I can guarantee that sparing with me would be more fun than sex with blondie over there."

I pointed at the blonde who had been following her around earlier. His name was Harry, and Harry was busy trying to kill me with his mind while rubbing his sore neck. He would probably have bruises in the morning. His wife would think they were hickies. Yeah, I knew he was married, and Liz probably did too. I research everyone who has power, especially ones from rival covens. He couldn't kill me with his mind, but I could probably kill him with mine.

"Hold that thought," she said as the man who was once her date screamed and cradled the wrist of his right hand, the hand that spiked the drink.

Liz looked back at me and asked, "Are you sure you want to challenge me?"

"I am now, Sorceress. I am now."

She smiled like she knew what I meant. I may be gay, but I didn't do anything soft and easy. I was married for thirteen years to a living vampire with sadomasochistic tendencies. Not only could I handle a little pain, but I loved it. It had been a while since I had tested my mettle against a worthy opponent.

I took the napkin under her drink, levitated a pen from behind the bar, wrote an address, date, and time, then handed it to her. She tucked it in her bra with the empty flask.

"I look forward to seeing you again, Sorceress. I like how your brain thinks. Well, mostly."

"You truly are gay, Sorcerer?"

"I am, but if that ever changes, you'll be the first to know, Sorceress."

I slid off the stool and left Liz to finish her drink. I could have stayed, but I was feeling a strange connection to her that had nothing to do with my alien powers or the vibes she was giving. I locked eyes with my friend from earlier and crooked a finger at him. He practically ran to my side, and after a little whisper in the ear, he followed me into the bar's tiny kitchen. I couldn't disappoint the poor boy; he had been so lovely in his offer. I realized when I had gotten close enough to whisper that he had points on his ears under his curly brown hair. Elf, not alien, blood ran through his veins. You had to be careful with Fae of any flavor, but in this case, he wasn't offering a favor; he was asking for one.

If you think I chose to allow the elf to give me a blowjob to prove a point to Liz Key that I prefer men, well, you would be half right. Something about her had me rattled. My father would say that she'd walked across my grave, but he was insane. He was insane, and I followed his advice because he never advised me about the future. He never guided or told me what to do…until now.

Liz

The bar's loud music was drilling my skull; the lights tested my patience while I finished my drink, and my tank top felt too tight around my chest. It was hot too. I could not put my finger on the reason why. My magic was shifting uncomfortably through my body, like wanting to go somewhere. I looked up to the mirror just in time to see the red-haired sorcerer, who was wearing an expensive silky purple shirt that looked amazing on him, with black Levi jeans that embraced his perfect body very well, walk away with his companion. That made me chuckle softly as I welcomed the cold feeling in my mouth from the iced drink. No one comes to this bar to leave alone. If this one drink were spiked, I would be in trouble because I just wasted my antidote on him. Good thing I have something extra to help me fight any potion or drug ever created. I play with my ring, my thoughts racing. My mother would slap my hands right now. 'Do not show your insecurities!' she would say. I am still not sorry about how she ended up.

Alaric Weird. Sorcerer. Extremely powerful. Dangerous. Player, some said. Pregnant girlfriend and out of the market, others said. Lone wolf, which made him dangerous. I should know this better than anyone, and Alaric Weird was the definition of a lone wolf, according to what I heard. I was assuming it was by his choice. The list played in my mind. I had heard about him alright, but I never had the pleasure…until now. It had been a while since anyone talked to me with that cockiness. Hell, it had been a while since any man took the initiative and did not run the other way when they found out I was a Key, the well-known family of potent dark magic users. The stories of my family would make your skin crawl; I knew it made mine crawl when I was a child. So, when they found I was a Key, precisely, Elizabeth Key, Sorceress, the 'Angel of Death,' the "Black Widow" -how do they come up with these nicknames, anyway- most of them ran. Little did they know I killed a Grim Reaper not too long ago. That memory made me smile. I needed that rush again; I needed that power again. Until that day, killing a Grim Reaper was a myth, impossible to achieve; no one could do it. But I did it. I fucking did it! I did not care what domino effect I started that day; I knew there would be consequences; there always are. But that rush…

Alaric Weird was gone, and the uncomfortable feeling was gone too. Frustration was the only thing left. I was not sure the sorcerer had the best intentions. I had a job to do, but he ruined it. It was fun to watch, do not get me wrong, but he had a hidden agenda. He looked and felt too much like me, and I had a hidden agenda. My company whimpering about his broken wrist was my current hidden agenda. I was ready for the spiked drink. Hell, I was prepared for a lot worse from Harry, but he could have had the information I desperately needed. I'm not usually so subtle. I attack first and think later. After that play of Alaric, I did not have a chance in hell to bring Harry home with me and perform some not very pleasant torture.

No matter what I wanted to do, I always seemed to attract people's attention, especially the attention of the men in the room. Sometimes it was motivated by fear, sometimes it was sex, but invariably, they stare. I took a deep breath, got off the bar stool, and left almost unnoticed.

I felt the night's fresh air hit my skin as I stepped outside the bar; the cold breeze caressed my face, and I took a deep breath. This was not how I expected the night to end; if Harry was a no-show today, I might have fished someone to do some sweaty cardio, hopefully with a happy end, but I just wanted to go home and shower.

I made sure no one was near or watching. I pictured my home in my mind as I invoked a magical portal that formed in seconds, glowing in purple. That was, once upon a time, my favorite part of the magic. I remembered feeling so free because I could go anywhere only by thinking of the place. If you had spent all your childhood trying to run away from a home where you felt like an alien, you would understand what I mean. Alien… I retrieved the napkin from inside my bra and thought of the sorcerer again. Why had he bothered me so much? I had no idea what made me touch him and, worse, what made me taste him. Yes, that little act was more than flirting. There were other ways to feel or taste the magic of another being, but I unconsciously chose that one.

"We will see each other again, Sorcerer," I mumbled, going towards the portal. On the other side, I would find my home, my living room, to be precise. I needed a shower; men like Harry disgust me.

Putting the empty flask and napkin on the center table, I undressed as I walked upstairs, directly to my shower. Why would I flirt with some warlock I find disgusting, you might have asked? Men like him were so easy; you just let them think they may be able to earn your favor. They made assumptions about women who look like me. Well, he got a taste of what it's like to spend time with Liz Key. I probably wouldn't be seeing him anytime soon.

I set the water for the shower, almost instantly seeing the steam the hot water created, and I steadied myself with my hands on the bathroom sink cabinet, watching myself in the mirror. I'd tied my hair up in an elegant ponytail, my heavy makeup was still perfect, and my gaze fell to my scar, the only mark on my flawless skin.

I liked to consider myself a woman of action; I followed the blood trail; I didn't sit and complain. I searched for revenge. Harry could have helped me with that, so I was with him tonight. As I said, I followed the blood trail from Temp, my ex–let's say ex-boyfriend–and found out Harry knew someone that knew who the big boss was, the one pulling the strings to put a price on the head of one of my friends and kill the other. Okay, not a friend, exactly, but someone I needed for now. I didn't do the friendship thing anymore. The truth was, we were friends once, but I changed. I knew now that friendship, love, and trust were a joke. We were either essential or expendable, and there is nothing more to it. Nothing more was vital, don't let anyone fool you.

Harry was going to tell me who the big bad wolf was. Yes, I was positive he would have. They always did, either when I used my female charms or reveal myself as the dark Sorceress. I always won in the end. I was once different from this, believe it or not. My parents tried hard to turn me into this, and I tried harder to be the opposite. I was Elizabeth Key, the only child of Magus and Morana Key. I was the one needed to keep the bloodline strong. But I did not want that power, or an arranged marriage with a powerful Sorcerer. I didn't want to have a child that could be the chosen one. I could not believe they still went for a make-believe story. No one knew if it was true or not. I was the shame of the Key family, the outcast, the witch who blocked her power because the energy was dark. No, I was Lizzie, a non-practicing witch with a degree in Psychology; I had friends and a cute human boyfriend, Daniel Costa. I even fell in love. But your destiny catches you, no matter how long or far you run. Yes, I was weak once; being weak almost cost me my life. Never again! I proved myself, I had my revenge, and I have become one of the most potent Sorceresses alive, possibly the only one, since the community was so patriarchal.

I entered the shower, feeling the hot water warm my naked body, taking away all frustrations of the day, and I stayed under the water for a long time. No one got away with taking someone I cared for, no matter how I felt for them now! I would need a new plan, soon.

Finishing my exaggerated shower, I wrapped in a clean purple towel and stepped out. Taking some time to brush my wet hair, I felt slow and drunk, but it didn't make sense; I had one drink and not a very strong one. My tolerance was better than that. Trying to shake off this feeling, I made a mental note to get a warm coffee after getting dressed. It was going to be a long night anyway. I had to develop a whole new plan and dig up a little more dirt about the entire group. I already knew it was not a group of mages; it was more significant than that. There were some dangerous beings in the mix. Someone powerful wanted Sophie, and I needed to know why.

When my hair was mostly dry, I put it in a messy bun, which made me think of Dan. He loved to watch me as I rubbed the vanilla-scented lotion on my skin. He loved the scent, and so did I. It was the one thing I kept from my old life. Some would say it was too innocent for a Sorceress with the fame of being a killer, a soulless person, but why should I care? It worked in my favor, after all.

I pulled on my black silk robe and loosened my hair a little, thinking about how much work I had ahead of me. No matter how much I enjoyed our tease, I could not let myself be distracted by any handsome man. I was starting to see why he appealed to me. I had to keep digging. I needed to find out who gave the order that resulted in Daniel's death. I needed to keep Sophie Smith, once my (I believed at that time) best friend, safe. She was the one they were looking for; she was the white witch carrying a deadly curse until, surprise, surprise, Alaric Weird got in the middle and changed destiny. I do love a good kick in the ass of Destiny! What would make me go through so much trouble when I did not care about anyone? It is a long story, so take a seat, get comfortable, and grab some popcorn.

I was a defiant child. If my parents said to walk, I would run or stay still. If my parents said to burn something, I would ice it. If my parents said I should stay up late to recharge my energy with the moon's power, I would go to bed earlier. You think I was an impossible child, but you only know half the story. As I said before, I was destined for great things, excellent in a typically seen lousy way. My parents wanted me to be a breeder. Some psychotic seer told them their line would produce the most powerful sorcerer. My parents forced me to train in defensive and offensive magic. Everything taught to me was dark magic and evil.

I had other plans. I wanted an everyday life, friends, or at least acquaintances that I didn't want to kill. I tried to date without focusing on my companion's family name or how strong they were, and I mostly wanted a life away from magic. So, I rebelled, and they hated it. It worsened as I got older, and they saw it was not a phase. I did not want to be dark; I did not want to be the Sorceress they wanted me to be. They turned my life into a nightmare hoping the hatred would make me use dark magic. They would have me train, go to bed without dinner, and cut all ties they didn't approve of–family and friends–getting hit by solid magic. They tried, but I would not fight back. I took everything from them without tears, without complaint.

The one light in my life back then was Alma, the family's alchemist. Her compassionate heart saw something in me that I didn't know was there. Alma would treat my burns, broken bones, and internal bleeding after a day of training or torture, as I recall. She and I bonded like a family over it, a strange but strong bond. She looked at me with pride, unlike my parents, who looked at me with disgust. It was Alma who rescued me from the torture of my childhood. She risked everything to save me from my own family. She risked her own family and her own life; she hid me and took care of me the way I assume a parent would take care of their daughter. She pulled me away from dark magic, and because I refused to use even light magic, she only taught me potions, promising it was safe. I always knew she needed to feel I could protect myself. Alma kept me away from almost everyone except Sophie Smith, the neighbor from a human family. Sophie was the one who introduced me to Daniel Costa, my first love and an ordinary human. He was not the reason I didn't date anymore, but he was the reason I steered clear of humans. When I embraced the darkness, Daniel turned his back on me, and I turned my back on him. I would only hurt them.

Sophie Smith had been a good friend, and Alma unofficially adopted her when we started hanging out. Alma believed Sophie and Daniel would keep me on the light path. Alma made me promise to protect her and guide her as she did for me once when I confessed what was happening. I explained Sophie's curse and that the Weird family cured it. Now I was searching for those who wanted to kill her, or worse. I keep my promises, especially those made to Alma. Some would say I trained Sophie too harshly, but she is still alive thanks to that, and I have kept her safe, even when she did not know. Safe from physical harm, not heartbreak. It was a big blow to her to find that her fiancé had died, and I was glad to not feel those kinds of things anymore.

I sat on the dinner table chair and turned on my laptop, seeing I had not closed any internet tabs since I started the research about Harry, and I saw all the organized documents on my dinner table. One of the documents was the family history, all critical information that Alma could find, and a picture of Tempest Griffin, the mage that killed Daniel thinking he was the targeted witch of their search. What they sensed on him was Sophie's curse that Daniel, along with Alaric, transferred to him, and I suspect that Alphonse Weird, Alaric's father, had misinformed them too. I did not understand the magic and science behind that accomplishment with the curse, but I would, one day.

Alma became more than an alchemist when she took me under her wing. She became a role model and teacher. More recently, I discovered just how good she was at obtaining needed information. She knew a lot about the magic community, things even I did not know. No wonder my parents kept her so close all those years. The big black wood table had never seen a dinner party or a family dinner since the interior designer put it in this house. Its job was to support all my papers, books, and laptop for me to work on. Well, at least it saw some potions being made. Did that count? I usually ate outside or in the kitchen, so it was more of a big desk than a dinner table since I loved to work next to the fireplace, even on hot days. The fireplace was handy today since it had been a cold night. It was not raining, but the wind was frigid.

I heard a sound coming from the room behind me and immediately invoked a magic fireball. Strange. I still felt my wards strong around the house, and I did not feel any energy interference. Out of the corner of my eyes, I saw someone walking in my direction carrying something I couldn't quite figure out.

"Lizzie, my child. It is just me," said the warm voice of the only person that could get in and out of the Key mansion without being attacked by my magic. Call me crazy, but I wanted to keep breathing for a while. I had many people who did not like me and wanted me dead, either because they knew me personally, or just because of my surname.

"I brought you my famous lasagna. You need to stop working so hard and eat. You are too skinny!"

Alma was the mother of the mothers, in all senses. I absorbed the energy back, making the magic fireball disappear from my hand while I watch her put the tray on the dinner table next to the spread of documents. If the lasagna looked good with that melted cheese, it smelled even better. She stared at the picture of Tempest Griffin. She knew he was dead, burned alive, on the same night a Grim Reaper died, both by my hands. She also knew he would have killed me if I had not killed him first. Her expression changed from horror to worry.

"Lizzie, why are you still looking for trouble, my child? Stay away from all of this," she said, moving the papers around to see how much information I had since she dropped off her research.

"I tried so hard–"

"To keep you from this." I finished the sentence as she would have, then gathered the documents into a pile and put them face down. In that pile was someone she feared– Alaric Weird. "I know, I know. I can still be saved. From what, Ma? From the power that keeps me alive? From myself? From destiny? From my early death? I cannot."

"Lizzie, you do not know…"

"Yes, I do know, Ma. And do not call me Lizzie. Lizzie died," I interrupted. "I might not know exactly when or why, but I know how. I never expected any other kind of death. So let me have fun now!"

"My sweet child," she murmured with a tone that made me believe she was in tears, and then she hugged me. "You deserved so much better."

Okay, this is awkward. Crying people made me uncomfortable now. Funny how I had dealt so well with that before. When I accepted my dark magic, something inside me died. I was telling the truth when I said Lizzie died. Lizzie was a young girl, too scared of her parents, with many friends, studying psychology to help others, dating a human that helped everyone, and she locked magic inside. Lizzie was the daughter Alma raised, who hugged her back. Lizzie died.

"Okay, Ma. I need to put the lasagna in the fridge. And you need to keep the visits short. I do not want anyone to see you with me, or you will be a target. We talked about this."

I broke from her embrace and picked up the tray with the lasagna. But I felt her hand on my forearm, keeping me from moving.

"Lizzie, please, stay away from them. Please, stay away from the Sorcerer," she pleaded.

News traveled fast, especially for her. She knew things instantly. And this visit has nothing to do with the lasagna and all to do with Alaric. Alma knew about Alaric and my interaction; she probably knew everything that happened and what was said. She was keeping something from me; all she told me was what everyone in the community knew. He was powerful and dangerous, and a lot more than the stories I'd heard because I had felt his magic from a distance. But so was I, and we were not enemies. I was just…curious. I was something. Something was pulling me toward his magic; something made his invitation impossible to refuse.

"Ma, you worry too much. You, indeed, raised a warrior!" I smirked at her, but I only saw the concern in her eyes. "I will play a little with his ego; that is it. And I cannot wait."

Sophie

I woke up almost refreshed for the first time in over a month. The silence scared me; Violet had been crying all night, every night, since Dan…since Dan, left us. His parents and mine had taken shifts helping me the first couple of weeks. They had their own lives, and I couldn't keep them here. I felt alone with or without them. Liz was looking in on me every day with the excuse of keeping my training going. I think she liked that I was a little like her, but my power was more in healing than throwing balls of fire. I didn't care about magic; I only wanted my life back, I wanted Dan back, but that wasn't going to happen.

I found Violet playing with the lavender socks that were no longer on her feet. She giggled when she saw me and offered me the sock in her left hand. It was a game she would play with Dan every morning. He would tickle her bare feet before putting her socks back on. Her smile was infectious, and I found myself smiling back. I tickled a foot until she grabbed my index finger.

"No, Mama!" She huffed.

I wasn't the one she wanted tickling her feet. I sighed and put her socks back on. She held her hands out to be lifted, though she knew how to climb out on her own. I carried her to the kitchen to get her something to eat. I may not care about myself, but she was my one last piece of Daniel, and I wouldn't let anything happen to her.

She was still drinking breast milk from the mother's milk bank I found online, but she had taken to solid food well. She was definitely a better eater than I was. She took after her father in that way. I didn't even know her birth mother; I had only met her once when we signed the papers making me Violet's mother. I didn't know her eating habits.

After Violet finished her cereal and milk, we had a quick shower. It was spring on our little island, though the rest of the northern hemisphere still suffered from winter weather. It was too nice to be inside, and I couldn't keep hiding away in my house wishing to die. I had to live for that beautiful little girl, so I got dressed in all black, again, as a sign of grief. Everyone kept telling me it was time to move on and let Daniel rest in peace. I didn't care what they said, my grief was my business, not theirs. I dressed Violet in purple because I liked it. She had her way of grieving. She climbed into the stroller the moment I put her down. She knew what I had in mind. A stroll in the park would probably do us both some good. Everyone seemed determined for me to get some sun. I glanced at her in the stroller, ready for the planned park trip, while I put on my jacket. Sure, now she was calm. She had cried all night. And every night before this one. But she just cried at night, so bye-bye theory of teeth coming in. I took a deep breath, mentally calming myself down and checking to see if I had everything I needed. I checked the mirror too, and I didn't like the face looking back at me. She looked tired and lost, but I knew Dan wouldn't think so. He always told me how beautiful I was, even when I was the worst mess ever.

The park was bustling in the early morning. I pushed the stroller, paying extra attention to everything surrounding us. I was searching for magic like Liz had taught me repeatedly. Maybe I shouldn't have left the house. Everything looked safe, though. I promised myself I would not be this person, a single mother, having to leave the house alone with a baby and all her stuff to go to the park full of mothers and their children…but here I was. Gosh, I wished I could make magic portals like Liz, but at least I could make a decent shield. Good for me, because when Liz trained, she did not hold back. She hit with everything she had, and my body suffered the consequences.

I was looking for a quieter space in the park, so I kept walking. I had just passed a blooming cherry tree when I saw him. Immediately, I stopped, watching the back of the tall man with a weird tattoo – or was it a scar - that reminded me of dark veins over his skin and a scythe in his right hand. He was looking for something or expecting something…someone. I felt goosebumps all over my skin; I did not need Liz's voice in my head to know that it meant danger.

Slowly and quietly, I tried to back away, pulling the stroller away from the man. I had to keep Violet safe! The goosebumps were not just a warning of danger. As I looked around me, the air was suddenly cold. The happy giggles of children were gone. The toddler tantrums and upset mothers became silent now. I did not see any living beings at the park, whereas before, it was full of life. In my head, a voice yelled, "Run!"

My eyes went back to the tall man in black, the Reaper. No one was there, just Violet and me. At that thought, I froze. He came for Violet, just like in my dream. Not Violet too! She was all I had left. Violet cooed softly, then said, "Dada." followed by a happy squeal. The tall man turned slowly, his body seemed to be wreathed in smoke or mist, but I recognized the face, even through all that darkness. I could never forget that face. The face of the man I loved more than life. I was not sleeping; I was not doped on sleeping pills. The Reaper was wearing my Dan's face and mocking my pain. That bastard!

More as an instinct, I invoked a shield around Violet and myself that closed just in time for me to see his scythe spinning in our direction. He was coming for Violet! The bastard came for Violet! Not Violet, not today, and not using HIS FACE. I needed to keep him away. Closing my eyes, I did what Liz had taught me. I imagine my anger traveling through my body and arm, forming a fire in my right hand. Without thinking, I threw it at him. He thought I would not attack the man I loved, but it was just a mask; Daniel was gone. Before I knew it, I was throwing everything my body could make in his direction. I needed to keep him away!

The Reaper took every hit, every energy ball, every impact bolt, every fireball, and he never returned the fight. Alton said the Grim Reaper used magic, and Liz said they were powerful. Why didn't he attack?

Finally, he raised his hand, and I was expecting retribution, but it never came. Instead, the scythe appeared in his hand, and he looked at me like he was smiling, mocking me like I was not even worth the concern. In a panic, I boosted the shield and fired again. I was not Liz, I was not as good or strong as her, but she taught me well. He walked towards me, confident.

"Show me your true face, you coward bastard!" I yelled, attacking him with all I had. All that Liz taught me was in action. The closer he got, the better I could see him. He was bruised, scraped, and bleeding but did not stop or even slow down. Alias told me how he tried to take little Aliyah, the tiniest of the Weird triplets. He almost took Rainn's baby from her; he would not take Violet from me! He would not take an innocent baby, not if I could help it. I did not care what face he wore!

He kept taking hit after hit like he was being hit by snowballs and not by magic. Liz taught me things, bad things, dark magic things. She said my life depended on it. I knew how to hurt them now; I knew how to kill. I did not want to. God, please, do not make me do it because I will! Dan would understand. My Dan, not the thing that was approaching my shield.

He threw his scythe again, and it arched way over my shield this time. He was a terrible shot! He had missed two...no, three times. This time he did not hesitate to make the scythe reappear, then he threw it again. I watched it, barely touching the edge of my shield but not doing anything to it. The scythe impaled a man behind me, someone I hadn't felt or seen before. Was he the one the Reaper came to collect? Am I in the wrong place at the wrong time? No, Liz taught me that too. There were no coincidences.

I rushed to pick up Violet and started to back away from the Reaper with Dan's face. Why? Why was he wearing Dan's face if it was not to call the baby when he was collecting her or to make me weak? He was so close, but he was no longer looking at us or smiling. He lifted his left hand, and a scythe flew into it. It was not his scythe; it was plain, less bony. He looked at it with repulsion and tossed it aside. The ground swallowed it where it fell.

"Are you okay, Soph?" he asked in a booming voice that was unlike Dan's voice, yet so familiar it made me shiver.

59

"Why?" I whisper. "Why are you doing this to me? Why him? Why Dan? Couldn't you pick anyone else's face...anyone else's body?"

He looked me in the eyes, and suddenly his eyes were Dan's blue eyes. They looked black just a moment ago. The veins I saw earlier were less prominent now, more like a tattoo. He was on guard, walking around my shield with his back to it. He was giving me a target. Why? Why did it look like he was protecting me? Did he just kill another Reaper?

"Dan?" I breathed. "Daniel Costa?"

"Is that it? Is that my name? Sounds strange. I don't like it."

He sounded more like my Dan now, less booming, more human. He was not Daniel, though. He was not human; I could feel magic. It was a powerful, electrifying, and a terrible force. He could not be Dan, could he?

The Reaper cradled his midsection like it was hurting him, breathed out a sigh, flicked his wrist, and the scythe disappeared. He looked at Violet, then smiled that teasing smile again. "Damn, I think you broke my rib, woman! That is gonna hurt for hours! Good job!"

"Dan?" I whispered again, wishing so hard it was him, that it hurt.

Violet started crying, and the Reaper held out his hands. He took her from me with magic, making me hold my breath as he bounced her on his shoulder.

"It's okay, Vi. It's okay, sweet pea. Daddy's here. Shhh."

He looked back at me, his eyes making me see Dan. He was rocking Violet just like Dan did so many times.

"Sorry, Soph. I couldn't remember, and then Liz told me I would only hurt you, and I knew that she was right...is right, but I couldn't let them take you! Violet needs you. They didn't even send someone worthy; he was weak! I think you could've taken him if he'd come alone. Don't tell Liz; she thinks she's hot stuff because she killed one of us."

Breathing hard, I stepped closer to the Reaper, gently took Violet from his arms, and slipped her back into the stroller. After she was settled, I turned to Dan Grim and punched him in the face, clipping his chin. The blow was just human, so it barely knocked his head back and probably hurt me more than it did him, but he rubbed his chin anyway, then burst out laughing.

"Idiot!" I said, angrily fighting the tears. He stopped laughing.

"What? What did I do?"

"You...you died! You left me! You...you are the Grim Reaper? As in Death? As in, takes souls to their final rest, Reaper? And what did Liz do?"

Dan Grim seemed to ignore me as he looked around the park that was teeming with life again. He seemed to be looking for something, or someone again.

"Let's get back to the house and Liz's wards. They might not keep all of them out, but they sting. I know that for a fact," he said as he popped my shield like a soap bubble.

I looked to where my shield had been, my best shield, the one that protected me from Liz's worst blows, and my jaw dropped. He had popped it like a soap bubble!

"Sorry, the scythe gave me a lot of juice. Your shield is great, baby! You can punch me again in the safety of home. Now shut that gorgeous mouth of yours, and let's go."

I was ready to give him another punch when he slipped an arm around me, a movement once so ordinary and familiar, and surrounded us with mist.

"Hold on, gorgeous," I heard him say, making me remember even more, the Dan I knew.

When the air cleared, we were outside our island home. Dan had one hand on my waist and the other on the stroller. Violet was cooing, the birds were chirping, and Liz was tapping her foot on the sand so hard it was melting into glass.

"Did we have a fun outing at the park, Deathripper? Sophie, I thought I told you to stay in the bounds of the ward!"

"Take your hands off me!" I growled, pushing him away–even when it was the last thing I wanted. I grabbed Violet from the stroller and walked towards the house.

"C'mon, Soph. Let's talk," he said, materializing in front of me and making me jump. Violet just smiled.

"God! Don't do that!"

I went around him and kept walking. I handed Violet to Liz when I got to the porch. She looked at me disgustedly, like I just gave her fresh crap to hold.

"Take Vi to her grandparents, please?" I asked.

"I am not your fucking servant."

"Liz, please? You know I do not know how to use magical portals yet," I explained.

"Ugh, fine! Sophie, be careful. He's a reaper, before he's Dan," she warned, giving him a deadly look, and then conjuring the portal and disappearing into it.

I put my hands in my jacket pocket to hide my trembling, leaned against the porch rail, and looked up to the blue sky, trying to calm myself. The weight of what happened finally settled down, making my knees weak. Dan–My Dan–for whom I cried every night until I fell asleep the past month, was there. Alive. I chuckled in my head. Not alive. But there. At my reach. To touch. To kiss. I closed my eyes, keeping my face up to be kissed by the sun.

"How long?" I asked, feeling him standing near me.

"What, Soph?"

"How long have you been away from me, knowing who I was?" I asked, a tear rolling down my face.

"I did not remember for a long time," he answered, reaching out to wipe away my tear.

I jerked away. "Do not dare touch me!" Was I mad or afraid? "You left," I breathed.

He sighed. "I'm sorry. It wasn't by choice, Soph." He took my hand in his and placed it over his heart. "It is still me in here, Coração," he said.

I looked into his eyes. "One more week, and you would find me married and with a bunch of kids," I joked, trying to keep my distance. He was a Reaper. What did that even mean? He laughed, the same rich and honest laugh I was used to.

"You broke my rib; now you want to break my heart, woman?" he said, still laughing. But then he went serious; his hand cupped my jaw to make me look straight into his eyes.

"You're stronger. Strong enough to fight some of us. But not all. You're in danger, Soph."

I jerked away. Some of us. The reality hit me like a blow from a wrecking ball. He was not my Dan; he was not human. He is a Reaper.

"Don't worry. I will never let them take you," he added, trying to get close again. I kept the distance between us.

"How do I know you are not trying to do the same?" I ask, voice shaking at the realization. He looked hurt by my question. He closed the space between us, catching me by my waist.

"Soph, you don't think that, do you?"

I rested my forehead on his chest, he flinched, probably from pain, and he held me. I was tired. I had been tired for a long time. What if he was here to take me? Why should I care? At least he was merciful enough to take me by the hand, painlessly, I hoped. At least I could feel his touch once again, smell him, hear him. I thought about our months together, love, like Liz taught me, and I put my hand on his chest, invoking what I needed to try to heal him. He was a Reaper; I didn't know if it would work.

"Don't," he said, stopping me. "I'll wear them proudly!"

I felt him kiss the top of my head, "Let's get inside so we can talk about all of this," he whispered. We made our way through the porch towards the entrance of our once-upon-a-time home. I didn't know what to expect, but I was too tired to fight anymore. I want to let this dream run its course so I can once again wake up alone and cry my eyes out, I thought.

"It's not a dream, Soph," he said as if answering my thoughts.

"You can read my mind?" I asked as I stepped away from him.

"I can read your face. I've known you most of my life," he replied, taking a step closer to me.

"No, you're not him!"

"I'm not, not completely. I don't know what I am, but I know I'm nothing without you. I'm just another dead guy."

"I'm tired, Reaper. I don't know what you are trying to do to me, but I will not let you take my daughter!"

"I would never do that. I gave her to you." He sighed.

The Reaper with Dan's face, voice, smell, and well-muscled body picked me up before I could protest. He popped us into my bedroom and laid me on the bed. I was about to object and leave the bed, but he sat beside me and kissed my forehead. It was like my sleeping pills had just kicked in, only it was daytime, and I hadn't taken any pills. I couldn't hold my eyes open; I drifted off with his arms around my shoulders and my head on his chest.

Al

Every city has a place where no one likes to go after dark. I chose Seattle, Washington, because it was close to her, often foggy, and within three soft areas.

I could have chosen any city on the coast for early morning fog, but Seattle has a Ley line running straight through, that belonged to the West Coast triangle. The triangle is a magical gateway, a port to other worlds.

Liz Key and I would meet up in the foggy abandoned parking lot, but we wouldn't be sparring there. It's not like I cared that it was forbidden to do magic in the human world. Breaking the rules was something we Weirds had been doing for centuries. Hell, my existence broke the rules, I am half-alien, and mages breed with mages only. Sure, sometimes there was an accidental Fae/Mage pairing. The Sidhe were attractive and attracted to the magic of humans. Occasionally someone would breed with an unmagical human. Still, in all of mage history, written and unwritten, there had yet to be a magic-using alien hybrid until I came along.

Mages would duel in a realm they had deemed safe for themselves. It would be another world free of any magical beings but full of magic. We wouldn't be in the Magic

Realm; it would be worse than sparring in the human world. Liz was as transparent as a window, but I was still in the closet, magically speaking. She didn't seem too upset to find out I was gay, but she was surprised. Most people were amazed, considering I had seven children and had never been with a woman. It's a long boring story about alien abduction and magical clones.

The place I chose was one I accidentally encountered while searching for what I call soft spaces. It existed in two areas at once, but the best thing about it was it also didn't exist anywhere; It didn't exist any when. It was a place without time. Once we entered, we could be there for days, weeks, or months, if we didn't need to eat. And we would leave the place when we entered. It was a safe place, but it wasn't huge. The entire realm was the size of the abandoned parking lot that marked it in the human world. Sometimes people would vanish there. Periodically, they would return, old and gray. It didn't have just one entrance and one exit, but I hadn't explored it fully. It was a hub, a waypoint to other worlds, but it was perfect for our sparring.

I parked my Tesla in the furthest parking spot from the center. The lights of the parking lot were mostly gone. Vandalism, not creatures from another world, caused the lighting to be spotty. It didn't matter; this was only the address, not the place. You're probably wondering why the fog is essential. You try parking a Tesla in an abandoned parking lot without attracting attention. I had to wait for Liz to arrive; she couldn't go into this waypoint, not that I knew. This spar was a test to see what she could do. Rumors were not enough to base an alliance on, and other than a few general statistics, all I had were rumors. I'm sure she was dealing with the same thing as me.

I sat down under a lamp post with my back to the soft spot and listened to the sounds around me. With fog came a susurration that made you feel like you'd already stepped into another world. Everything was silent until I felt the buzz of the portal behind me. I could barely hear her footsteps; if I were more human, her silence would be complete. I don't have superpowers, just big, pointed ears.

She stopped near my car, and I could feel her eyes on my vulnerable back. Any other person would seem cocky turning their back on a potential enemy, but again, ears. I could hear her breathing even with the fog dampening the sounds around.

"You just keep getting better and better," she whispered.

I'm sure she was talking to my Tesla Model Three since she was standing closer to it than me. She was a pretty impressive car for the price. She'd been a gift from an old lover. He was among the many lovers that were murdered by the vampire soul that was possessing a portion of my body.

"She gets software updates nearly every week," I replied without turning to her. We weren't completely alone; trolls, goblins, and some lesser Fae knew about this spot.

"Pretty, but the million-dollar question is, are you ready to lose this duel?"

"Her beauty is on the inside, but we didn't come here to talk about cars. This is just a spar, not a duel, but don't think I'll hold back just because you're a girl. I'm an equal rights kind of guy."

I stood and brushed the rocks and pavement off my clothes, such as they were. We'd both dressed in less than usual. You never knew what someone would throw at you; skin healed better than clothing.

"I would be disappointed any other way, but you still will not beat me. It will be fun seeing you try, though."

She shrugged off a little leather jacket to reveal a lacey one-piece body suit. She looked ready for end-of-date activities, but I probably did too. Neither of us was a virgin when it came to fighting with magic. I didn't know her body count, but I knew one of them had been a Reaper. I hadn't had that pleasure yet, but maybe one day. The new Reaper was off-limits for now, not just because he and Alton had been friends. I still owed his scythe a debt for my life. Liz's confidence impressed me. She lived up to her reputation. My reputation was more private, and few knew what I could do.

I froze time and whispered some words. There were no actual magic words. Any sound in any language would do. It's the intention of the terms that count. Most people use Latin or other dead languages to avoid accidentally doing magic during a heated conversation. I've never had that problem, but I still liked to say silly things like, "Open sesame." The time freeze was more important than the words.

The scenery didn't change, but the fog was thicker, and the air was frigid. We were in winter territory now, even though it was April. She shivered as soon as I released time. She glanced to where my car had been, where she had left her coat. The realization filled her face at the same time as curiosity. She would want to know how, but not now. I gave her a slight bow and said, "Ladies first." Her quizzical look turned to anger immediately, and she sent a hot blast of fire at my face. That probably was not the smartest thing to do; the second shot hit me in the shoulder, burning a baseball-sized wound. I ducked just in time and laughed.

"That smarts a little," I quipped as I returned her fire with my own. I wasn't trying to hit my mark; I was testing her reflexes. She anticipated the shot perfectly and pivoted into the line of fire instead of away. It barely grazed the top of her left shoulder, but it did catch her clothes on fire for a moment. That was why I wore only boxer briefs and boxers.

I would have apologized if I had been nice, but no one had ever accused me of being nice. She returned my fire with a bolt of lightning. I danced out of the way quickly, inhumanly quickly. "Dammit, Alias," I whispered to myself. He was aching to join the fight, but it was between Liz and me. Carrying the soul of my dead ex-husband was not precisely the easiest thing to do. He loves blood and violence. I wasn't ready to explain him to Liz either.

Liz didn't hesitate long enough for me to think about how to explain my parasitic souls. She hit me in the chest with something that left a bruise. If it weren't for a particular contract with a Reaper, that one probably would have ripped through my chest and taken me out. Anyone else would worry that she was trying to kill them, but she knew about the contract. It was her Grim's mark on my body. I didn't choose these tattoos out of a flash book. Any magic user who dealt with a Reaper would know that I was immune to magic death, but that doesn't mean the blow didn't hurt. It also pissed me off.

"Oh, you want to play dirty, Sorceress?" I returned her force magic with my own, clipping her in the left hip as she tried to dance away. It made her stumble and stop for a breath, but she was still on her feet and smiling like a cat who had cornered a mouse. She took three deep breaths and threw another fireball in my direction. She clipped my left side, sending pain through my ribcage. I would have been excited by the foreplay if she were a man.

"I always play dirty, Sorcerer, especially when someone underestimates me. What is the problem? I thought you were not going easy on me."

I could see that fire was her favorite element, but there were three more, and I liked to play with earth myself. The ground looked solid as the asphalt of a parking lot, but that was an illusion to confuse anyone who accidentally opened the way gate. I decided to throw a few mud balls in her direction. She had to allow a few to hit, or she would have to put up a shield to stop them. She chose the painful road. Five of the twenty hit their mark, one on her forehead, leaving it scraped and bleeding. The blood made her look even more dangerous, but maybe that was Alias' opinion. I could feel the fangs sliding into my mouth. They weren't real, at least not totally. My magic created them for him. I ran my tongue over them, feeling the foreignness of the points. I really couldn't understand how he didn't cut his tongue every day of his life. His fangs never retracted.

I smiled at Liz, letting her see how happy I was to see her bleeding. She looked a little surprised, but it didn't stop her. She chose wind since I was showing off. It was my turn to bleed as she pummeled me with the detritus picked up by the force of the blow. The cuts stung a little, but that only made it better. I couldn't remember the last time I had so much fun with magic.

"Fangs? That is a new one. Who is playing dirty now, Sorcerer?"

I licked my lips, cutting my tongue on the needle-sharp upper fangs. Alias was itching to take over, especially after tasting my blood. I had to cheat a little to get him under control, so I froze time. She would never notice if I didn't do something stupid. Then again, I had the soul of a serial killing vampire in my body. It took a few moments and deep breathing before I could get him calmed down enough for the fangs to disappear. I was in basically the same position when time started again. It wasn't easy to freeze time in a timeless place, taking more of my power than I wanted to use.

"I'll introduce you to my ex later since you are partially responsible for him being here, Sorceress."

I needed to rethink my strategy since we needed to be more evenly matched. I was not going to allow Alias to ruin my fun, but he was already putting the thought in my head that she would taste delicious…and I was not sure he was thinking about her blood. I must have given my thoughts away in my facial expression because she stopped for a moment.

"You are a new kind of interesting, aren't you, Sorcerer?"

I took advantage of her curiosity and threw all four elements toward her simultaneously, ending in a downpour of water. Water dampens magic, allowing me to close the distance between us while she fought to see through the water and drenched hair in her eyes. The sight of her wet body gave me a flash of vision. She was projecting again, this time, we were in a shower, naked, and I was kissing her. I could almost feel her lips against mine. She had no idea that we had this connection or that her thoughts were bleeding through to me. It threw me for a moment, and she took advantage; she hit me with another force blow, then used the water against me before I could return the impact. First, my face, then my hair; she knew how to hurt a guy. Nothing to do for the moment but spar with words.

"You've never met my kind of interesting, Sorceress; I'm a bit out of this world, but don't worry, the body is all me, no blue skin underneath. The fanged parasite infesting me is Alias; watch out, he bites."

I cheated, I used Alias's power to move behind her and grab her around the waist. I pinned her against the wall of a utility shed–or at least it was in reality. My left hand was around her delicate throat, and my right was holding her hands above her head. I imagined what would happen if I squeezed until I crushed her windpipe. If you think those thoughts were coming from Alias, you're wrong. I loved the sound of bones breaking…when I caused the breakage. Alias wanted me to bite; I could feel the fangs coming in. I could crush her throat, leave her for whatever passed by, or bite her and drain her of all that delicious magic-spiced blood. With the blood would come her power–the power of a Grimslayer.

I squeezed her neck tighter and leaned toward her. My eyes, reflected in hers, were flashing from lavender to emerald, green. Yeah, Alias wanted her blood. I had to let go of my grip to turn her head, exposing her taut neck. I leaned in slowly as her breath caught in her throat. She knew I had her, that I could kill her in more ways than one. Most people would be afraid, but she wasn't; she was turned on. Her skin was flush with heat, and her eyes were dilated, so I could barely see the lavender iris.

I continued to move slowly, but at the last moment, I pressed my lips to hers and kissed her roughly. The fangs tore at my lips and hers as I forced her mouth open with my tongue. She kissed me back with as much enthusiasm as my kiss. Sparks popped between the two of us and a thick oily feel of black magic filled the air. I could feel a storm building between us, and it was trying to pull me into its vortex. I let go of her hands and wrapped both of my hands behind her head, kissing deeper. I needed more of that sweet magic. Or was it the blood?

I didn't feel her hand on my chest until she dug her nails in and hit me with a forceful blow that threw me across the parking lot. I landed on my ass, but it could have been worse. There aren't many sorcerer-level magic users in the world, and she could have taken any of them out with that blow. Except me.

"Not bad. Not bad at all. For a gay man, or whatever you are."

That last blow made me understand why my father thought she would be a good ally; even someone with immunity to most magic would die if you crushed their heart. My rib cage was broken, and I could tell I was bleeding internally, but I felt fucking great! Whatever she did to me during the kiss was like a drug. She was talking cocky, but I could tell she felt it too. Her magic was inside me, energizing me like a line of cocaine. I stood slowly, not because I was in pain, but because the magic was pushing me toward her, or pulling…both.

"Gay, alien, vampire, sorcerer, and part-time archeologist. I don't know what you did to me, but I will find out! This challenge is your win, Sorceress; I guess that means I buy breakfast. I want to do this again, but I should tell you more about myself, so you know when I'm cheating."

She touched her lip and gave me a quizzical look. She didn't know what had happened either. Did she feel the magic, or did I manage to drain her without her consent?

"Did you just ask me on a date, gay alien, vampire Sorcerer?"

I had to think about that for a moment. I had no idea what people did on dates, and I don't just mean straight people.

"I don't date as a rule, but what makes you think this has earned you a date?"

She touched her left hand to her bleeding forehead, then showed me the blood on her hand.

"Anyone but you would owe me sex for this foreplay. I'll settle for pancakes and some answers, this time."

Answers were going to be tricky. She would probably understand Alias and Alton; she did kill the Grim who held us hostage. I wanted some answers, too, like why I felt as if I'd kissed a live wire or a lightning bolt. I dropped us back into the real world with a whisper, then grabbed some clothes from my trunk and pulled them on. Liz put on her jacket; it was all she had. Liz was already getting into the passenger's seat, which surprised me. After I admitted defeat, I would have thought she would want to drive. I was still hesitating about opening the connection between us. She's already been bleeding into my thoughts with her fantasies.

Al

The IHOP on East Madison in Seattle was open twenty-four hours. Liz wanted pancakes. Where else would we go at two on a Monday morning? The drive through the city was quiet inside and outside the car. I left the music off, in case she wanted to talk. I guess talking about nothing isn't her thing, or my car was just that impressive. It was fine with me; all the small talk people did to pass the time bored me. The silence allowed me to think, which was actually my favorite pastime.

The one thing I hated about any city was the people. They were constantly moving and always in the wrong direction. All of the lights were there to give them the illusion of safety. Humans feared the dark and what lurks inside. I'd always preferred the darkness. But I'm a lurker.

There were only a few cars in the IHOP parking lot. I guess two in the morning wasn't their happy hour. Liz was out the door quickly, and she led the way inside. I didn't know if she wanted me to look at her ass or prove that she wasn't afraid of me. She did have a nice ass, for a woman. She marched past the sign requesting that she wait to be seated.

She picked the most defensible position in the place, secure for two. If you thought she was all sweet and trusting, you were wrong. It was a test; I would say she had something in mind, from her demeanor. Her seating choice left me with my back to the door. Most people would have a problem, but my hearing was better than my sight, and thanks to the soul of a vampire, I had fast reflexes. You might have wondered why Liz was so paranoid unless you knew that the name "Grimslayer" made an excellent big target on a person's back.

"First time?" she asked as her eyes scanned the room.

I sat down hard on the seat, causing it to creak loudly. I threw a quick glamor over us before the waiter made it to our table. He was hesitating as if he knew we needed to talk worse than eat. He probably knew Liz because he looked scared.

"I've been here a few times; the omelets are pretty good," I replied as I searched the room. Liz's paranoia was rubbing off on me. I knew she wasn't asking about the restaurant, but I've never been an information volunteer. My answer frustrated her; it showed on her face.

"First time getting your ass kicked by a woman? The first time you revealed your secret powers? The first time you've stolen power with a kiss?"

I'd felt that at first, she was stealing power, but then I felt the magic grow. That was the first time I'd ever had my ass kicked…by anyone. I rubbed the considerable bruise forming on my chest and said, "My first ass-kicking ever. No one else lives to tell a different story."

"Cute; tell me about the fangs, Dracula."

"I could kill you with a thought, and you are worried about some fangs?" Yeah, I was stalling. Liz was more than just a stranger; she was a potential danger. And now I knew just how dangerous she was.

"If you believe in what you said, then why didn't you?" She hesitated for a moment, then added, "Kill me?"

"I owed you an ass-kicking, not a death. You just caught me off guard. I don't want to kill you, but I am possessed by someone who might." I ran my tongue over normal canines as if I was willing the fangs to appear. It never worked that way, but it didn't stop me from trying.

"I've never met a vampire Sorcerer before," she said, watching me carefully. Either I was projecting, or she was reading my thoughts–probably both.

"And you still haven't. Hold on..." I don't like to release control of my body, but the only way I could explain Alias was to allow him to explain himself. I could only hope Liz didn't kill me while I was away. Never trust a vampire, seriously!

I could feel the change as my body tried its best to reflect the soul which was now taking charge. What I hated most was his brown hair; his eyes were a gorgeous green. I knew I would regret letting him out to play, but it was the only way.

"Hello, Gorgeous," I said to the woman sitting across from me. She looked me over like I was a strange exhibit in a museum, then glanced at the window. I looked over at my own reflection–could have been worse. I yawned just to show off all four fangs; they were sharper and longer in this body. Many things were more considerable in this body, and it was tempting to touch all of them. Al didn't let me out to play much, probably because I tended to kill people…mostly the ones who love him. I wondered if this sweet blonde would be the next on my list. I already knew she tasted sweet and spicy. I wouldn't kill her now, though, not after just one kiss. She'd have to love him first, and she didn't seem like someone who loved quickly or easily. I held out a hand that I knew she wouldn't take. She was paranoid, just like him.

"Alias Weird-Durant, alien-vampire hybrid, born vampire, not turned. I died about eight months ago and was a prisoner in the shadow realm where your Reaper friend now lives. You set me free, Gorgeous; I guess that gives you a free pass on the fangs. He doesn't usually let me introduce myself. Never has actually. Not even when we were married. He doesn't let me out to play much."

"So, you possess Alaric's body? I have heard of you, by reputation, vampire."

"Actually, he possesses my soul, and I am just along for the ride. It was that, or let your Grim friend end my existence, and I kind of like not being ended."

The waiter got brave enough to approach the table, so I had to exit quickly. I was not the man she arrived with, and he would notice. I nodded a quick good-bye as I felt Al take over.

I was myself again before the waiter made it to the table. He was young, in his early twenties, blonde with ice-blue eyes. He was probably working the night shift to pay for college. He stopped at the table, looked at the window, then at me. He must have noticed something. Shit! I should have frozen time, but I didn't want Liz to learn that secret. No one living knew I could do that, not even family. Liz was brilliant; she would figure it out sooner or later.

"Can I take your order, Miss Key, and you too, Sir?"

So, she was a regular, or at least she had the attention of our young, very human waiter. Poor boy, I had more chances with her than he did, and I was gay.

"You know what I want, Carl. Al will have the same; only bring him some meat to go with it. I gave him a good workout, and he needs the protein; he's a big boy,"

Carl glanced at me, and his ears turned red. Liz had given him the idea that we'd had sex, and I wasn't going to disagree. She had her reasons for breaking the poor boy's heart. I'd been with a human or two, they didn't have the stamina to keep up with a sorcerer, and they broke easily. I didn't add anything to the order; I figured the usual would mean coffee, which was magic.

Liz started laughing when the waiter was gone; she only stopped to ask, "So you are insane? Multiple personalities, or am I missing something?"

"Yes, to all of that. I'm not introducing you to Alton, but you met him the night you killed the Grim. He doesn't come out to play with strangers normally."

The waiter returned with two coffees and some creamer cups. Neither of us went for the cream. We were silent until he was out of hearing range.

"Now tell me what you did to me with that kiss and why you kissed me, gay, Alien Sorcerer!"

I held my hand flat on the table and looked her in the eyes. She was curious but guarded, just like me. I could see in her thoughts that she believed I had put a spell on her, a mark. It was something she would do to her lovers.

"This is rare, but I will apologize for the kiss. I'm not sure why I did that, but I didn't do anything more than kiss you."

I didn't want to do this, but I sent her an image of her touching my hand. She followed her vision self as if in a trance. When her hand was over mine, not quite touching, a lightning storm of magic erupted between our hands. She pulled her hand back and rubbed it on her jacket sleeve.

"Is that some alien thing?"

"I've been an alien since birth, a sorcerer for a few years, but nothing like this has ever happened to me. It's like an electromagnetic field being generated between us."

"Now you're talking like an alien."

"Like a scientist, but there's not much difference, especially in my family."

"It's still magic even if you know how it's done," she said, quoting Pratchett.

"So, you do read," I said while sipping the hot coffee. There are quicker ways to get caffeine in your system, but nothing is as good as a cup of coffee.

She took up her cup, sniffed it, then took a sip. "Funny, Mister Scientist. I do read. I have no idea how magic worked for you, but I had to learn everything myself. I didn't keep myself alive by ignoring something like that kiss. You say you didn't do anything to me, magically, and I know I didn't do anything magical. I don't trust you, and I doubt you are stupid enough to trust me, but I want to know what that was. I can feel your oily magic inside me." She took another sip of hot coffee and winced as if in pain. She tried to hide the reaction by blowing on the steaming liquid, but I knew it wasn't that hot.

"Sorry about the cuts; they'll heal quickly if that helps."

"Tasting my blood, was that you, or Alias? Because you looked like you," she said twirling her index finger in a circle in front of my face. I resisted the urge to bite it. That was probably Alias's thought and not my own.

"It's all magic, the fangs, the glamour. Sometimes I forget which of us is me. I do magic; he drinks blood. It's nothing new, I was always living under his shadow," I sighed.

The waiter brought two stacks of pancakes and a plate of breakfast meat. I'm a meat eater, which Liz noticed. You don't get a body like mine grazing on vegetation, but the pancakes looked good. Another side effect of magic is the extreme craving for carbs. The waiter stepped away and returned with caramel sauce. He set it in front of Liz and walked away without a word. He got the message.

"Always?"

"Since the day I was born. He is my stepbrother; in case you are thinking incest. Most people go there eventually."

"Scientist father, alien mother, vampire brother–sorry, stepbrother. Did you have elves for cousins?"

"Children. Three, one-quarter elf. Alton's not mine," I replied jokingly. Rainn had given birth to triplets the night that Liz killed the Grim and released Alias and me from the shadowlands. Thanks to their genetics the three girls would all be hiding pointed ears.

"All I had were parents who wanted me to be like them or die," Liz mumbled.

"Sophie Smith, Daniel Costa. Alma? I do my homework. You still spend time with Soph; I've seen you at her house."

"Debts owed from another lifetime. I assume you understand these things, family man?"

"The difference is, they owe me; I don't owe anyone a debt…except your Reaper. I can live with that one."

She knew what I meant; my tattoos told anyone who knew about Reapers that I belonged to one, like an indentured servant. Deathripper could call on me to do favors, but there is not much a Reaper needs from someone living like me. Alive, it didn't mean much. When dead I become a battery of endless magic and the possibility of becoming one of them. No one told me that part when I signed the contract in my blood. Alias also carried a contract, but his body was charcoal now. No Grim would bring him back. He was too long dead for that.

We stopped talking to eat the food. I was trying to figure out how to ask questions without giving away any secrets I wanted to keep. She was an open book. What I didn't know before, she was projecting in her thoughts. I tried to avoid sending my thoughts back.

"So, gay alien, vampire, sorcerer, top or bottom?"

"Top, always, unless there has been an arrangement made. I don't relinquish control easily. You?"

"Same, I've never met a person who is strong enough to dominate me, and I have never been submissive…in any way. You could ask my parents for confirmation, but they are unavailable unless you're a medium. "

"I dabble in necromancy, but I'm not interested in contacting the dead."

Liz was about to answer, but she glanced up, and a smile filled her face. It wasn't a friendly smile, and I was glad she hadn't aimed it at me. The reflection in the window showed an angry-looking blonde. I could tell she was a mage by her aura.

Liz sipped her coffee thoughtfully while the recipient of the Cheshire cat grin scanned the restaurant with her eyes. Once she settled her gaze on Liz, she started marching toward us.

"Trouble in 3-2-1," Liz whispered as she watched the woman approach.

I waited until she was within earshot, then asked, "She looks pissed…what did you do, fuck her boyfriend?"

"And then killed him," she said when the woman stopped at our table.

"Bitch!" the woman screamed.

"Always so eloquent, Judith," she said, turning her attention away from the raging woman to me.

"Al, this is Judith, one of Temp's pets" Liz said indicating the woman.

I knew Temp Griffin; he was like a capo for the magic mob. Though I didn't know the young woman standing next to our table twitching like an addict. She smelled of expensive alcohol and even more costly perfume. She couldn't have seen her thirtieth birthday, and she wasn't likely to the way she was going. Liz was paying close attention to the woman's hands but didn't look worried; she looked as if she was amused while she sipped her coffee.

"Be careful of what you do with your pretty hands. You can end like Temp, honey."

Judith looked at her hands, then at me for some reason. She didn't know me or of me; I could tell by how her demeanor suddenly became very seductive.

"Are you the latest victim of the Black Widow, cutie? She'll kill you too and drink your blood while she dances away to the next victim," she said.

I might have been amused, but I don't like being called 'cutie' by anyone but my alien stepmother. Her concern over her dead lover seemed to melt away at the thought of 'stealing' me from Liz. Her motivation was as clear as the window; she wanted what she couldn't have or what Liz had. Temp meant nothing more to Judith than a dress or piece of jewelry that Liz possessed. He was an asshole who deserved to die, but I hate people who thought of people as possessions. I'm evil, but even I am not that evil.

I glanced at her briefly while she did her best to look sexy, then I returned my gaze to my companion before addressing her. "Judith, you are not my type, and I have no fear of Elizabeth Key, but you should. I saw your boyfriend after Liz finished him. If you are smart, you would leave and let us finish our breakfast."

Liz hid her smirk with the coffee mug, but I couldn't hide mine. Judith was fuming, either because I didn't heed her warning, or I refused to look at her while addressing her. Maybe it was telling her she wasn't my type. I've been told I don't act gay. I never apologized for not fitting a stereotype.

I felt Liz weave a subtle protection spell that no one else in the room could notice. I didn't know if I was more sensitive to her magic because of the mental connection or if it had to do with whatever happened with that kiss. All I knew for sure was that Liz was ready for a fight, and so was Judith. It wasn't my concern, so I returned to my cooling breakfast and tried to ignore the two women.

The strike came moments after Liz's shield was up. I could sense the greasy aura of the death curse aimed at Liz. It was subtle, but it would have caused a scene had Liz not been prepared. I noticed that she shielded more to control the situation than protect herself. I had sent worse at her earlier, during our sparring, and she hadn't even tried to shield. Judith continued to throw curses and a few lethal but subtle fireballs toward Liz with her right hand. Liz was in tears from laughter, but she didn't raise a finger to stop the woman. Watching Liz laugh at the young woman using everything she could conjure was entertaining until the waiter stepped out of the back. There are rules about what humans are allowed to see, and should a human see someone slinging magic around, well, they shouldn't live to tell about it. Judith started to aim her next spell at Carl, and that was when Liz stopped her, with my favorite Vader force choke. Liz was not quite strong enough to lift Judith off the ground, but she stopped her magic for the moment. It was just long enough for Judith to pull a gun from behind her back and aim it toward Liz. I had two choices: freeze time to get Liz out of the bullet's path or do something more lethal. The first choice would reveal a secret I wasn't ready to tell two people, since Carl would also be in the path of the bullet since he rushed over to see what was going on.

I knew what to do when I saw a familiar face in that darkened window. A human would never notice him even if they could see him. He didn't wear the typical robes of a Reaper. He wore black jeans, a T-shirt, and a black leather coat. They called him Deathripper because he didn't follow the rules… He killed. He was here because someone would die, and I would do the killing. No one else would see him– well, Liz might. She had a connection to this particular Grim.

Judith already had one hand on her throat, which made it look like she was choking, so when I used my magic to explode her heart it looked as if she had a heart attack, especially since Liz released her the moment blood obscured the light in her eyes. Carl rushed over to give aid to the fallen woman while he used his cell phone to call 911. Liz used her foot to pull the gun under the table so no one would see.

She leaned over the table and whispered, "You ruined my fun."

"I got bored, and the coffee was getting cold," I whispered back.

I could have saved Carl from overhearing by using our telepathic connection, but I wasn't quite ready to reveal that.

The paramedics showed up quicker than I thought they would and took over the resuscitation attempts while Carl crawled away to puke. It was probably the first time he'd witnessed a death, especially a magical one. The paramedics gave up quicker than Carl had as they realized Judith's lungs were filled with blood. None of them paid much attention to us as they worked. The police car that pulled up in the parking spot next to the ambulance held the two who would ask questions.

"Now, where were we?" Liz asked, pulling me away from the action.

I had to think for a moment before I replied. "I believe you were asking about my favorite sexual position or role."

We were both laughing when the two policemen stepped up to our table. Thanks to the glamor, we just looked like two people having breakfast after a late night of partying. In preparation for the interrogation, I had already pulled my driver's license out of my wallet. The officers were typical Pacific Northwesterners, one tall, fit, and blonde, the other shorter, stocky, and from his looks, a mix of Anglo and Haida or possibly another Pacific Northwest tribe. The blonde, Officer Kennedy, was hot and gay, but I don't think he was out of the closet with his partner. He was trying too hard to look straight until he met my gaze. I gave him my most charming smile, saying, 'I like what I see.' He practically melted but regained his composure before his partner noticed. He was living in the closet, for sure.

Kennedy took my license, looked it over, then looked me in the eye and asked, "Weird? Seriously?"

The question was part curiosity and part flirty from the tone of his voice. I'd never been with a vanilla human before, but he was sending signals, or maybe it was just me. Killing Judith and flirting with Liz made me feel more horny than usual. Liz was not getting the same interest from Officer West. He looked at her ID, passed it back, and was already getting her statement about what had happened. It's not like we had much to say; she came in, started ranting, and collapsed.

Officer Kennedy was leaning on the table pretending to listen to Liz, but he held on to my driver's license and kept his eyes on me.

"So, do you go by Al or Rick?"

"My friends call me Al. Are we friends, Officer Kennedy?"

I was trying to listen to Liz's fascinating story about how this crazy drunk woman came up to us, started screaming, then collapsed. She made it sound dull enough that I stifled a yawn. Officer Kennedy was trying to decide whether I was coming on to him or not. He wasn't sure of me, I was sitting in a restaurant with a scantily clothed woman, and I had failed at buttoning my shirt. He had no idea I was cut, burned, and bruised from my night with that scantily clad woman. I would be immobile within a day if I didn't do something. Even magic bruises don't go away by magic. Luckily no human could see through my glamour. Otherwise, there would be questions about my ears. I never learned to hide them as a child, or the nickname elf-boy would never have stuck with me.

"So, Al, you're a long way from home. Do you have anything to add to Miss Key's statement?" Officer Kennedy pulled me out of my thoughts, and I looked down at the body as they slipped it into a bag. It was obvious to everyone that she had died a natural death; well, magic is natural to me. An average person would feel remorse, but that wasn't my way. I don't do guilt.

"What could I add? That I used my magic powers to cause a woman to have a heart attack at my table, spoiling my breakfast with my colleague? Maybe she was just overwhelmed by my stunning good looks?" I joked.

I didn't expect him to laugh, so it surprised his partner and me when he did. Liz watched us like we were just putting on a show for her. Officer Kennedy slid my license across the table, and I returned it to my wallet. I slipped my card into Officer Kennedy's hand with a handshake that lasted longer than appropriate. He put it in his breast pocket without looking at it.

When the excitement died down, I returned my attention to Liz, still grinning at me. "What?" I asked when I noticed her silently giggling.

"You turned the charm on high," she said with a smirk, "Officer Hottie was seconds away from asking you to spank him. Tell me, Sorcerer Alaric, how much do you want to spank him?"

"I did slip him my card with my cell number on it. I've never been with a vanilla human before. Do they break easily?"

"What makes you think I would know?"

"The late Daniel Costa."

"Another time, another life. If you know about Dan, then you know I was almost human myself back then, and he was alive and in one piece when I left him. Are you telling me that you have never been with a human before, or are you just trying to get information about me without asking the questions?"

"I lost my virginity to a vampire; everyone else has been on my downward slide. I play rough."

I dropped a C-note on the table, which was more than twice the bill, but I did make a mess. Judith had been kind enough to do her bleeding internally, at least mostly. Liz was watching me like I was an interesting bug.

"You're totally serious, aren't you? Vampires?"

"Alias and Pedro were vampires. I been with a few of the Fae. They are fun, but I wouldn't recommend them unless you are good at negotiation. I usually stick with those who can heal themselves, at least a little."

We both stood and headed toward the parking lot. When we got to the car, she handed me a business card. I thought she was giving me her number until I read the card. It belonged to Officer Kennedy–Brandon. Officer West must have given her both cards while I entertained his partner.

"Call him, and don't break him…too much."

She slipped my phone out of my jeans pocket and turned it on. She looked at me for a moment, then typed in four numbers, my unlock code. She typed something into the phone, then handed it back to me. She had sent herself a message, but the message was for me. It read "Elite?" My password, and not one a non-gamer would understand. It didn't answer my unasked question of whether she was reading my mind or only guessing PIN. Afterward, she turned and created a portal right there in the parking lot. I stood looking down at my phone as she stepped through the doorway. I needed to learn how to do that. It would probably take me an hour to get home from here. I had to find the nearest soft spot that was big enough for a Tesla Model Three. The Policeman's business card went into my pocket with the phone. I don't date, and I never have, but something about this guy was different. It wasn't just his slightly sociopathic laugh. He was hot and gay and should have been totally off my menu. Liz had me thinking about things other than just magic. This alliance would be more fun and dangerous than I had imagined when my father suggested it.

Liz

Wolf's breath on my cheekbone mixed a mix of fresh mint and alcohol. Mojito, to be more specific. A mage like him only drank the Mojito because it was what I was drinking at the bar. I let him talk me into going to his place; he didn't have to talk much. Wolf, and do not let the name fool you, was a powerful mage with a strong bloodline and a taste for knowledge. With delicious dark skin, black short hair, and green eyes, he was, once upon a time, a suitor of mine. His tight navy-blue shirt showed how well he worked out at the gym, and his black suit pants showed he was enjoying his time with me. I could do worse; I've fucked worse. I would not be an incubator and then a teacher to some brat child that could steal my magic, or at least my will to live. I didn't come here for this; I was here for information and maybe a little fun. I liked Wolf because he usually provided me with both.

"I don't have the answers for you, Elizabeth," he replied breathlessly, a side-effect of my hand over his intimate parts. I smirked at him, giving him a squeeze that made him shudder.

"Are you sure, Wolf?" I whispered into his ear, nibbling his earlobe. "You knew Temp, you know Harry…and you know rumors."

I prefer to use other torture methods to get information, but Wolf and I go back. He, too, was not interested in procreating for the well of the bloodline. And damn it, he was hot!

"I just need to know for whom they were working," I said, stealing a kiss, "But I have to cut our night short if you don't know anything. I have a lot of research to do. You know me, time is precious." I squeezed his firm package once more, then backed away from him.

"Wait!" Wolf whispered the moment I reached for my jacket I had left it on the floor. I turned to him with a smile on my face. "They are dangerous beings, Elizabeth. Run the other way."

"Charming," I said, moving closer to unbuckle his belt. "Charming how you forget I am one of the dangerous beings." He did not need any more encouragement to talk. He would spill the beans no matter what, but now I wanted him. I was only a magic being.

"It is true, what they are saying? You killed a Grim Reaper?" he asked, moving his hands to my butt cheeks and squeezing me. "Elizabeth, if that is true…."

He lost his train of thought when I unbuttoned his pants and slid my hand inside his underwear.

"True," I answered, not wanting to waste more time or give any more details. "So whoever it is they were working for, I can handle. Talk."

"Elizabeth," he whined.

I should slow down, or he would not be coherent, but I did not like to stretch sex, and that just got up on my wishlist for this night.

"I can make this feel very good for you while you talk, Wolf," I told him softly against his ear as I shoved his pants to his ankles and nibbled his neck. "Tell me, Wolf. Give me what I want, and I will give you what you need."

"Fuck, Elizabeth, I hope that no one ever finds out the hold you have on me, or no one will tell me anything again!" I slowly teased my hand up and down his cock, giving him a little incentive and allowing him to keep talking. "Why don't you take on my purpose? Why don't you let me treat you like a fucking Queen like you deserve?"

I was not expecting this, not right now. I had my hand on Wolf's shaft, damn it. I didn't need this. He wasn't the first person to offer me a position in his family, a family name, protection–like I needed money or safety.

"Wolf, the Boss?" I demanded, utterly aware of his heavy breathing.

He'd had enough because, in seconds, he'd brusquely grabbed me by my waist, turned my back to him and pressed me down so my upper body lay over the ceremonial alter. One of his hands held me still against the altar, and the other worked up from my knee to my thigh, harshly. He began searching under my skirt for something that was not there.

"Elizabeth, you are mad? You went to a bar, in a dress, without underwear," he said, with a malice tone in his voice as he teased me with his fingers.

I shrugged my shoulders. "I forgot?" But I gasped when Wolf's finger entered me, and I closed my eyes and stopped fighting him. His torturous fingers inside me, and his hard lock on my back made it hard to concentrate.

"Wolf–" but he interrupted me.

"You can't let go of control, can you? You were planning how to escape already, weren't you? Elizabeth, why don't you let go for once?"

"Because you want to marry me, and all I want is this!" I said, grabbing his hard cock, and he shivered. "Now, fuck me, and if I get anything, I will fucking burn you alive!"

"Will I get something?"

"Fuck you, Wolf!" But I smirked at the audacity. He knew what he was allowed to say.

He loosened his grip on me, and I supported myself on my elbows, lifting my chest from the uncomfortable altar. I felt him at my entrance and didn't wait for the rest; I forced my body back and he filled me. Immediately his hands were on my breasts and squeezing painfully. I let my head fall back to his shoulder and try to get my hand to his waist, to pull him harder against me, to scratch him, anything. His thrusts were rough, deep and I let out a moan.

"Elizabeth," he said, letting a high laugh escape his mouth. "You killed Temp's boss. The Reapers are not neutral anymore. Some do not care about the Universe's balance."

Wolf didn't slow down; he couldn't stop. He kept squeezing, biting my shoulder and neck, thrusting hard, while holding me steady with one arm around my waist.

The harsh strokes forced me to hold onto the altar and the light candles collapsed to the floor and set the small altar cover on fire. Ignoring the little flames, I tried to hold onto his neck. I needed to scratch something, squeeze, hurt, and get hurt, so I dug my fingernails into his arm, making him thrust harder.

"Think of the most powerful beings we know, all together to end one person…someone who endangers them all. Tell me is not you, Elizabeth. Tell me it is not you that they are after." He pulled me into a painful kiss, and his hand slipped lower to caress me between my legs.

"No," I moaned, responding to his question, unable to do anything else. I would think straight about all he is saying after. Now, I needed the release.

The fire that had started with the fallen candles was now considered a danger to a human, but Wolf did not see or care. He kept thrusting, ensuring I was steady enough to take him. With my release seconds away, I held my hand in the direction of the fire and absorbed its energy, lowering the flames until they vanished altogether.

I felt his hand on my neck, pinning me against his chest, and he moaned, "That was so hot!" With that, I let my release take full force while holding onto the altar. I felt my whole body shake and lost all my strength, almost falling. Everything disappeared for a few seconds before I was back in my body in time to experience his release too. He was still inside me, still holding me in place. There were burn marks on the altar where my hands rested. I had done this. I released more than an orgasm; no wonder he asked if it was me they wanted. But I was not the one they want; they wanted Sophie.

"That is why we do not do this more often, Wolf," I said breathlessly, pushing him away from me. "You are too eager. It is never enough for you."

I put my clothes straight, thinking how grateful I was for my home being a portal away, while he got dressed. I needed a shower, but after the questions I had.

"Wolf, what do you know about the person they are searching for?"

"Besides the rumor that you are that person or that you are protecting the person?" he asked, proud of himself. "A purifying power that can turn darkness into light. It threatens any living creature that is dark or has dark in itself. Be careful before you get purified yourself, in case the rumors are true."

I scowl. "I'm afraid those assholes will be disappointed. What more do you know?" I asked, sitting on the altar, which moments before was the only thing keeping me up.

"Powerful beings want that person dead, Elizabeth. People say that the person has the power of an angel. They believe this kind of power does not belong here and that no one should have so much. The good ones are afraid also, and they are starting to want the person dead too. If that power goes dark for some reason, it will be too dangerous. Temp's boss was the Reaper you killed; I do not know who Harry's boss is, Elizabeth. But whoever they are, you should stay away from all of this."

He started to look at me strangely. "What, Wolf?"

"Are you sure it is not you?"

I started laughing, and I could not stop. "The power-. The power of an angel. A pure- Angel. Me?" I said between laughs. "Shut up, Wolf."

"I will get you more names of who was involved with Temp and who is involved with Harry. It will take a few days. Stay low, Elizabeth. Humans… The cops are involved in this mess too. Stay clean, stay safe."

He was still unsure about my innocence in all of this, but I didn't care.

"Well, this was fun." I created a portal, not waiting for Wolf to answer and not interested in what he was beginning to say. I picked up my phone and scrolled to my last text message from Alaric, and texted back.

Liz: Do you believe in angels, Sorcerer?

Al: Biblical?

I put the phone away. I'd wait until I had more time to discuss this matter in depth with him and turned to Wolf.

"Let's do this again," I said, jumping off the altar. I stepped through the portal without looking back. Wolf was always fun, but he wanted more than I was willing to give.

Al

I'd said this before, but I don't date. I came out as aromantic while still married. Don't get me wrong; I enjoyed sex almost as much as magic. I just didn't do relationships or love. I didn't know why I was sitting in my living room with my phone in one hand and Officer Kennedy's card in the other. I also never took advice, but Liz's text had me thinking. It read, "Have you tried out the handcuffs yet?" It wasn't her first text about Officer Hottie. She'd been encouraging me to call for nearly two weeks. Liz hadn't been hiding in a house with an overworked mother of three newborn girls and twin toddlers, but she knew I had been.

Usually, I would just zone out and let Alton take over...There's more than one reason I never sleep. The body was mine, so I had more control than they did, and right now, I didn't feel like giving up control. Liz had made it clear that Alias was not invited to play, and one phone conversation with Alton was enough for her to text questions before calling me. Her interest in babies stopped at not causing them harm. It was getting crowded inside my head.

I was just about to dial the number on the card when my phone rang. The area code was Seattle, Washington, and it didn't take my genius to figure out who it was.

"Officer Kennedy, I wondered when I would hear from you." I had only guessed that it was him by the area code. I don't give out my number often.

"Brandon, Al. We're friends, remember?" He had the charm turned on high for a first phone call.

"Alaric, Brandon, we're not that friendly…yet." I know it was a little late to play hard to get. I had more than one reason to be reserved with him. He was a human who would be curious about me because of his profession. I could only assume he had been spending the last two weeks doing what I had been–investigating. I knew more about him than he could learn about me. My birth certificate had been faked; it's not like my father walked into a hospital to give birth; he would have been sent to Area 51. The place of birth was correct, Inverness Scotland. My father had been on vacation for three months. His co-workers at the lab had started noticing his weight gain, and he knew he wouldn't be able to hide me from them. I was born blue–literally. Think Avatar without the tail.

"Alaric, no middle name, Weird, born in Inverness Scotland. Thirty-five years old, but you don't look over twenty-five. Former junior Professor of Archeology in Argentina. You studied under Pedro Gonzales, a minor celebrity in his country. You speak five languages."

I laughed. "Seven, and that doesn't include Klingon." That made him laugh. Other than Klingon, I only included the human languages.

"And you're a geek."

I preferred nerd; geek sounded like a carnival entertainer who self-harmed. I didn't want to correct him and sound more like a geek.

"Is that it? My tailor knows more about me."

"You live with a woman named Rainn Rivers and her three children whose father is listed as Alton Weird, but his picture is the spitting image of you. Twin?"

"Something like that," I replied. How did you explain a magical clone?

"And you are listed as the father of twins with the last name Fabian."

"Their only surviving father, the other five, are dead, and I have officially adopted them; they are Weirds now."

"Yes, a fire in San Francisco, where your two brothers and four lovers mysteriously died. I believe Pedro owned the building."

"It was determined to be a freak accident, and they all had a reason to be there. I was late to the party, fortunately for me."

"I'm not your type, am I?"

"German mother, Irish father. You have a master's degree in law, which you don't use as a beat cop. You are the youngest child of three, and your two sisters are lawyers, following in your late father's footsteps. You're still in the closet with your Catholic family and coworkers, including dating the women they set you up with. And you're completely human. You're not my usual type."

"Let me guess; you're half Klingon?"

"Vulcan, actually, on my mother's side," I said, continuing the Star Trek theme.

"That explains the pictures with the pointed ears. I thought they were fake." I didn't have an answer to that. When I was young, I hid them with hair, but I looked silly with long hair. Glamours were easy to pull off for human eyes, but cameras tended to reveal the truth.

"The small talk is fascinating," I lied; I couldn't keep the sarcasm from my voice. "But were you going to ask me out, or just tell me all the things you've discovered about me? Is this call business or pleasure, Brandon?"

"You are confusing. Your social media says that you're gay, but you live with one woman and date another. Are you sure you're out of the closet?"

"Okay, so more small talk; I don't date anyone. Liz and I are friends, and I owe it to my brother to help raise his children."

"Don't date? Your breakfast looked a lot like a date to me. My friends wear more clothes."

"Midnight paintball match." It was only a little lie. "You can't expect us to get paint all over the restaurant."

"Okay, so how about drinks next time you are in town? We can call it whatever you want."

"Friday. Eight. I choose the place. I'll pick you up, and don't complain about the car. I know she's small, but she's fast." I knew where I wanted to take him. It wasn't somewhere he would be seen by friends or family, and it wasn't a gay bar. In every city around the world, you would find a place that only those who lived on the edges of human society can see. They used glamour to hide them; It wasn't wise to take a human there, but I had other motives. I tended to avoid places with too many humans.

"I would expect a guy as big as you to drive a Model Y, at least," Brandon said, bringing me out of my thoughts.

"It was a gift. It has sentimental value," I replied, which was accurate; I was sentimental about the car but not the giver. I was relieved he was gone.

"So, Friday. Drinks, your choice of venue, and you drive. I think I get why you don't date. Always in charge?"

"I'm a busy man and like to be on top. Is that a problem?"

"A relief, actually," he sighed. I guess everyone expected the cop to be in charge. Some people just needed a break, not me, but some people.

"Good. Bring your handcuffs," I said, then hung up without saying goodbye.

I texted Liz, "Testing Friday." She would know what I meant. She always seemed to know, and I was beginning to wonder if she was learning about our connection already. That she guessed my phone's PIN in less than a minute said that she either knew a lot about me or was reading my mind. We usually couldn't connect like that with humans, but Liz was no ordinary human. I chose the place and time of the date because I was hoping to run into Liz. She had been the one who told me about it. It was a good place for people like us to meet others like us. I wouldn't be popular after taking a human cop, but I was used to being unpopular with the magical community. The majority of them looked down on anyone who was not pure blood. I was the least pure of anyone I knew besides my siblings. Someone had found out that my father could see the future. They'd used him to find and kill Daniel Costa. The torture he received cost him his life. I wasn't after revenge because I had been fond of my father; I had other reasons to take them out, and so did Liz. Her loyalty was her only weakness; mine was more complicated.

My family curse was both a weakness and a strength. Nearly two thousand years ago, a dark sorcerer cursed one of my ancestors. It was a particular curse designed to take her mind out of time. It made her a helpful scrying tool, like the Oracles of Delphi, only she was cursed instead of drugged. The sorcerer meant for the curse to weaken the bloodline, but her children, three girls, were each only cursed with one third: one to see the past, one to see the present, and one to see the future. My father had been born with stunted magical abilities. His main magic had been his future sight, something he hid from the paranormal community. Only one man outside the family knew, and I was ready to take the fight to him and his cohorts.

My father had seen this battle in his visions, so he wanted me to seek Liz as an ally. I had family, siblings, and children that Officer Hottie didn't know. A few hours later I received a responding text.

Liz: No backing out, Sorcerer.

I spent two days dreading the "date". I'd already spent twenty minutes on the phone with Brandon doing the small talk thing. Talking was the main reason I didn't date. I don't care about someone's day or their family. I research what I want to know. I might drink with someone at the bar, but the discussion is more of how, where, and when…and that I was on top. Once those things were established, there is no need for chatter. I didn't even talk that way with Liz; we just teased each other or talked about magic. If I wanted to know something about her, I wouldn't ask her, I would have to pay for information. She was searching for something, just as I was.

My brain was stalling on this. I was thirty-six years old, too old to be going on my first date, especially with a human. I'd packed a small rucksack with healing potions–some to numb–a pack of lubricated condoms, and a forget potion just in case. It was illegal in both worlds to make someone forget a lousy date, but in this case, it wouldn't be the sex he would find bad; it'd be what he would see before and after. I only hoped everyone at the bar would be on their best behavior. I was going to make Liz pay for daring me to do this.

Officer Hottie lived in a section of town that was being taken over by those modern but industrial-style apartment complexes. I'd texted him my arrival time down to the second. He was waiting when I arrived, leaning against the wall, trying to look sexy. He didn't need to try so hard, especially with his forefinger hooked into his handcuffs. Using the handcuffs to drum out a tune in his head, he looked up as I drove over, and I realized he was wearing earbuds. Those might come in handy in case there was screaming.

He started moving as soon as he saw my car. You must have ears the size of mine to hear her coming. But he recognized the vehicle. How many Midnight Silver Tesla Model Threes have custom Hawaiian plates with "WYRD" on them?

Once in the car, there was plenty of room; the trick was getting in. He took a few seconds to get the seat adjusted and the seatbelt attached. He had no problem opening the unusual door. He was a big guy like me, and I could tell by his discomfort that he was used to driving.

He reached out and traced a finger around the edge of my ear, and only then did I realize that I hadn't thrown a glamour. I grabbed his hand and looked him in the eye. That was enough to make him pull his arm from my grip and backpedal in his seat, hugging the door.

"Fuck, your eyes are purple, and you're not wearing contacts!"

"I call it lavender; Liz calls it violet. And no, they are not this color because I am an alien. The ears are a different story. The ears are sensitive; I will need a few drinks and some ground rules before you touch."

"No love, no relationship, you like to play rough. I read your blog too. I thought it was fiction, but now I am wondering. Alien, vampire… And your brother, you created your twin?"

I created a ball of light, just a small one. It was something a child could do, but impressive for human eyes that have not seen real magic. I took his left hand and spilled the ball into it. It was primarily harmless magic and felt like holding a solid static electric charge.

"How long does it last? Is this alien? People don't do real magic."

"People do, magic people. And you will see a few magical people tonight."

I reached into the back seat and unzipped the rucksack. I took out two potion vials and held them out to Brandon.

"What is this? Drugs? I'm a cop. I can't, not even weed!"

I put my hand over the light ball to extinguish it, then I put both hands on the wheel. It was time to move. I couldn't explain it to him while sitting in front of his home. He wanted to be in the closet, and being seen with me wouldn't help.

"The first one is for stamina, and I'm not talking Viagra style; your body can't handle what mine can. I twisted a little strength in there; you won't get high. You will just be less breakable for a while," I said. I pulled the car into the traffic and headed toward the bar. Liz would be there; she had bet me that I wouldn't make it to the end of the date. I was beginning to think she was going to win. I thought about the forget potion. It would make him forget the entire night. The problem is it only wipes out a day, from sunset to sunset.

"The second?"

"Healing. It will take care of bruises and most internal damage. It's not as good as having a healer and won't replace blood loss. I don't– I can't heal. I don't do that kind of magic anymore."

"That kind?"

"White magic, light magic, pure magic. Think Gandalf."

"You're a–?" He asked as I slowed to a stop at the light. He looked ready to bolt; his thumb was on the door release button.

"I prefer the term Sorcerer."

"But like blood and death, curses, hexes?"

"I can turn the car around; it's only going to cost me fifty bucks and maybe some information."

"You did it. You killed that woman in IHOP? Her heart exploded like it had been squeezed. Fuck! You fucking told me? A cop?"

"There is another potion in there, all voluntary, you take it, and you forget a day…today. You won't remember any of this," I whispered as the traffic started moving. I was waiting for him to tell me to turn around. He just glanced at the back seat, then stared at the road ahead. I could tell he was thinking about everything I'd said. At least he was a thinker. I hated talking to people with empty heads.

"You can't just zap me with a spell? Sorry, but I usually avoid drinking unless I know the ingredients."

"If I use a spell, I make you forget everything…your whole life. It's a curse, a black magic spell. It's not meant to be for friends." I pulled the car up to a seemingly empty building. It had signs in the window advertising its availability for lease.

Are we friends, Al? The voices in my head were speaking up. Al doesn't have friends. I might have to introduce Brandon to Alias and Alton if he lasts the night. He was religious, at least a little. If he could handle fucking an alien, learning that a vampire possessed me, and my clone, shouldn't be too difficult to handle.

"A month ago, I would tell you that I have no friends. I'm not going to poison you or kill you if I can help it. I don't do the relationship thing anymore; people expect emotional attachment. I play rough, and it's not for everyone. I don't do safe words; fear is part of the fun."

We both got out of the car as a young man, who looked to be around fifteen years old, approached. I handed him a black card from my wallet; it was blank except for the Tesla "T" symbol on the front. I didn't ever use the key card, but it came in handy for valet service. If Brandon was surprised, he didn't show it or ask if the kid had a driver's license. The kid was at least twenty years older than Brandon and probably had a thing about his looks. He was an elf, but one of those who tried to fit in by rounding his ears.

Outside the car, I could see that Brandon had dressed much like I had when we'd first met. Black jeans, a black button-up dress shirt, probably short-sleeved for a warm spring night. He'd topped it off with a black suede jacket and running shoes. I didn't know what that meant for a human, but in my circle, black meant that you weren't afraid to bleed. I doubted Brandon knew the rules, but the thought that he might turned me on.

Brandon arrived at the door first. I stopped him from pulling it open. It wasn't dangerous; the danger came after. I was intrigued by this human; I wanted to see how he took to my world. I turned him and pushed him into the brick wall. I'd told him the potions were voluntary, but I couldn't do what I wanted if he refused. He tried to push me away when I pried his hand open and took the vials from him. I'm all for asking permission regarding sex; this wasn't about that.

I popped the tops off both vials and tipped them into my mouth. Brandon thought I was about to force drugs or poison down his throat, not mine. The moment his lips parted to ask what the fuck I was doing, I kissed him hard. He didn't need much encouragement to kiss me back, but I spit both potions into his mouth once he gave in. He had to swallow the liquid or stop kissing me. He put his hands on my hips and pulled me closer. He didn't need any encouragement to continue kissing, but this was not what we were here for. I don't do back-alley sex, so I gut-punched him. The punch knocked his breath out and caused him to bite down hard on my lower lip. Blood. It had been a while since I let Alias out to play.

The fangs always came first, but the eyes were what people noticed most. Alias's eyes were emerald green, like his biological father's. Brandon took one look at me and started crab-walking away along the wall. The fangs were there, the bright green eyes and the curly brown hair he could never tame. The fangs were as real as any spell, but you couldn't find them on an x-ray or by any scientific means. The look was just a glamour made by Alias' soul and my magic.

"What the fuck are you?"

"The scientific term is insane. Dissociative Identity Disorder. The religious term would be possessed, and the magical term, vampire. Don't worry. It's not your blood I want; it's Al's. I'm not really into humans. The name is Alias, and if you love him, I will kill you."

Alias simply slipped into the back of my mind. He and Alton were always there but usually kept their opinions to themselves. Alias just wanted to scare Brandon, and he succeeded.

"Holy shit!" Brandon screamed when he looked up to see me back to myself. He was on the ground, scared enough that he was shaking. His fear was delicious but not what I wanted yet. I held out a hand to help him to his feet. We hadn't even made it inside the bar, and already I thought he needed that forget potion. Inside the bar, glamour was optional. If Alias freaked him out, I couldn't allow him to go inside. He took my hand tentatively and allowed me to pull him to his feet.

"My brothers aren't dead in the traditional sense of the word. I have three different personalities; well, Alton isn't that different. My world, this world, has different rules. We can go inside and have drinks, or I can take you home, and you can forget all of this."

He looked down at our clasped hands, then pulled me in for another kiss. He didn't hold back this time; his kiss was rough. He licked the blood off the outside of my lip before pulling away and letting go of my hand. He then removed the blood on my chin by swiping his thumb and licking that off.

"I don't scare easily, and you scare me. I like it, don't get me wrong. I don't want to forget this!"

"You haven't seen what is inside, and they won't be happy with you being here. I'm not supposed to bring a human here," I said as I opened the door and gestured for Brandon to go ahead.

The bar was packed, but no one seemed to notice Brandon. I had a reputation, especially after what happened with Judith. Her death wasn't Liz's style; it was mine. Thanks to a string of dead lovers and a tough Reaper, she may have a few nicknames, but I had mine too– Heartbreaker. It wasn't just my devastatingly handsome face and hot body; I had a thing for hearts. They were the most vulnerable organ in the human body. The brain had that hard shell encasing it, but the heart sat in a cage of bones, surrounded by more vulnerability. I also didn't like that people talked about the heart and love synonymously. There was more than one reason that I didn't date.

I usually head to the bar for drinks, but Liz sat next to her 'nighttime snack' in a back booth. He was better looking than her last date, with no visible scars. Her date also gave off an aura of power that was impressive. I knew him– Klaus Dahl. He was on the magic council, a group of politicians who dabbled in human and Spellcaster politics. He was sitting next to Liz, but not close. She was much scarier than I was, but she always seemed to have someone to keep her entertained. She was waving me over to her table as if we'd planned to meet. My plan was for Liz to casually run into us, not for her to beckon us to her table. Brandon noticed her and started heading for her table before I could stop him. He sat and introduced himself to Klaus first thing with a handshake. If I had offered my hand to the wizard, it would have been slapped away or broken. Klaus minded his manners, probably with a promise from

Liz that he wouldn't regret it. He might regret it one day, but not today.

Brandon slid over so I could sit next to him on the padded bench. There were already two beers sweating on the table in front of us. Liz knew when we would arrive, but she hadn't known I would be forcing potions down Brandon's throat for fifteen minutes. We'd discussed what was safe to order for a human. Liz had more dealings with humans than she would admit. She lived half of her life with them, as one of them. I might have gone to a human school, but I was never one of them.

"You're late, Al, and you started the party without us," she said as she handed me a napkin and pointed at her lower lip. Thanks to the second kiss, it was still bleeding, or maybe again.

"I didn't know this was going to be a double date," Brandon commented. He was watching me for my reaction to Liz. He still wasn't convinced that we hadn't had sex. We had kissed, and just the touch of her hand as she handed me the napkin reminded me of that deep thrum of magic between us.

"This isn't a date, Officer Hottie; I brought Klaus here for the entertainment…when everyone in this room tries to kill you, and Al for bringing you. I gave you thirty minutes before you do something to piss them off."

I looked around the room; most people there were magical humans. Spellcasters, mages, and those with magical talent didn't like to call themselves humans. They thought the magic made them more, somehow. I was, in their definition, an anomaly. Aliens don't do magic, not at all. They have their mental powers, telepathy the main one, but as a rule, they weren't magical. My sister Alie and my brother Len were the only other family members with real magic. It kept them safe and off of the magical grid. I was reasonably sure no one would bother us inside the bar. It was after that I would have to watch my back. This was my idea and my fault; Liz wouldn't help me with this, nor would I ask her to–but no one in the bar knew that. Grimslayer, AKA The Black Widow sitting with The Heartbreaker. Who wouldn't think we had each other's backs? I loved the names; they made us seem like supervillains in a DC comic. Marvel had better terms for their bad guys.

"Not late, Liz, just introducing Brandon to the family."

Liz glanced at both sides of Brandon's neck; she knew what I meant by 'family.' Her date didn't know, though. He looked confused. I preferred to keep Alias a secret from everyone in the magic community. It was bad enough for an alien to have magic; a vampire was unheard of. Alias had access to my magic, which could give him an advantage in hunting my kind. And Spellcasters were his favorite prey.

"Neither of you likes small talk, do you?" Brandon asked after a long uncomfortable silence.

"Weird, can you make your pet stop barking?" Klaus asked. He was making me like this idea even more. Klaus would talk about this for months and liked the small talk. He also wanted to gossip and brag, which was why he was with Liz.

Brandon was ready to punch Liz's date, which would have been entertaining until I had to kill Klaus. I promised to stop interfering with Liz on her dates after our initial meeting. That meant crushing his heart was off the table– although there are exceptions. Instead of answering with words, I grabbed Brandon by the chin and turned his face toward mine. This kiss wasn't for him; it was for them. I kissed his lips softly, slowly opening his mouth with my tongue. He was just as eager as before, but he could sense it too. All eyes were on the two of us. The susurration of the room was broken only by Liz's cackling howl of laughter. Brandon put one hand on my cock, and the other behind my head; he held me tightly, not allowing me to stop, not that I planned to. This was a show, but it was also a dare. I was claiming Brandon in a way that they would understand, and I hope he understood, too, for his sake. Alias would kill him at the first hint of love; Brandon's not mine.

"Okay, Weird, you can stop, please? You're making me ill," Klaus sighed.

Klaus's comment didn't stop me, but Liz knocking my beer over into my lap worked. The cold beer hit Brandon's hand before I stopped time. I dropped a napkin on his hand and returned the rest of the beer to the glass. I paid attention to all the eyes on us, which were everyone in the bar. While everyone was frozen, I took the time to drink the beer. The cup would need to be empty before I started everything up again. I was about to return everyone to the timeline when Brandon suddenly gasped beside me. He waved a hand in front of Liz's eyes, flipped Klaus off, and looked at me. It sometimes happens when I'm too close or touching someone. If I touch them, they won't stop with time.

"You're a fucking god!" he whispered.

"Not yet, but one day. You have to forget about this." He flinched.

"That sounded ominous."

"Not a spell or potion; you can't tell anyone or show that you know. You had better be a good fuck, because you could fuck up my life if this got out."

"No one knows, not even Liz?"

"I plan to tell her, but it's not a conversation I can text. I was already hoping to get her alone for a moment, but I didn't know about her date. Klaus will not leave her side until he gets what he wants."

"He wants?"

"You are so gay. Look at her and think like a straight guy. He wants what she wants. We don't date, she and I. She plays with them, though. I just fuck 'em and forget 'em."

"That was the plan with this? Fuck and forget? I'm not going to say that I didn't think that myself at the beginning of this date, but I haven't had so much fun on a date since my first. I was eighteen."

"I don't date; I don't do humans. I don't have a plan, and no one is stupid enough to bring one of your kind here. No one but me."

"We are going to fuck, right? Because right now, you sound like that memory-erase thing will happen. I would like to feel like I had a good time."

"You want to do it now? We've got time. I can hold this for days." I could hold the time bubble for days as long as I kept still and didn't breathe much.

"You're serious, aren't you?"

"I've never done this for this long before. I don't know why I am telling you of all people. I can't let you remember this. I have to talk to her before I take you home." I'd found some information about who sent Temp after Dan Costa and my dad. Liz was looking for them, but they were looking for her, and Sophie Smith. I didn't know all the details; I didn't need to.

"That I can help you with. I'm not supposed to be in this place, and the big dumb blonde doesn't like me. Those fucking potions are making me feel like God damned Superman, and I need to fuck!"

I had to admit the thought of my date pounding Liz's date into the floor was hot. I was pretty sure Liz would agree. I couldn't tell if her date was business or pleasure, but he was at least more intelligent than the last one…for a homophobe.

"He can kill you with magic; the potion doesn't make you invincible." I had an ace regarding magical death, but I doubted Deathripper would let me extend that to a human I wasn't even attached to. I could never be sure about him; after all, he'd been a human once.

"Is he a pussy? Doesn't he know how to fight like a man? No offense."

"None taken. I know how to fight like a man and a woman. I have sisters too."

"So where were we?" Brandon asked. I had almost forgotten the time freeze. I held up my index finger and grabbed Brandon's beer. I knew Liz enough that she would knock over the other beer. The first one was still mainly on the table, but I'd saved my jeans from being doused. When the threat of soaking was gone, I kissed Brandon one more time before I releasing time. It was like popping a soap bubble. The noise of the bar was almost deafening to my ears.

Liz laughed too hard to notice that the only spilled beer was on the table. Her date was getting anxious, with everyone watching. Liz brought him along because she knew that I would make him uncomfortable. If that was her motivation, she was about to get more entertainment than she bargained for. I pulled away from Brandon slowly. I was giving him all the time he needed to cause a distraction.

"I assume this place has restrooms?" Brandon asked. I slid off the bench to let him out and pointed to the back corner of the bar where the restrooms were clearly marked with signs. I didn't know his plan, but I knew Officer Hottie had already established where everything was situated in the bar. He was more cop than human.

He slipped out of the booth and pretended to trip over my very large feet. He caught his balance with his left hand on Klaus' shoulder. He held there for a moment, then gave Klaus an affectionate squeeze. That was all it took to get Klaus to his feet. He knocked Brandon's hand off his shoulder and gut-punched him. He didn't go for a spell first, which meant he was more intelligent than most. I would have killed him for ruining my date.

Brandon doubled over like he was hurt, but the potions running through his system would dull the pain and heal him almost as quickly as he was injured. He didn't stay down for long; once upright, he threw a roundhouse kick to Klaus's head. That was my cue to start talking. I signaled to the waitress, who was doing everything to avoid the fight. She was reluctant to get close, but I held up a twenty-dollar bill, and that got her attention. When she finally reached the table, I asked for some popcorn and two Jack and Cokes. I pulled another twenty from my pocket and handed them both to her. It was enough incentive to dance her way around the fight, which had turned into a wrestling match. Brandon figured out that it wasn't easy to sling spells with your hands behind your back. Meanwhile, the bar patrons were betting on the outcome, and more than half backed Brandon for the win.

"So, what was so important, Al?"

It wasn't my idea, and Officer Hottie wasn't stupid. He'd managed to keep Klaus down with no more injuries than the gut punch and an elbow jab to the lower jaw.

"I assume this was your idea since Officer Hottie doesn't seem this stupid."

"I found them, or at least one. Kamei, a member of my coven and the council. My sources say he is, or was, Temp's boss." That information pulled a surprised look from her, just as the waitress returned with a bowl of popcorn and our drinks.

"Your coven? Like the ones who owe allegiance to you as the head?"

I wasn't surprised that Liz knew I was the head of a small coven of witches and wizards. I'd earned that responsibility by killing the former leader. I didn't murder him. He'd just decided to remove my impure blood from his coven, and I decided not to let him kill me for being an alien. Most positions in the magical community were decided by combat rather than voting. It was the only reason I didn't have a seat on the council. I couldn't kill my way there.

"Care to help me teach them a lesson?" I asked. She'd already started digging into the popcorn, so I had to wait a moment for the answer.

"Before or after tonight's entertainment? Really, you had better fuck that human stupid for this! Klaus is well versed in martial arts, but apparently, he wasn't on the wrestling team in high school." We both glanced at the fighters, who looked like two teenage boys fighting on the playground. It wasn't Brandon's fault; he was doing his best to avoid a deadly curse.

"Sorry about your date, he seemed like a nice homophobic bigot."

"Well, you know, all the best ones are married, or gay," she said with a smirk.

Brandon gave me a look that said he was getting bored trying to keep Klaus from killing him. I needed to get things settled. I gave him a thumbs-up, and he backed off a little. Klaus stood quickly and got ready to throw a deadly curse. I could feel the oily black magic coming from him. I froze the room for a second, everyone except Brandon and myself. I nodded, and he punched Klaus's beautifully straight nose. I let time resume just as the punch hit Klaus, breaking the delicate bones in his nose and upper jaw. The potion also gave Brandon a little extra strength, superhuman strength.

Klaus went down hard, probably with half his nose bones in his brain. Brandon was good enough to check his pulse and eyes before returning to the table and sitting next to me. Liz handed him a napkin for his bloody nose. The potion had already stopped the bleeding, but his face was still covered in fresh blood. He cleaned his face and dropped the napkin on the table. Liz beat me to the napkin. She dropped it into the empty glass and set it to flame. Brandon looked confused at the concern we shared.

"If he lives, he could use your blood to curse you," I explained.

Liz stood, stepped over the unconscious Klaus, and looked back at me. She mouthed, "fuck him," then walked over to a gorgeous woman with long raven hair and eyes

119

so dark they looked black. After whispering in her ear, Liz took the woman's hand and headed for the door. Before she left, she held her phone up for me to see. It was the signal to text her with details. Before she left, I texted, "fuck her stupid" and hit send. Liz left the bar laughing, and suddenly I was alone with Brandon. At least thirty other people were in the bar, but they stayed far away from us.

"Should we get out of here before someone eats us? I swear I saw someone with canines in the corner licking their lips."

"I should take you home. You made an impression, Klaus is strong with magic, and according to Liz, he knows how to fight like a man."

"Really? He should learn to fight like a girl. I've never been able to pin a girl like that; they bite and pull hair."

I dropped another twenty on the table for clean-up. We slid out of the booth and headed for the door with all eyes on us. I was used to the attention, but Brandon was on high alert. I couldn't blame him; I'd reacted that way when I first joined the magical community. Everyone wanted to kill me or fuck me. Some got their wish, and the others died.

My car was waiting outside the moment we stepped out the door. Brandon got in without a word, not even a comment about the small car. As I got behind the wheel, he set Spotify to my favorite playlist. The sound of Disturbed's Sound of Silence blared through the speakers until I turned it down with the steering wheel controls.

"Is this where you force that forget potion on me with a kiss?" Brandon asked. I had actually thought of doing that, but I really didn't want him to forget. I started driving without answering.

"Because I totally understand why you want me to forget that shit, not that I could tell anyone; I'd be locked up in a padded cell. Fuck, I'm having a hard time believing it," Brandon continued.

"I'm going to take you to your apartment. We are going to let all of your neighbors know that you are out of the closet, then I am going home to diapers full of baby shit and a tired mother of triplets."

"You make your life sound glamorous."

"Alton's soul is inside of me. He loves them but I can't. Love is a weakness I can't afford."

"I'm not looking for love. You're right, I'm still in the closet with practically everyone."

I pulled into the small parking area next to Brandon's apartment building. His apartment was on the second floor, with the entrance in the back. The night was fantastic, and many of his neighbors were out and about at ten o'clock. Several people nodded or waved as we walked up the flight of stairs. When our feet hit the landing, I pushed him against the wall and grabbed his neck with my left hand and his ass with my right. I leaned all of my weight on him to keep him in place. He put his hands in my back pockets and pulled me closer as we made out in plain sight of his neighbors.

After about five minutes of tongue-massaging each other's tonsils, he shoved me away. The heat in his gaze made me want to rip his clothes off and fuck him right there in front of his neighbors. He had other plans; he balled his fists and got into a fighter's stance. This was his show, his coming-out party, and we would do this his way.

121

I grew up in a small town of humans who didn't know what I was, just that I was weird. Boxing wasn't my thing, but I'd had my share of dirty fistfights.

"First rule, not the face; it's a bitch to heal," I said as I mirrored his stance.

"What's the second rule? No shots below the belt?"

"Last rule, don't let me kill you!"

"You know you're talking to a cop, right? You just admitted to an officer of the law that you intend to kill."

"I intended to fuck you until you can't stand, then make you forget this ever happened."

"And now, Vampire wizard?"

"That's sorcerer, and I'm not the vampire."

He punched me in the face, then danced away as I recovered from the surprise. He didn't hit hard enough to break anything, just enough to piss me off.

"Well, Sorcerer, I follow my own rules on my territory. You wanted me out of the closet. I'm out!"

I was still trying to get my jawbone back to its place when he came at me again. If I had known dating would be this fun, I would have done it long ago, but we were attracting negative attention from his concerned neighbors. I started avoiding his punches as he backed me toward his apartment door. The people around Officer Hottie felt safer with him there. If I fought back, they would either help or call for help. A few of the younger people were already grabbing some video that would be on the web later tonight. I froze time for everyone, including Brandon. I had to ruin a few phones, or he would be more than out of the closet. He would become a target in the war I was about to start. Three teenagers and one very concerned woman who probably called the police lost their phones.

I grabbed the fist he'd aimed at my face again. When I released time, he and I were at his door. I twisted his arm behind his back and shoved him through the door. It looked more violent than it was. I learned to pick locks with magic when I was a teen. Wards were tricky, but Brandon was a vanilla human.

He stumbled on the threshold and fell on his ass. I held out a hand to him to help him up. I needed to let his neighbors know that I meant him no harm. I did mean to harm him a little but only for fun. He took my hand and let me pull him into an embrace, then he spun me around and shoved me against the door frame. I expected him to tell me my rights. Instead, he turned me around and kissed me again. I heard the rattle of the handcuffs and then felt them lock onto my wrists. We moved out of the doorway, and he closed the door.

"This will be on the internet in about fifteen minutes," he sighed. The fight was gone, but he was still agitated. I would have to adjust the potions for human metabolism next time…if there was a next time.

"I killed a few cellphones tonight. I didn't do it to protect your reputation, but your life," I replied as I wiggled the handcuffs toward him; I could probably talk Alias into breaking the chain, but that would mean letting him out to play. I had access to the fangs since my magic created them, but the strength and speed belonged to his soul.

"Oh, no, the cuffs stay–my rules. I don't fucking know what you did to me, but I think I like it. How long does this spell last, midnight?" He was looking at his knuckles, which were already healed. I could feel cuts and bruises on my face; I wouldn't be healing without help.

123

"Twenty-four hours and your body will heal almost any wound within twenty minutes, maybe less for you."

"And you? How long until you heal?" he asked as he gently ran a thumb across my swollen lip. I was tempted to bite, but tenderness gave me the creeps. Yeah, I prefer to be punched.

"Oh, I'll keep this for days. That's why I made the rule about the face," I whispered. The situation started to feel uncomfortable until Brandon punched me in the diaphragm. I fell onto the floor in a heap because I couldn't use my hands to catch myself.

"Beg me to stop?"

"No fucking way," I gasped. "I haven't had this much fun in years." I laughed, and it hurt like hell. He was more potent, and his pain was registering as pleasure. I was wired this way from birth, or at least as long as I could remember. Alias loved me like no other person and hated me like no other person. If you're feeling sorry for that little redheaded toddler, don't. I wouldn't want to change a thing.

"I want you to bite me. You, not him. I've seen you with the fangs. I want you to fuck me, bite me, and drink my blood. I'm clean, get tested regularly, and always insist on condoms; sorry if that ruins it for you." He grabbed me by the shirt and sat me up against the wall. I'd never done anything sexual with handcuffs. I was always in charge from the first time, even when I was a prostitute. Oh, I had taken the submissive role on birthdays and special occasions, but Brandon wasn't asking me to suck his cock. He just wanted to keep me from killing him. He was following my final rule.

"I have condoms in my bag, along with that potion. I'm not sure I am immune to disease. I could probably make a cure, but why tempt fate?"

"Oh no, you may be the one doing the fucking, but you are not in charge here, buddy! My territory, my rules."

I found that sitting against a wall with my hands restrained behind my back was a very uncomfortable position. Maybe it was the considerable bruise forming across my abdomen and probably my diaphragm. Brandon seemed to sense my discomfort. He stepped into the living area, grabbed a sofa cushion, and slipped it between my arms and the wall. He straddled my pelvis, still fully clothed, and bent down to kiss me. There was no tenderness in his kiss; it was more teeth than lips. He was trying to make me bleed, that would bring on the vampire. I didn't know if I could keep Alias away once he tasted my blood. If I killed Brandon, around twenty people could identify me. I didn't use glamour all night. The ears might throw off his partner, but I had a distinct look even without them. I couldn't kill him; I might want to do this again. He moved the biting kisses to my chin and neck while slowly unbuttoning my shirt.

"Tear it," I whispered.

He balled his hands in the fabric at my shoulders and tore the shirt down the back. I leaned forward and let the material fall to my wrists. Brandon stood and removed his jacket. He started unbuttoning his shirt; he was teasing. I was a tease; I didn't have much patience for being teased. I leaned back against the sofa cushion and closed my eyes.

"No," Brandon growled. "You will look me in the eyes! I know that you are afraid of intimacy. I don't want romance; I want to look into your fucking purple eyes!"

"I can't do what you ask with my hands behind my back. I have to hold you still; I can't hypnotize you." I didn't want to tell him that I could get free. I was used to being underestimated; being treated as a threat was a rush.

"No offense, but the magic scares me more, and you all but admitted that you want to kill me. I prefer to keep breathing for a few decades." He slipped his shirt off, and I stared at his chest. He had a circular scar on his left shoulder that could only be from a bullet. The other scattered scars looked to be stab wounds. Given his profession, I could have assumed they were occupational, but they were old scars, white from age. It was no wonder he was cautious with me. He continued to undress without another word. He wanted me to watch, so I did. His scars fascinated me, all scars did. They were like a story written on the body if only you knew how to read. He had more scars on his pelvis, long lines, and short ones that looked like stab wounds. He was already hard with no encouragement from me…probably a good thing since he didn't want me to touch him.

"I could get out of these cuffs anytime I wanted, and I might not be able to crush your heart without my hands, but I can still do magic. Klaus is not half as powerful as I am."

He pretended to ignore me, but his heart was beating faster. I didn't need the soul of a vampire to hear it, only large, very pointed ears. He knelt between my knees and started working on the buttons of my jeans. I've always preferred button-fly jeans over zippered jeans, mostly because I rarely wear underwear; this night was no exception. My lack of excitement didn't seem to faze him, because it ended when his lips slid to the base of my cock.

I felt his tongue slide between my cock head and the tight foreskin bringing my cock to its full length and breadth with that one action. He was good, better than good, and far more experienced than he seemed. He found a slightly musical rhythm while I watched his head bob up and down over my pelvis. He wanted me to watch him and kept his turquoise eyes locked on mine. Suddenly he drove down fast and hard onto my cock and swallowed me whole, taking me into his throat. I could feel his breath against my crotch as the last inch of me went into his warm, inviting mouth. He was gifted, and I knew I couldn't hold out for long with the assault his mouth and throat were making on my cock. The pressure, the need to cum was almost too much…then he slowly pulled away. He kept his eyes locked on mine as he said, "Okay, Houdini, do your magic."

It took me a moment to realize what he meant; he had me so far aroused that I had forgotten the cuffs entirely. Subtle magic was the first thing I learned. Picking locks is not easy for most people. You have to be able to see the mechanism in your head, then use the subtle elements of your surroundings. I'd loosened the cuffs before he stopped sucking, and I held them in my hand. I let them drop to the floor with an audible clink.

Brandon stared at me with his mouth open. It was my turn to tease. I wrapped both hands around his neck and pulled myself to my knees to match his stance. I planted a hard kiss on him while I willed the fangs to appear. I had never done this before without Alias's interference, but it was my body and my magic. I had to kick my jeans off my ankles to move freely. That brought the long line of precum he'd left on my calf to my attention. I used the thumb of my left hand to wipe it off, then I pulled away from the kiss and stuck the thumb in his mouth, making him taste his juices. He'd begun to soften, but that one act had his soldier standing at attention.

I stood, grabbed the cuffs, and slipped behind him, holding him in place with a firm hand on his shoulder. He let me take his wrists and cuff them behind his back. It would be awkward, but I was big enough to accommodate the obstruction. Once he was cuffed, I pulled him against me and turned his head for another kiss. It was an awkward angle for him and painful. He shivered with excitement and the anticipation of pain. He wasn't afraid anymore.

Brandon's hands moved to my cock, and he grabbed it with both hands, one on top of the other. He squeezed hard as he leaned against my chest. I'm not a vampire; my stomach is not built for large amounts of raw blood any more than an average human. I also didn't have any talents vampires had to keep victims passive. Being bitten on the neck hurts a lot! If he fought, I would tear his throat open. I usually let Alias do the vampire stuff; he was born into it. I pulled his head to one side, causing his neck's skin to tighten. I held his head still with my left hand on his ear. I used my right to reach around and grab his cock. This wasn't as easy as it should have been. He and I were big men, but I wanted to feel his excitement when I bit him. I also wanted to make sure he stayed hard. If I took too much blood, he would lose his erection. I didn't want that to happen; the fun was just beginning.

I gently placed the top fangs on the bulging vein in his neck. I applied pressure and felt the pop as they entered first the skin, then the vein. Brandon gasped, but I couldn't tell if it was from pleasure or pain. Either way, his cock got harder, so I didn't stop. The hot blood rushed into my mouth, and I had to swallow fast to keep from wasting it. Something had changed about me since Alias's soul possessed my body. My saliva kept the blood from coagulating. There was nothing I could do on my own to stop the blood from flowing, but I still had my magic…blood magic. When I'd drunk more blood than my stomach could handle, I used my magic to entice the platelets in his blood to seal the wounds. I couldn't heal him, but I could stop him from bleeding to death. Blood still trickled down his chest, and his heart was pounding from the blood loss. He hadn't lost his erection, but that may have been more from my attention to his cock than from the blood in his body.

"Fuck, that's hot!" he whispered.

His body was feeling colder than before, and he was swaying a little like he was going to pass out. One of the perks of vampire venom for the victim is its narcotic effects. It wouldn't be much fun if he passed out before sex. I released the mechanism on the handcuffs, letting them drop to the floor, and stood, pulling him to his feet. The bedroom was visible from the front door. I wrapped his arm around my shoulder, and half dragged him toward the bed. The potions would kick in soon, reversing the weakness. Thoughts of my brews reminded me of the bag I'd left in the car. I wasn't great at portals and sucked at teleportation spells, but I needed the bag. I had to return to the living room to reach for my phone. My car wasn't magic, but sometimes it felt like it was. I used the app on my phone to lower the window and levitated the bag out, pulling it to me until it thumped against the door. Retrieving the bag, I took it into the bedroom, unzipped it, and drew out a water bottle. Brandon had flipped over and propped himself up against the padded headboard. I tossed him the bottle, and he caught it with ease.

"When was the last time you gave blood? Today? Yesterday?" It was just a guess, but I hadn't taken enough blood to cause his reaction.

"This morning, I didn't think you would be able to do that. I…"

I took a bottle of lube from the bag and a strip of condoms, setting them on the bedside table, then sat on the edge of the bed. I was used to hook-ups in hotels or occasionally a back room somewhere. The people I fuck didn't want to invite me to their homes; it was too dangerous. I hadn't been this invested in a night of sex since I was married. Brandon had almost lost his erection in the short time I was out of the room. I scooted closer and started to lower my head to his cock, but he stopped me with a firm hold on my shoulder. "No! Not that I haven't had fantasies about you sucking me off, but it's not you."

"You don't know me, and I have only told one person that I don't suck cock. Since she is still alive, I know you didn't torture that information from her."

I only had one living person in my life that knew my sexual hang-ups. I'd used my good looks and sex appeal in the past to make my life easier. Many men had paid me thousands just to suck their cock. I had done a lot of things that made me uncomfortable looking back on them. It was one of the many reasons I liked being in charge. It wasn't something I discussed with the people I have sex with.

"You talk about sex with Liz?" Another thing that made me uncomfortable was that Officer Hottie (as Liz liked to call him) was too intuitive. My life wasn't an open book; it was one of those diaries that you lock, then wrap in chains, drop in a lead-lined box, and bury in the desert somewhere. Liz knew quite a bit about me, but she didn't know everything. If we stayed friends, that would probably change pretty quickly. Thinking of that made me reach into the bag for the memory-erase potion. I put it next to the lube on the table.

"You know things that could get you killed," I said when he noticed.

"This has been too much fun to forget, but Al, fuck me and get the fuck out of my house. I think your potions are wearing off, my neck is still bleeding, and all of this warning about you is making me lose my boner."

"Grab your headboard and shut the fuck up; you talk too much," I said with a chuckle escaping me. Brandon moved slowly, and I could see that he was right. The potions were wearing off in just a few hours instead of a day, but then I never used them on a human, and the blood loss probably didn't help. His heart was still pounding, and I regretted the bite. I could have ended with that, but he wanted it, and I wanted sex. I twisted him around for a kiss. I wasn't crazy about sucking cock, but one thing I did like was kissing, and I did it well. It was enough to get us both ready to fuck. His heart calmed as I pulled away to grab the strip of condoms and rip the top packet open. I held his shoulder while I rolled the condom onto my cock. The condoms were lubricated, but that was more for my comfort than his. It took two hands for the lube bottle, and when I let go of Brandon, he started to sway. It wasn't the blood loss that caused it, my saliva was running through his system, and he was flying high. I use two fingers to lube and open his asshole. He released a relaxed sigh and bent a little lower.

I'm not a gentle lover. I thrust my cock into his ass without letting him relax first. I grabbed his cock with my left hand and put my right on his shoulder for balance. He tried to keep hold of the headboard, but my pounding put him on all fours. I stroked his cock with the same rhythm. He made noises that sounded like a wounded animal, but his backward thrust into my pelvis told me they were good sounds. I felt the pulsing of his cock as he came; his whole body convulsed, spraying his headboard with cum. I felt that sweet pressure of impending orgasm, then the even sweeter release. My body spasmed with pleasure, turning my legs into rubber. We both fell sideways onto the bed while panting like marathon runners at the end of a race. We stayed in an uncomfortable embrace until I noticed he was sleeping. His heart and breathing slowed, and his red face told me he'd live through the blood loss. I left the bed and went into his bathroom, dropped the condom into his trash and utilized his shower to clean myself up.

After the shower, I grabbed my jeans and shoes and slipped them on. My legs were still shaking from the exertion. I found a notepad and pen by his door and wrote out, "Drink this or call me." Then I took the note into the room and tucked it under the forget potion. I grabbed my phone and bag and left without making a sound, locked his door, then summoned my car to the bottom of the stairs. My phone started playing Santana's Black Magic Woman, my ringtone for Liz. I whispered, "Yes, I fucked him stupid."

"Too bad he won't remember it in the morning. I bet you're a fuck worth remembering."

"About that…"

"You didn't give him the potion?"

"Oh, I gave it to him; I just didn't make him take it."

"You're going soft on a human?"

"I'm a fuck worth remembering. He knows the risks."

"Do you? I looked up this Kamei guy. He has more connections in the business than Temp had," she said, changing the subject.

"He's just a small fish in a sea of sharks. He's the one who ordered the hit."

"I guess we are going fishing?"

"I'll bring the pole; you bring the net," I teased, and she laughed at the innuendo. She hung up after that, then texted me a thumbs-up emoji. I was relieved by the silence as I got into the car and closed the door.

Liz

We met in the same spot Al had chosen for the last spar. I was amazed we didn't break it the first time. I didn't usually enter other realms; not because of fear, but because the creatures dwelled in those places, feared me. This place felt like it welcomed us, with a cold breeze and foggy air, just like we both liked it. It felt alive and conscious of everything going on inside. I could almost hear it whisper on the wind, welcoming us.

I could not help but think the cold, light breeze felt suitable for our night of cardio. We would be doing more show-and-tell than competing, but we were going to have some fun too. Al and I had only ever fought our battles alone. We needed to learn to work together, and I needed to wipe that permanent smirk off his face. His confidence was hot but also a little irritating.

"Okay. Let's have some rules here," I announced. As last time, I had my hair in a ponytail, light to no make-up, and tight black clothes. I know better than to have anything restraining my movements. And, as last time, Al was dressed in an expensive shirt and his trademark Levis jeans that embraced his ass like an artist sculpted it. "Rule number one: No cheating. And I mean, no Alias! No vampire speed or anything like that. Sorcerer against Sorceress. The fun with fangs will have to wait for another night. Rule number two: I would like to request that you keep those clothes on. I like men as much as you do, especially men that look like you. No fair distracting me. Rule number three: If you cheat, I cheat."

"Rules ruin the fun," he said, unbuttoning his shirt. "But if you need a few rules to feel safe…"

I did not let him finish, and threw a fireball he easily dodged, laughing. I took my black jacket off and threw it next to the light post. "So I will take that as, no rules, like last time," I said, and an energy ball hit me in my right butt cheek. "Hey!" I complained.

"Watch your back, Liz, always. Now, stop stalling. Let's go." Al had a half-confident, half-teasing smile on his face and bounced an energy ball in his right hand.

"Oh, it is so on!" I rubbed my hands together and created a more significant fire blast than required. "Al," I warned softly. "Leave my ass alone."

And just as he said, "Make me," I threw one of the most potent fire blasts I had created in months. He could take it, but it never reached the target. He threw a blast of water in my direction that counter-balanced my fire blast in the middle of its journey, and just like that, the remains of both our hits were on the ground, steaming like spilled coffee. He made a smirk of 'try again' which pissed me off as much as it made me feel excited.

We walked to the center of the empty area, not taking our eyes off each other. Both of us were trying to anticipate the other's actions.

"Give me your best shot, Sorcerer," I said with a smile, while I formed an energy ball in my right hand. He grinned evilly and made the pavement between us break using only the movement of his hand, throwing the little pieces of the asphalt in my direction. Putting my hands at the height of my chest, with my palms facing him, I created a wall of air that stopped most of the projectiles. When the little rocks fell to the ground, I sent the blast of air in his direction, followed by a few fire blasts. He easily dodged every hit I threw.

"You call this an attack, Sorceress?" Al teased, holding my fire blast in the middle of us with his hand.

"I call that distraction, Sorcerer."

Fire and air were my strong talents, but I had others. I could have pounded him to the ground with an energy bolt or electrocuted him using one of his most vital talents against him. I knew he chose this place for the moisture in the air, but moisture conducts electricity. The fog was just clouds covering the ground, after all. I thickened the fog causing it to form the static electricity that lit up the sky in a rainstorm. I directed those bolts of lightning toward Al with the intent to knock that smirk off his face. He fought back with a simple, decisive blow of air that swept the clouds away and forced me to use my hands to keep balanced. We were each using the other's strengths against each other. With a supernatural speed, he was in front of me, grabbing my right wrist with his left hand. His movements slowed just before he was there. Smooth as a dancer and without letting go of my wrist, he turned me around so that he was behind me and grabbed my other wrist with his right hand, securing me against his chest.

"You are cheating simply by being a man," I teased, trying to free myself.

"I thought the deal was not to hold back, Sorceress." He spoke low, against my neck, provoking goosebumps all over my skin. And I was sure he was smirking.

"Oh, it is!" I said, sliding a little to my left. I tried to break his firm grip with a strong push so that my right elbow would hit him straight in the stomach.

"Nice try!" he chuckled when I failed, and I let my head fall back to his chest; his breathing was steady. I breathed deeply, wanting to inhale every spark of magic that flew around us.

"Al, just fuck me already," I sighed, and it created the second of confusion I wanted. It would have worked without those words, too, but where was the fun in that? I used my stiletto heel to stomp on his foot, and the moment he loosens his grip on me, I turn around, and with my hands, I use the same air blast he tried, knocking him off, then walked toward him as he scrambled to his feet. "No face, no hair. You did not say anything about your feet," I teased.

With a smug smile, and without a word, he moved far too quickly for me to react, throwing everything he had. I avoided most of the energy blasts, but not all; my skin is reddish where the hits struck. My upper thigh, shoulder, and chest were where the biggest ones found their target.

Breathless, I collapsed to the hands-on-knee position. "You are using vampire stamina, Sorcerer!"

"I am using my body's stamina," he chuckled, proud of himself. "Or have you forgotten my reputation?"

I am still breathing hard as I look at him and start to laugh. "I want to believe you…." I smirked back. Seeing an opportunity in the small talk, I lift my right hand from my knee, I pull the small rocks on the ground behind him in his direction and create a distraction. My left hand sends a jolt of electricity to his chest in a quick movement, making him stumble back a little. That jolt would burn anyone else, but I knew he could take it. And we promised not to restrain ourselves. "But I really cannot see it."

Al was showing me all his perfectly white teeth, but he wasn't smiling, at least not a friendly smile. I prepared for what was coming at me. I don't see the future, but I knew he was preparing to send some pain. The magic he chose was an oily curse that felt like death. He knew it wouldn't kill me, but I am not sure how he knew. I didn't have many secrets, but I did have one I didn't talk about. I had my form of protection that worked better than a shield. I threw up a shield anyway; I didn't want the black oily mess on my skin. I might have to make him clean it off in the shower.

Al danced away like a boxer in a fight and came at me again quickly. I was prepared for magic, but he grabbed me around the waist. This move was one I knew how to escape; every male lover liked to pull that on me at least once in an evening of fun. He had my arms pinned and was taller than my usual sparing partners, but I managed to slam my head into his chin. That loosened his grip enough for me to drop out of his embrace and turn around to face him. Grabbing a fistful of his hair, his head tilted back slightly, forcing him to his knees in front of me. He looked up at me and just waited.

The idea was to make him surrender, but my smirk disappeared as I looked into his lavender eyes. Powerful magic around him had my body vibrating like we were submerged in the ocean. The waves sent my body back and forward. I grabbed his jaw with my left hand and kissed him hard, feeling like a firework had just started inside my body. It was pure power, a sea of unlimited power. I felt every crack and spark of it, and I just wanted more. I needed more. I could not tell how many people I had kissed before, but it never felt like this. He was a source of pure magic within my reach. My lips tingled with it; my whole body absorbed it. The rougher I was, the more of his power I felt, so I finished the kiss with a bite on his lip. I let go of his hair slowly, reluctantly. I'd never felt more alive, and my magic was overflowing. With my guard down, he swept his arm into the back of my knees, and I fell on my ass, only to be pinned by his body. He just grinned at me, keeping my arms pinned to the ground, and for a moment, I thought he would kiss me again. My body wanted it. My body completely forgot that this Sorcerer was very much gay, and I reacted with lust. Breathing hard, feeling my face burn with desire, wanting to get us close, wishing he would just fuck me right there, right then. He moved closer, and at the last moment, he whispers to my ear, "I win hot stuff!"

He pulled himself to his feet, gloating the entire time. I let myself sit on the ground, just laughing, with my forearm over my face. "You are a pain in my ass, Sorcerer!" I said. I'd let my guard down and made it too easy. That would sting later. I usually would be angry about something like this, but I was too drunk on power. His power.

He offered me his hand to help me get up. "That is the only pain in the ass you will get from me. Now, you are buying breakfast today!"

I thought about slapping his hand away, but I was enjoying the buzz of magic, the feeling of electricity with every touch. Accepting his hand, I stood and while trying to brush all the dirt from my clothes, he slipped on his shirt and started buttoning.

"That is the deal. IHOP, on me. Let's go." Getting near, I stilled his hand, making sure he did not cover his chest. "A consolation prize, Al. For me." I opened the portal that would make us travel to our favorite place to eat.

He stood still, his expression thoughtful. "Liz, I have a better idea. Meet me at my house in two hours." And he just started to walk away.

"Al, that is not how a gentleman asks a lady to go on a date!" I yelled behind his back.

"Good thing I am not a gentleman, and you are not a lady!" he yelled in reply and just waved goodbye without looking back.

Well, I guess it was settled then.

Al

I won the rematch with Liz, but it's only because I cheated…again. The tradition we set was for the loser to pay for pancakes, but I had another idea. I had the house to myself for the weekend, no babies, no…whatever Rainn was to me. Thanks to my association with Pedro, my dead ex-boyfriend, I had other properties, but none had a gourmet kitchen stocked with everything needed to make the perfect pancakes. I planned to introduce Liz to a different version of her favorite meal. My family called them German Pancakes, but I had no idea if that was the origin. I only knew that you needed an oven and a lot of butter. The texture was not something Liz was used to, but the taste was much better.

Breakfast was not my only reason for inviting her. I finally had the plan to strike back at the organization that had been plaguing both of us for some time. I knew at least one of the factions who had ordered the death or capture of the one who carried the bloodline curse that nearly killed Sophie Smith. The hunt for Sophie resulted in the death of her fiancé, Dan Costa. Thanks to my family and me, he was the one bearing the curse. It took me a while to figure out who would search for Sophie. I still had no idea why they wanted her, dead or alive. That mystery was going to have to wait.

Usually, I would sit and wait for my enemies to make a mistake—which was attacking me first. This time I would take the fight to them, or the biggest group of them. I needed Liz at my side because there were too many for me to take on my own, and she had a reason to want them dead, too…two reasons. I would need them too, but I didn't know how to ask. Deathripper held my leash, not the other way around. I owed him my soul; he was contractually obligated to raise me from the dead should I die from magic. In case you were wondering, death had its limit, but I figured that a few thousand times would be all I needed. I didn't want to live forever–no one did. I just didn't want to die before I was ready…no one ever wanted that either, right?

I checked the oven one last time to ensure the pancakes were on time. I learned to give Liz at least fifteen minutes to be safe. I understood that too. She wanted to do things in her time, on her terms. If I had faulted her for that, I would be a hypocrite. I could feel her portal open as she arrived. She came bearing caramel sauce and champagne to celebrate our victory in the battle we were about to wage. I knew that because she had leaked it into my head when she arrived. I would have to explain the connection, but first, we had to figure out why we both acted like a live wire in a rainstorm when we touched. A little magic sharing was standard for sex, but we hadn't done that or even talked about it. We teased, and both flirted with all genders, but usually, it was just that–flirting. There was also the issue that I'm gay…so we don't talk about it.

"Nice place. It's so…feminine!" Liz remarked.

The place was filled with purple, my favorite color, but nearly everything had flowers on it, even the sofa. The compromise was Alton's, not mine, but since I had to share a body with him, he got a vote…and he loved Rainn. I had been sharing my body with my dead clone and my dead stepbrother for a while now. I rarely allowed them to take control because I had no idea what they would do. Alton was my alter ego, but he was bisexual and in love with Rainn Rivers. Alias was a vampire whose main goal in death was to kill everyone who loved me. Alias was why Alton no longer had a body of his own. Both of them were the reason I rarely slept.

"I would offer to show you my bedroom, but we aren't here for that," I teased. I didn't invite anyone home for sex; it was one of my rules. Even when I lived with five other men, my room was always off-limits for sex and for them to sleep.

"One day, your teasing will get you in trouble, Alaric," Liz replied as she took a seat at the bar. My home on the island was a hybrid of a Greek palatial-style home and a beach house. My sanctum was the attic, but it was open to the elements. The islands rarely got too hot or cold, and I enjoyed the view.

"Not today, temptress. I plan to pleasure you with my culinary skills." I carefully took the cast iron skillets out of the oven and sat them on the glass stovetop. I had two large plates waiting to slide the pancakes onto. There was no need for butter; they were practically swimming in it already. I slid a plate to Liz and pulled out two champagne flutes. The bottle had gotten warm, but chilling it was easy enough. I enjoyed the incredible feeling of the frost on my hands. Controlling temperature was an easy spell, but sometimes those were the most fun. I was still working on freezing an entire room or a living body, but I never needed ice.

I popped the cork and poured two glasses, setting one in front of Liz, and the other I set with my plate at the seat next to hers. I had one more thing to give before I sat to eat. As Liz poured her caramel sauce in a spiral on her pancake, I reached beneath the bar and pulled out a long thin box. It looked something like something an expensive bracelet would come in if the recipient had large wrists. It was black with a purple ribbon tied around it. I hadn't chosen the box, only the contents.

"Plying me with alcohol and gifts? Are you sure I am not seeing your bedroom today, Sorcerer?" she said, chuckling. She hesitated a moment before pulling the box closer.

"Not today, Sorceress. This is a family tradition, so I am told. I'm sure you will like it."

"I don't think I am that sort of friend; I don't accept gifts from anyone, especially ones that I haven't had the pleasure of some rigorous playtime."

"And I don't give gifts to anyone. Think of it as a down payment for your service in our upcoming battle. My family would gift their allies with something similar before a battle."

She slid the ribbon off the box and opened the top. Inside was a dagger that, in Gaelic, was called a Sgian Dubh. It had a five-inch blade and a hilt made for a small hand. The pommel held a deep purple amethyst with a faceted cut like a diamond.

"Just what every woman needs when going into battle. I know how you feel about thanking, so I won't."

She closed the box reverently and began slicing away at her pancake. I joined her in silence, waiting for her reaction. When she rolled her eyes, I knew I'd gotten it right. The secret is vanilla and a pinch of nutmeg. The fresh cream butter takes care of the rest. My father would put powdered sugar and lemons on his pancake, but I preferred old-fashioned maple syrup from Canada.

"I don't think you will be able to use that in battle, Sorceress Key," I said while pointing at the box with my fork.

"Oh, I know that the only way men like them want to be up close and personal with me, is in the bedroom." She sighed disappointedly. I wouldn't want to be the one she got up close and personal with if she had that knife in her hands. With the right amount of force, the blade could slip between a man's ribs and into the heart. If the attacker managed to get her beneath them, she could use their weight against them. There were faster ways to stab a person, but they took force that Liz didn't have yet.

Before I could reply, I heard Rainn's Tesla Model X pulling up. Liz hadn't noticed anything with her human ears, but my bat wings could pick up the sound of toddlers giggling. It was my turn, or Alton's, to watch the twins. The moment Rainn walked in through the front door, I froze time. Liz's elbow had been touching my arm, so for her, time never stopped.

"Uh, sorry. She wasn't supposed to bring them yet," I stammered like a teen caught necking in the living room.

"Forget that! What is this? I've studied nearly every book on dark magic and with some of the best Sages in the world. None of them taught me how to freeze time."

"None of them will; it's a curse," I replied. I grabbed the box with the knife and pushed Liz toward the stairs. I guess she would get to see my bedroom after all. She started to protest, but I wanted her up there before Rainn got any ideas. Once she was heading up the second stairwell, I returned to the kitchen. The scraps went into the bin next to the trash. The cast iron pans resided in the oven, and the rest of the dishes went into the dishwasher. I could have used magic, but I preferred not to when the time was frozen, sometimes it slipped.

I finished the cleaning, then allowed time to start up slowly. Corbin was walking well, but Coraline always wanted to be held. Rainn came in with one toddler holding on to her shorts and the other on her left hip. She had a gym bag with her because I refused to touch a diaper bag. Her sensitive nose sniffed the air. She was a new mom, and her nose was nearly as good as a dog's.

"German pancakes?" she asked as she placed Cora on the floor. Both toddlers ran to me and wrapped their tiny arms around my legs.

"Breakfast of champions," I replied. I followed her gaze as it moved across the kitchen to the caramel sauce and the bottle of champagne. I didn't owe her any explanation, and I wasn't giving her one. I pried the toddlers from my legs and carried them to the sofa.

"Celebrating?" she asked, suspiciously. She walked to the bar and sat the bag down then bent and plucked the ribbon off the floor where it had fallen.

"Business meeting," I replied, which was the truth. We didn't have a reason to celebrate yet.

"I interrupted by coming back early. I will take the twins down to the beach so you can conclude your…business."

"No need," I said, then I made a small-time bubble downstairs, freezing Rainn and the toddlers. After everyone was stuck blissfully unaware, I ran up the stairs to my bedroom. Liz was stretched out on my bed looking up at the skylight above. It was a better sight at night with the starlight shining through.

"I haven't hidden in a guy's bedroom since high school. Daniel's parents didn't like me much," she said as she rolled over to the left side of the bed and patted the right. I sat on the edge of the bed, kicked off my shoes, and leaned back against the headboard. I could hold the time bubble for a while since it was only Rainn and the twins trapped inside. Now that my secret was out Liz would want to know how I did it. No one knew about it, not even family.

"If it helps, this is a first for me."

"I didn't think you were in the habit of inviting women into your bedroom…or library," she said as she gestured around the room. The room's walls were bookshelves with glass doors to protect the books from the moist salt air. The glass had a UV coating to further protect the books. Even the doors to the bathroom and walk-in closet looked like bookshelves, but they were fake. What can I say? I like books. I had a small desk in the corner opposite the stairs that held my laptop. The room did look like a library if you ignored the king-sized bed with a royal purple duvet covering it. The headboard was made of Redwood because of the moisture from the ocean right outside. The place was a paradise, but it felt like a prison.

"Thanks, I couldn't explain why I was here alone with a woman. She has accepted that I am not Alton but…"

"If she saw me, she would want sex…from you?"

"Yes, sort of; it's complicated, " I whispered. It was a sore subject; I looked, talked, and even acted the same as Alton, but I couldn't live a lie.

"So, tell me more about this curse that gives you such a unique power," she said as she moved to sit next to me against the headboard. She'd left her feet dangling off the edge of the bed to avoid removing her knee-high boots.

"You've heard of the Wyrd sisters or Norns?"

"The myth of the three sisters who either see or control fate, yes."

"They were real and one was my ancestor. The seer of the present. She was the only one of the three to produce children."

"They were cursed?"

"Their mother was. The curse drove her mad because she could see the past, present, and future all at once. She bore triplets, and the curse split into three."

"Others in your family…?"

"My father could see the future and was diagnosed as a schizophrenic as a teen, but those records were lost. My brother sees the past. He is married to a three-hundred-year-old vampire who was once a ghost that haunted our family home."

"Another vampire?"

"They used his DNA to create Alias, and I used necromancy to raise Tom from the dead," I explained. My stepbrother was what some would call a test-tube baby. He was created using alien technology because his father was sterile. No one bothered to tell Alias's mother that she was an experiment. Alena didn't know how she had given birth to a vampire until her youngest son let everyone know that he could see the past. I raised our family ghost for him and for Alias.

"Another thing that I can't do," Liz sighed. I could teach her the secret, but it involved finding a fresh bleeding heart…from a human. I'd only ever used the spell a few times. Despite being a dark sorcerer, I am not a natural killer.

"I studied with the Grim you killed. He owned my soul, and it seems ownership was transferred to your ex-boyfriend," I said as I looked down at the elaborate tattoos on my arms. Each tattoo was a codicil of the pact I had made with the late Grim Reaper.

"My family was once in possession of a Grimoire of curses," she whispered. I knew of the book she spoke of. It was something I had once been very interested in finding.

"I believe your ancestor cursed mine," I replied. It was another rumor, but I would know for sure if I could find that book.

"Well, as curses go, it doesn't seem so bad. I would think that more people would want to be cursed."

"Oh, they do! Everyone with the tiniest bit of Weird blood wants it."

"And they will kill to get it?"

"If they knew that Len and I had it… He is half alien too."

"Your dad must have spent a lot of time on the spaceship."

"In this case, no. Len is my half-brother. His mom is Alias's mom. My dad was in a polyamorous relationship with Alias's parents," I remarked. My family was a very uncomfortable subject for me. We all had very complicated relationships with each other. It didn't help matters that I was carrying the soul of my dead clone and my ex-husband/stepbrother. See? Complicated!

"Weird is a good name for your family," she said with a snicker. It made me smile to hear her joke about what I said instead of getting uncomfortable.

"I will use this power in the battle, but no one will know, not even you. Deathripper will notice, but I can't stop death."

"If your father could see the future, why was he there? Why did he allow himself to be taken by Temp?"

"I asked him once why he didn't stop bad things from happening; he said because there was always something worse that could happen. He didn't just allow Temp to capture him; he made it easier for him to do it."

"Seeing the future and not being able to change the outcome would drive anyone insane."

"Oh, he changed the outcome…Grimslayer."

"You are saying he died for me?"

"No, he died for me, for his family. You and the Grim just happened to be in the right place at the right time."

"If he hadn't told me to kill the Grim, I never would have tried."

"If you hadn't killed him, he would have killed you. He would have collected you as a grim candidate, contract or not. Not everyone is a willing candidate. He was very high in the hierarchy of Grims."

"They call me 'Grimslayer' after I killed one Reaper. Does that mean he was THE Reaper?"

"All I know for sure is that he was centuries old and that no mortal being has ever killed a Reaper. They police their own."

"All anyone needs is a scythe," she replied.

"Normally, a living being can't touch a scythe, it burns, and not every scythe can kill a Reaper, or there would be more need for candidates."

"So I'm hot shit! Better watch it, Sorcerer, I might just be number one."

"Might is the keyword there, no pun intended."

"Meanwhile, I have other things to do before tonight, and you have babies to sit."

She stood and then created a portal in the middle of my bedroom. That was another thing she could do that I couldn't. I could teleport short distances and use rifts to travel, but it meant going into the realms of the Fae. It also used more energy than necessary.

When Liz was gone, I strolled down the stairs and stood in the spot I had been before I froze time. The chat had taken nearly an hour, but Rainn hadn't noticed. She kissed the twins goodbye and left without another word. I also needed to prepare for battle, but I couldn't explain that to Rainn or the toddlers. Luckily the twins could entertain each other for hours. I put on a video for them and finished cleaning the kitchen. Battle plans could wait until after The Little Mermaid. It was moments like this that I wished I had found a way to keep Alton alive.

Sophie

My friends were preparing for battle against the people responsible for Dan's death. I knew they wanted me to stay out of it, but I couldn't. Lizzie was my high school BFF. Him? He looked like Dan, talked like Dan, and even acted like Dan. I couldn't lose him either, could I? Alaric, I didn't know well, but I heard he was the reason I was no longer cursed…and a little the reason Dan was dead. Liz trusted him, though, or she said she did. I knew it took a lot for Liz to say those words about anyone! I'm no daredevil superhero, either. I'm smart enough to be scared. They all acted like we were going out for a coffee at Starbucks…with knives and scythes. I had already puked twice just thinking about what could happen. They were all sitting in my kitchen eating breakfast. Da…Deathripper had even made pancakes for us. Dan used to do that for Lizzie and me on Saturday mornings. I couldn't eat; the smell made me feel like I would puke again.

They called him Deathripper because he killed a few Grims, so he said. He told me he was already dead, so he couldn't be killed, but Liz killed the Grim before him. I saw my Dan whenever he looked at me, and I heard his voice. My vision came back to me…Dan was in pain, lying in the street, dying from magic. My Dan, my fiancé, died. He was gone, and then the Reaper showed up wearing his face, his body, speaking in his voice. I wanted to believe that it was him, some part of me did, but Dan promised he would never leave me, and he did. And he was still gone.

Everyone was wearing black, some makeshift army fatigues for Deathripper and Al, and Liz was dressed in a bodysuit that hugged her curves but still allowed her to move. She always wore boots, she said she liked that the heals could be used as weapons, and they made her butt look nice. I liked boots too, but I had no idea if my butt looked good in them. Dan always seemed to think so. Deathripper didn't comment on my appearance as much; maybe it was because he knew I didn't trust him. He was a creature of magic; he could look like anyone.

I also chose black, added a red blouse, and wore flat-heeled shoes. I wasn't going to fight; I was going to keep them alive, even the dead guy. Liz had tried to teach me to fight, but mostly what I learned was how to defend.

The plans had already been laid; Al would go first, as bait. He had already checked the place out earlier in the day. He was sure that they would be there and ready for him. The plan seemed risky, but Liz assured me that Al didn't do anything without a plan, a backup plan, and an escape route.

"Don't have too much fun before we get there, Sorcerer," Liz teased as she opened a portal.

"I'll leave one or two for you to play with, Sorceress," Al replied, then he stepped through the portal, and it closed behind him. Liz returned to picking at the pancakes on her plate, and Deathripper finished the bacon. He didn't need to eat, but he seemed to enjoy it. I felt the bile rising on my empty stomach, but I held it down. I would pay for this later, but I would not be a burden. I wanted to be there to make sure they all came home.

153

Deathripper wanted ten minutes, then wrapped an arm around my waist and took me there. It's difficult to explain the feeling of traveling this way. It was like having an out-of-body experience. The first time he did it, I was angry and scared. Some Grims had attacked us in the park where I took Violet to play. I hadn't known him then; he was just a Grim Reaper. I thought he was trying to take Violet from me like he took Dan…or I thought he took him. It was the first time I had ever attacked anyone, the first time I tried to use magic to kill. It still scared me that I could feel the cold dark creeping inside me. It was oily and uncomfortable, and I wondered how Liz could stand that feeling. She said she didn't mind, but she wasn't the Lizzie I knew before. She was cold, almost uncaring, and sometimes cruel. It wasn't her fault; she told me once how her parents treated her. We were having a sleepover, and we had been drinking alcohol. My parents would have killed me if they found out, and Alma, she would scold me, but she was lovely. Lizzie had loved her like a mother.

When we appeared on the scene, Al was standing in front of a doorway, the double doors looked like a strong wind had blown them off their hinges.

"Damn, Weird, you could just knock," Deathripper said while laughing loudly.

I was looking at the now open doors waiting for the flood of trouble that should have been coming at us. I was scared, but then they should have been too. They were planning to kill people and maybe Grims as well. That was the other reason I was there; I wasn't safe at home. The Grims were coming for me, according to Deathripper. I'm sure it was his fault, but I didn't say it. I didn't like to see hurt in his eyes…Dan's eyes.

I had sent Violet to my parent's house. They were worried about me being alone in my grief, but I told them that Lizzie was there for me. They never approved of our friendship when I was younger, but they allowed it anyway. I didn't have that many friends growing up. Mom said I was just shy, but most people were mean to me until Lizzie and Dan came along. After I met them, they never let anyone be mean or bully me. When they fell in love, I was a little jealous, but I loved them both so much. They barely spoke to each other now, not since Liz chose to do black magic. Dan tried his best to keep her away from me, until the curse.

"I huffed, and I puffed, and I blew the doors down," Al said, pulling me out of my thoughts. He was wearing a strangely evil grin that made him look more dangerous. With his red hair and his handsome features, he looked like someone who would be nice, like the boy next door. Like Dan. That smirk of a grin made him look more like something you don't want to meet in a dark place. His eyes darkened to purple, too; it gave me chills.

Liz arrived just after we did. She liked to be what she called "fashionably late." I think she had her own preparation to do, and she wanted to do it privately. Since she became a dark sorceress, she did many things alone. It made me sad and scared for her. No one should be alone. But then Al came along. I wasn't thinking anything romantic about the two of them; he was gay. Everyone on the island knew he was gay, especially Rainn, the woman he lived with. Dan and I could hear them fighting even over the sound of the ocean. I knew about Al's magical clone, partially from Liz and partially from the yelling. I also knew that Alton was the father of those three tiny girls.

Still, Liz hadn't paid much attention to anyone since she left us. The two had a relationship, or else we wouldn't be here. Liz didn't ask for favors, and she didn't do favors. That had been a rule even before the magic.

"Here they come," Deathripper said as a crowd began filing in. They were dressed much like Al and Deathripper–ready for a fight. Behind them came at least twenty Grim Reapers in tattered black robes. These were the ones that Deathripper called cannon fodder. He had explained that only a hundred or so Grims were a danger to him. When he saw the group, he started whispering to his scythe, which always freaked me out. He treated it like a living being; sometimes, I could feel life in it.

I started the incantation that Liz taught me to raise a shield between them and us. I usually only made a small bubble around myself to ward off Liz's spells, but I was not taking chances. Soon enough, everyone would be out of range, and I would have to pull the shield in. The air around my shield crackled with power, and I could smell the ozone. Something about this always gave me a little thrill. Liz always told me I was powerful, but I didn't feel like that; I felt clumsy. This time, though, something was different. The Warlocks were surrounding us, I could feel them testing my shield. Orange sparks and the occasional deep purple sparks were appearing all around us. Al and Liz were smiling at the assembled crowd like a couple of alley cats. Deathripper spun his scythe around like a baton twirler in a marching band.

The big men rushed at the Reaper and Al, knowing that they were the most significant threat and that maybe they just didn't like to hit girls, maybe. They started hitting my shield hard, but they were just testing me. The grunts charged Al and Deathripper as soon as my magic shield failed; they were trying to use physical force to distract us from their magic. Deathripper sent his scythe away into the void and cracked his knuckles. I hadn't seen him smile like that since… before he died.

The warlocks started attacking Liz with spells that felt like oil on water to me. They were the black magic that made my skin crawl. It should have scared me even more, but it made me angry. Liz might be practically a stranger to me now, but once, we would sit up all night eating cookies and talking about boys. Mostly Dan. She knew I liked him back then, but I also wanted them to be happy. He was my friend too before he became more. I saw Deathripper fighting bare fisted with men bigger than him but not more challenging. He wouldn't kill them with the scythe, even though they were probably just magical clones. Al wasn't so friendly, he was playing with them, but everyone eventually fell to the ground dead, clutching their chests and looking like a fish out of water. He usually looked like someone you would see in the centerfold of Vogue magazine or a men's underwear ad, but when he fought, his eyes burned with purple fire, and his face was twisted with a deranged smirk. He was enjoying the killing. I had to look away as the spell casters started hitting us harder. Liz was using her favorite magic, air, and elemental fire, which glowed purple in the near dark of the building. It was that magic she was pushing me to learn, but my magic tended to be more explosive when I used fire.

It was challenging to watch all three of my companions at once. I had to admit I concentrated on Liz and Deathripper–Lizzie and Daniel–even if I wasn't sure it was him.

Deathripper and Al were nearly back-to-back in a dance that was both a physical fight and a little magic on Al's part. They were so concentrated on the big grunts that they didn't notice the Grims approaching, scythes ready. I started to scream a warning, but Deathripper's scythe appeared before I could make a sound. He mowed the black-robed figures down as if they were a field of tall grass. He was not my Daniel, not totally, anyway. He was born with a scythe in his hand, and it showed. His eyes were black, not Daniel's ocean blue. His face was frightening but in a different way. It wasn't me who was afraid; it was them. They stopped coming at him from the front and tried to discorporate and appear out of sight. Al caught many of them, but without a scythe, he could only fend them off or send them to Deathripper to finish off.

I had been so worried about them that I overlooked one of the Grims appearing behind Liz. I tried to send a firebolt to fight him off, but he sliced her stomach open with his scythe. It should have killed her instantly. I threw a shield around her and ran to her side. There was so much blood, and she was turning pale. I put my hand on her stomach and willed my magic to heal her. It was the one thing I could do that the others couldn't. I hadn't embraced the darkness, and even though I had a Reaper for a shadow, I hadn't embraced death.

The spellcasters stopped sending spells our way and concentrated on Al. He laughed maniacally as the spells rolled off him like water on a duck's back. He was giving them hell in return, concentrating only on the ones closest. They were shielding from his magic, but it wasn't doing them much good; his spell was laced with death. I couldn't explain how I knew that other than his aura was a near match for Deathripper's. Liz, too, had black ribbons running through her purple aura. She was on her feet but still breathing hard.

"Thanks, Soph," she said just before another Grim appeared.

"Deathripper, a little help here?" she yelled over the cacophonous roar of people. Deathripper sent his scythe sailing through the air, and it slid into Liz's outstretched hand as if magnetically attracted to her. She cut down the Grim who cut her, and another while still trying to catch her breath. When they were gone, the scythe appeared in Deathripper's hand as if it had been there all along. He concentrated on a couple of black-robed figures when another popped behind him. This was not the black-robed pawns that had been there before. He was wearing the face and body of my late fiancé. He looked like Deathripper.

"Pathetic human, I will rip that scythe from your hands, and then I will have my way with your little pet!" The doppelganger cried as he brought his scythe toward Deathripper.

"No!" I screamed, then I started hitting him with everything I had.

"Soph, stop it's me!" he yelled, but I didn't stop. I didn't care if he was the real Deathripper; he was not my Dan! I hit him blow after blow, just like Liz had taught me. I had done this to the other Deathripper, the one fighting him. I got confused after a moment, so I hit them with force blows that Liz said would break bones. It didn't matter to me that one was on our side. I couldn't kill either one with magic; only a scythe could kill them. When one of them fell, the other sliced off his head neatly. The scythe fell to the ground, and I continued to hit the survivor until Al stepped in front of him. The body of the other Reaper disappeared, but the scythe remained. The standing Deathripper grabbed the scythe and sent it in Liz's direction. I held my breath, thinking he was going to kill her, but she reached out, and the scythe slipped into her hand just as another robed figure appeared next to her. She lopped his head off like she was cutting dandelions. The remaining Grims backed away from her in fear. She had earned the name Grimslayer by just killing one; now that she was holding the scythe of one of their bosses, they didn't know what to do. Deathripper had told me that a scythe would burn the hands of a living person, but if Liz's hands were wounded, she didn't show it. Her eyes blazed with that deep purple that matched Al's.

The magic users were all that was left as the Grims all disappeared. Deathripper was chuckling loudly as he watched him go. There were only a handful of spellcasters left. They had fear in their eyes, but they weren't leaving. They started pummeling my shield again, trying to take me out. Deathripper disappeared and reappeared behind one of them without his scythe. He wrapped his hands around the man's throat and twisted his head off. I had to look away to keep from puking. My Daniel couldn't do that to another human being, but Deathripper wasn't Dan, nor was he a human being. I puked anyway, even though I had only seen a glimpse of the gore.

Somehow Al and Liz appeared in the group of spellcasters. I was given a reprieve as everyone concentrated on the three of them. My magic was still strong, but I was more tired than I should have been. The smell of blood and other things was making me dizzy and nauseous. Liz used the scythe on one of the spellcasters, then dropped it to the ground as if it burned her.

Deathripper picked it up and made both scythes disappear. I tried to close my eyes to avoid any more nightmare-creating action, but I managed to see Liz burn one man alive, Deathripper crush another man's windpipe, and finally, Al punched his way through the last man's chest and ripped his heart out. The room was suddenly silent until Liz said, "That was so hot, Sorcerer!"

"Have a heart, Sorceress," Al replied as he held the bloody heart to Liz.

"Alaric Weird, men usually wait until after sex to give me their heart," she laughed.

Deathripper appeared next to me and caught me as I wavered. The room was spinning, and I felt faint. The Reaper held me close and covered my eyes, but it didn't matter; the sight had been burned into my brain. I didn't watch horror movies for this reason, not that they scared me that much, but my mind would make up new nightmares with the information it had received that night. Maybe I would have nightmares about strangers and not about my Daniel. Maybe not. But I knew that I was too sick for it just to be this.

I felt Liz open a portal and force Deathripper to let me see what was happening. She held a hand to Al, and he took it and allowed her to lead him through. She had a strange look on her face, and her aura was laced with red. I had no idea what was on her mind, but it wasn't the battle. I loved watching her just step through the swirl of purple into another place.

When the portal closed, Deathripper waved his hand in the air, and all of the bodies disappeared. You could still see the destruction, but anything could have caused that.

The blood, everything, was gone as if it had never been there.

"Let's get you home, Soph; you did well today. I think I will have to soak for a week to heal the bruises you gave me this time," he said. Then suddenly we were in my living room as if we had never left. I rushed to the bathroom and puked again. I felt like I had already hurled my toenails, but I was still sick. I looked up at the medicine cabinet. Earlier in the week, I had picked up a pregnancy test at the pharmacy. I didn't know what made me think I could be pregnant; I just had a feeling. I hadn't been with anyone since the night before Dan had died. I'd been grieving for months and hadn't felt well. Nothing unusual for someone grieving the death of their fiancé, or so I thought. I opened the pregnancy test pack and pulled out the stick. I didn't feel like I needed to pee, but I managed a little trickle.

Deathripper was right outside the door; I could hear him breathing, which I always thought was strange since he didn't need to. "Soph, are you okay?" he whispered. I didn't know what to say; what would he say? If I was pregnant, the baby was Dan's. If he is Dan, like he said, then the baby would be his. Can Reapers be fathers? Violet seemed to think so; she was enamored with him. He was "papá" to her, even when he appeared in her room bearing that awful scythe.

"Just give me a minute," I replied. I could hear him move away from the door. The wait seemed to be forever, but as I watched, a faint blue line began darkening immediately. I chose a two-pack for a reason, so I took out another just to be sure. I managed to pee a little more the second time. The line showed up faster than the first. How do you tell a Reaper that you are pregnant?

I picked up the second stick and opened the bathroom door. The Reaper was in the kitchen cleaning up the mess from earlier. He looked just like my Daniel. It was always a thing for him to clean as he cooked, but we didn't have time before the battle. I walked over and placed the stick on the counter next to him. He looked at it, then at me.

"I've known for a while. I could hear the heartbeat, and I felt the life," he said.

"Don't tell me if you know the gender; I want to see for myself," I replied. Of course, The Grim Reaper would know that I was pregnant. Deathripper was the end of life, and the baby was at the beginning.

"It's mine?" He asked hesitantly.

"It's Dan's," I replied, then turned away when I saw the hurt in his eyes. I wasn't ready to admit that I sometimes believed he was my Daniel. I wanted this to be real; I couldn't raise two children alone. Dan would understand, so I hoped that if this Reaper were him, he would understand too.

"We'll get you an appointment with an OBGYN in the morning. You can call your mom to go with you."

"But…"

"No one can see me. I'm not alive. Don't worry; I'm not leaving your side."

I yawned, and he took that as an invitation to sweep me off my feet and take me into my room. He pulled back the covers and tucked me in, kissing me on the forehead. Daniel would do that when we were only friends, but suddenly it felt like more than just a friendly kiss. My eyes closed as if weighted with lead.

"Don't leave me, please?" I asked with another yawn. I held my hand out to him, and he took it. I could hear the springs in the mattress as he settled beside me. I rolled over and put my head on his chest. He stroked my hair, relaxing me even more. I don't know what happened after that, only that I slept like the dead.

Deathripper

Time doesn't mean much anymore, I sometimes wear a watch, but I never look at it. I looked at her; she was my window into life, into a world I didn't belong in anymore. She was tired and always said beautiful things when she was sleepy.

She held out a hand to me, but I pulled her into a hug. I held her next to my beating heart; it meant something…it beat only when she was near. She rested her head on my chest and listened; I knew she was trying to decide whether I was real.

I needed to touch her. I know I did… But I needed more. For a little while, she was real and mine.

"I'm proud of you; I am really proud of you, Soph." I wanted to say that I (Deathripper) may love her, but I didn't want to scare her. I'm not her Daniel not anymore. We were strangers now.

I just sat there silently, waiting for her to say something. I'd never met anyone like her before in my life. She thought she was a pushover, but when it comes to the ones she loved, she fought! I wanted to tell her that I needed her; in every way, I needed her.

She put a hand on my knee, and I flinched. I didn't want her to know that she made my pants get a lot tighter when she did that. She took it as a bad thing. I knew she wasn't ready to hop in the sack with a Reaper, I wasn't even a man anymore, but I had desires. I couldn't hide it forever…or could I? How long would I live? I could ask how long she would live, but I knew it down to the last breath of her life.

"I know you don't feel the same way about me, Soph, not right now, but I'll wait for you. And even if this is all you want us to have, I prefer this to nothing," I said as I took her hand in mine.

"Soft hands for a Reaper," she sighed sleepily. She moved her head to my shoulder and lay there in silence. I was glad the blanket was there to keep her from noticing how happy I was just to hold her. I couldn't lose her. It wasn't about being alone, and it wasn't about her making me wait… I would wait an eternity for a chance to hold her like this and make everything alright.

I existed for her alone; she kept me grounded, solid, and real. Without her, I was a Grim Reaper, a tool for death... nothing.

How in the world had this happened, and what would happen to the baby? This wasn't supposed to happen; she was supposed to be barren. I couldn't keep the smile off my face. I was going to be a dad again. I never wanted kids; I did my best to avoid creating them when I was alive. Violet had changed everything for me; now, she would have a sibling to grow up with, something her mother never had.

I usually didn't sleep, death never slept, but I closed my eyes and enjoyed the sound of Soph's breathing and her strong heartbeat. I knew one day she would stop doing that. She would grow old and grey while I stayed like this. I imagined her with silver hair and wrinkles; she was still gorgeous.

AI

I stood staring at the portal Liz had just made; I could only make out a little of what lay beyond. She wasn't taking me into a trap, or her lair, AKA her bedroom. That didn't matter. For the first time, I was nervous. We didn't plan this with words, but we both wanted to know how far we could push this energy that ran between us. I couldn't help thinking Liz would be hot if she were a man. I expected the voices of Alias and Alton to say something, but all I could hear were the sounds the dead made and the magic crackling from the portal. I should have hesitated but didn't want to. I knew what she wanted; I knew because I wanted it too. She pulled me into a familiar room, like something I'd seen in a dream. She was waiting for me to make the first move. Of course, she was; I was out of my element. She could probably feel my insecurity; our connection was wide open. I had one of those vulnerable moments, but it was just that...a moment.

I put Kamei's heart on the pedestal before me then I moved toward her. It was that same damned pull that had happened before; only this was more intense. I wasn't thinking; I wasn't feeling. The magic was in control, and it knew what we needed.

I slammed her body against the wall using mine, pressing my hands on either side of her head as I kissed her hard. The blood on my face smeared onto hers. The magic started flowing as soon as our bodies touched. She wrapped her hands around my head and pulled me in closer. I had a moment of uncertainty that passed quickly when I felt the hum of magic as I slid my right hand down the wall to grab her firm ass. Magic poured from Liz's right hand as she moved it slowly down my chest and onto my already solid erection. She held her hand there and pulled away from the kiss to look me in the eyes. Her eyes were like mine, another sign of the powerful dark magic running through our souls.

"Are you sure about this?" she whispered.

She didn't sound like Elizabeth Key Sorceress Supreme. I could hear uncertainty and desire flowing from every word, along with the magic. To answer her question, I put my hands on her waist and spun around so my back was against the wall. Then I slid both hands to her firm, round ass and pulled her into me. Her thoughts leaked into my head as she kissed me.

I've wanted this for some time now. I've craved this feeling since sparring day. It's power, pure ecstasy in every single touch. I need his magic. I want to share mine.

I know he liked my hard kisses, the way I pull his head down to me and bite his lip. The way he shudders as I scratch his torso.

Those are my nail marks on his skin. It is so hot, the way they scratched through all the blood. I know he likes the pain, just like I do.

I am not waiting any longer. I cannot. It was time to get rid of these clothes!

Her thoughts didn't distract me from the blood singing in my veins. It beat to the magic running through us like an electrical current. Liz was in a hurry to get into my pants, and I was willing to help, but she pushed my hands away.

I was confused about what to do until I remembered she was also wearing pants. They were tight, and I couldn't find a button or zipper, so I tore them, causing a gasp to escape her mouth that could have been from pain or pleasure. It didn't matter. She continued to devour my face and neck with her kisses while her underwear suffered the same fate as the pants.

The magic was ebbing and flowing like the tides, and I realized it was us, pushing and pulling it.

Another jolt of magic hit me when she dropped my jeans to find that I didn't wear underwear into battle.

I flipped her around, pressing her chest against the wall. I knew she was aching for me to touch her breasts, but I wanted to tease her. She didn't expect me to turn her away, and she struggled, but I held her waist with my left hand and her hand against the wall with my right. I rubbed my hard cock in the chasm spanning from her asshole to her clit. She gasped and fought some more, trying to angle her body to force my cock in, but she wasn't getting it that way. I knew my gentle thrusts would not be good enough for her, for the magic she was spinning through me.

I pulled her into me and grabbed her breasts, squeezing them. It was not something I had ever done on purpose, but I could tell by the sounds she made that I'd done well. I leaned in close to her ear and whispered, "Liz…Elizabeth Key. Fuck me, please?" She didn't answer my question; her mind was too busy.

I feel so powerful with him. His pleas, his magic. The feeling of being in control and chaos is euphoric. I cannot do this for much longer. I can hardly breathe; he feels so good. My body is vibrating with pleasure.

The magic makes me dizzy. And him, sliding against me. It is not enough. I want...

He is so strong. The hold he has on me. Does he feel it too?

I need to move my hips and press him inside. I want it hard; need it to hurt.

I crave his magic. Now! Feeling him in my brain and my body at the same time is so intimate.

"My magic, my whole body is yours now. Only you, Alaric, and only now. Just make it hurt, big Al!"

Pain, magic, and pleasure almost blinds me with his harsh thrust. I feel like I will explode. Our synced magic flows through me and around us. I can almost see it, but I focus on him and the orgasm building in my core. I pulsed faster, my impending climax threatens to follow. His hard cock fills me with deep thrusts and the sound of our bodies acts as a trigger. My muscles tense as the orgasm took control. I feel nothing and everything simultaneously, squeezing him inside me. It is hard to breathe and see, as wave after wave of pleasure takes over my body. His thrusts inside me falter a little as he felt my muscles tighten around him.

"Do not dare to fucking stop!" she growled, spinning to face me while she pushed me down and climbed on my lap. Her head fell back as she took me in again and her thoughts bled into my mind again.

More eager and insistent; that's better. The magic is building too. Was this the sex magic? It's unlike any magic I'd felt with another mage. I arch my back and bury my nails into his thighs. He is hissing in pain but there was pleasure on his face. He slams his penis inside me, and the pressure of orgasm returns. Rapture spills over me and I struggle to catch my breath. I look down at him, expecting a smirk, but his eyes are filled with desire, need, and magic. Every thrust built a purple haze, a black magic.

His hands on my breasts, I leaned down for a kiss. He squeezes hard enough to bruise, and here is my third orgasm, this one making me squirm and buck as he holds me firmly.

Magic became a tangible object around us as Liz's body devoured my cock. I hesitated momentarily as her pelvic muscles worked to crush my penis, but the magic caught me and drew me back to my rhythm. She didn't want me to stop, and the magic wouldn't let me. I held her by her ass cheeks, lifting her so I could thrust deeper. I wanted to feel that sensation again. It was better the second time, and I almost lost it. The magic was building to an intensity that burned. The vibrations kept me shy of climax, it would have been frustrating, but I didn't want it to end just yet. I grabbed her breasts and squeezed them roughly. She screamed and began writhing in an uneven rhythm; it was what the magic awaited. The pressure that had been building in my body burst. My climax hit me over and over like the shockwaves of an earthquake or an explosion.

I had to breathe hard, and blink through the shattering peak of my latest orgasm. My body, mind, and magic tangled in an incredible delirium and euphoria. In ecstasy, I almost missed the extra blast of magic our bodies released in a purple wave of pure power and destruction, making the bliss we felt inside us visible.

I took deep gasping breaths and tried to wrap my brain around what had just happened. There was dust in the air and debris all around. I'd seen what happened during a magical explosion; usually, the mage is part of the debris.

There was no sound except the high-pitched whining noise that seemed to be coming from my eyeballs. Liz had collapsed on my chest, and I suddenly felt panic. What was that? I didn't feel fear. I didn't feel…I didn't feel them. Alias and Alton! I must have tensed because Liz pushed up and stared into my eyes. Her eyes, so much like mine… Nope, not going there; this was not me! I was feeling things, and my head was silent.

 No teasing, no 'I told you so'. Nothing. My thoughts were all my own. I had to break the silence and get her eyes off mine before Liz saw what I felt.

 "Please tell me it is always like this with you?" I asked. I'd meant it to sound like a joke, but I could hear the awe in my breathless voice. I had never experienced anything like that before. That wasn't sex; it was more. I couldn't move, every nerve in my body vibrated, and my legs were weak. I had to look away from her again because she was studying me intently as she pushed herself off me. She knew something was off. I couldn't hide everything. I had never been alone, just me, since she had known me. I raised myself on my elbows and watched her look around for clothes that were now torn rags. She didn't reply or speak, but her thoughts were bleeding into mine as she collapsed onto my chest again.

I'm breathless. Every inch of my skin feels alive and sore.

What the fuck just happened? We did this? My body is filled with so much power I feel unstoppable, and the best part–we did not steal it. I gave it to him willingly, and I took some back. The power still buzzed between us; we were still connected.

His face. He felt it, too; I knew he did. Our surroundings show he did.

What is going on inside your head Alaric? He is saying something, but I can not focus. I do not know what to say. Where are my clothes? Oh, I remember, they are gone… Look at him, all naked and bruised, watching me. That must be how gods look, damn me! The best magic sex I ever had was with a gay sorcerer. It would be hilarious if it were not tragic.

I was just about to answer her thoughts when she rose and started looking for clothes.

"Honey, I am good, but I have never been this good."

Having had sex with magical people and some Fae-bloods, nothing would compare to that. I would have said more, but her thoughts flooded my head with concern.

We don't trust, her voice in my head whispered. That one hit me hard, and I didn't know why, but seriously, that took a lot of trust on both our parts. And then, 'The best magic sex I'd ever had, and it was with a gay sorcerer. It would be hilarious if it were not tragic.' That last thought stung, and I couldn't stop the words from tumbling from my mouth.

"I do trust you, Liz. I couldn't do that with you if I didn't. And yeah, I'm gay, but that was the best sex I've ever had. If I'd thought this was what straight sex was like, I would be arrow straight in a heartbeat." I realized too late I had just answered her thoughts. She was staring at me intently now like I was an interesting bug.

"Dammit, are you reading my mind? Did you hear everything I was thinking?"

"You were projecting a lot. It was like watching football and listening to the commentary. I won't tell anyone that your best sex was with a gay man if you don't tell them that my best was with you," I said, then laughed. She tried to hide her smile, but it didn't work. Instead, she picked up the remnants of her pants and hit me in the face with them.

"I need a shower, some clothes that aren't shredded, and some pancakes. I'm starving!"

"I need meat after a workout like that!" I replied.

She picked up the heart and tossed it into my hands. I had almost forgotten about it. I had a reputation that I was sure Liz knew. I took the hearts of my enemies. I had three of them in a jar at home, though one of those was not an enemy. I held the heart to my mouth and took a bite. I could feel the magic flow down my throat with the blood. Liz smiled, and her eyes sparkled in the darkness. I held the heart out to her, but she shook her head.

"You have your meat. I need an explanation, mind reader!"

She created a portal without hesitation and held out her hand. I took it without thinking and let her pull me through. I'm not sure I could have resisted her at that moment even if I wanted to, which I didn't. I wasn't sure of anything anymore, which should have made me nervous. I was too high on whatever this was to care.

AI

Liz's ability to make a stable portal, and hold it open for several minutes, was a desirable skill. She could do it right after explosive sex, which was even more impressive. It looked so easy when she did it, but my attempts had been a bust. I didn't do subtle things well. She stood in front of the portal, reaching out to me. I took her outstretched hand and let her pull me through the portal into her lair. We ended up in a kitchen that was all black and stainless steel. It reminded me of one of my acquired properties; I assumed the same designer had their hand in decorating both places. I wondered if the designer was still alive.

The feeling of her magic surrounded my body and left me tingling again. The magic crackled and popped between us with just the slightest touch. I let go of her hand when we stepped into her home. If continued contact caused another explosion, I didn't want her house to suffer. I would be lying to myself if I didn't admit my first time with a woman had been the best sex I'd ever had. It was a little overwhelming. But no, it was more than just sex.

I distracted myself from that thought by looking around the place while she went to the fridge. Everything was modern, and a reminiscence of Le Corbusier's style abounded, but with the paranoia of the magic community, I doubted he was the architect of this beauty. The predominant color was black, which some would find cold and uninviting, much like the house owner. There were bits of purple, scattered around the open space in the form of throw pillows and blankets. We shared a passion for purple and black. I could feel her watching me assess my surroundings. She probably thought that I was paranoid or overly cautious. I could tell a lot about someone by seeing how they live. Liz was a very private person. There were no photos or personal decorations that spoke of attachments. I even had pictures of myself on my walls–but I was a little narcissistic.

"Nice place! Did you steal it from Dracula?" I asked.

She opened the fridge as I continued to snoop. I turned back to her as she shut the door, holding two water bottles in her hands. We were both naked and bloody, but I didn't even notice my thirst until I saw the water she offered.

"This Dracula answered to the name Dad. Catch!"

She tossed a bottle at me, and with a goofy smile, I stopped it mid-air and spun it around. I felt giddy, almost high from the magic that still tingled my skin. I leaned against her bar and opened the bottle. I didn't usually drink water from plastic bottles, but I didn't usually stand nude in a woman's kitchen either. I downed the water without taking a breath. I'm not good at small talk, and that seemed to be where we both stuck.

"Yeah, I know it's your family property. The Key Lair...kind of big for just you, isn't it?"

"I like my space, and I like being alone. Usually. Now tell me more about this mind reading trick of yours."

"It isn't a trick; it's an alien thing."

She leaned against the cabinet and opened her water bottle. The magic jumped from her to me and back again like we were playing ping-pong. She was studying me, not just because I was hotter than any straight man she knew. I could have taken a peek at what she was thinking, but that was one of the reasons we were here. I needed to explain our mental connection. Her blood was pure magic; she had no alien blood that I could detect. I shouldn't have tasted her blood. If I had taken more than a sip from her, she would have me hooked like a heroin addict. Bodies are just meat puppets; the soul makes you who you are. I had three souls, one of which was a vampire. Alias was born craving blood, and I just gave him a taste of the best.

Liz took a sip of water before speaking. "I should know by now that you hold a lot of information on me. How much do you know? What did your spies say about Elizabeth Key?"

That was a loaded question and one I couldn't answer yet. I'd gathered a lot of intel on potential enemies, especially the most dangerous ones. I may have been immune to magic death, but there were other ways. I wanted to trust her completely, which was why I didn't. She had some power to make me confess all my secrets. I didn't know if it was magic or just her personality. I was leaning heavily toward the magic explanation.

"I don't have spies. I deal with digital or magical information. My research mostly told me the basics, like what happened to your parents, that you lived alone, that the men who fucked you don't live long after."

I put that last part out there, knowing I had added myself to that long list of fucked. I wasn't too worried; I might have been naked and vulnerable in Liz's kitchen, where she had more knives than anyone needed for cooking, but she was also naked. She was, however, covering the scar on her lower abdomen self-consciously. Interestingly, she preferred hiding that from my eyes over everything else. She didn't want me to notice it, so I didn't stare.

After a dramatic pause, she laughed. "It's not my fault that they decided to...stop breathing."

Her laughter invoked a genuine smile from me. It took the tension down a little. I was pretty sure she didn't think I was a threat, at least not at the moment. She stood next to the knives, but I was quicker and deadlier. We needed to work on that too. She had been the one to say the sex would be just once; she was the one who invoked a spell that had my head silent. I couldn't feel or hear them, but Alias and Alton were still there.

Her kitchen had me thinking about something else. I didn't know if it was my thoughts or the two bisexual souls inside my head. The damned magic was still threading its way through my nerves. Also, all the straight porn I'd watched with Alias over the years came to mind. I could feel my ears warming to that thought, and I could only hope I wasn't blushing like a teenage boy. I looked at her, looking into her eyes, which were concentrating on me. She was trying to make me read her mind, damn it. I realized just then that the thought of setting her on the countertop and repeating the early morning sex was not mine, at least not entirely.

"Nice one, but we should get the blood off. I do believe you promised a shower?"

She gave me that sultry look that Alena called *bedroom eyes*. I'd gotten that look from hundreds of men, but this was the first time it made me nervous. She'd gotten through my mental blocks and put her thoughts in my head. I couldn't tell if she was doing it intentionally or by accident.

I must stop thinking of that damned magical charge, the pure orgasmic power. I want to do it again. I wonder if it would happen now if I just touched him, I heard in my head.

She pushed off the counter and walked past me. "Follow me," she said as she climbed the stairs. She took them slowly, doing her best to ensure I would look. She was just projecting a lot. She did have a nice ass…for a girl.

"Yes, you have a nice ass; you can stop thinking about it now. I'm beginning to think you know more about my ability than you let on."

She stopped at the top step, looked back at me, and smirked. The mischievous look on her face was hot, and I realized that the connection was still open. I was not only getting her thoughts, but her emotions, too; yeah, we still had those.

"Just testing, but you better block what I think next," she said as she opened the door closest to the stairs. She was still flirting with me. I couldn't fault her; I wasn't protesting either. She had reason for forgetting that I was gay; I didn't. Guilt was leaking through, and that was not my emotion or hers. My constant companions were silent, but I still suffered from their feelings. Luckily my thoughts were my own…mostly.

I barely registered that we were walking through her bedroom. The decor had the same theme as the rest of the house, only this room had deep purple accents. Velvet throw pillows and a royal purple blanket decorated the bed.

"Make me!" I replied to her earlier demand of blocking her thoughts. It sounded playful, but I'd meant it as a challenge. It was time to see just how much of a connection we had.

The bathroom was her–dark with flecks of gold and purple, some sort of volcanic granite, maybe? The shower was big enough for a group of people. It had a large showerhead that would mimic rain, and the entire front was glass with a large glass door. Time to show her this went both ways. I stopped blocking and let her see all my thoughts.

"It's okay; I am just me; Alaric Weird. Alone, naked, with a woman. Men died to be with me." She was staring at my ass this time. I wasn't trying to be overly cautious, but the sexual tension made the mental connection a little awkward, and she was getting that too. She gave me the most mischievous smile, letting me know she could hear my thoughts.

"I can let you in any time I want, and I can teach you to keep me out if you want that too. It's just an easier way to communicate with my people. Until they started abducting humans, my mother's people had no voice boxes."

She studied my face seriously, making me feel like I was the one being the test subject. I usually controlled everything. It's what made me suck at science.

"How-" She started to ask with words, then shut her mouth quickly. Her thoughts bled into my brain.

This is no magic, but it sure as hell could be! Breathe, steady yourself, Liz; whatever he is doing, he doesn't even have to touch me to make me feel...I want to run to him, kiss him hard...No, that's over. We said just once, for the power. Breathe.

After hearing her thoughts, her words startled me. "You need to teach me that!"

Her thoughts told me that she was concerned about my sexual orientation. She'd been the one to say it would be just once about sex, because I was gay. I admit I had some conflicting feelings, but that didn't diminish the high I felt from my first time with a woman. It was more than sex; it was magic, the main area we shared a common interest.

She asked me to teach her about telepathy. She had no idea how much of a boon it was, but it was an ability coded in my alien DNA. I could no more teach it than a fish to breathe. Liz gave me a quizzical look and realized I had been projecting my thoughts again. It was too easy to let her in and too challenging to shut her out. She had everything she needed to get into my head.

"I can teach you to block or let me in when you want. My clone, Alton, connected with you on the night you killed the Grim. He didn't know the connection would remain with you after that night."

"Is that good? A pain in the ass? Or both?"

I had to laugh; she'd left that wide open. "Babe when I give you a pain in the ass, it's going to be good. Better than good."

She threw a shampoo bottle at my head without even blinking. There was the Liz Key I knew. I caught it, this time with only vampire reflexes, no magic.

"You already are a pain in the ass, Alaric Weird," she said as she joined my laughter.

She started thinking again without realizing we were both open.

I do not remember the last time I talked to someone about magic like this, a basic discussion with someone smart and powerful. With the body of a god. Just control yourself, Liz!

"Do you want to go first or…?"

The only way I could explain this connection was to open up and show her how connected we were. So, I answered her in my mind.

"Showering together saves water and time. And it's big enough for two, and you know you are goddess material yourself."

I stepped into the shower, and she followed. Her thoughts were as loud as if she was speaking them. I hadn't done this with anyone for any length of time. No one ever told me I could do it with a human.

Oh, the hot water burns. My skin is sore from the blood. The heat feels good, like a warm day at the beach. Probably the afterglow. Sharing a shower is a first for me; I am usually out the door by now, and if they were lucky, they would never see me again. I'm exhausted. Another unusual thing–I never let my guard down near someone. Especially not someone as powerful as Al. And he's staring at me.

"What?"

I blocked her from my thoughts for a moment. She was incredible, and I was seriously having a life crisis. I didn't dare brush up against her; I could still feel the magnetic pull. Running water dampened all magic, but enough could leak through, and her house was too nice to become a ruin. But my mind was half alien. My alien powers and my seer powers worked independently of my magical abilities. I'd never let this secret out before, not even to non-alien family members or lovers. It wasn't just reading thoughts; I could *create* thoughts and feelings. What I showed her would happen in her mind as if it was real…but I had another talent as well. I opened my mind entirely and slowed until the water barely moved. She wouldn't know anything was happening; the time was slow for her, but not for me. The exciting thing about humanoid brains was they didn't exist in time. They could dream an entire lifetime in a matter of moments, but do it while awake. I had to make this dream in my head, then give it to her.

I had never done this before with anyone, not like this. I opened my thoughts to Liz and let her see. No words, just action. She was closer to the glass than I was and already looking at me. I leaned over, touched the glass, and slowly kissed her. I wasn't doing this for magic. This was for sex. But I had to know she wanted this. There was no magic compelling it; it only me. She let herself go faster than I thought she would. She wrapped her hands in my hair and pulled me down, thrusting her tongue into my mouth. I was ready for this, and I repeated my actions from earlier in the morning, only this time facing her, looking into her violet eyes. I rubbed my erect cock across her clit slowly. She again tried to squirm to get me inside, but I fought this time; this wasn't for the magic.

I continued to stroke until her body flushed and vibrated with the oncoming orgasm. I felt her release arrive, and her body pulse to the rhythm of pleasure. I let her go in that instant and allowed time to resume as the glass of the door shattered around us. I was standing nearly a meter away with no sign of erection, but even my body was pulsing to the beat of magic. I quickly pulled her by the arm into the water to dampen her magic and avoid any glass shards that might have rebound into the shower.

Liz

In a flash, I felt him again. His skin on mine, his lips were crashing into mine with the same harshness that had happened before. It took only seconds to feel a rush of pleasure with his hard cock against me, and I instantly felt wet. Seconds. Second after second of him massaging me, my orgasm took control. Seconds? How was that possible? Mere seconds passed, and I was gasping for air as he releases me from the vision. I felt my electrified power burning under my skin. His hand pulled me under the shower's raining water, and I slowly felt the power melt away.

"Thanks," I whispered. I could not fight this lust; I did not want to. I felt a door slam inside my head, or at least that was how it seemed. He apologized for ruining my shower door, but I would sacrifice the whole bathroom to feel that again, and he didn't even touch me! I was about to protest him shutting me out when I heard his thoughts.

It wasn't supposed to happen that way. I wasn't supposed to get carried along for the ride, and she wasn't supposed to go nuclear. *We didn't even touch! It wasn't like I did this all the time, but I know my power, and it was not like that.* It should have been just a quick daydream. I wasn't supposed to get caught in it too! It's good that I was standing in the running water, or Liz would need more than just a shower door. *What is happening between us?*

"No need to thank me. You saved my ass; I saved yours. No problem," he said out loud.

"Pancakes?" I asked, my voice cracking like a pre-teen boy's. I turned off the water and carefully went to the towel rack outside the shattered glass. I always had two black towels hanging there, but I only needed one. I had to step carefully around the glass. I could have just swept it away with the wind; the excess magic running through my system would simplify it. Instead, I held the power inside like the last drop of wine in a bottle. I didn't want to lose the special kind of high that created.

I felt comfortable around Sorcerer Alaric, which was strange. Showering with someone was almost as intimate as sleeping with them. I didn't usually allow myself to show vulnerability, but that felt natural. I hadn't felt secure with anyone since I chose darkness over life as a human. This was not good. Al is gay, and that felt way too good.

I tossed the other towel to Al as he picked his way through the glass. Neither of us wanted to release any of the magic highs. My bedroom seemed a bit hot, and it was also humid. I walked around the bed to my wardrobe inside the walk-in closet. My clothes were primarily monotone black, but I had a few colorful things. Purple and red were the main accents, but I looked best in purple. I had other clothes with more color, but they were in the cedar chest in the corner. Those clothes were from another life.

"I have something you can wear," I called back to him as I started searching the wardrobe. I opened drawers and searched through the shelves pulling out items, finding jeans, a button shirt, and shoes that would fit him.

"Yes, these will be right on you," I added as I tossed the clothing onto the bed.

He had a strange look on his face as he glanced at the clothing. He was wondering who the items belonged to before…almost like he was jealous. He snapped the connection between us closed when the word *jealous* appeared in my mind.

That was fine with me; I could enjoy him getting dressed without his thoughts tainting my own. I loved watching men dress and undress, though I'd rarely known the pleasure of either.

I gathered some clothes for myself as he sorted the ones I gave him. I did not date, but I had men's clothes around. They were left behind by the ones that ran afraid of my requests, or the others that had accidents. I stepped in front of him to look him in the eyes. I saw him watching when I straightened, but he interrupted any thought with a simple question.

"Nice shirt. Eight hundred bucks nice. Is he going to be upset that I'm wearing it, or did he decide to stop breathing?" he asked with a wicked smile. He was teasing me to cover his feelings. I understood, he knew about the others, and knew they were silent.

"The clothes aren't haunted; the former owner is very much alive," I began as I put on underwear and a bra. "But it is a shame to cover such a masterpiece," I continued as I pulled my pants on.

With any other person, I would tease first by slipping on a skirt after everything that happened, or not. But this wasn't a normal situation. I finished pulling my boots on and passed my hands through my hair, drying it. Magic had a lot of benefits, especially when you did not care about consequences.

I created a portal for the IHOP parking lot. It was later in the morning than I usually arrived, and the place was a little busy. I allowed the waiter to seat us since he was new, and I felt generous. I looked him over, memorizing his walk and appearance. He was too thin, his blond hair a little too dirty for working in a restaurant with food. His hands were dry, and his cuticles were torn. They were probably desperate for staff since the pandemic. He looked harmless enough, and I relaxed a little. I was feeling high as a kite and horny as hell. It didn't help matters that Al was there looking like a god. His aura shone like a beacon, and I wondered if mine also looked like that. If I could feel guilty, I would have, but I mostly felt sorry for every woman in the restaurant staring at him.

"Are they staring at you or me?" Al asked as we settled into the booth.

"Women don't usually stare at me like that unless they are lesbians."

Ian, the waiter, gave us our menus and took out his pen and pad. He was giving Al a heated gaze as well. It was like the man didn't even know how stunning he was, even under glamour.

"Can I get any drinks started for you, sir?" Ian purred at Al.

Al didn't acknowledge that the waiter had spoken. I didn't bother to look at him either. I hated new waiters; they always deferred to my male companion as if we were still living in the twentieth century.

"Al will have the bacon sausage combo, eggs sunny side up with black coffee. I want just a plain ordinary stack of pancakes with caramel sauce, and before you tell me you don't have it, you do, and a coffee as well," I said to the waiter. He looked at Al again, then wrote everything down. He walked away without another word.

"Stupid humans. Do I look like a wilting flower?"

"I won't tell you what you look like to me right now. I'm not sure the words from my mouth would be something you'd want to hear."

The comment almost made me angry until I looked into his eyes. There was a heat there that I'd seen many times before. Alaric Weird was an enigma. I tried to tap into his thoughts, but he had everything on lockdown. It was either that, or I wasn't as good at this as he said I was.

"Because I'm still tingly from our exercise, I will take that as a compliment, not an insult."

"Not an insult. You're something different, something dangerous."

"Then I will take that as high praise coming from you, my alien, vampire, sorcerer, friend."

"We're friends?"

"I don't have friends now, but it felt a lot like this back when I did."

The waiter returned with a pot of coffee and two cups. He sat the cream beside Al and a bottle of caramel sauce near me. I knew they had some in the back! When he left, I poured out two cups of the steaming beverage and added some caramel sauce and one of the tiny creamer cups.

"I don't know what is happening between us, but I have never had a connection to anyone like this," Al said as he blew the steam from his coffee. I looked around to see if anyone was listening. I wasn't used to talking magic in a room full of humans.

"It was like I took your magic and gave you mine," I replied. Thanks to the cream and caramel, my coffee was at the perfect temperature.

"Do you think it is our power?" His thoughts in my head made me tingle.

"I have been with powerful mages, never have I blown up a building."

"I've been with many magical creatures. I don't know what this is, but I'd like to find out."

"Is that an invitation, Mister Gay Alien, vampire, sorcerer?"

"If we had done this before battle, would there even have been a fight?"

The waiter, Ian, brought our food on a large round tray. He sat a stand down and put the tray on. Our mind conversation stopped at the smell of food. Building up that much magic had given us both an appetite, and I still needed to learn what we would do with the surplus. Al grabbed a sausage and started chewing on it like he'd been starving for days. I took my time with the pancakes. I didn't eat a lot of food, but I loved pancakes.

"I guess we will never know, Sorcerer."

"Oh, my father taught me never to say never, Sorceress."

I picked at my food but didn't eat much. It had nothing to do with what he said, my lack of understanding, or how the food looked. It looked tasty and smelled amazing. No, the last day's exhaustion had finally hit me like a tsunami.

"Again, you are an enigma, Alaric Weird."

"You need to eat to get your blood sugar up; just sex will deplete you, and what we did... Well, that wasn't just sex," he said aloud. He stared at the mess I had made by digging my fork into the pancakes. I took a bite of the crumbled food and nearly moaned with pleasure at the taste. He was doing something to me again and didn't even notice.

"You mentioned blood, but you didn't tell me how I taste, not a vampire."

"You taste like danger. There is a reason we don't do that. I may not be the vampire, but I still have his soul and cravings, even if I don't feel or hear him," he said, taking a sip of coffee. His thoughts were on his face, but I couldn't feel him in my mind.

"Danger, I like that," I said as I snagged a piece of bacon from his plate and chewed on it.

"Not the fun kind, the addictive kind."

"I am exhausted from this night, and yet I still feel the magic all around us," I said as I waved a hand in the air. A faint purple glow trailed from my fingers as I moved them. I could see the same glow in Al's aura.

"Careful, we don't want to blow up your favorite restaurant!"

"No, we don't, so one of us should probably go before I start thinking again," I said as I rose from the table. It was my turn to pay, so I took some cash from my pocket, enough to pay for the meal and tip, then dropped it on the table. I stepped close to Al and leaned close to his ear while touching his shoulder.

"Sorcerer," I whispered, inviting him into my mind. I imagined myself in front of him, sitting on his lap, looking into his amazing eyes. I ripped his shirt open in the middle of the restaurant to see his naked chest, and my hands snaked over his skin down to his firm abs. My thought faded there. "It was truly a pleasure," I continued aloud, took my hand from his shoulder where it had left it in reality, and straightened. I could hear him loudly blow out a held breath as I walked to the door.

"The feeling is mutual, Sorceress," he said in my mind as I left the restaurant. A smile reached my lips as I created the portal to my home. I could have offered to send him home, but he was a big boy, a very big boy, and he would find his way.

Al

My life always seemed to be moving boxes, and boxes of stuff that had no value to anyone but myself. I was at least taking my clothes this time. The rest would go to the manor for the parents to deal with, including Rainn and the kids. I couldn't be with her, with them, anymore. It wouldn't be safe. I was just waiting for the next battle, ambush, and death to happen at any time.

I was packing the last box, the books, and the most essential Grimoires. I'd acquired around thirty rare Tomes and Grimoires. I had a healthy stack of manuscripts to go with them. How I obtained the books was not as crucial as the reason. I was searching for a clue to my family curse. Much of my life had been devoted to finding answers to that riddle, and I still had only rumors and gossip to go on. My university study in archeology, specializing in archaic languages, and my ties to the black market, helped me find some of the rarest books. Acquiring my new home gave me an entire library of magical tomes. I hadn't had the time to look through even half of them.

The Mage Tower was a hang-out for all the magical community, but nowadays, you wouldn't catch anyone over thirty years in there. It was a place for the young, not the old. The security there was out of this world–literally. The tower was new, modern, and a Svartalve construction. The entire first floor was dedicated to a dance club. The subsequent floors from the second to the twelfth were reserved for more intimate entertainment. You could rent a room to sleep in, a room for play, or a companion for your evening entertainment. It was not exactly the family fun center, or the place for a business meeting, though that never stopped anyone.

The thirteenth floor was reserved for the penthouse suite. I liked to call it home. It sounded like a vast mansion but was a very open, intimate space. The whole of it took up less of a footprint than the rest of the building, but instead of four sides, it had five and a private elevator that went from the first floor to the living area. Some in the community would think this was a cowardly move, but I liked my sleep when I could get it and needed the environment for which the Tower was famous. Magic was forbidden in the tower, everyone there had it, but it was not the place to use it.

I teleported the thirteen large boxes to the center of the penthouse. It took a lot of energy to move that much mass, but since my last encounter with Liz Key, I had been humming with energy. Teleporting myself was even more complex and took more power than I wanted to expend. I still had to use magical hotspots to get where I needed to go. That is why I needed to learn to make a portal. I needed Liz to teach me. It's not like I would ask for a favor; I would teach her in return. I was used to being the teacher, I had done it most of my life, but I was always a reluctant student. I thought it was not worth learning if I couldn't figure out how it was done. Then I saw her portals.

I was exhausted by the time I arrived at the penthouse. I had no wish to unpack the boxes that had only been packed moments before. It was eerily quiet for such a lively building. I could only hear the water from the decorative fountain near the bathroom door. The architect thought putting a water feature near the toilet was cute.

The place was spartan, with uncomfortable black and white furniture. That was going to be the first thing to go. I liked my home to be a place to relax, not a place to show how stinking rich I was. I hadn't amassed wealth; I'd survived. I couldn't even say I'd inherited it. I just managed to be the last man standing.

The only room I was comfortable in was the study. The previous owner was someone like me. The desk was a mahogany piece that was a century old. It had many secret drawers but no keys to unlock them. You were out of luck if you didn't know the right magic. Good thing knowing magic was my thing. The study walls were filled with wooden shelves polished to an excellent gloss. They were coated well with a bar finish epoxy to keep the wood oils from seeping into thirsty books. The desk chair was dark leather and worn in the seat but not torn. It probably had seen a lot of use by someone nearly as tall as me.

The previous owner had amassed an extensive collection of antique tomes and grimoires. I grabbed an interesting-looking book off the shelf and almost dropped it. It was humming with magic that was so strong it had a purple aura. I opened it expecting to see something different than the runes the book was written in. I set the book inside one of the boxes I'd brought so I could study it later. I was tempted to float the books into the shelve storybook-style, but I needed to rest. Unfortunately, the bed matched the rest of the place. The slightly soft brick reminded me of an altar…which reminded me of her.

Time for a cold shower and drink. The thought of a shower was another reminder. I couldn't get her out of my head, so I decided to skip the shower and go straight to the bar. I needed a drink and maybe some noise. It was fun walking into a room and having all eyes on me; some wanted me, some were curious about my ears, and others were frightened.

The private elevator looked like a service elevator next to the four others. For a change, no one noticed me enter or travel across the dance floor to the bar. The music was so loud that I could feel more than I could hear. It pulsed in my head so violently that I *almost* didn't feel the magic in the room.

She was at the bar, sitting conspicuously alone. Every male in the room was staring at her, including me. The women were looking everywhere but in her direction. She was dressed in her usual fashion, like a lacey Dominatrix. Her demeanor suggested that she wasn't there for company.

She had to know I was there, but she kept her back to me and the rest of the room as if she were the only one in the bar. I couldn't stop the arrogant smirk from forming as I approached her. Her thoughts were running at breakneck speeds, and I heard them all.

Research was only fun in movies, with pages turning, coffee on the table, and background music. It was tedious and frustrating in real life, especially when you ended up with nothing! I have spent all my free time researching Al's and my magic connection with nothing to show off. I'm glad I've decided to drop it for the night and go out for a drink instead of wasting magic…again.

I'm glad to be here and not in my usual hangout place for a drink. There was so much talk about it, and let's face it, I was done with the same people flirting with me repeatedly.

I expected the 'fuck off' expression on my face meant I would not have to keep brushing off people who did not get the meaning. I don't enjoy drinking alcohol, it makes me feel too slow to react, but there are times when I do drink; today was one of those rare nights.

His presence gives a sudden, undeniable surge of magic. It is a power that surpasses anything I have ever felt, intertwining with my own in a way that is both thrilling and perplexing. As my research progresses, the realization of our shared connection grows and I need his help to understand it.

He liked to have fun as I did, so finding him in these kinds of places is not surprising, though I am surprised to find him here. I'm not sure why.

I know it seems like we are stalking each other, but we are not. A meeting like this is a pleasant surprise that keeps happening.

I need to block everyone else, every magic, every sound, and focus on his steps and the feeling of him getting closer.

"Come here often?" I asked to interrupt her thoughts. She already knew I was there, so the cheesy pick-up line wasn't necessary.

"Alaric Weird. What a pleasant surprise."

Liz stared at me like I was dessert, and she was starving. It was still a little unnerving. I kept clinging to my sexual identity even though it had been tested and found wanting. Yeah, I wanted more of Liz Key. Call me crazy or bisexual. Her thoughts were still in my head, giving my ego a boost, not that it needed it.

At least half the room is disappointed just because he chose to talk to me instead of with any of them. I can feel it. Even with his cocky smile and never-ending sex appeal, he is told me he is used to living in this kind of world. And now, with him close, I can see he looks tired.

"Long night, Sorcerer?"

Her question made me realize I was holding in a lot of tension. She could feel it through the connection. I sat on the stool next to her and turned to lean my back against the bar. All eyes were on us now. Two gorgeous and powerful sorcerers walk into a bar… Sounded like the beginning of a joke.

Her mind was closed now, but it didn't matter. Her voice told me she was tired and mentally drained as well, though not from lack of sleep. I get it; I was drained too. Just because the first battle was over, it didn't mean that we hadn't started a war. If I hadn't controlled my stray emotions, I would feel guilty for dragging her into my mess. I'd painted a target on her back by asking her to join me, but I needed the backup.

"Long life, Sorceress. I never expected to see you here."

I waved a hand at the bartender. Jon knew exactly what I wanted without a word from me. When I had first turned to the darkness, this was my place to relax. The tension coming from the current patrons was anything but relaxing now. It would have been entertaining on another day. I could almost read their thoughts. The rumor was that people die when Al Weird and Elizabeth Key got together. Her thoughts suddenly screamed at me, but I don't think she realized it.

This is not his first time here. I wonder if what keeps him awake is the same thing that keeps me awake. Probably

197

not. Probably parties and men. But if it was as powerful to him as it was to me, he had to at least be curious about it. I need to know what is happening with our magic; even now, I feel high when we are not touching each other. It is like my power feeds from his magic.

"Why? Did I give you the impression of having a boring life?" she asked playfully.

I decided to remind her of the connection and play a little with our audience. I opened my mind to her. They would only see her back to them and my eyes daring them to make a move.

"You are scaring them all just by sitting there, but the two of us together terrify them. I can only assume that you are not a regular here. As enjoyable as it is when you tease, please don't do it right now. I don't want to blow the place up. After I've finished my drink, and if you want to chat, we can go upstairs."

I could tell by the amused look on her face that she thought I was inviting her to one of the rooms for private entertainment. It had been a long time since I invited anyone into my home. Somehow that seemed more intimate to me than asking her to have sex.

"Is that an invitation, Sorcerer? You know I never say no to an interesting conversation. And you, honey, are fascinating. Lead the way, Al." she said out loud for all to hear.

"You aren't much of a people person, then again neither am I. I just came here to watch them watch me, but they seem to be less turned on by my handsome face tonight. I love the scent of raw fear, but I believe, I invited you to join me upstairs." I cleared a path through the bar just by walking through the crowd. Yeah, our reputation was getting severe. When you had as many enemies as I had, you rarely let someone walk behind you, but I knew Liz was enjoying the show.

I stopped briefly at the bank of elevators that led from the parking garage to the twelfth floor. I couldn't resist the tease. But being too weary to push it further, I led her to the unmarked elevator near the restrooms. I waved the key card over the laser light, and the doors opened. This time I gestured for her to enter first. She seemed a little surprised, but true to form, she was also amused. The penthouse suite was not visible from the ground or air. You had to know that it was there.

She sauntered and gave me a show on the way onto the elevator. It wasn't so much flirting as just her nature. The most beautiful creatures were usually the most dangerous, but the sparks she was putting off made me relax more than the alcohol in my stomach. When the doors closed, she sent me a little vision of her leaning me into the elevator's corner and kissing me. It was a chaste vision, but my heart sped at the thought.

"Not here, not now," I sighed.

I was too tired to explain the restrictions. Once inside my wards, only my rules apply. I had no plans to repeat our explosive sex, but my body wasn't protesting the idea either.

When the elevator doors opened, I gestured for her to enter first. It was a test. I wanted to see if the magic recognized her as a friend. She stepped into the living area without a spark or even a breeze…interesting.

"Welcome to Castle Weird, my new home. It's not me yet. The previous owner did not enjoy creature comforts," I explained, letting her wander around to look at the place.

It isn't huge; it was meant for a single reclusive person like myself. The only private room in the place was the bathroom. I enjoyed listening to Liz's thoughts as she walked around the perimeter.

I'm inside the penthouse of the freaking Mage Tower. My parents talked non-stop about this place, and they had never set foot in it. Rumor had it, the most powerful sorcerer in centuries had built the penthouse at the top of the tower as his fortress. There is only one way in–the elevator–and those who leave by other means don't live to speak about their experience.

I could see the magical field generated by the wards from every window. The decor of whites and blacks didn't seem like him. The pile of boxes in the center of the living area said he is still moving in, but I have heard the stories. It takes some serious power to keep the wards going and the place invisible to those who don't run in the highest magical circles. It is not the tallest building I'd been in, but it dwarfs everything around it. The lights below seem like tiny fireflies frozen in time. I want to take my time observing the place because I can feel his eyes on me. If he were straight, I would say he was fucking me with his eyes, but he is probably looking at me with his scientist's brain. I'm nothing more than an exciting specimen under his microscope. That's fine; I am here to learn, too; he had already said he had things to teach me. I never turn down a chance to discover new magic.

It was interesting watching Sorceress Elizabeth Key wandering around my new home like a kid in a candy store. I was just about to tease her when she asked a serious question.

"You? You are the powerful sorcerer that owns this penthouse?"

There had been three tower owners since its construction; I was the third.

"No, I killed that guy," I said, waiting to see how she reacted.

"How?" she asked in a tone of slight disbelief and awe.

"Research, Sorceress Key, research," I chuckled.

"Did you hit him with one of your dusty old books in this box?"

She kicked the bottom box of one stack, and they all tumbled like a house of cards. The book I wanted to show her slid to the top of the pile as if guided by an unseen hand. Magic books and some magical talismans often gained sentience after a few centuries. I was not surprised that this one was begging to be touched by her dark magic. It started to glow a deep purple, thrumming in a beat identical to hers. It recognized her in some way. I thought it might.

She stared at the book for a moment, then reached down and plucked it off the pile. She held it like a mother holds a child. It was then I knew I was right; she was my *Key* to unlocking my family curse.

That book was written by a powerful sorceress nearly two millennia ago, I explained in thought.

She opened the book reverently and caressed the worn pages. It would have disintegrated at her touch if it were an ordinary book, but it was made from skin and bound in magic. It was indestructible, though I never wanted to try. It was written in Nordic Runes, the language of my ancestors. I doubted Liz could read it, but that didn't stop her from trying. I could tell the book was talking to her, but I couldn't tell if she understood.

I leaned against the bar and watched her turn pages like a scholar in an ancient library. Getting her interested in being a test subject for my experiment would be easier. If I could give her my power, I could choose who would get which ability, maybe even one day have all three myself. It had happened before. Liz was my only hope to get all the power the magic world leaders craved. I watched as she lifted the book to inhale its scent.

"If you'd like me to step out and give you two some privacy, just let me know," I teased.

She glared at me angrily, then threw the book at my head. She gave the toss a boost with magic so that when it impacted, it would hurt. I stopped time on instinct. It wasn't my face I wanted to save; that book was more important. I just plucked it out of the air centimeters from my face. I let the time flow free when my hand touched the book. It would look like I moved faster than vampire speed to save it, but I had hardly moved at all. Either way, she would see it as cheating, but we weren't sparring, and she was lost in thought again.

That book looks familiar; it's freaking calling me. I know better; I ran across a few curses at the beginning of my magical journey, and I had learned not to touch anything that hummed magic. But this book...this book feels different. It feels like it belongs to me, which makes no sense. I have never seen it. Looking through the pages, it feels so familiar, like I already used it before, but that is impossible. Suddenly the high pitch makes my heart jump. I close the book. He knew about this, that was the reason he invited me here. And that is, at least, the second test he made me pass since we entered that elevator. I pisses me off. How long has he had that book? How much does he really know about me? About my family? How much does he know that even I do not? I'll wipe that smirk off his face with this book. It's heavy enough to leave a mark when it hit his pretty face.

"What is the meaning of this?"

I touch my ring with my thumb, searching for security. He can not possibly know about this amulet, can he? No one knew except the person who gave it to me. I need to hide the shock but I'm doing a terrible job. I avoided any teaching from the Key family; I never claimed anything from them. I hate them all. Though from the Key bloodline, all my power had grown without guidance from the Key family. I need to sit and try not to draw much attention from him. My mother wanted me to learn more about our family history, and I never wanted to. Did she know about this? Too late to ask.

There must be something out the window, something to focus on, so I can control my thoughts and avoid his gaze.

Anger was not the reaction I expected from Liz when she touched the book. When I caught it, the magic ceased to thrum as if I had snuffed a candle with my fingers. The book wasn't concerned with me anymore; it had found its owner. I lowered the book from my face slowly as if overcompensating for what would have looked like a super-human power. I'd been keeping an eye on Liz. I knew she was looking for answers, just like I was, but I'd found what I was looking for. She waited for my response.

"What is this?"

But I had no idea what the meaning was. I only knew that she heard the whispers. She knew the spell, or it knew her.

"I was hoping you would shed some light on the subject. Have you ever seen that book before? I've had it in my possession for five years, and today it woke and started whispering to me. I could still hear it until I caught it in my hand.

"In case you needed to ask, I acquired it the same way I acquired this penthouse; I believe the book's previous owner was your cousin. I could tell you that it never woke in his hands, or I wouldn't be at war right now. I'd probably be dead."

"I never saw it… But there were rumors."

Was her reply almost a whisper of reverence? I set the book on the bar and went to the tiny fridge in the back. The kitchen wasn't stocked yet, but there was always some alcohol in the penthouse. It had been in my possession for a couple of years, and I was the only one with a key, but things happened when no one was there; things appeared, disappeared, and moved. It might have been haunted, but I'd lived in a haunted house most of my life and it hadn't felt like this.

"Drink?" I offered.

I pulled out a bottle of fireball whiskey without waiting for an answer; I poured three fingers of the cinnamon-flavored liquid into two glasses, then walked over and handed one to her. As our fingers touched, purple sparks jumped back and forth between them and around them. It was nothing like that night, but it was still there. I knew we could re-access the power, but I wanted to know what she knew about the book. I still needed to experiment on her, but if we got the results, she would be even more powerful. It was a risk I was willing to take.

"Definitely!"

I need the drink; I don't even want to wait for him to pour it. That book is filled with curses from my ancestors, and I know what it means to me and anyone who would use it. It's evil, but also intriguing.

"I heard several versions. The one I heard the most was how a Key feared for our existence and made a curse to survive. A very tricky and very dark curse that was only possible by sacrificing the person she loved. I thought it was ridiculous; we did not love, not the family Key. But perhaps at that time, we did. The curse was meant to attack and wipe out another potent family, the only family strong enough to threaten us. It was said they would end the family bloodline. At that point, I guess it was them or us."

"Us?" I asked in thought. We were getting more comfortable communicating without words. She knew that the connection went both ways.

"That book already made me say 'us' when discussing my ancestors. Rumor was that it worked, but not quite like we wanted. Magic, as you know, was very delicate. The curse made them more powerful, and we almost died out. If we were not a target before the curse settled, we were after."

She paused to pour herself another drink and slam it down her throat. She'd realized that communicating in thought with me made it easier to drink.

"There was another version. That the curse was created as a punishment. A Key fell in love, or maybe just joined forces with a member of the other family. At this point, who cares what they did? But there was also a rumor that it was love, weakness, something that put the Key bloodline at risk, which was the real reason for the creation of the curse, they say. One thing was sure, a curse was made, and ironically, it cursed us too. The book disappeared for generations sometime after our family was attacked. I did not think it was real, not until today."

Liz touched the book with reverence, just as I had. She knew it had power, our kind of power. The rumors meant nothing; they were there to entice or warn would-be seekers of the knowledge inside. I'd read the book enough times to know what each page said, and it was all innocuous poetry for the most part, but then most curses were hidden in rhyme and poetry. It was strange for me to communicate in thought when we were alone but speaking aloud about the book seemed wrong.

"I am sure all the rumors you've heard are true. There was more than one curse in the book and more than one way to activate them. I don't know if the very dark curse you speak of was the one I was seeking, but it was meant to be a punishment and a way of controlling the victim. It was created to drive an ancestor of mine insane while keeping her alive as a slave to the magic created inside her. A Key sorcerer cursed her, and she controlled the curse. The bookbinding is made from the skin of one of your ancestors killed by the sorcerer's wife. You are a true Key...more than anyone in centuries."

She winced a bit at the comment, but I had meant it as a compliment. I shouldn't have forgotten that family was a sore subject for her. It had been a while since someone in the bloodline had risen to the rank of a sorcerer; the last had been a distant cousin. Her parents were powerful, but they had no idea what they'd created or what they tried to destroy.

I downed the whiskey and resisted the cough that was tickling its way from my lungs–they don't call it *Fireball* for no reason. I would have worried about Liz's comment, but she was deep in thought, and I hadn't been invited to share. I gave her some time to let all of it sink in. The next part would be even more difficult for me to say.

"So…my family cursed yours? Go figure. Is that what our magic was reacting to? You do not want me dead, at least not at this moment, or I would not be standing here," Liz said, interrupting my thoughts.

How do you ask someone to allow you to curse them? It sounded insane, yet I knew she would want it and that she, of all people, would be able to handle it.

I couldn't tell if she was asking me or herself the questions. I didn't want her dead, far from it; I wanted her to be like me. It's lonely at the top, and I felt she and I were at the very top—the only ones left with enough power to do the spells and curses in that book. I'd known a few people who called themselves sorcerers, but none of them could do what we could. No one in recorded history had ever done a power exchange as we had. The book didn't recognize me anymore, but I thought the book had gotten a taste of the real deal, and I was just not as appetizing any longer.

"I don't know what our magic is reacting to; my research has never discussed this. I have read of others 'pulling power' through each other like electricity through a line, but that was something else. Liz, do you trust me? I don't want you dead; I don't bring people into my home to kill them. I rarely bring the men I fuck into my home. Since I acquired the place, you have been the first guest to enter here. I want to do some magic with you."

I handed her the book, took her hand, and led her to the bed. I knew by the devilish smile on her face that she thought I meant sex. I did want to see if what happened was a unique experience, but tonight I had other things in mind.

I wanted to try to recreate the curse that put my family at the top of the magical food chain and on the most wanted dead list.

I turned her back to the bed and pushed her on. She crab-crawled back to make room for me. It was a California king-sized bed, which was interesting since the last owner was a small man. I sat on the bed, scooted a bit, then turned to face her as I sat cross-legged near the center. I held my hands out to her, and she took them, mirroring my stance. I retrieved the book from the edge of the bed and sat it on her lap. In her hands, it had hummed; in her lap, it was swirling with a purple aura.

"Liz, I want you to open the book and slowly turn the pages until you hear a sound like angels singing. Don't look at me that way; it's what the text says. That will be the curse put on my family, the reason I can control time. I want to give you that power. I think you can handle the power without going mad. If anything goes wrong, I will take the curse. I'm already a madman."

Before she could answer, I invoked the inlaid circle into the wood floor. It was copper and silver, perfect protection for anything that wanted to get in through the line we would tap.

"If this goes the way I think, you will have the power to stop time and see the present, the power of a god in the hands of a Key Sorceress. You will be unstoppable, and we will have everything the others desire."

She rested the book on my shins and opened it to the first page. I heard the faint voices again, but to me, it was gibberish. Liz was listening. She turned the pages slowly, one by one. The sound never changed for my ears, but she stopped on the thirteenth page. It might have been that one.

I had to get this right, or I would do to her what her ancestor did to mine. The words on the page were in Ogham, the ancient language of the Druidic cultures. Those looked like tally marks. Most people noticed the Nordic people's runes—one language for instruction, the other for the spell.

I finally understand the meaning of so much information that your head feels numb. I never thought it was literally.

"Liz, do you trust me? I want to do some magic with you."

"I would usually say no to that question, but you are not normal, and we are not ordinary. I only trust one other soul more," she replied, shocking me.

She stopped when she got to the curse I thought was the one. She had her hand over the text, but I knew the words. It wasn't just words that this spell needed, though. A curse required a sacrifice, blood, or flesh, and not just ordinary blood. It required Key blood…a lot of it. We could use the book as a substitute, flesh for blood, but it would consume it. I needed the ability to do this again.

"Liz, I have to ask you for total trust. This is a black curse, and it requires blood, Key blood. It requires more than I would take from you, and I will alter the spell. I won't ask for more than I am willing to give."

I waited for her answer. After a moment, she gave me a curt nod. I wouldn't have taken that as consent if she were anyone else. I took her left hand and held it over the book. I had no ceremonial knife but something sharper and more fun. I bit into the vein that pulsed beneath her soft skin, then licked the wound to keep the blood flowing onto the book. She held it steady as her life force poured into the gap between the pages. It was my turn next.

I found it awkward trying to bite my own wrist. They do it so quickly in the movies, but fangs and jaws don't allow for self-feeding…unless you are half-alien. The bottom fangs are as sharp as the top, maybe more so. My blood flowed easily into the book as I wove my fingers into hers. It was an intimate gesture, holding hands, but we were not following instructions. The sacrifice would have had been to cutthroat, and the potential curse victim would have been forced to keep the book to catch the blood. I never was good at following instructions to the letter.

There was something sensual about doing curses; the words flowed like poetry. I had read these words a hundred times, trying to decipher them. Each rune in Elder Futhark had a sound but also its meaning. You had to employ the rune's sound and intent to get the desired results. I had to do one more, take the spell apart to give only what I wanted to share and hold back the madness that the past and future would bring. No one could live sanely in all three at once. Or so I had been told.

I said the words that would bring out the present and held back those that would give her the entire curse; it was like the abridged version of the spell. I could feel the magic in the air like a warm mist filled with static electricity. I could see why the instructions said to sit to do the spell. I hadn't used a protection circle since I first learned black magic, but the sparks jumping off the invisible shell told me something was trying to join us. A good curse taps into the ley lines that surround the planet. Ley lines are portals in their own right; they are fractures between this world and countless others. You never knew what you would get when you tapped one.

Liz seemed oblivious to what was going on around us, but then I realized, at that moment, I was freezing time without noticing. I was hesitating. *What if it went wrong? What if I destroyed the only interesting person I had ever met?* The Liz Key I'd heard about would never trust someone to curse her. I was feeling Alias' guilt again. I put that out of my mind and concentrated on the spell. She didn't matter; only the magic mattered.

I finished speaking the words and felt the curse creep out of the book and surround Liz in a greasy purple haze. I was witnessing something that no one had seen in millennia. The music was the Key; I could hear it now, I would call it more a siren song than Angels, but that was more my lack of religion than a difference in tune. I was confident in the changes I'd made until the tune changed, the song was still singing, but it was sad and chaotic. I knew this tune, and it was the sound of madness. She would get the whole curse, and I couldn't allow that. I needed her sanity more than I needed my own. I was already crazy, not just for trying to give away magic to someone powerful enough to kill me in my sleep–even with my immunity to magical death.

I grabbed the book and wrenched it from her hands. She gasped as the spell broke off. I heard the sounds of screaming and wailing, and I heard them–Alias and Alton!

"This is the end, stupid fucker; you'll be stuck here with us."

I could feel myself losing consciousness and falling back on the bed. The screams and wails were loud and endlessly pounded on my brain. I could feel the book leave my hands, but I couldn't see anything but magic or hear anything but the noise of madness. She straightened my legs and sat on my stomach. I could feel the crackle of magic that somehow tied us together. I couldn't tell if she was speaking to me, but suddenly everything stopped. It wasn't just sight and sound; the world had stopped. I knew this feeling; it was the magic of time. She had stopped time and taken me inside with her.

"Thanks," I croaked. My voice sounded strange in the silence. I could see images of Liz as a child, sitting on a boy, punching him as he taunted her. He was so dark that his aura felt greasy, evil. I saw Alton's triplets graduating from high school, all smiling except Aliyah; she would have a hard life just as Alias did. I should have felt guilty, but I felt a sense of pride; I had forged them with magic, not sex. They were all perfect creations of my power. The vision faded, and I was back with Liz as she slapped my face hard enough to knock a tooth loose. Yep, that was the Liz Key I'd read about. Hit them hard when they are down, and make sure they don't get up to try again. She was okay…well, as okay as we could have been, and she was already using the power as if born to it. My family curse was now hers, and she was invested in keeping it out of the hands of my enemies…our enemies.

I tried to focus my eyes; my mind was fractured, slipping from the past to the future. The magic hadn't stopped, though I felt nothing from the book. There was something on the bed; her ring was lying against my leg, and I could feel her aura within it. I floated it in the air and felt the charm on it. Images started flowing in my head, and I shut them down cold. Thanks to my alien mother, I had something no other Weird had ever had. I had control. I had gambled on all of this; I thought it might happen this way. I did nothing without thinking of it from all angles, running through all scenarios.

"That was extremely stupid of us," she said with an evil grin. I didn't know if she felt anything different, but I did.

"Yeah, no kidding. There are things you shouldn't do before cursing someone with a spell like that. Drinking alcohol is high on the list."

"Let's do it again!"

Like I had the strength to sit up, I hadn't spent that much magic since I raised Rainn and the triplets from the dead. She seemed energized from the curse, probably because she only got a third of it. Liz was close enough to my face that I could just lift my head and kiss her lips. The cinnamon of the Fireball was a pleasant aroma mixed with her perfume. I wanted to do exactly what she was asking me. It was just a kiss; what harm could it do? It's not like I could move more than my head, and my left arm. I pulled her face to mine and kissed her deeply, tasting the alcohol on her breath. It was just a kiss, but the magic it was creating drained the rest of my strength. I released her head and held the ring to her face as she slowly pulled away. She took it and slipped it on her finger without explanation. I didn't need one; I could just open my mind and learn all the secrets the ring held. I wouldn't, though; if she wanted me to know, she would tell me. She fucking trusted me to curse her with a spell that could have made her my mindless slave. It's what happened to my ancestor.

I patted the bed to the left of me and said in the most sultry voice my weary throat could manage, "Sleep with me, Liz." She laid down next to me with my arm trapped under her shoulders. She didn't weigh much; her frame was smaller than my usual bed companions. That she understood, even with my flirting, that I actually wanted to sleep, stung a little, but it also made me feel safe. She was my friend, not my lover. We didn't have to follow anyone's rules but our own.

I watched as she tossed the ring into the air and froze it into place. She would release it and freeze it again. I remember doing that for hours when I first discovered the power. I grabbed the ring from her time bubble, then opened my fist to show her it was gone. She gasped and glared at me.

"Look on your finger," I said. She lifted her hand to find the ring on the finger where she always wore it. I also learned that if a seer of the present can control that moment, someone with all three sights can send a tiny ring a few moments into the future. It was enough of a drain that I felt my eyes closing of their own accord. I'd have to wait until morning to see what else I could do.

Al

I woke in the late morning, ten twenty-six. No, I didn't look at a clock or my phone. I just knew precisely what time it was. Liz had curled up next to me and was using me as a pillow. I knew she was not used to sleeping with another person any more than me. I was a child the last time I shared a bed for sleep. It was strange, and a little uncomfortable, not just because my arm had gone to sleep. It had wrapped around her back…for my comfort, not hers.

The magic that usually jumped between us was silent, but it wasn't gone; it was just sleeping like she was.

I slowly slid my arm out from under her and tucked a pillow under her head so she could continue sleeping. She would probably have a headache equal to mine, if not worse, when she opened her eyes. The ability to control time took a lot out of a person, as I well knew, and she was practicing when I passed out for the night. The ring she'd used was back on her finger. I knew it was some form of protection charm, but as powerful as she was, I doubted it was necessary. There was a story behind it, of that, I was sure.

I needed a shower. I would have woken her for it, but as much as she wanted to be reckless with magic, we needed to set some boundaries first, for her sake and mine. I also didn't want to dance around the broken glass in my bathroom. She didn't seem upset about her shower, but my home was hidden for a reason; I couldn't have movers or repair people in without wiping memories. I could do it quickly, but if they had weak minds, they would have a psychotic break; if they had strong minds, they could break the spell, even if they were nonmagical humans. I didn't have the advantage of a reputation that kept Liz reasonably safe. My notoriety as a minor celebrity, a model, and a gay half-alien made me seem less of a threat to the stupid. I was saving lives by keeping my residence hidden. I got bored killing people who thought they could beat me because of my inferior breeding. Worse were the ones who believed that gay meant soft. I was born hard, and I was not just talking about my dick.

My bathroom was more significant than my sister's living room. The shower was custom-built; again, it seemed to be made for a larger man than the previous owner. I didn't recall the first owner being described as a big man, either. Maybe they just thought they were bigger. The shower was much like Liz's, with stone and glass walls. My first thought was to take a quick shower, but I needed to practice myself, so I stopped time. I didn't usually do this for fun or convenience, but Liz would be angry if I didn't invite her to join me. Anger was not quite right; she would be distrustful, which was worse than anger. A friend who stopped trusting you could quickly become an enemy, and I was not sure if either of us would survive a real fight against each other.

There was another power she would take issue with if she found out I had used it. I just needed to try something without anyone around. So, I took a three-hour hot shower from a water heater that couldn't support much more than thirty minutes.

My skin was red, and my fingers wrinkled when I finally decided to stop. I was about to release time, but I had a better idea. I wrapped my deep purple towel around my waist and entered the kitchen. It was built for someone who liked to cook, which again, resembled me. The cabinets and appliances were stainless steel, and the countertop was a deep black granite with walnut-sized chunks of amethyst strewn throughout the surface. Just as I thought, there were pots and pans and the basic needs inside the cabinets. The main fridge was stocked with fresh milk, eggs, cheese, and two huge sirloins wrapped in the paper my favorite butcher used. I'd have to remember all this later in case I accidentally changed the future by forgetting the eggs.

I'd wondered for days why everything I needed seemed to show up at the right place, at the perfect time. They could be from charms, brownies, or even hauntings. Last night I realized I had been doing this all along. If only I had thought to surprise myself with new decor, but then I was never much of a do-it-yourself person. Alias was the architect, artist, and designer. I preferred to get my hands dirty in other ways, like digging into the past.

I'd find a way to make the place more me later. Right at that moment, it was my turn to provide breakfast, and I liked to cook sometimes. Pancakes were my specialty, and I seemed to have provided maple syrup, fruit, and whipped cream in a spray can. I didn't recall them being there before; my grocery list grew. My scientific mind was thinking of how the future changed just by me noticing there were originally two shopping trips I now shortened to one. I wondered if I would notice anything else showing up just when I needed it.

I released time just as I finished the noisiest part of cooking, mixing the batter. I figured it would be much nicer to wake up to the smell of pancakes than the whine of the electric mixer, which I didn't remember seeing in the cabinet earlier. I must have hit a big box store to get all the preparations for this. Knowing that I was the one making things appear in my home didn't help much. I could only assume I would start remembering in reverse. I really needed to know if this time traveling was normal, or if it was something that only I could do.

I could feel Liz's eyes on me as soon as she woke. The magic needed us both to be conscious; interesting. She was quiet, but I could hear her breathing, and I could feel her stare. I was about to say something when I heard her in my mind.

"Nice view. Do you get naked and cook for all the women you invite to sleep with you?"

She gave me an image of what she was seeing. I had not even thought about clothing, it was my house, and I was always alone. Well, almost always.

"As a matter of fact, I do. And I am not naked."

If she were anyone else, I would think her question was laced with jealousy, but she knew without telling me, she was the only woman to sleep in my bed. She was being playful, a side effect of the magic flowing between us. Whatever this was, acted like an aphrodisiac; I felt it too. It would be easy to give in to it, but before I could indulge, I needed to know what our new powers would do in combination with the explosive magic we created together.

Liz needed to stop worrying about my sexual orientation. It was bothering her a lot more than it affected me. Labels were not really my thing; it was just me. I wasn't going to change my whole life because I had sex with a woman. We both knew that what we did was more than just carnal pleasure. Somehow sleeping with her seemed more intimate anyway. It was probably something we should talk about, but for some reasons words just wouldn't form in my mouth. I decided to stick to thought.

"There is another towel in the bathroom if you wish to clean up. I promise I won't peek."

Even my mind had a case of foot-in-mouth. I realized too late that I had given her a slight insult. She crawled off the bed and marched to the shower without a thought. She wasn't hurt or angry, just disappointed and for the wrong reason. Damn! We were going to have to talk about that. The problem with both of us was we didn't know how to relate to other people, except regarding sex. Sex was easy, just two people using each other to get off. The other stuff, well, we both had friends when we were younger, but if she was anything like me, and I was sure she was, she didn't trust them entirely.

Liz didn't spend much time in the shower; she came out in a towel identical to mine, using a brush on her long hair that wasn't mine–and her hair was dry. She was learning to freeze time too quickly; worse, I hadn't even noticed. That was a bit worrying. It meant that she could do what I had done to her, and I wouldn't know. It could have been possible that she showered and dried her hair in less than five minutes, but then she wouldn't be female in my experience, not to mention human.

I dished out a healthy stack of pancakes already bathing in butter. I set out several toppings and chose maple syrup for mine. Real Canadian maple syrup was something you wouldn't find in box superstores. "Waking up to a breakfast like this, a girl could get used to it."

Her words brought my focus back; I had an eternity to figure this out. I didn't know where to start. She had taken a seat on the end stool and had started loading her pancakes with fruit and a small amount of syrup. She began to reach for the whipped cream until I accidentally sent her what I was thinking. It's not my fault that many of my bedroom activities involved whipped cream cans. The fact that she was dessert in my vision didn't help my problem.

I sat on the stool next to hers and pulled my plate closer. I was thinking of how to say what I needed without causing more issues. The "I just want to be friends" speech wouldn't work here because that wasn't true.

The act of sitting caused my towel to fall, but I pretended not to notice. She'd seen it all before, if not close up, I'm sure she's seen photos. I glanced at her, and she was staring with a smile slowly turning into a smirk.

"I'm still unsure which view is better–you or the breakfast." She stuck a healthy bite of pancakes in her mouth, probably trying to disguise her cheeky grin. She moaned like a professional porn star with the first bite.

"As you can tell, the pancakes, as sexy as they are, taste better than they look. It's a Weird secret family recipe from the more alien side of the family. No one would ever let my father near the kitchen."

She stopped chewing when I mentioned Alphonse, then shrugged it off and continued eating. I didn't have the problems with my family she had with hers, but then I was also no more attached to them than she was to hers. Some people called her evil, but at least her parents deserved her ambivalence.

"Be careful. A woman could fall in love with this. Not me, but some woman."

That was the opening I needed. She was teasing, and I wasn't upset. If she were anyone else, I would be worried…maybe even scared.

"If you were a man, I would use the 'I just want to be friends' line; I've been thinking about this for about four hours, and I want to know how long you took in the shower when I am done talking." I always hated talking about this shit; that was why I leave or get kicked out. Having someone sleep in my house made me feel strange, but not as much as I thought it should.

"You and I are unique in at least this world, and there are some things I need to deal with if we are going to do more magic together. It's not the gay thing. Well, maybe a little. But it's all of this." I gestured with an open-palmed circle which caused sparks to jump between us. She started leaning away from me, so I held her elbow. That stopped her for the moment, and me, and the clock. Shit, I was afraid this would happen. I wasn't stopping time, she was, and I couldn't tell how big the bubble was. I wasn't frozen this time; I wasn't in the bubble. I was in the eye of the storm. I let go of her elbow and leaned back; the bubble broke as soon as I let go. She straightened, shrugged her shoulders, and tossed her hair onto her back.

"Al, don't hurt yourself. I'm not accepting a proposal," she joked. "I mean, the sex was good, better than good, it was magical. Literally. But I don't expect anything from you."

I laughed. "Could you imagine what the magical world would do if I did propose to you?"

She didn't laugh, but I could tell by the twinkle in her eye that she wanted to. Instead, she punched me on the arm hard enough to bruise. We both broke out in laughter for a few moments. I wrapped the towel around my waist and stood. Taking her hand, I guided her off the stool. She must have felt the charge just as much as me because she stumbled but caught herself before she fell.

"I can't imagine you proposing to anyone, Alaric Weird," she said, then yanked her hand from mine.

"There will be clean clothes in the top drawer of the closet, your size, your style, and no; I haven't had any other female house guests."

Make that five shopping trips, or was it six now? I followed her to my closet, and when she slid the door, I grabbed my jeans and an old t-shirt off the floor. The T-shirt was a gift from my friend Marcello, a fellow alien. It had a rainbow alien head on the front with the word 'Homosexualien' underneath. The alien was wearing a wizard hat just to complete the description of my lifestyle. I didn't wear it to remind her, or anything, but when she saw it, she started laughing hysterically. Hey, what could I say? It was one of my favorite T-shirts. Once we were dressed, she started walking toward the elevator. I used vampire speed to block her path. "Not yet, I have two steaks in the fridge and some wine chilling. You're going to stay for dinner," I said matter-of-factly.

Liz crossed her arms and glared at me, angry this time. I opened my hand to show her that I had her ring in it. I knew she would think I froze time on her; the proof was on her face.

"Sometime in the future, I will go shopping for groceries, kitchen gadgets, and women's clothing. I don't know when, but I know you are supposed to eat steak here today. You don't get a steak from Antonio's and let it sit for more than a few hours. It has already been aged to perfection. I thought it would be dinner time because I need to warm them to room temperature…and know how long you had me frozen," I blurted. I didn't want her to leave, and I was pretty sure she wouldn't. I knew the full curse came with the ability to see the future, but I hadn't gotten the hang of controlling it yet. I was actually a little afraid of what I would see. Liz looked confused but walked over to the uncomfortable sofa and sat down.

"Steak? Right. I will answer your questions. It was maybe twenty to thirty minutes; I'm not sure," she replied. She was more relaxed and not running out the door.

I took a seat on the chair next to the sofa. This furniture was not made for the likes of me, the chairs were too low, and the backs barely reached my kidneys. I sighed trying to wrap my head around all of this. I was a freaking time traveler! I was still working out how I did it or would do it in the near future. I closed my eyes, and I could see myself at the local Walmart. I didn't want to tell Liz her clothes were off the discount rack of a big box store. At least I had stuck to her goth chick black on black theme she preferred.

"I froze time on you for about four hours, and that is not all. I traveled back in time–and will again–to get breakfast, dinner, and some clothes for you," I explained. It was difficult to tell her exactly what I meant since I didn't understand it myself. I wished I could talk to someone who knew more about my family curse, but everyone who knew anything had died before I was born. Explaining what was happening wouldn't be easy until I understood myself.

"You froze time for four hours? Under running water?" she asked. She walked toward the kitchen as if she wanted to sit, but she stopped and leaned on the pillar near the elevator doors. I loved how she could go from angry to curious in less than a minute. Most of the women I knew, even the alien ones, didn't have that much control over their emotions.

"That is why I am worried about doing more magic, not sex. I'm not going to pick out china with you, and I will not use the term 'friends with benefits,' but that does fit," I explained.

"Again, you mention marriage. Don't worry, I am not that sort either, and if I wanted to be married it wouldn't be to a gay alien who has a vampire living in his head. The bite was fun, but not something I want to make a habit," she said as she slid down the pillar to rest on the floor.

"If there were instructions on this, if I even thought that someone had ever done it before, I wouldn't be so worried. In all my research on the power of sight, it was always just that–sight. I thought maybe my being an alien was the reason I could affect time, but unless your father was abducted and gave birth to you, I think we can rule that out. It makes me a little nervous that you can use your power on me, but I trust you to have my back, and I hope you won't do it again without telling me first. I promise to do the same. I've never had a friend or an ally, and no one has ever slept in my bed. As a rule, you and I don't do relationships, but I would rather be your friend than your enemy."

"Friend, huh? I like the sound of that, for some reason. I haven't slept in someone else's bed since– Well, that's not important," she said. She forgot that I tended to get glimpses of her thoughts when she didn't shut me out. She was thinking of Dan and Sophie, the two people she had once called friends. I felt a little sting of jealousy, not about her past relationship with Dan, but that she had experienced true friendship. Alias had been my only friend growing up.

I pulled out a black key card and handed it to her. She looked at it as if it were a bomb that might go off if she shook it too hard. I had to explain. "You have enemies thanks to your alliance with me. This place is safer than yours, even with your wards. No one has to know this place is here, that I own it, and that you have access. Only the most powerful can even see it from the air. I'm not asking you to move in; just use this as a safe house if you need to. If I wanted to look, I could tell you what the future holds for you, but that is the real madness of the curse. I don't want to know how you die or how you live." She looked at the card briefly, then handed it back to me.

"Thanks, but no thanks; I'm a big girl. I can take care of myself like I always have. I don't need a safe place, and I don't need you to protect me."

I didn't know how to tell her I wouldn't already have the card if she didn't need it. The locks were read by a laser and a biometric scanner that detected the DNA of the cardholder. No one else could use that card, not even me. Liz had to be holding the card and have a pulse to use it. She couldn't be coerced into allowing anyone to ride the elevator with her. My wards would destroy anyone not connected to me through magic. I slipped the card into my pocket for the moment. She wasn't going anywhere without it.

The look on her face told me she wanted to say something or bolt. The whole time she kept turning that ring on her finger. Until last night I had never seen her take it off. I left her to her thoughts. If she wanted to let me in, she would. Liz didn't believe in secrets; I envied that in her. My family was all about secrets. I had to hide my magic, alien form, lie about my ears. Alias had it worse. Revealing my secrets put a target on my back, making it challenging to sleep…except last night.

* * *

Liz

Secrets were weaknesses; that has always been my motto.

Al had said, "I don't want to know how you die."

That sentence kept playing in my head. I trusted him with my body, in battle, in bed, and more recently, with a curse. Maybe he deserved to learn what I knew.

Secrets were weaknesses. I looked for the Key family book, which I thought was a myth until recently, and found it lying on the table. I didn't want protection after he knew the truth; I could handle everything myself. I always had. But if we trusted each other, he deserves to know that part of my life. I did not want him to find out through an accidental connection between us or in any way other than me telling him.

The truth was I knew how I would die; I knew since I accepted my magic–yes, the dark magic–that it would not be a comfortable and warm death in bed. I didn't know why the vision happened or what triggered it, just that it happened. But knowing how did not mean I knew when.

I'd had that ring for twelve years now. It was given by someone who loved me, and then 'blessed' by the person who tried to save me from my family and my fate–the Key family alchemist named Alma. Amulets do not need to be beautiful masterpieces, full of symbols, and made of specific crystals. They could be everyday objects if we gave enough power and intent.

Some people said we made our destiny and that we could change it. I believed in that too, but I still needed to stand a chance. I was marked by darkness and death as soon as my lungs filled with air for the first time. My magic would never be white. My path would always end there, as a dark sorceress fully aware of her inevitable end. We will all die, won't we? But I would not go without a fight. A fight that was mine and mine alone. Not his.

I kept silent, feeling his gaze on me, studying me. It was what he did; it was his nature. He was a scientist. But he did not break his promise, nor try to connect, and did not try to force the truth.

I took my ring off–and like every time I did, I felt like I was missing a member–and gently launched it to him. He caught it with ease. I opened myself to him, ultimately, hoping he'd accept the connection. This was the only time I felt vulnerable and intimate with anyone since I went dark. I had never shared this with anyone before and allowing him to live what had happened through me was a little strange. I let him see my memories.

Dan gave me that ring full of love and hope for a future that never happened. At nineteen, I thought I was free from the Key name; I was in love and away from magic. I believed in fairy tales back then. I have no shame in admitting I was weak once. That memory vanished, and another one took place.

The second was about the moment I'd used black magic for the first time. I was dying, bleeding on a cold floor after being tortured and stabbed, in a dark alley, in the middle of nowhere. I was a twenty-one-year-old woman, so proud of myself for finishing my courses and living an everyday, non-magic life.

I went to the next memory, and somehow, I thought I was feeling the physical pain torturing me at the moment of my recovery years ago. That was not right. I was not there. These were memories, but it hurt as it hurt then. The alchemist, Alma was the only person from the Key mansion that treated me like a typical child/teenager, and not like an incubator for the most powerful mage alive, like I was just a prize. She was trying potion after potion to stop the poison the blade of Dagon had thrust into my bloodstream. Finally, when almost all had failed, she was successful with one potion and an incantation. A protection incantation was put on the ring that represented hope, love, and happiness. My promise ring. The ring in the hands of the most potent Sorcerer alive. The potion and the ring worked like a cleansing process. The ring guarded my dark magic. Not only did it keep my darkness, but it also made me and my magic invisible to my parents and everyone that they hired to finish me. And it worked until the day I cursed them. It was still working like an invisible shield; it still protected me from anyone who wanted to harm me.

The next memory was the first time the ring worked. It had changed with me, as I started to accept my life as a dark witch. Once locked inside the ring, the darkness began flowing inside me. From an amulet, the ring became a second life too. For me to be killed, the ring had to be destroyed as well, and it obliterated anyone with bad intentions; so, someone would need a lot of good luck getting it from my finger. The ring carried a little of my life force, soul, my aura. When I started to learn and use black magic, the ring was all I had left from the person that supposedly loved me. He was afraid; he wanted distance from magic, especially this kind of magic. Love and black magic were like water and oil; they did not mix.

"Sorry, Al, I am getting away from the topic," I thought in my head.

It had been like wearing a bomb that only went off whenever anyone intended to harm me. The first time it happened, the guy burst into flames the moment he touched me. Maybe that was because I used fire so much. And I did not feel anything. Not remorse, not sadness. He was going to kill me and paid the price for that desire with his life.

And the last memory was the vision of my fate; my death. A high-pitched sound made me cover my ears and fall to my knees. Images flashed before my eyes while I had them closed. A book–the book. The ring was gone, my magic drained. A black figure in front of me had a ceremonial blade. The smell of blood. Life left my body with every drop of my blood, which had already puddled on the floor. Words spoken in Latin. My blood, the Key blood. They needed my blood to complete the spell. And that would be my death. I could swear I felt myself losing consciousness as I was losing our connection.

Our communication broke, and I avoided his gaze. Looking at the book, I tried to hide the fact that it had terrified me to my core like it had the first time I saw them,

229

and I was shaking like a pathetic little girl. I knew the last memory was my future end. My ancestor created the curse that made the Weird family famous. There had been a few Keys with the curse of prophecy, and one of them was me. A terrible thought crashed into my brain: Did they want it all? Did they want both the Weird and the Key power?

I quickly stood to leave. That book, and these memories… "I need to go," I said, snatching my ring from his hand as I bypassed him, not looking back.

He gave me a curse, a power I could–but I would never– use against him. And I gave him the entire 'How to kill me' freaking guidebook.

* * *

Al

Before I could process the visions, she closed off, stood quickly, took her ring, and stomped to the elevator.

"I need to go," she said uncertainly.

That was the other reason for the key card; she was my prisoner without it. I held the card up and asked, "Going somewhere?" with the cheekiest grin I could manage. She wasn't leaving without that card. I could let her out, but that would require her to ask. I was having too much fun with this to hold back my laughter. She strode over to me as I sat in the chair, laughing my ass off. The vision had her rattled, but I could see that she was relaxing already. She grabbed the card and turned to leave. Hesitating momentarily, she turned back to face me and slid the card into her bra.

"I believe you promised to cook me a steak dinner and ply me with alcohol. Who knows what could happen after that," she said coyly.

"Not sex," I replied curtly. "Not here; I can't do that here," I said a little too quickly.

"Oh, I see; my place it is, then. I am not afraid of a little magic."

I was sure I looked as surprised as I felt, especially when she started laughing herself. The tension in the room dwindled to nothing as our laughter faded.

"I don't need to be saved, Al. But I did get the best sleep I have had in ages last night, or this morning. I haven't slept in the same bed as another person since…well, it's been a while."

I knew what she meant; I hadn't slept with anyone since I was a teen. Not since I outgrew the coffin. What do you do when the vampire you call big brother is afraid to sleep alone?

"I can promise that you will never interrupt me here. I don't plan to entertain anyone in this place; it's too important. Besides, I hate altering my wards. You already know your way around them. Listen, I have that card made sometime in the future, so there must be another reason than the occasional sleepover. I don't do things impulsively, it's not my nature."

She looked at me, confused for a moment. "You aren't joking about the time travel, are you?"

I stood and stretched as she watched me like a cat watched a mouse. It was okay; I was used to women looking at me that way. I went to the fridge and pulled out the package of steaks. They needed time, and we did too. Now that she wasn't ready to storm out, we needed to try the vision thing again. I had no plan to change the past, I'm not sure I could, but I could learn from it, and so could she. My brother Len taught us that the past could come back to haunt you, but sometimes that could be a good thing.

Liz

"Come on, Al. This is not a favor; you won't owe me anything," I told him as I pulled him outside the house.

As usually happened, we stumbled upon each other at the bar. Again, as commonly occurred, we were the most exciting people, meaning we told everyone to piss off.

The only lights that allowed us to see anything were from my house. The night was dark, just like I liked it, and the moon was nowhere to be seen. A new moon? We were in my backyard and couldn't see anything besides my house and the woods for miles. Alaric Weird was the only living thing I have allowed in my home in years besides Alma. There was the Grim Reaper, but that was a different story. He could but never did come here. He was tied to me, so I could not do anything about it. But to be honest, I never looked for a way to break the bond. I don't mind Deathripper being around. It's like Death was on our side, literally. Sophie was a different story, she always called me, not the other way around, and she didn't come to my house. Also, she hadn't learned to make a portal yet, but that was just because defensive magic was more urgent. I taught her almost everything I could, and she was reluctant to learn the black curses. Especially the ones that kill.

Magical portals were something I could help Al learn though, since he didn't know how to do it yet. It was funny how he knew how to teleport, which was much more complex and magically consuming, but not how to create a simple portal. I guess it was all a side effect of not having an everyday magical life with teachers and people who cared. It's not like I had an everyday life either, or people who cared, but I did have teachers and learned some precious lessons from them. Mainly I learned not to trust anyone, but here I was, trusting and teaching.

An intelligent and powerful sorcerer like him would eventually figure out how to create a magical portal alone. I did; I had to, but why spoil it? And this could be fun. He was used to teaching others, not being taught. I could see this was all new territory to him, but then again, when it came to us, everything was new territory.

I circled around him, my hand barely touching his hard abdomen and muscular lower back as I walked. Magic from my hand seeped directly to his body. It had been a while since I felt this kind of proximity with someone. What people would call friendship, we called an alliance. Someone to talk with–even though we didn't like small talk–someone to tease, and someone that had our back.

"What is the matter, Sorcerer? Are you becoming shy on me?" I teased. I didn't think he was very fond of being taught. But that did the trick; he raised his hand toward the forest. I noticed he wanted to tease back, but he did not. I saw his chest rise and fall as he breathed, his hand steady. He was remarkable!

"Imagine hard where you want to go; see it in your mind. Use the need to run away from me," I joked. But I became serious before continuing. "See it in your mind, Sorcerer. The view from the window, the lights of the building around your penthouse. The smell of the old books in your impressive library, the dark, old desk you love to use for work. See it and wish to be there. Make that wish true; put your will into the portal. Let the magic serve you, Sorcerer. Make it your bitch."

I slowly stepped back a few inches. The magic was powerful around him, emanating from him like a sweet fragrance in a beautiful package. Just the kind of power I was so attracted to.

A portal started to form in front of our eyes, and I smirked. For his first time, creating a portal was impressive, but it quickly disappeared. I was not helping him with my thoughts. He needed to focus, and my mind was racing to an intoxicated lust for power-his power. Now was my time to put what he taught me into practice, and I blocked my thoughts.

"Home, Sorcerer. The safety of home, your wards will not block you, not your magic. Unless you secretly want to stay here, in the lair of the Black Widow," I teased.

He went for it again; I could feel the magic being channeled. The portal started to appear this time, and it is more stable; I could feel that too. The buzzing sound, the light coming through it, his black mark on the portal, and his signature magic were scorching even when it faded before it was completely formed and ready for travel.

I felt him look at me, but my gaze was still on the place the portal was a few seconds ago. If he was teasing, and I thought he was, he'd be very disappointed. We teased, that was how we worked, but when I was in teaching mode, I was different. I was serious.

"Again," I said calmly, with no other words.

"Or?" he threw back, and I rolled my eyes.

"Men!"

He called for the portal again, created it almost wholly formed that time and a sense of pride moved me. He was so close, and it was impressive how strong and steady he was, even using this much energy.

I remembered that portals were the first thing I learned. The need to run away was strong, and the portals were a must, not a cool thing to know. But it was hard, so damn hard. It took so much from me. Sure, I was still learning. I was still waking up my magic, but still, I remember it drained me. And sharing with Al was a pleasure. My advice would help me speed up the process as much as his power.

But what if I showed him instead of just using words?

I moved closer to him and took his hand, intertwining our fingers, and opened my mind entirely to him. This simple gesture felt weird and ordinary at the same time. We'd had sex, and we teased each other any chance we could, but this felt more intimate, and he probably had the same first instinct I did–run away. But neither of us did. Magic immediately flowed between us, and that was what I wanted; that was what I expected to happen.

Mentally, I focus on the inside of the place he called home, where he kept the Key grimoire, my grimoire.

"Do it now," I said, sending him my muscular memories through our connection. He would know how to do it, use it, and never need my direction to open a portal again. The cracking sound of a completely formed magic portal caught my attention. I had not seen him move or the beginning of its formation, but there it was. Holding on, with a mix of black and purple around it, I saw the library on the other side. He'd done it almost effortlessly. The magic was stable and robust, the portal safe to travel. Being around magic as much as the two of us were, we could sense these things.

"Miss Key?" I heard Alma's scared voice from inside the house, just near the backdoor, and I loosened my grip on his hand. But before I could answer her or take my hand away from his, Al pulled me into the portal, to travel to his penthouse, leaving her behind. Had he not given me the key to his penthouse, I would have been more burned than Temp's body. That would have been a sucky way to go.

Miss Key was what Alma uses as a cover-up anytime I had company, making her pass as an employer only. She was not keen about my alliance with Alaric Weird; he knew it very well. To her, the Weird family meant death to everyone around. But if we were going to be honest, so did the Key family.

"You did that on purpose, Sorcerer," I told him, amused, as I felt him let go of my hand and pull away. "You cannot leave my staff alone, can you?"

He just smirked. "Damsel in distress disagrees with you, Sorceress. She should know that."

"Next time you kidnap me like that, I expect to be f–" A sound interrupted my teasing. The high pitch of that damn book pulled my complete attention over to the bookshelf. It was calling me. The need to get close was overwhelming; touching it was too strong a desire to resist, and as if in a trance, I start to walk towards it. I could not understand what it is saying, only that it wanted to be touched.

A harsh grip on my upper arm stopped me, and I saw Al's lavender eyes looking at me with interest. He, too, was curious about my connection to the Grimoire.

"Again, Sorcerer, next time you grab me like this, I expect to be fucked," I teased, but I was glad he interrupted the connection. I shook away the powerless feeling of fighting off the book. "Now, I have to make sure you did not kill the best housekeeper I have."

I couldn't use magic to leave his penthouse, so I took the keycard from my bra and went to the elevator. "Call me when you find yourself in the middle of the Pacific Ocean," I teased, getting inside the elevator. Once outside the building, I would create my own portal home. Al probably didn't understand why I did this, but I owed him a lesson or two. He was the teacher, but even a teacher can learn from his student once in a while.

Al

Have you ever done something so foolish, and it turned out to be cool? A few weeks ago, I decided to curse my only friend with my family bloodline curse. It seemed fitting since her ancestor was the one to curse my ancestor. The curse was older than both families, but it was written down on Key flesh, with Key blood mixed in ink. The curse was meant to make an Oracle or seer of all time. The cursed one would go insane but would also be a valuable tool for the Sorcerer powerful enough to do the curse.

I acquired a penthouse apartment on top of a club called The Mage Tower. The penthouse could only be owned by powerful sorcerers. In order to possess it you must have killed the owner in a magic duel to get your deed to the place. I didn't set out to commit murder, he shot first. There had only been two owners before me. Sorcerers are rare, and most don't live long lives. Great power comes with many enemies, as I was learning all too well.

It wasn't until the day I moved into my new penthouse at the mage tower that I realized what the book was. When I took it off the shelf and felt the magic–her magic–I knew it had the key, no pun intended, to my family curse. It needed the magic of a Key sorcerer, and I happened to have some of that. I could still hear the words she spoke to me as she brought me back from the edge of the abyss. "That was really, *really*, stupid of us. Let's do it again!"

I'd fucked three different magic users since the night after the battle, and not one of them gave me more than a tingle of magic. Nothing like the nuclear bomb that went off when she and I were together, or the rush that lasted for days after. Magic, power. It was like a drug; I was the addict. It was a weakness, being addicted to power, or so I'd been told. Most addicts sought help eventually, but even had I wanted to be free of this, what would I say? Hi, my name is Alaric; I'm a gay man addicted to magical sex with a woman. No, not with just any woman, but the last Key sorceress alive. I should probably stop referring to myself as gay, even if the term applies to everyone else in several worlds. I just don't know what to say. *Bisexual with extreme exclusivity?* Just thinking about it made me want to accept her invitation.

Thoughts of the magic had me pacing like a tiger in a cage. The book lying on my desk didn't help matters. I'd studied it for hours, but even the curse we'd performed hadn't made sense. The words are nonsense; the instructions were the same for every spell. They all needed the blood of a Key sorcerer. Any curse done required Liz's blood, either willingly given or taken. Our connection allowed me to see glimpses of a vision she imagined was her end. I couldn't let it happen. I needed her alive. Listen to me saying that I needed her. You'd probably think that I loved her. If I did, it was like an addict who loved heroin.

My eyes kept going to that damned book; I could still hear the noises in my head, though it had been quiet since she left. I picked it up and shoved it in the bookcase with the hundreds of other books in my library. The previous owner left most of the books when he stopped breathing. That one book was worth more than the whole library, and not just in monetary value.

I'd given Liz my family curse. I had meant to give her just the present if only to see if she could do what I could do. Since the first casting, no one had held all three aspects of the curse. I knew that Liz's mind couldn't handle the madness as well as mine could. That was why I forced the curse to move to me rather than curse my only friend with insanity. Her insights into the human mind, thanks to a doctorate in Psychology, might have helped her cope, but I couldn't take that chance. I may have looked mostly human, but my mind worked differently.

None of that thinking helped matters at all. Liz had learned to block our connection. Privacy was complex for both of us now. She knew that I was not always in control. She'd blocked my sight, too; she was the only person alive who could do that.

I stopped pacing the floor and grabbed my key card. I needed a drink, I had to stop thinking of her, and someone was always willing to distract me downstairs. They might not be human, but neither was I. Usually, I would have put on more than underwear and a loose robe, but I needed to be away from that damned book. It just kept reminding me that Liz had asked for more. She asked for what I shouldn't want to give.

The moment I stepped out of the elevator, I was assaulted by the sounds of Electronica. I liked most music, but the cacophonous beat didn't improve my mood. I was restless and irritable–like a junkie needing a fix.

One of the regulars approached me as soon as I entered the bar. I was dressed for bedroom activities, but that wasn't my intention. Sebastian was Sidhe, what some unknowing people labeled as an elf or faery. The Sidhe were the most human of the Fae and the most beautiful. He should have been precisely what I needed. His purple hair was as long as his torso, and he had to move it aside to take a seat at the bar. I sat next to him, avoiding his deep purple eyes. I'd seen everything he had to offer, and it was tempting. He was the only person I knew with skin paler than mine with no freckles. Seb was addicted to sex and magic.

"Looking for company, Alaric?" he asked as he eyed my attire. There was no dress code at the Mage Tower, and patrons would often be seen in the bar with less clothing on. I had thrown on a silk robe that matched the silk boxers. The black canvas shoes clashed with the purples, but I wasn't there to impress.

I ordered my usual drink and did my best to ignore my unwanted companion. He wasn't buying my act. I had never turned him down before. It was considered a great insult to his kind. He was winter court, Unseelie Sidhe. His queen would take the slight personally, but he wasn't the distraction I needed.

"Can I get a rain check on that, Seb? I just came here for a drink and some quiet." Yeah, leave it to me to insult while trying not to insult. He laughed anyway; I guess he didn't miss the irony. The music was muted in the bar, but it was still difficult to talk without raising your voice.

"I would be insulted if it was anyone but you, Alaric. I've been told that you have turned a new page in your life story. You were seen going upstairs with a beautiful woman. Am I no longer your type?"

Another thing that is slight to the Sidhe is to lie to them outright. They never lie, and they never tell the truth. You had to learn to untwist any information you got from them. I had to tell him the truth without giving any information. It was a slippery slope that I didn't have time for. My mind was racing, and so was my heart. His words made my brain itch, and I didn't want to answer his questions.

"A friend, nothing more." Okay, so I am not a good liar.

"And your friend left alone, over twenty-four hours from when you went up in the unmarked elevator. And she was wearing different clothing when she left. I asked around; you have been seeing a lot of Sorceress Key. Do you still want to call her a friend and nothing more to my face?"

He had me there; she was more than a friend, but he was fishing for information, and I caught him in the act. With the Fae, information was currency, and I would not pay without getting something in return.

"I don't owe you any explanation, Seb. Liz is my friend and ally. I came here for a drink and peace, and I have had my drink; I will leave you to yours. I may take you up on the offer some other time, but I will not give you what you seek tonight. Tell your queen I owe her no favors. If she wants to know about me, it will cost her a favor, and more than your body, as hot as you may be," I said as I got up to leave. I'd only guessed that Maeve, the winter queen, was behind his questions. She knew I valued my privacy, and that I didn't do pillow talk. As I said, information was currency, and the knowledge she sought would have bought her a huge favor from my enemies. I might fuck them, but I am no friend of the Fae.

I walked away toward the elevators with Seb fast on my heels. Well, there was something he didn't know about me. Vampires are faster than Fae. I turned at the last moment and ran as fast as a living vampire out of the tower's entrance. The crisp air in the magic realm helped me focus, but it all came crashing back when I realized I couldn't go back inside. I had let Sebastian chase me away from my own home. To return was to admit defeat, but I didn't need to worry; he had followed me. I could feel the magic in his hands as he touched my shoulder. He was powerful even though he would never beat me. He turned me to face him and pulled me closer for a kiss. His lips, which were always cold, touched mine, and I felt a spark. It was nothing like the feeling I got from Liz, but it made me want more. I kissed him hard, my tongue lashing at his teeth and tongue. I bit his lip and tasted the sweet blood of a full-blood Sidhe. He started pulling his t-shirt off, but I stopped him. I turned him away from me and started kissing his neck. He was expecting me to take charge, but what came next was a surprise. I stretched his neck away from me, and I bit down with all four magically sharp canines. I held him tight while he struggled, but after a few moments, the vampire venom kicked in. He was as pliant as a sleeping baby. His blood filled me with power and magic. It was taboo for vampires to bite the Sidhe, but I am not a vampire. His hard cock went soft quickly as I swallowed a whole mouth full of blood, then another and another. I'd never done this, not with a Sidhe, and never on my own. I wanted to finish him, drink every drop, and toss him to the ground, but I was Alaric Weird, not Alias. I slowed his heart and set him up against one of the sad-looking trees someone had planted outside the tower. I would have to pay reparations to the queen, but he was alive.

My eyes were glowing, and the blood on my chest was burning my new tattoo. It felt like someone was running their nails over my raw chest–someone who smelled and tasted pure power. Just the thought of her touching me made me hard. I was buzzing from the blood and the magic, but all I could think about was her lips on mine, her breasts pressed against my chest as she ran those nails down my back until the blood trickled into my ass crack.

I opened my sight; I wanted to see her with someone. I wanted to watch her fuck another man until he screamed her name. I wanted to know that she wasn't alone. But she was.

I wiped the blood from my mouth with the back of my hand and created a portal. It wasn't as elegant as the ones Liz made. She made it look easy, but then she made everything look easy. I would never admit it to her face, but she was better than me. The magic that surrounded the edges was black, much like my aura since the day I cursed myself with insanity. It didn't matter; the portal served its purpose. It wouldn't take me inside the wards, but that didn't matter. I'd never found a ward that I couldn't break with enough power. I had plenty of power, thanks to the Sidhe blood. I didn't even attempt to bypass the magic; I threw everything at the wards, and the magic dissolved like sugar in water. Door locks were easy in comparison. Manipulating the physical was something I'd been doing since childhood. The door was even more accessible than the lock.

"Gold star for you, Al," she said, smirking. She was sitting on her kitchen counter wearing nothing but a very short black silk robe…and knee-high black boots.

"Those were some powerful wards you just broke, but you are not a normal sorcerer, are you? You are lucky I know your magic, or you would be a little bit burned right now."

I ignored her words; I wasn't there to talk. I wasn't sure I could speak. I closed the distance between us and wrapped her in my arms. I kissed her deeply, and she returned the kiss without hesitation. Her tongue stroking mine caused sparks to crackle and pop inside my mouth. It was just like last time, only now I was in charge. I didn't ask; I didn't need to. She wanted this as much as I needed it.

Liz dug the heels of her boots into my ass cheeks and managed to drop my boxers to the floor without touching them. She used one hand to hold herself steady and another to dig at my back with her nails. The pain mixed with pleasure caught my breath as my blood ran down my back, burning with released magic.

I moved my attention to her neck, not kissing but nibbling. I didn't want to feed, but my fangs extended anyway, and I nicked her delicate skin, causing trickles of blood to cascade down her chest. I couldn't let it go to waste. I pulled the robe open, exposing her breasts. She leaned back to give me access to her body. This was not for magic anymore; I wanted her. I wanted to pleasure her. A voice in my head tried to remind me that I was gay, but since that voice was mine, and not Alias or Alton, I ignored it. I could worry about my sexual orientation later when my body wasn't vibrating with the need to ravish the woman in my arms.

I licked at the blood trail that ended in the valley between her breasts. Her erect nipples seemed to beg for attention, so I moved to them, nibbling and sucking, first the right, then the left. She was gasping for air, each quick breath driving my need further. I kissed lower, moving my way down toward the mound of her pelvis. She laced her fingers through my hair, stopping me from moving any further.

My vanity won over madness, and I let her pull me back to her sweet mouth. We were two tops with no bottom. The thought of her bottom entered my head, and I grabbed it with both hands and pulled her to the edge of the counter. I slid my throbbing cock into her easily. She moaned and moved closer, urging me to go deeper.

The magic was as thick as morning fog around us, and it was building—my black mixed with her deep purple. We had barely started, and I could feel the impending explosion. My rational mind told me to slow down and let the magic dissipate a little. Too bad I wasn't listening to the rational thoughts. I gave her what she was whimpering for; I thrust myself as deeply as possible. I was on the larger side of average, and though she was very wet, she was tight. Her moans told me to continue, and again my crazy took over. I didn't want to be gentle, and she seemed to agree. My pounding rhythm caused her to make some of the strangest noises I had ever heard from human vocal cords.

Liz tried to lie on the countertop, but I could not allow that; I had to know that she understood this. I had to look her in the eyes so she would know I didn't come here for the magic; that was just a bonus. She was my drug; she was my addiction…and she was my high. I'd tried with others, but nothing like this ever happened. Dishes rattled in the cabinets, and it felt like an earthquake was rolling through, with her kitchen as its epicenter. I was so close to climax, but I held on, although the pressure to release was intense. I wanted to hear her scream my name. I wanted her to rip the flesh off my back until the blood pooled on her kitchen floor. She had both hands there now, digging in, scraping and scratching, then digging again.

I felt it when she climaxed, the pulse and the wetness, but she seemed eager for more. I pulled her face close and kissed her. My magically created fangs were razor-sharp, cutting and piercing her lips. She growled at me like a lioness and started biting my neck. The dishes started crashing to the floor, and the furniture started dancing out of place. I didn't care if we brought the whole house down; the magic and sex felt too good to stop. I didn't want to ever stop. I needed more. I wanted more.

She tore into my neck with her blunt teeth and lapped at the blood with her tongue. It caused my rhythm to falter, and I almost lost control. I could hear the house moaning with her, we were going to cause severe damage, and I didn't care. I would buy or build her a new house. She had other ideas about that, and I realized as she pulled away from my neck that she had frozen time around us. Nothing was moving in the house except for her and me. She grabbed my hair again and forced me to face her this time.

"Al, fuck me. I can't hold this as long as you can!"

Her words brought me back, and my brain tried to understand what she said. I had been fucking her this whole time, but the last time, the explosion, happened at the moment we both climaxed. She didn't scream my name, but she said it. I returned to pounding my pelvis into her groin until it felt bruised. I waited for her to build up again while she made urgent noises.

When she started shaking like she was having a seizure, my body decided it was time. The dam broke, and I felt weightlessness along with the waves of pleasure as my body fluids flowed into her, and hers flowed over me. She held the bubble well, but I reinforced it as we both screamed and writhed with the waves of ecstasy. I pulled her off the counter with my penis still inside her. She'd chosen the boots well, and it was only a little uncomfortable, mostly because she had both stiletto heels digging into my feet. Her legs gave way as she released time to let it flow again. I gathered her in my arms and carried her up the stairs to the room at the end of the hall. She was shivering from pleasure, and so was I, but I had to hold the magic in; time couldn't resume until it was safe. Liz had saved us and her home by freezing time. I didn't know how long she could keep us in the time bubble, but while she contained our magic, I poked at the invisible barrier to see if I could affect it. It held up to my prodding, which was interesting. I could control it as if it was my own. Curses were strange creatures, unlike your average spell or ritual. They sometimes seemed to be sentient like the Reaper's scythe. It was too bad the only people who knew anything about it were long gone. The Keys had written the instructions, but I could find no evidence that anyone had ever used it before we did.

Liz was limp in my arms as I laid her in her bed. Her body was feverishly hot, so I didn't bother to cover her, but I pulled her robe closed and retied it. She turned on her side and pulled a pillow under her head. The magic was still visible around her, and I could feel its vibration as I sat on the bed. I tested Liz's bubble again, managed to let it go, then bring it back up until I could sense that the pressure was gone. No explosion this time, but only because Liz had kept her wits.

When I finally let go, the weight of everything hit me. I slid down on the bed and grabbed one of the pillows. I shoved it under my head and lay facing away from Liz. I meant to close my eyes for a moment, but when I woke, it was morning. I was on my back, and Liz was curled up next to me with her head on my chest. She had dried blood in her hair and on her neck. I didn't like seeing her like that…vulnerable. I could kill her in her sleep, and she would be powerless to stop me. This was why she took so many precautions, the marks, the ring, always kicking the men out right after sex. I couldn't blame her, and I was usually on the other end, but any other time I would have been long gone.

I slowly edged my way out from under her and went downstairs. My boxers were still at the end of the bar and dotted with blood–mine. I slipped them on and left through the front door. I locked the locks and reset the wards refusing to leave her vulnerable. I made a portal to the tower without looking back. I didn't want to explain myself; I couldn't. I'd used her for magic and sex. Yeah, I probably should have rethought my sexuality, but at that point, I had reparations to make, and that would either mean giving blood, information, or sex. One of my rules is never to share my blood with the Fae; information is too costly to me.

I walked in through the front door of the tower, the place never closed, but there weren't many people milling about. Those that remained had passed out sometime in the night, and no one bothered to wake them. I felt the chill as soon as I approached the bar. The Fae woman wasn't the queen, just a vassal. Her hair was as red as mine and long. I knew before she turned that her eyes would be the same bright green as Alias'. It was a terrible time to do this, but the Fae didn't live in linear time as humans did; that is the one thing I did have in common with them. She was drinking a mint julep, and the smell of mint reminded me that I needed to brush my teeth. I smelled like blood and other bodily fluids, but mostly like sex.

I sat on the stool next to her and asked for a single malt scotch. The bartender was thrown for a moment, but he took one look at my blood-covered body, took down a bottle, and poured two fingers into a glass. I tossed the liquid into my mouth and swallowed hard.

"Rhoslyn, to what do I owe the pleasure?" I knew what she was doing there at nine in the morning, but I couldn't give anything away. I'd left enough life in Seb for him to tell them all that I was the vampire who bit him. The problem was I didn't look, feel, or smell like a vampire. She would want to know more than I wanted to tell.

"You know why I am here, Alaric. I can wait if you wish to wash it away. I don't mind; I love the smell of fresh sex and your companion's scent. I had heard that she was a great lay, but she didn't do my kind." She was waiting for me to be surprised or to deny being with Liz. The Fae had noses like dogs; to lie now would be a worse slight than trying to drain Seb of all his blood.

"She's bisexual, so I am assuming you mean Sidhe. Yeah, she is smarter than I am."

She laughed, or cackled at my comment, then leaned close to my ear, her breath tickling as she spoke. "You could kill two birds with one stone, as they say, Alaric. Could I taste your companion and you? Maybe in your lair upstairs? Now that you have broadened your horizons."

She ran a finger over the bite mark on my neck, then tried to put her finger in her mouth. I stopped her using the speed and strength Alias' soul provided. I stuck the finger in my mouth and sucked the blood off. It was mine, no one else's.

When I let go of her hand, I stood, started to walk away, and then turned to the bartender.

"Rico, when Sebastian arrives tonight, have someone take him to room three thirteen and give me a call." I glanced at Rhoslyn, and she nodded. Sex it was, and I would enjoy it almost as much as he did. Hopefully, it would be enough to get the Queen of Air and Darkness, also known as Maeve, off my back.

Liz

I returned home, as I always do after my magic training, through a portal straight to my living room. Magic was like a muscle: the more you worked at it, the more it grew. Or at least, that's what it was like with me. And to be honest, I had a lot of magic to burn after another encounter with Sorcerer Al Weird. It was the second time it ended up like that, filling me with so much power and energy I had to burn the extra. I felt like a glass of water, almost overflowing. He had yet to learn what an unreal and impressive source of magic he was. He was like a walking, living recharging station. I still needed to find out why that connection was there but until then, being friends with someone as sarcastic, witty, and powerful as he is had been great.

I slid my hand along my neck, where he had nibbled a few nights before. Never, ever, had I allowed anyone to bite me or taste any drop of my blood, but with him, I did not mind. I may have even wanted him to. It was like I lost control over my body with him. Yes, I liked the danger, but it was not that. Not entirely. He didn't make me weak, he made me more powerful, and this girl loved some power, even more than a good orgasm.

Some magical users would say I had enough and that the search for more power would be my end. I am afraid I disagree with all of them.

As soon as I set foot at home, my senses tingled like I was standing too close to a live wire. There was something wrong here. My wards were down. A quick scan through my surroundings showed me that everything was out of place. Empty drawers on the floor, papers everywhere, my plants were lying down like fallen soldiers; even the pillows were cut open. Whatever someone was looking for, they were meticulous.

Almost on instinct, I readied my shields to investigate who just signed their death certificate. I was still determining what I was up against. Whatever it was, it felt familiar and potent. But no one had bested me yet. And definitely not in my own damn home!

I had seen enough horror movies; I knew I should have run or asked for help, but that was not my nature. I was walking towards the kitchen when I saw the first one. The robust and pale man was waiting. He looked like the head of the mafia in those movies, wearing an expensive black suit with hints of dark purple, and dark hair. It all made me think I had seen him before.

"Sorceress Elizabeth Key," the pale man said, spitting my name. The I saw at least five more people around my kitchen. "The chosen one," he continued with disdain, and the only woman in the group scowled.

"Just look at that. A group of fans," I reply, getting a bottle of fresh water from the fridge. They were powerful, very powerful–I could sense it. But Hell would freeze over before I allowed anyone to intimidate me in my own damn house. The Key lair, Alaric Weird once said. Cocky, cocky Sorcerer. I let out a chuckle before taking a sip of the water.

With no warning, and still with the bottle in my left hand, I raised my right in their direction, and from a distance, made the pale man's throat close slowly. "I am deciding which one will burn first for the intrusion." His hands flew to his throat, and he gasped for air, but the others did not react. They seemed amused.

Their magic was similar to mine, but I could not understand why. My wards had gotten stronger since the episode with Al, not because I did not enjoy that particular night but because I needed to prove myself. It was not easy to lower my wards down, yet this was the second time it had happened in less than a week! How had these morons gotten in?

"I would listen first if I were you," the woman said. She slowly put a flask on my kitchen center island which contained a gray liquid. She, I believed, was the mastermind behind this act. "You will drink that tasty potion someone extraordinary made for you, Key." Her lips curled into an ugly smile, and she continued. "I promise it will not hurt. Much."

With long, straight hair, and fair skin, that woman reminded me of my mother. Not only physically but also with her cold voice and threatening gaze. She was at my home, not fearing my power. Why?

"The fuck I will," I reply, not releasing my grip on the neck of the pale man.

"Now, now. Do you kiss your mother with that mouth?" the woman said, entertaining the rest of the gang.

At the mention of my mother, my anger took over. I took a deep breath and, in an instant, had them all gasping for air on their knees, except the woman. It took a lot more energy than normal; I had been using a lot of magic all afternoon. But I had enough to face these miserable assholes.

"I killed my mother, and maybe I will give you the same death. But I must warn you, it will sting a little."

"Not mommy Key," she said, with a wicked smile, and I felt my blood go cold. I watched as another man brought Alma in, my family alchemist, the woman who'd saved me from my family, from death; her hands were tied behind her back. Like the men in front of me, she was gasping for air.

"Please! Stop." Alma fought to let her words be heard. Her white clothes had spots of blood and dirt. Tears rolled down her red and bruised face. It made new spots on the already dirty clothes. I was boiling inside now, my anger making me shake. How dare they!

"Cool magic, isn't it? Everything you do to us, mama Alma feels. If you kill any of us, you will say goodbye to your sweet innocent mommy."

Anger made me grip them harder, but I knew the woman was telling the truth when I saw Alma's face become more red. I loosened my grip and let my hand fall. I should do it; I should finish them right there, but not if it costs me Alma. I would not let her die. Her gaze locked on me.

"Forgive me, my sweet child. I tried. I tried. They have Ava. They will hurt Ava!"

The other woman laughed, and a shiver traveled through my body.

"You made a mistake, not just with the clothes you chose for today. What makes you think I care about anyone?" I asked, hoping that my voice would not betray me.

She made a movement with her hand, and I instinctively created a shield between the elegant woman and Alma, but it was a bluff; she did not do any magic at all. I just showed my hand.

"Bitch!" I breathed out, and she just smiled. "I am going to burn you!"

"Here is the deal, Key. We have something you want; you have something we want. This can easily be a business transaction with no casualties. Give us the book, and this beautiful family that adopted you will be reunited," she proposed, walking towards me.

"Kiss. My. Ass." I replied, fighting my instinct to burn her where she stood, but she was just a distraction. I had eyes on all of them, or so I thought. I felt something teleporting in at my back, but before I could react, I heard Alma yell my name. The sharp, hard blow to the back of my head came before I was able to freeze time. Everything went dark.

* * *

The sharp pain in my skull made it hard to open my eyes as I regained consciousness. I noticed a terrible taste in my mouth. My arms were numb from being tied to the kitchen island like I was damn Jesus Christ, but I felt my ass cold from sitting on the kitchen floor. This was embarrassing. Fighting the pain behind my eyes from the light and trying to focus on anything, I search for Alma and the group. I finally found her, sitting on the floor like me, but still with her hands behind her back. Two men were guarding her, one standing and the other squatting beside her. Dark hair, dark skin, and dark eyes; those two looked nothing like the others who had fair skin and light brown or blond hair. All of them, except for the one missing, had muscular builds, like they hit the gym a lot–or dealt with making dead bodies disappear. I felt magic from all of them, but the strange woman's magic was different.

The pale man, another large and tall man, and the elegant woman were waiting for me to wake up. Their faces became clearer as the focus returned to my eyes. I did not see the other one; he was probably still searching.

"Welcome back, sleepyhead," the woman said. She was pissing me off. "See? That was not that bad, was it?"

I tried to burn through the ropes, but my magic–I could not access it. They had blocked my magic.

"You stupid useless bitch! What did you do to me?" I tried to wiggle the ropes loose, but all I did was hurt my wrists. She slowly squatted in front of me and then slapped me hard. I felt my left side burning with the impact, but I looked her in the eyes. I was not afraid of her, not even now.

"Where is the book, 'Sorceress'?" she asked with a controlled and mocking voice. Although her physical violence showed quite a lack of control.

"Let me tell you something," I smirked, not breaking our gaze, using my tongue to taste my own blood from the slit in my lip. "After how I was fucked in this very spot here not too long ago, you will have to do better than that to turn me on, honey." In seconds, her hand struck my face again. Blood rushed to the area from the new impact, making it red and hot. I heard Alma pleading for her to stop.

"Kali, that will not work on her; let me do my job," the pale man whispered to the woman, probably not knowing I would hear, or thinking it was unimportant because I would not survive this to tell a soul. He handed her a knife.

Fantastic, I thought, watching her play with the blade of the knife.

"Is the book in this house?"

"No, 'Kali. I do not have coloring books at home. Why don't you try a kid's store? I am sure they have books appropriate to your mental age. Let's start slow, shall we?" I retaliated, knowing I was playing with my life, but I did not care enough to stop. I smiled at her.

The teasing was cut by her hook on my left side, expelling all the air of my lungs.

"I am not going to tell you anything," I said, looking at her in defiance.

"Let's try again," she said, too calm for my taste.

I have no idea how much time had passed since the beating stopped and the carving Liz game started. The same question, different spots on my body. Deep enough to scorch and bleed, but not deep enough to kill. I felt my body hurt and burned, and I still could not invoke my magic. But it was here; I could feel it. It was with me. A slap brought me back to the present as I focused on my captor's face.

"Where is the book?" she asked, passing the blade over me again.

I held my breath because of the pain. Warm blood rolled down my skin, and I smiled, feeling all the muscles of my face hurt and not caring. "This is just foreplay to me. Come on. Bring the big guns," I teased. I would not let them see weakness. I would rather die, but I knew this was not that day. The book they sought was not here. It would be with me when I died. I had seen that in a vision. Unlike the Weird family, I couldn't control psychic visions. I rarely got any glimpse of the future, and it was never happy moments. Kali's torture was a walk in the park to what I knew my end would be.

"Last chance, Key. Where did you put the book?" she asked again, dragging the blunt side of the blade over my upper body without cutting.

"Go to Hell, bitch," I hissed. She had no idea how much pain I had taught myself to endure. My parents had hurt me worse when I was just a toddler.

She rose to her feet, looking down at me with a mischievous smile on her face. Without taking her gaze from mine, she said, "Kill her."

Everything happened in slow motion. I was expecting the 'her' to be me, but it was not. The 'her' was Alma, and I saw one of the brunette men end her life like she was nothing.

Numb, I watched her body go limp on my kitchen floor. I tried to get to her, to get up, but my wrists were still tied, and I couldn't move. On my knees, I looked up at Kali, suddenly feeling my anger burn through my veins, and then it was like someone else was commanding my body. The earth under me started to shake, everywhere around us became dark, and my eyes shone with a purple glow. I drew energy from everything and everyone. At least, that was what I felt. My body visibly pulled in the magic and the light. Surely it was a power so broad and strong that no one alone could take it. Yet, I did.

"Stella," I said with a voice that was not mine, and the ropes fell like they were made of petals. "Moritur!" The same voice came from my mouth again. I felt myself levitate like I was watching from above, and a blast from within me ignited a source that caught everything, and everyone, around me, burning it all down.

I crash to my knees and hands, bleeding, everywhere. I tried to get up slowly. My magic was utterly drained. I look around my house; it was not a house anymore. My home was gone. Alma… I try to find her, but all I see was dust, burned wood, and shattered glass. I wondered, stumbling. "Alma?" No one answered. No one would. No one would have survived that blast. What had happened to me?

I could not find the other man alone, not like this. And I would find him, and I would kill him! I did not want to admit it, but I needed help. I stumbled and fell to my knees again.

Still bleeding and feeling dizzy from the hemorrhaging, my anger could not keep me up any longer. I searched inside my right boot for the key card I kept with the dagger Al gifted me. I tried three times and failed to invoke a portal to the Mage Tower. The fourth time was the charm. Stumbling, I fell into the portal that could lead me anywhere by this point. My magic was weak, and I was disoriented. When I saw the lights of the well-known Mage Tower, I stepped out of the portal and walked towards it. If anyone could help me, it was Alaric Weird. It would cost me, but I did not care now. Ignoring the looks of everyone there, I walked to the elevator and supported myself against the wall as I was granted access by the keycard. Finally, the door opened. My vision was blurring and becoming darker by the minute; I didn't know if I could get to the thirteen-floor conscious. Blood pooled around my boots as I felt the elevator ascend, and I struggled to stay upright. Finally, the doors opened, and I stumbled to the living room. Al was at home, cooking pancakes, by the smell. At least I'd have a nice last view before death, I thought.

"Please, keep the blood off the rugs; they are hell to clean," he casually said, like this happens every Tuesday, and I scoffed in my mind. I looked down and saw I was losing more blood than I thought.

I smirked at him and said softly, "I would say bite me, but I don't think I have even enough left to quench your thirst," I teased. And that is the last thing I remember before my vision went completely dark.

Alma

Still, with my eyes closed, my brain starts to piece everything that happened together. Bad people hurting my Liz. Bad people hurting me to get to my Liz. It was my fault they got in; I had to let them in because they said they had my daughter and my granddaughter. These people did not lie and did not threaten in vain. They would hurt and kill, even if it were not necessary. My sweet Ava. They made me choose between my innocent toddler and my loved daughter. They made me break down Liz's wards, and only after that had they let my Ava go from where they had taken her. They said it was a token of goodwill, but I knew they were planning on using and killing my Liz. She was mine, Liz was mine. I raised her; I loved her and still did, even with her darkness. That sweet child, who loved kittens and cotton candy, never had a chance; she tried to but could not outrun her blood destiny. Her sin was being born a Key.

I knew, for sure, that I had not been here for a very long time, and I was still baffled about what happened. The first time I was conscious, I had two potions and some clean clothes beside me in an unknown bed. From what I could see through the open space and expansive windows, I was on the top of the Mage Tower, and that means Sorcerer Alaric Weird.

Lizzie was nowhere to be found, leaving me with a bad feeling that only a mother could describe. I gathered the two potions and left them on the side table. The clothes I humbled accepted, ending up changing in his bathroom, grateful I could get out of my bloody rags. I only dealt with blood when people reach out to me to help them with healing potions. Alaric Weird kept his distance and was respectful with the little words we exchanged. I did not try to form a conversation either since I was not sure I was a prisoner in his penthouse. My distrust of him was not his fault. Like my Liz, his only sin was being born a Weird, and I could overlook that if not for my need to protect my child above anything. And my child was buried up to her neck with this Sorcerer.

The sound of kitchen tools made the headache worse, and the smell of something cooking made my stomach burn, reminding me that I had not eaten all day. I was not alone; that was the first thing that got my attention. Then the little buzzing as the elevator stopped on the penthouse floor made my eyes opened in fear as I sat on the bed. I fought the pain of that sudden movement. Everyone I dealt with in the past 24 hours was deadly dangerous. Alaric Weird also was deadly dangerous. People I had tried to avoid since the night I picked up that blonde mistreated little girl and ran from the Key mansion had surrounded me.

My body was throbbing; everything hurt. I needed to make sure I left this penthouse alive and got to Lizzie.

When the elevator door opened, I saw her again, the scared and hurt little girl I had carried on my lap that night. She was hurt again, but this time her face did not express fear, only determination, maybe a little relief.

Why, Lizzie? Why are you always bruised? Why are you always bleeding?

I almost immediately got up, but I heard a male voice, the voice of the red-haired sorcerer I had warned her about so many times. Rumors abound that the Weird family was as powerful as the Key family, as dangerous and deadly. Rumors say that the few allies of Sorcerer Weird drop dead, or more precisely, end in accidental house fires.

"Please, keep the blood off the rugs; they are hell to clean," I heard him say to my Liz, my hurt, burned, and bleeding Liz. She was pale from the ongoing blood loss. Her face was swollen from the violence they used to coerce her to take them to the book. That book, he had right there, in my eyesight. They hurt my Liz because of that damn book on his desk. I would recognize it anywhere; Mrs. Key had been looking for it, too, before she went missing. The entire Key family was looking for it. Lizzie needed a healer, and he was making jokes. Alaric Weird. I wouldn't let the false rumors trick me, and I knew how dangerous he could be. I knew what he was.

"I would say bite me, but I don't think I have enough left even to quench your thirst," Liz answered, her gaze focusing on me for a few seconds, and she smirked before collapsing into unconsciousness.

I tried to get up from the bed again, and I winced in pain. They had not hurt me as much as they'd hurt her, but it was enough to keep me quiet for a while. Alaric Weird never looked in my direction as I watched him. He slowly took the pan from the stove, cleans his hands with a purple kitchen towel, and approached Liz only after that.

"Sir," I said, my throat hurting and my voice failing while I watched him pick up Liz like she was a bag of potatoes

265

and put her over his shoulder. I tried, for the last time to get up, to get his attention. "Mister Weird, please. She needs a healer. Let us go home; I can take care of her." But he was gone, locking the door behind him. I was a light magic user, an alchemist, and I could not face a powerful sorcerer, not even on my good days. Lizzie trusted him; I did not! I looked back to the family grimoire, the Key grimoire that lay open on Alaric's desk. Very slowly, and holding onto things, I went to the book. It was an unholy old book with the family Key insignia on the cover. With my scarf, I closed it and wrapped it up, taking it back to the bed. I heard water running from the closed door and strained to hear something. I wished I were powerful enough to get Liz and myself away to safety. If anything indicated Liz was in trouble, I would try whatever it took to get her out, even if that meant my life. She needed a potion, a healer; we were wasting precious time here.

I put the book inside the bag Alaric provided for my bloody clothes, hiding it between the layers as I waited. They hurt her because of that book; she was not safe with that Sorcerer and the book in the same space. She would never be safe with this book around. I needed to keep it away from all of them and find a way of destroying it. The world would be safer without it. I waited a little more, making sure again that the book was well hidden. It was not stealing; it belonged to the Key family and Liz. I was not doing anything wrong; I was keeping my Lizzie safe.

The door opening pulled me from my thoughts. I could see my Liz, now with wet hair, wearing an oversized deep purple t-shirt that could only belong to the Sorcerer. I hated where my mind took me, so I stopped thinking and tried to get up to help her, but I was useless today. I noticed Alaric was touching her, and Liz pushed him away as she walked. He quickly put his hands up and laugh.

"Do I look like an eighty-year-old grandmother?"

"You know I don't lie, Liz. Do you want me to answer that question right now?" he said, still laughing.

"Oh, please, Supreme Sorcerer. Do answer," she replied mockingly.

I hated the connection I felt between them. Like he was an old friend. But they did not have friends. My Liz said so. And I had only seen it that day before, how she had fully accepted the darkness and used it. I only saw that comfort with another male, her now ex-boyfriend.

"Maybe I should conjure you a wheelchair?" he started saying, but Liz interrupted with a smile as she walked towards me.

"Bite me, Al."

"You keep offering but biting you wouldn't be much fun right now; you're a few pints low already. And you got some on the rug!" Alaric was still in the same spot. My presence seemed unnoticed, but Liz came close enough to put a hand on my shoulder and squeeze it.

"If you ask me, it was an improvement. But you can send me the bill, Al," she said, smiling, moving her hand away from me quickly. She did not comfort others now, did not love, and did not let anyone see she could still feel human at times.

"Get your ass in the bed before you pass out. I don't want to carry you again and drop you on it. I'll need you alive to send you the bill," he said, walking to his library, the library the book was in just a few minutes ago. My heart started to race.

"Al, wait," Liz said, walking towards him while holding her right rib cage. She needed a healer. Why was no one listening to me? She stood on tiptoes and gave the Sorcerer a small kiss. Not the kind of kiss I was used to seeing her give to some overconfident, over-lucky stinking mages she sometimes brought home. But I could hate this one more. My Liz was better than this. "For her," Liz whispered so low I almost couldn't hear it. Then returned to my side.

I didn't hide my disapproval of any of this, and I wanted my Liz away from that Sorcerer. He was smirking at her like she was just a piece of meat; from what I knew about Alaric Weird, he was used to everyone throwing themselves at him. But he must have noticed my unhappiness because the Sorcerer simply nodded to her and turned away.

"Lizzie, tell me you did not do it!" I whispered, pulling her to me by her arm. I held my breath waiting for an answer that never came. She waited for the Sorcerer to be out of sight and hugged me, and the wince of pain she let out did not go unnoticed. Hugging was another thing she had not done in years. "Tell me you did not offer yourself to that man, Liz! What is going on with you?"

She slipped away from my embrace and looked at me with that damn joking expression of a girl in trouble and enjoying it.

"Offer myself to him? Really? What year do you think we are in? And I did not have sex with Al, Ma." And I could finally breathe. "Tonight."

She laughed at the horrified look on my face after hearing that statement. Lizzie loved to shock me with her wildness, but I could tell she was being honest. She'd let a demon touch her. They got into people's heads, changed their memories, and altered their reality. He was only half alien, and his father was a good man, but still…

"Oh, my sweet child," I murmured more to myself than to her. "I will fix this. Let's go home, Lizzie. Portal us out of here; portal us home! I can heal you there but let's get out of here."

"We are safer here, Ma," she replied, getting into bed with difficulty. "Besides, Al took care of me already."

I did not want to know what that meant; I only knew I did not like the implications. Liz was getting comfortable in the expensive lavender silky sheets; like we didn't almost die. Like she had not confessed to me she had been with the Sorcerer intimately, like we were among friends.

"Ma, come rest. I would really prefer to be asleep when the potions kick in," Liz said, patting the bed and closing her eyes. She was fighting sleep and I knew it. The blood loss and the day's events had taken almost everything from her. I could feel it. Like I could feel that her energy was different, similar to his.

"Lizzie, you accepted potions from him? You are smarter than that." I heard the disappointment in my voice, and I immediately regretted it. If she was under his influence somehow, she could not help herself.

"Ma, Al saved you," she murmured with her eyes closed, almost falling asleep. "I trust Al with my life."

That was what I was afraid of, I thought, looking back to where the Sorcerer had disappeared moments ago. "And he heard your overreaction about us having sex. Be nice!" Liz added with a laugh.

He could hear that far? So, I was right. She was in more danger than she knew. I took her from her parents to keep her safe from men like him, men like her father. She should have been wise to him and guarded against anyone who could use her for that book. I drove my attention back to her and saw she was finally asleep, her breathing steady and slow.

I tried Lizzie, to keep you safe. I wanted to keep you free and good. I am so sorry, I thought to myself, getting into bed.

The hours seemed to go by slowly; maybe that was because I feared having our throats cut open during sleep, even though I knew it was not his style. I was overreacting, alright. The exhaustion of the last 24 hours finally caught up, and I fell into dark dreams.

"I cannot believe you let them sneak up behind you. How human of you!" I heard the male voice say, laughing. I opened my eyes in time to see Liz playfully slap his shoulder.

"Mister, you can hear everything within a three-mile radius; I cannot! They caught me off guard," she answered, laughing too. Liz was sitting on the kitchen stool, wearing only his shirt, showing most of her bare leg. Her hair was in a high ponytail, and I could see her neck and jaw still bruised, but other than that, she looked better. I still didn't trust him.

"I can't help that my alien ears hear dog whistles from two blocks over. Anyway, you have to admit you've gone soft, Liz," he teased her. I had seen her hurt many people for a lot less, but she allowed it. Like she had accepted everything from him.

"Who, me? The woman who normally has people hard, and sweating, and on their knees?" she flirted, her voice becoming more hushed and smoother as she delicately nipped a piece of bacon. I refused to witness what might come next, so I sat up, clearing my throat.

"Not here, and not with your keeper in my bed, anyway. I'd like my shower to stay intact, and the rest of my house. You have a nasty habit of causing explosions."

The day following the attack, my body hurt more. I never thought it could be possible, but here we were. I could feel it in every inch as I got to my feet. I was getting too old for this sort of thing. I needed to retire before one of these mages finished me off.

"Lizzie, we should go home. We have already taken too much of Mister Weird's time," I said, forcing a smile. We had to get out before the Sorcerer found the book with me, or before I had to see more of whatever mind control was happening between them. As soon as the book was in a safe place, I would take care of that. Liz slid off the kitchen stool. She looked much better already, but she bounced back quickly thanks to the Key blood. Bringing me a glass of orange juice, she took a sip and offered me the rest.

"Drink, Ma. You need your strength. Al said you didn't take any potion or eat anything yesterday." My clever girl knew I did not accept because I did not trust him, and she just took some to make me see it was safe. I took the orange juice from her to gain some time.

"No offense, Mister Weird. I always made my own potions," I said politely, passing the glass from one hand to the other. It was not a lie.

"None taken. I respect someone being cautious, and call me Alaric," he replied, giving me a charming smile and returning to his food.

"Lizzie, I need to see if you're healing properly," I said, if anything, to force her distance from him. In another lifetime, in another world, where I did not think my child was in danger for being so close to one of them, I would have admired how respectful and educated Alaric Weird was. Still, this was my child, probably being mind controlled by a demon.

"Okay," she answered, pulling the shirt up without hesitation, leaving little to the imagination. I saw the Sorcerer smirk at what was happening.

"Lizzie!" I said, astounded, trying to cover her again with the shirt already too revealing for my taste. She was always a defiant child. A strong, motivated, defiant child.

"What? It is not like Al hasn't seen everything already," she replied with a twinkle in her eye.

"Twice," he added, putting two fingers up but still too focused on the food in front of him.

"Well, three counting yesterday," he said shyly. The information I had on Alphonse Weird's eldest child was that he was gay. It seemed my research was wrong. I could almost hear the conceited grin he must have been wearing. *Was he teasing me as Lizzie was?*

"Maybe four? Or was the shower included on that first time?" Liz added, looking like she was enjoying this too much. She was not acting like my Lizzie, or maybe she was, just not the grown-up Lizzie who knew that the world was cruel, and no one was to be trusted.

"Lydia Elizabeth!" I scolded, putting the glass of orange juice down so hard on the kitchen counter that the noise almost made me think I had broken it. I pulled her by her forearm. I had no idea how I was managing to keep my hair from fading to white! "Lizzie, listen to me carefully. He's a demon!" I whispered, and she looked at me like I was crazy, until she broke into laughter.

"He sure gives orgasms like one," she retorted, looking at him like she memorized every aspect of him. She was testing me. "Ma, seriously. Look at that ass!"

"Liz, that is enough! We are leaving," I announced, taking the bag from the floor and grabbing her hand. "Mister Weird, I appreciate the hospitality."

"Mister Weird was my father. You can call me Al; I prefer it to "demon", though I know why you call me that. It's not the first time I've heard it," he replied. He knew what he was, and he was proud of it. He was more a demon spawn than a demon, though. I could see through a disguise; they always disguise themselves to look human.

"Al, I am keeping this, by the way," Liz said without allowing me to answer him and pinching the shirt to make it move.

"You better bring that back, Liz, without blood on it. It is one of my favorites, and it was expensive!" he replied, now looking in our direction and pointing his finger at her.

"Unless you come here taking it from my naked body, too bad! Put it on my bill," she retorted, giving him a wink. "Next, let's say three times, breakfast is on me, Al."

"Make it five, and don't forget you owe me a rug." He started cleaning the dirty dishes. Liz just crossed her arms over her chest, smiling at me.

"Ma, you will have to ask Al to create a portal for us to leave, unless you want all guests at the bar downstairs to watch your precious baby girl in only a shirt. I do not mind; this shirt looks better on me than on Al anyway," she said after a while, amused.

"Is the mighty Sorceress Key afraid of doing the walk of shame?" Al dared, with a devilish smile on his face, stopping the cleaning for just a few seconds to look at her.

"Oh, I will do it! You should know better than to dare me, Sorcerer. But I might be the cause of a scene downstairs," she answered as she fixed the shirt, and I knew she would do it. We knew our children to the core.

"Liz," I said with my best mother's tone to show my disapproval. She was not just a grownup, self-sufficient woman. She was a powerful Sorceress. But that didn't mean I still couldn't get to her. She still respected me, and I would never give up on her. Lizzie was still there, no matter how many times she said otherwise. There was still some good in her. I saw it in little moments.

Her expression changed from a taunting grin to a sweet smile exchange between them. It was like a secret language shared through their eyes and I was not invited to participate. She nodded, still smiling, and he created a portal before us.

"Safe travels," he said respectfully to both of us. Unlike my Liz, Alaric Weird showed himself to be a respectful person. I had a problem with him disregarding Liz earlier. It may have just been my motherly instincts, but I felt disrespected by it. I didn't trust him, and it wasn't his fault. He was raised by demons, and they have no civility when it comes to humans.

My house was on the other side of the portal, not Liz's, and I wondered why. It was not as safe as any of Liz's properties, but she could lift powerful wards in minutes here, too. It was better this way; the book must be destroyed. I pulled the bag closer to my chest as if hugging it, and I felt for her hand in mine before stepping toward the portal.

"See ya, Al," she said in a sexy tone.

"Alaric, my door will be open for you to collect my debt," I said, having a hard time forgetting the manners. In all my years, mages and Sorcerers demanded respect from a poor alchemist like me. It made me feel strange to say it, but judging by his smile it was the right thing for him. I added, "But if we ever meet again, I hope it is under better circumstances."

I wanted this to be my debt, not Liz's. She said his saving me was just helping. But she looked so much better already. That wasn't just help.

He gave me a courtesy nod, and we stepped into the portal toward an old-looking small house I call home. A home where there was nothing but safety and where Liz would get back on her feet and then find another way to dig her own early grave.

I just hoped Alaric Weird was not the reason.

Al

My notification alert for Liz went off. She didn't usually text during the day. Sleeping during the day is easier for people like us. And vampires.

Liz: Code Red: Your boyfriend just called. He has questions about my late-night adventure with the toasted marshmallow. I thought you had fucked him mindless, Sorcerer. Watch your step!

I was staring at that text from Liz when my phone rang. The caller ID said Seattle PD, but I knew who it was thanks to Liz. I was going to hit the red button to hang up. I had confessed many secrets to Officer Kennedy, but he never called after our date. He took the potion to forget me as I hoped he would. Okay, part of me wished he would have called me instead. It's not like the sex was the best I had ever had. Lately, that subject was up for debate.

I hit the green button to answer, but I didn't say anything. The silence went on for over a minute. He still remembered me as the guy he flirted with at the IHOP.

"Mister Weird? Alaric Weird?" he asked. His voice was trembling; he was afraid to talk to me. I could almost taste his fear. Whatever happened when Liz and I fucked, made me more vampire than I ever was. I almost missed having three separate personalities. I had Liz to thank for that. She accidentally spelled Alias and Alton silent when she asked for me alone.

"We're friends, Officer Kennedy. You can call me Al," I replied. I could hear his heart slowing, and his breathing slowed with it.

"It's Detective Kennedy; I got a promotion yesterday. Listen, Mister Weird, we need you to assist us in a recent case. Your father's wallet was found at the scene of a possible homicide."

"You're a homicide detective?"

"No, it's not my case. I– I'm the low man on the totem pole who makes the phone calls. Hey, I'm sorry I never called after. I couldn't do it. I can't be part of your world, and I can't forget."

"You didn't drink the potion, and you didn't call? I must be losing my touch, " I teased.

"Yeah, so… I heard you are living in Vancouver now, or is it Portland? Your address is a little vague, considering it's a building that doesn't exist. I convinced them that it was probably a typo."

"I'll be in tomorrow to give your Detective colleagues whatever information they need," I said, changing the subject. I'd registered my home as an abandoned building that is technically in Washington state, but the address is in Portland, Oregon. The Columbia River separates the two cities, so it's not like my home is on the border. You see, the entrance to the Tower is in Portland, but the Tower is actually across the river. It's magic, but I had explained enough about magic to this human for his lifetime.

"Did you kill him? He was burned beyond recognition, just like your brothers and lovers."

His tone was severe; he believed I killed them all. I suppose I was responsible for my lovers' and brothers' deaths, but Temp was accountable for his death. I called it 'suicide by Liz.'

"A wise Grim Reaper once gave me some good advice that I should have heeded when you and I first met. I won't confess to anything. You use your detective skills on this one, Brandon."

"Please tell me you are kidding about knowing the Grim Reaper."

"A Reaper, and you can call him Deathripper."

"Long hooded robes and scythe kind of thing?"

"You and your freaking questions, Brandon. No, he wears black but no robes. He's a bit of a rebel. He does have a scythe."

"Death? You are friends with freaking Death?"

"Don't get jealous; I haven't fucked him. Ripper and I aren't that friendly." Sometimes you can almost read the thoughts of someone in the long silence of a conversation. I had said too much again. One day I would have to learn to stop oversharing with humans.

"Tomorrow afternoon, at the station. I've asked Miss Key to answer some questions, too," he said after the uncomfortable silence.

"She told me," I replied. I hadn't read the whole text from Liz, but I got the message. The cops had found Temp's body, and though I wasn't there the day he died, my body was. I had no idea what sort of evidence Alton had left behind. When I created him, he got most of my emotions but not my logic.

"Please tell me you didn't do this. I'll do what I can, but–"

I hung up the phone before he could talk more. I liked talking to him, which wasn't like me. I didn't do small talk, but he was almost as curious as Liz. I liked curiosity; it was one of the reasons I took the job as an archeology professor. Students who took archeology were some of the most curious and interesting people.

I texted Liz a reply to her earlier communication.

Alaric: He's not my boyfriend!

It would make her laugh and probably argue the fact with me. She didn't respond right away, which meant that she was occupied. I could have, if I wanted, found out how occupied and with whom, but I didn't want to go there. Something about our night after the battle had changed me. I didn't hear the voices of Alton and Alias, nor did I feel their presence, but I did feel their feelings. That was another reason I had just talked to a policeman like he was a friend.

Some people would sit and worry about the upcoming future, but all I had to do was meditate. No one ever taught my father to control his gifts because no one alive knew how. One of the perks of having the entire Wyrd curse was I could learn from the past. My Grandfather was the one who saw the future. Learning from him was like talking to his force ghost; only we couldn't communicate. I hadn't figured out how to travel with a body into the past before I was born. I didn't even know if it was possible. I was doing this quantum leap style, only jumping into my past self. My Grandfather could see the future, and I could see the long past. It was confusing the first time we tried communicating until I thought of writing things down. He had a small slate board that probably belonged to my aunt. I had my dry-erase board that had seen better days.

So, Grandpa, Alistair, taught me how to control my visions. It was too bad he never lived long enough to teach my dad. In case you were wondering, I got my stunning looks from gramps. I was rambling again. I sat in a lotus position, closed my eyes, and willed my thoughts into tomorrow. Any scientist would tell you that you could change the outcome just by observing an experiment. The future is the same, or as the wise Yoda said, "Always in motion is the future."

I'm not practiced at seeing a fluid timeline. I got glimpses of the future, and since I was looking for a specific time, I had to have something to focus on. Since a person triggered my original gift, I chose Brandon. He was sitting on the edge of a desk chatting with a young woman. He was wearing a suit which seemed odd to me. The fact that he seemed to be flirting with a girl just like he'd flirted with me was a little odd. His social media bios all listed him as gay. I was curious; he was my first human. And my last. He looked up in my direction with a look of recognition, but the look was for Liz, not me. She'd probably portal in. I loved driving my Tesla too much to waste energy on a portal.

Time skipped ahead, and I saw myself sitting in a room behind a solid-looking table. Two men were sitting across from me. They had photos on the table and four plastic bags marked as 'evidence.' I thought I had lost my pocketknife, my dad's wallet, an ugly-looking amulet, and bloody rope.

Time skipped again, and I saw myself sitting in a large room with several other men. I was on a bench near the bars; the others were huddled in the corner. I had called a flame to my hand, playing with it like a little rubber ball. My usual reaction to bullies–all animals fear fire.

I shook myself out of the vision and stood. I knew their evidence against me, but I wasn't there. It wouldn't help matters because my body had been there. I had all the time in the world to figure out what to do. I thought letting the humans have a go at me might be fun. It had been years since I'd been in trouble with human law. I didn't want to look further into the future. Alistair had warned me that using the sight too many times led to madness–of course, those were the words of a madman.

I rarely ever sleep, but seeing the future took a lot out of me. I woke late, which explains why Liz beat me to the station. I still didn't rush the process of showering and dressing. I wore comfortable clothes since they would probably be detaining me that day. I thought about just not going in and making them hunt me down, but playing innocent seemed wise. It was so ironic that I would get in trouble for a murder I didn't commit and not even get questioned about the ones I had.

Liz was sitting in a waiting area when I arrived. She patted the chair next to hers, then pointed at Brandon and made kissing noises with her puckered lips.

"He's moved on," I commented as I watched the scene of Brandon flirting for the second time. He glanced my way, then he locked eyes with Liz. She chose that moment to put her hand on my knee and slowly slide it to my cock. It made my whole body vibrate with magic. I couldn't hide the pleasure if I wanted to. She was giving Hottie some of his own medicine. She knew what she was doing to me too, and I was not just talking about the tight pants. I would

281

have moved her hand, but the confused and slightly disappointed look Brandon had given me was fascinating. I gave Liz a hands-off look, and she laughed loudly while slowly pulling her hand away from my crotch. I had to adjust quickly or risk the whole station noticing the semi she'd given me.

Liz was asked to follow an officer while I was still getting comfortable. That left me alone in the line of chairs. Detective Kennedy removed his ass from the woman's desk and walked toward me. He sat a chair away so it wouldn't look like we were being friendly. I was a possible killer, not his lover.

"I'm sorry, Al. I didn't know what they– You need a lawyer," he said so quietly that no one else could hear him, even if they were sitting next to him. He remembered the ears. I wondered what he did with that forget potion.

"Janice or Rebecca? Which of your sisters is the better at defending a murderer?" I joked.

"Shit, you did it? You killed a fucking Councilman?" he whispered.

I didn't answer, I couldn't. If I told him no, his next question would be who did it. All the evidence pointed to me, not her. I was the one with the criminal record. I wasn't being selfless, just practical. If I told him Liz did it, he would work to get evidence on her. Sitting beside me showed me he wasn't thinking like a cop.

A woman called my name and gestured for me to follow her. She led me into a room with a solid-looking metal table. Deja Vu. I sat down, and detective one and detective two (the same men from my vision) showed up with some files and bags. They didn't need to ask me anything; they were stalling for an arrest warrant. The evidence was enough to place me at the crime scene, and with my history, they didn't need to look any further.

"Mister Weird, this is Detective Marsh, and I am Detective Young," the first guy said. They were wearing matching blue suits. Young was old, probably in his late fifties. His hair was gray, and so were his eyes. Marsh was in his early forties, with black hair, black eyes, and beautifully dark skin. I usually didn't go for older guys, but physically he was my type. He hadn't let the desk job ruin his physique.

"Alaric, please, my dad is…was Mister Weird," I lied. Dad was like me; in public, he always went by Al.

They spread the evidence in front of me. I knew they were trying to make me feel comfortable so I would confess or slip up. This was still a new thing for me, though. Normally I would be cuffed and stuck in the back of a cruiser that smelled like vomit and disinfectant cleaners.

"Do you recognize any of this?" Young asked.

"Dad's wallet, my pocketknife, some rope, and a gaudy necklace," I replied.

"Your knife?" Marsh asked.

"Where were you on the night of April fifteenth?" Young asked.

"In another realm hanging out with my dead ex-husband," I said truthfully. Only my body was at the scene of the murder with Alton in the driver's seat.

"We are just asking for information, Mister Weird," Young said as he slid a picture across the table.

"I prefer my meat rare, thanks," I joked. I hadn't seen Temp's body before, but I recognized the signs of magic fire. I'd used the same kind to burn the room my lovers, clone, and ex died in. I'd removed all evidence from that scene, but since I had cheated the Reaper of his prize (AKA Alton's soul), he refused to help me clean up the mess. Liz killed that Reaper, so he hadn't helped her with the mess either. Deathripper was too new to the job. Liz didn't have the same deal with him as I had, but they had a history. Ripper and I had some issues to work out. All of that meant that the corpse of Tempest Griffin had been left to rot.

"Can you explain how Councilman Griffin came to be in the well-done condition?" Marsh asked.

"Well, too much heat or too long on the barbecue. I would guess it was too much heat since it looks like nothing wanted to eat him but the worms." Yeah, I was having too much fun.

"The six bodies found in a building owned by your-" Marsh began.

"The term used is lover, but the love was all him. I was just in it for the sex," I replied. I could tell he was trying to be politically correct. Straight people were either homophobic or overly cautious regarding LGBTQIA+ issues.

"The term is sociopath," Marsh murmured.

"Sometimes, but it doesn't interfere with my social life," I replied. The look on his face was priceless; his partner hadn't heard a thing.

"Mister Weird, did you kill Councilman Griffith?" Young asked.

At that moment, the woman who showed me to the room stepped in and handed Detective Young a piece of paper. It was time to ask for a lawyer, but I didn't have one. I had never had one. I was joking with Brandon about his sisters, but they were the only lawyers I even knew of.

"I'm not answering any more questions until I talk to a lawyer, and I can only assume that you have a warrant for my arrest," I said as they both glanced at the paper.

"Alaric Weird, you have the right to remain silent," Young began as his partner rose and pulled out some handcuffs.

"I have a right, but I don't think I have that ability," I replied. Marsh walked around the table and gave me a look. "You going to make this easy, or hard?" he asked as his partner continued to drone out the Miranda rights.

"You use those cuffs on me, and I might get a little hard, but they aren't necessary. I am not going to resist," I replied. I had both hands on top of the table; I know how cautious the police can be even when they think you're a whore, or a drug dealer. These two thought I was a murderer.

Marsh slipped one cuff on my left and the other on my right. I never moved, so he felt brave enough to let me keep my hands in front of me. Detective Hottie would have known better. If I could see where I was aiming, I could burn them all to a crisp, crush their hearts, or even do something more fun. When Young got to the "if you can't afford a lawyer," point in his monotonous speech, I interrupted. "Seriously, my shirt cost more than your weekly wage; I can afford ten lawyers."

Marsh lifted me out of the chair by slipping an arm under my armpit and wrenching me to my feet. I knew he was in shape, but that impressed me; I'm not a petite guy.

"Handcuffs, and you know I like it rough. If you want a date, I can pencil you in my calendar," I teased. He tensed; he was straight, maybe bordering on homophobia.

"You're not my type, sweetheart," he replied. He guided me toward the door.

"The last man who called me sweetheart sucked my cock first. You can call me Alaric until you suck my cock, Roy," I joked. Marsh didn't like my comment, and he showed it by pulling me hard enough to dislocate my shoulder if I was human, but only half of my DNA was human. I think it surprised him that I didn't even make a sound.

"You're going to be popular in prison, pretty boy." He led me down a hallway into an elevator that went down a floor, then down another hallway until we were at a large holding cell. A uniformed officer walked up to the cell door and opened it. Marsh took the handcuffs off and pushed me inside the cell. It was big enough to hold at least twenty people sitting. The Benches looked uncomfortable, but it was not a place meant for long-term storage. The men sitting on the benches were what I like to call 'catch and release' criminals. Whores, petty thieves, drug addicts, vandals, and some low-volume drug dealers would be my new friends until they had a room in whatever jail they sent me to. I found an empty spot on the left bench. Marsh gave me a dirty look, so I blew him a kiss. That made every man in the cell laugh or make rude noises until the uniform yelled for them to quiet down.

"Watch that one," Marsh told the uniform as he walked out. Uniform walked over to the cage and asked, "Why am I watching you? Are you a stripper?"

"You're the one dressed like a stripper, Officer Johnson, and before you think about it, you are not my type," I replied as a nearby clone of Officer Johnson walked into the room. Detective Kennedy looked at me like I was about to get guillotined. He whispered, "Take a break," to the officer. The uniform scampered away quickly, leaving me alone with Brandon and eleven other guys. We were the center of attention. I guess not many people received visits from hot young detectives. He looked good in the suit but better in the uniform.

"Not your type, huh?" Brandon asked as he pulled a chair closer. The room smelled of piss, sweat, and vomit; not a place I envisioned for a second date with Hottie.

"Hot, blonde, thinks I'm hot? No, not my type at all. Anyway, I have already marked 'fuck a uniformed cop' off my bucket list."

"Fuck, Al!"

"Yeah, that is what I'm talking about. What do you want, Detective Kennedy?"

I leaned back, closed my eyes, and waited for him to start talking. I could hear the other men creeping closer so that they could listen to what we were saying. I froze them for a moment and wrapped a bubble around myself and Brandon. We had all the time in the world.

Liz

The air conditioner inside the precinct was cold. Specifically, inside the small room I was led to. Even though I should have felt chilled, all the magic tingling from my body gave me a sense of suffocating heat. This always happened when I experienced physical contact with Alaric. Power recognized power, I guess. We would figure that out some other time.

The white space was empty, aside from a table and three chairs. How I avoided something like this for so long was not a mystery, it was always because of my sense of caution. I was reckless, but not that reckless. Until Temp. He was a pain in my ass, even after his death.

The tall young officer pointed to the only chair facing the door. "Take a seat, Miss Key. The detectives will be right with you," he said nervously. Interesting. A human, with no knowledge of what a member of the family Key means, was afraid of me. I could feel it in my bones. What did he know that I didn't? I took the seat he'd indicated, facing him, not the metal desk.

If I hated one thing more than chitchat, it was wasting time waiting for something to happen. If I was going to stay, I may have a little fun.

"Officer?" I asked, crossing my legs in a sexy way and looking at him from top to bottom. He seemed very young to be trusted with a murder suspect, which made me think

I was not on that list. Probably. Or not yet. I smiled at him, slowly biting my lower lip.

"Hart, Miss Key," he replied, flushing. "Please, let me know if I can assist in any way."

"I could think of a few things," I started saying, with a smirk, when I was interrupted by two detectives entering the room.

"Thank you, Officer Hart," the older detective in a blue suit said. "You can go now."

I watched the brown-haired man walk toward the door and gave him a wink that made him blush before he left the room.

"Miss Key, we are sorry for the delay. Thank you for taking the time to speak with us," the other detective said, sitting in one of the two chairs in front of me and laying a stack of paperwork on the table. "My name is Detective Wells, and my partner is Detective Garcia." The older detective only nodded when I looked at him, not showing any emotion. "Miss Key, we called you to assist us on a murder case. We first want to give you our condolences on the loss of your…boyfriend?" Detective Wells paused to let me confirm or deny the statement while reviewing the documents in the folder.

"My boyfriend, you say?" I replied, amused, resting my arms on the table. I knew exactly who they were talking about, but why not play a little bit? "Detective, I am afraid you are mistaken. The only boyfriend I had was years ago, and your co-workers mysteriously lost his body without finding his murderer. I believe there was an internal investigation, but your detectives never gave closure to his poor fiancé. It has been four months now, is that the 'boyfriend,'" I said, making air quotes with my fingers, "that the Detectives want to talk about?"

"Miss Key, we cannot give information about an ongoing case that is not ours. I am sure my coworkers are doing the best given the unfortunate circumstance, but we understand the frustration of the family and friends of the victim."

Frustration? Oh, my frustration and anger were released, on bastard Temp. I avenged Daniel Costa in the process. Too bad about Temp, though; he was hot and not that bad in bed. I closed my eyes to hide my thoughts, but the two detectives already assumed I was innocent.

The Detective recovered fast from my affirmation. Not only did I throw him off his game for a few seconds, but he looked like he was about to apologize.

"Miss Key, do you recognize this piece of jewelry?" Detective Wells asked, while Detective Garcia only observed. He slid a picture to me of the necklace Temp always used; it was a dark amulet I knew too well. That should not have survived my flames, my magic.

"Detective, why don't you ask what you want and stop the theater? I am a very busy woman. Yes, I know the necklace. It belongs to Tempest Griffin," I replied, not breaking his gaze.

"The mortal remains of Councilman Tempest Griffin were found. Miss Key was in a relationship with the victim, am I correct?" Detective Garcia finally joined the interrogation. He had remained standing.

"Detective Garcia," I said, not breaking the gaze of Detective Wells. "Councilman Griffin and I were never in a relationship. We went to the same nightclub, enjoyed the same…exercise, and talked a few times until he, as men do, never bothered to show up again. I moved on as women do." I smiled at Detective Wells, who showed a hint of a smile that he quickly hid, clearing his throat. "Miss Key, in those conversations or…exercises, did Councilman Griffin express concerns about someone threatening him?"

"Detective," I said slowly, with charm, my fingers brushing against his as I slid the picture of Temp's amulet back across the table. "Why would Councilman Griffin say to a poor woman like me, that he was being threatened?"

"Please, answer the question," Detective Garcia said impatiently.

"No, Detective. Temp never told me anything about being threatened or even seemed afraid of anything when we hung out."

"There is no need to show such an atrocity to a young woman like yourself. Miss Key," Detective Wells began to say, flipping the burned corpse picture upside down and clearing his throat when I nodded, trying to pass a thank you instead of a fuck you, and adjusting my top. "One last thing before you go. Where were you the night of April fifteenth?"

"Should I be worried about that question, Detective Wells?" I said, flirting.

"You can call me Ryan, Miss Key. And not at all," he flirted back. "We want to make sure you are not bothered again."

"I appreciate it, Ryan. It was a long time ago, but it was around when I was trying to comfort a friend who had just lost her fiancé. I spent a lot of nights there; someone probably saw me," I answered. Not all was a lie. I spent most of that time helping Sophie control her magic.

Detective Ryan got up from his chair, searched for a business card inside his pockets, and wrote something down with a pen. He handed me the card and helped me get up from my chair.

"Miss Key, that is my private number. If you think of any more information that might be useful, or if you need anything, just call me. Thank you again for your time." Detective Wells offered his hand to give me a shake that lasted a little longer than appropriate. "Can we get you a ride, Miss Key?" he asked, still holding my hand.

"Maybe some other time, Detective. Especially if you can use handcuffs," I said in a low voice, taking my hand back and walking out of the interrogation room.

I returned to the waiting area after asking Officer Hart if Al was done with his interrogation. I was not surprised to learn that it was still going. Knowing Al, he probably was already fucking a Detective in one of the precinct rooms. That thought made me smile to myself. After what I felt like an hour, I got up to find a terrible cup of coffee from one of those vending machines. As I was walking, I felt a firm hand grab my elbow and was directed from the building via the nearest exit. Looking up, I saw Detective Hottie. Okay, Detective Brandon Kennedy.

"Keep walking," Detective Kennedy murmured, not letting go of my arm while he dragged me out. His grip was surprisingly firm.

"Detective Hottie, foreplay already?" I teased in response to his harsh touch, but I let him guide me outside. "No wonder Al had such a fun time with you."

Outside, far away from the attentive eyes of the Police Station, he stopped us and looked at me with a puzzled gaze, probably thinking I was crazy.

"What is wrong with you? Both of you?" he asked.

"Oh, honey, you haven't seen anything yet," I answered. Detective Brandon Kennedy did not look like someone who appreciated being called honey, but I was who I was. "Where is Al?" I Asked.

"Not here," he answered, watching his surroundings. "If you care about what is happening, meet me at IHOP tonight. Say, 3 AM. I don't care; make it work for you."

And I watch him walk back towards the precinct.

Al, what fun did you get yourself into this time, I thought to myself as I searched for a dark alley to invoke my portal.

Brandon

I was in the camera room watching Al's interrogation. It was clear he was hosed from the beginning. Roy and Dave were at the top of the food chain regarding the Seattle PD. They had an eighty percent close rate. No one else had near that, but those other cops also followed the rules, like 'innocent until proven guilty.' I was a shit person, but a damned good police officer. I knew that Protect and Serve was the number one job of any policeman.

I'd been convinced that Al was guilty until I learned about the evidence. The Alaric Weird I knew, albeit it a short acquaintance, would not be so careless, so stupid with evidence. He'd killed that woman in IHOP, confessed to me, and I had laughed it off. There was no evidence. She had no visible marks on the outside of her body; the only signs were the hemorrhaging in her eyes, and blood in her mouth and nose. Even the coroner ruled it a natural death. Like having your heart crushed from inside your body is natural. That still gave me nightmares, or sometimes a wet dream. Shit, he was hot, even in the glamour that hid his ears.

I could hear nearly everything being said, but my mother taught me to listen to what people weren't saying. Al, in particular, was not saying he murdered a Councilman. He fucking admitted to being a sociopath, but not the death. I expected him to use a Jedi mind trick or some spell that knocks out the power and people, or that he'd freeze time and just walk out, and no one would know. He just sat there until Roy cuffed him, then he slowly walked out. He didn't even flinch when Roy tried to dislocate his shoulder. Shit, he took it easy on me. If I ever got the chance again, I'd take a two-week vacation and recover.

I was planning my next date with a suspected murderer– a known murderer to me. Shit, I was so confused about this.

I followed them down to holding and waited until Roy left. Roy didn't like me much, not because I was white, blonde, or gay. He thought I was too young to make Detective and thought my late father's occupation influenced the decision. He was probably right, but I was a damned good cop.

I asked Will, the officer on duty, to take a break. He and I were friends; we went to the academy together. He was straight, but he was also a flirt. I laughed when he asked Al if he was a stripper. If only he knew what Alaric Weird was. His juvenile record was sealed, but cops talked. I wished I'd known him back then, when he was just a prostitute.

"Not your type, huh?" I asked. I grabbed a chair and pulled it closer to the cell. Al was sitting far away from the others.

"Why do you think a hot, blonde, human, cop would be my type? Anyway, I have already marked 'fuck a uniformed cop' off my bucket list," he replied with a devilish grin. He always seemed to take serious shit like it was one big joke. I admired that, but at the same time, that sent me down the Sociopath line of thinking.

"Fuck, Al." I didn't know where to begin. I wanted him to tell me he didn't do it. I wanted a reason to feel like he was being set up. I wanted to do exactly what I told him I didn't want. I wanted to be a part of his world of vampires and sorcerers. It was hot, and it was dangerous. It made being a cop seem tame, especially now that I was riding a desk. I liked investigation, but the thrill of knowing you could die from the next call…I missed that already.

"Yeah, that is what I'm talking about. What do you want, Detective Kennedy?"

He did that spooky thing where he went all still and closes his eyes. I didn't know if he was about to blow the place up or do something monotonous. I watched as everything stopped moving, the clock on the wall, the other detainees, the air. It freaked me out the first time he did that, but it was so cool.

"I love it when you do that! If humans knew that your kind could control time…." I resisted the urge to wave my hand in front of the closest man's face. It was just like someone had paused a video.

"My kind is just me, sorry. I am unique."

"You're the only one who can freeze time?"

"No, someone else bears my curse, but until she was cursed, I was the only one," he replied. I knew who he meant when he said she. I'd seen them together; you didn't let a friend touch you like that.

"Liz…so you and her…you had sex with her?" I wasn't sure I wanted the answer, mostly because I was sure it was a yes.

"Sometimes I forget how human you are. Anyone else would worry about the word 'curse.' Your jealousy is flattering, but Liz and I are just friends," he said.

"Like you and I are friends?" I don't know why I kept asking; something about this made me irrationally angry. I didn't love him, but I liked that he was gay, not bi, but gay… he was.

"Well, maybe she is a little friendlier than you; she at least called me after sex," he joked. He was making fun of me, and that was Al. I was overly jealous, but she was from his world, and they were close. Closer than just friends, obviously.

"Sorry, it was a lot of… It was a lot to take in. You and Liz live things I have only read about in fantasy books or watched in movies."

"If you assume that you hurt my feelings or made me feel anything by avoiding me, then don't worry. The sex was good, but you chose to continue the nightmare, and now you are chatting like we are not separated by bars. What do you want, Brandon?"

"I want you to look me in the eye and tell me you killed the Councilman. I want you to tell me to walk away and not try to get you out of here."

"Walk away, and don't try to get me out of here. You have a career and a life to think of."

I knew he didn't do it! He would have told me as he did with the lady in the IHOP.

"You didn't do it, but you know who did, and you are trying to take the fall. Why?"

"I'm not taking the fall. The evidence points at me; I was there, sort of, and in the eyes of the law, that means I am guilty."

"Is it Liz? Are you protecting her?"

"No one but Liz protects Liz. She is not a frail human; she doesn't need my protection."

"Shit! It was your dad, the one tied to the tree. He died there, not in the car accident. You fucking cut the ropes, and that substance they think is synthetic blood is you! You don't have a freaking blood type?"

"Actually, I don't know anything other than it is different. My dads were into that genetics shit. Blood doesn't stop the species from mingling. It's been happening for hundreds of years."

"Sorry, I have difficulty mixing fantasy with sci-fi. The alien thing should be easier to swallow than the magic, but shit, like aliens?"

"They have my phone and wallet. You could be a bad cop and sneak a peek at my phone photo gallery. Most have opted to change to human form permanently, but moms and dad number two prefer to be themselves."

"Do you–? Are you–? Is this just some skin or disguise?"

"I think we've been down this road. You've seen the real me. I haven't been blue since I was a baby. Ears are all that is alien about me."

"It wasn't you there; it was one of them?"

"It was my body, blood, knife, father. He killed my father. He killed a good man."

"You've never talked about your family. It's good to know that you thought of your father as a good man; mine wasn't."

"Oh, no, my father was a lunatic and an asshole. The good man was Daniel Costa."

"Liz's high school sweetheart?"

"Oh, Detective. Were you so jealous that you investigated her too, or were you just thinking of swinging your gate both ways?"

"I'm not jealous, but you were the first guy I had been with who never fucked a girl. I guess I was hoping you…"

"Would stay pure for you? I'm still gay. I'm not going to lie and say I didn't like it, but it wasn't about sex. I'm not going to explain because I don't fully understand."

"It's none of my business, is it?"

"Neither is this! You go find a crime that you can solve. This one is an open-and-shut case. I fucked up trying to pretend to care, and now I am fucked."

"Care about Liz?"

"You have more of a hard-on for her than you do for me. Stop looking for a substitute. I'm done here. Is there something else you want? A goodbye kiss?"

"Not through bars and chain link, man."

Al made a gesture, and a freaking hole opened up in the center of the door. It had a purple and black haze around it. He stepped through and stood in front of me, grabbed the back of my neck, and pulled me into a rough kiss that instantly made my pants tight. Damn, that man could kiss. I leaned into him as he teased my throat with his tongue. I hadn't forgotten this. He pulled away slowly, smiling like a cat. He spun us around and shoved me against the bars hard enough to hurt. It took me a minute to catch my breath. He started kissing me again with one hand on my neck and the other on my growing erection. He'd mentioned before that he couldn't hold time and do this, but he fucking was. Just when I thought we were going to fuck, he stopped and backed away with his hands in the air.

"Goodbye, Detective Kennedy. Don't come back."

He stepped back through the hole, and it disappeared behind him. I looked at him; his jeans were hanging loose at the crotch. The kiss that nearly had me busting a nut did nothing for him, but one touch from Liz made him adjust. He always claimed to tell the truth, but there was more between those two than friendship. Time resumed, and the detainees were a little confused since I was standing instead of sitting. I turned quickly and headed for the restroom. I needed time to recover before I decided what to do next.

When I returned to the first floor, I saw Liz waiting. I knew I should just go back to my desk and catch up on the paperwork. I wouldn't be assigned to anything major right away, being the rookie. I should never have taken the tests or put myself up for promotion. I should have called him. Al wouldn't let me help him, and it wasn't selflessness; that wasn't him. He acted like he wanted to go down for this murder. He'd already proved to me that he could just walk out of the cell anytime, so why didn't he? Was it Liz? She knew something, or she wouldn't be there. I needed to find out what she knew; I needed to find out if she did it. I needed to know why she could touch him and turn him on. That kiss was hot–scorching. He didn't even get a semi. I don't know why I cared, either. He was hot, exciting, fucking brilliant, and the sex was literally magic, but it was a one-night stand.

I noticed Liz was still waiting–probably for Al–in the waiting area. If nothing else, I could ask her to get him a lawyer because my sisters hadn't practiced criminal law in ages. It didn't matter because they would ask why I cared about a murder, and I still hadn't told them I was gay. My mother would have a heart attack.

None of that mattered; I knew that Al hadn't killed the councilman, and I believed in innocent until proven guilty, not the other way around. In that case, I couldn't be like Marsh and Young. I had to give Liz a chance to confirm or deny. I would do my little investigation on this. No one was acting as they should. Al was just fucking weird, no pun intended. The freezing time I could see, but he just fucking made some dimensional portal in the fucking jail cell, then sat his ass back down inside like he was on the beach. He could get out any time he wanted, but he stayed. Hell, he could make himself look like anyone and just walk out. I've seen his real face; it's hotter than the one they see.

Liz may not have all the answers I need, but she sure as hell had some I wanted. Why her? Why her and not me? Was I too human? I had to get to her before she left, and I had to talk to her outside of the station, maybe somewhere else. I felt like they were always watching me now. Whenever a hot gay man came through the doors, they would watch to see what I did, like I was some sort of entertainment. That was why every other gay cop in the building stayed in the closet.

Liz was the key to unlocking all the mysteries. And that pun I did intend.

Brandon

y co-workers used to pick on me because I drove a Prius. Behind closed doors, they would tell me my car was gay. I knew that I could turn them in for that. They knew it too, so they stopped when I walked in for wearing rainbows on pride day. I bought one of those T-shirts that read 'Let's get something straight. I'm not!' My car was white originally, but I wrapped her in a pearlescent purple that reminded me of Al's eyes now. Even my car had to remind me that I was stupid not to call him, but I couldn't let go of the feeling that he had drugged me. I got jealous when Liz touched his junk and again when I saw her waiting for him. They didn't arrive together, and though Liz had a valid driver's license, she had no car registered in her name. I waited in my car to see if I was right.

I only had to wait about five minutes to see a portal open in the darkest spot in the parking lot. The lights were always broken there, even the night after they were replaced. The stories ran from ghosts to gang members. My guess would be they pissed Liz off one night. It was the perfect place for her dark, mysterious hole in the universe. Sometimes, I had to remind myself that this was real, not a dream. She stepped out looking like she was on a date, but all four times I had seen her, she looked ready to fuck. I got out of my car, shut the door, and waited for her to join me.

She fucking walked like she was on the catwalk with spotlights and cameras all around.

She was putting on a show for me, probably. She looked well-manicured and spoiled, but it was an act. I had seen her hands dirty the last time I was at this IHOP. Maybe only Al was pulling a glamour that night. Yeah, I talk like this now, portals, glamours. Did you know fucking fairies are real? If my co-workers knew that my research on my particular case took place in the mythology section of the library, they would probably lock me up. In a padded cell!

"Do you always have to make an entrance?" I asked as she walked past me toward the restaurant door. Any other woman would wait for me to open the door, but she walked right up to it, turned around, and leaned on it, putting the sole of her left boot on the glass.

"Do you like what you see, Hottie? The last gay guy that looked at me like that, I fucked him raw!"

"It's strange how what I like about him is what I hate about you. I know you fucked him; I know it was after he and I-"

"After he fucked you, stupid? You're welcome; I made him promise he would," she said with a smirk as she spun around and pulled the door open. I had to catch it before it smashed against the wall because she had used magic to slam it behind her. I could feel the bruise beginning in my palm where the door had caught me, or I had caught it. If we broke the door at IHOP, I would never live it down at work. She marched over to the table where she and Al had been the night we met. Shit, if I had never called him that first time, I wouldn't know any of this existed. And I would still be swiping right for a date. I swear all the men on Grindr are robots. I know, it's just for sex, not for relationships. I didn't even want a relationship; I just wanted to talk about interesting stuff, then fuck.

I sat across from Liz, right in the spot Al had been in. I swallowed hard when I thought about that night. A woman had died just to my left on the floor. Her heart had been crushed, and her killer had confessed to me, a uniformed cop responding to the call, and I had laughed. I wasn't laughing tonight. If Liz didn't kill the councilman, I bet she would have killed others; she had the look of an alligator just waiting for her next meal to wander too close.

"So, what does this mean? Are you like fuck buddies? Friends with benefits?"

I know. I was showing her just what she wanted to see. She played cat and mouse with me, and I was a good little mouse. I couldn't stop looking at her hands, though. I knew Al told me that he didn't need hands to do magic, but hers looked, I don't know, more magical. Maybe it was the ring on her finger. She wasn't married and didn't date; she was like Al in female form. She noticed that I was looking at her hands. She flipped her right hand over, and there was a small ball of purple flames in her palm. She put her left hand over the ball and extinguished it, but I could feel the heat before she did. That tiny ball could have set me on fire, maybe not burned me to a crisp, but enough that I would need to visit the burn unit.

"I'm not going to steal your boyfriend, Hottie, but I'm not done playing with him either. He's not going to pick out curtains with you. We aren't wired that way; he would only break your heart–or crush it. He told me he ate a heart raw once, and I watched him rip a man's heart out of his chest. That was so hot!"

"I'm not even going to ask if you are kidding me. So, did you kill the councilman?" The question was out of my mouth before I thought it was a bad idea. She didn't need weapons; she was the weapon.

"Why do I feel like I have been through this before? Temp is dead, and so many people are better for it. It only matters that he can't hurt anyone anymore," she said with a yawn.

"It's not like I'm going to walk in there and tell them I know you can make a fire in your palm that could burn a man to charcoal without it harming you."

I had to stop talking as the waiter approached–or at least I thought I did. Carl stopped moving about four feet from our table, and everything else stopped but her and me. She freaking stopped time, just like Al!

"I need more time to decide what to order," she said flippantly when I noticed.

"Al told me that he…that you–. He called it a curse."

"A curse is a spell that takes life's blood, a death, sometimes heart's blood. It's what we do. Are we here to talk shop? I already have a student, and she can do magic."

"Al needs a lawyer," I said to clear the air.

"Al needs a good fuck, and maybe a psychologist. Oh, another thing I can do for him that you can't."

"He only needs a psychologist because of what you did to him."

"He cursed himself. Our exercise cured him of his multiple personality issues. You need to get caught up with the previous episodes before you get too many spoilers."

"Alias and Alton? Did you kill them too? That means…"

"He can still do your favorite foreplay, Hottie, just like before. Only Alias won't crash the party."

305

"Something is wrong; he is taking the fall for this murder, he doesn't want my help, and you are fucking flirting with me. What is going on? Why won't you take this seriously?"

She waved a hand, and time started again. In the movies, someone would stumble or show in some way that their flow had been interrupted. Carl kept walking smoothly toward us as if he hadn't been frozen for nearly ten minutes.

"Miss Key, I haven't seen you in here since…." Carl began, then he looked at where the woman Al killed had been. Many people would have quit after witnessing a death, but Carl stayed.

"Yes, Carl. Such a tragedy. Detective Kennedy and I are here to celebrate his promotion. I think he will have the usual, and so will I," Liz replied in a sweet tone that was not like her.

Carl scribbled something down and walked away nervously. Maybe he was getting that creepy cobra stare of hers too. Something was off about Elizabeth Key, something dangerously off. She might say she could see what Al sees in me, but I could see what he saw in her. If she were a man, I would be right there with him—probably. She wasn't a man, and I didn't like her. It wasn't the danger, it was the way she seemed to not care about her supposed friend. She stretched like a cat, showing off her chest, even though she knew it did nothing for me.

"I'm on a low-carb diet," I commented after Carl returned to the kitchen.

"You are paying; if you want meat, ask for it. I don't order meat for a man unless they've earned it," she replied with a wide grin. She knew I was thinking about the morning we met. Al was eating meat, and so was she. I know what she meant by earning too, but Al had said they hadn't had sex then…or had he? He never really said they hadn't. Shit, why was I feeling like this?

"You've got it bad! That is why I don't let vampires bite me," she said as if answering my thoughts.

"What do you mean?"

"Their venom is a drug. Too much of it kills you, and I have the kind of blood a vampire craves, according to Al."

"You–. He–He never bit you?"

"Oh, all over, Hottie. Just no deep drinks. I've tasted his blood, too; you should try it sometime. Or maybe not. It could be toxic to humans."

"We were talking about a lawyer. And maybe you can tell me what happened that night," I said to change the subject. I touched the small scars on my neck where Al had bitten me. They seemed to tingle when I was around him and now her.

"Temp killed an old flame of mine, and he used Al's father to find him. I killed Temp, and when the Grim came to revive Temp, I killed him too," she replied thoughtfully.

"Grim, as in Reaper?"

"One of them, yes."

"Al's friend?"

"Al's jailer. He did tell you too much. I hope we don't have to kill you. I would miss that cute pouty face you make every time you think of Al and me together."

"I can't be involved in this."

"Relax, Hottie. My family has a lawyer on retainer. Well, I do, since I am all the family I have. Al will be out tomorrow."

"Bail was set this afternoon at half a mil. How?"

"Magic!"

"If you already took care of everything, why meet me?"

"I would never stand up a date as hot as you, cookie! Now be a good boy and eat your carbs," she said as Carl returned with a tray laden with coffee and pancakes. He had added a side of bacon without me asking. I was also a regular here; the omelets were terrific.

"I'm not having sex with you."

"Oh honey, Al went easy on you. I would break your frail human body. Anyway, I don't do humans anymore."

"What did he do, record the whole thing for you to watch?"

"No, we weren't like this then, but he thinks about it all of the time. I get glimpses, a few details he dwells on," she said with a sly grin that made me feel a little dirty.

"You're a mind reader?"

"Oh, not me, honey. I am not the alien. He invaded my mind first."

I got a text from the station. I was on call, so they weren't worried about waking me. There was a disturbance at the coroner's office. That usually meant uniformed police, not detectives. Something weird was going on.

"I gotta go; I guess they don't have enough Uni's to cover a disturbance," I said, then took out my wallet and dropped two twenties on the table. If she wanted more, she could pay for it herself. I tried to hurry away before she had time to comment, but…

"Your ass looked better in uniform, Hottie!" She yelled loud enough for everyone in the building to hear. I got into my Prius just in time to see Liz walk out of the restaurant and head toward the dark corner of the parking lot. I was paying too much attention to her, and I almost hit some blond guy in a black suit. He looked familiar, but not. He continued walking in the direction Liz had gone. He didn't hit my creep vibes, but Liz did. I was worried for him if he were after Liz. That would be like a garter snake going after a full-grown eagle.

I resisted the urge to warn him as I drove away. If I saw the man in the morgue tomorrow, I would know who did it. Listen to me talk about someone getting murdered like it was nothing. I either needed to rethink my morality or ask for a demotion to Uniform. I didn't want to be like the old farts who liked to close cases before there was any evidence.

Al

I was sitting in the cell with about a dozen other men, and everything smelled like rotten garbage. While I was there, many came in and went away, but there were always at least ten. I recognized the latest one when they slipped him through the doorway. The magical mafia and the Magic Council worked hand in hand with each other. They pretended they didn't, but the crime was down if the bad guys policed the bad guys and the good guys kept each other in line. This guy was rough Benjamin Greer, otherwise known as Benny Grim. He wasn't a real Grim, but he dealt with death nearly as much. He was a magical assassin. He kept his long black hair tied back with one of those girly-looking barrettes with a unicorn and dressed like he was at the Dojo, complete with a black belt. He was a little taller than average and wiry, not a hulk like me. He wasn't there for pleasantries, and neither was I. I learned long ago that sometimes cheating is the best way to win. I froze for half a second before he took his first shot at me, or should I say his last. I used Liz's favorite, the violet flames that burn like the inside of a volcano. I returned to normal for a split second before it engulfed him in flames. The entire pack of humans fled to the other corner of the cell. Meanwhile, it smelled like barbeque, and there was a mess with witnesses.

I closed my eyes and willed Deathripper to show his face and gorgeous ass. He always showed up in the same clothes: dark black jeans, a black t-shirt, and a black leather jacket.

"This had better be good, Weird."

"Clean up on aisle nine?" I asked playfully.

"You summon me to a jail cell that smells like piss and vomit, and you want me to clean up your mess?" the Reaper asked. He was leaning against the wall with his arms crossed, waiting for my response.

"What if I said please?"

"I think I would drop dead again from the shock," he replied, then chuckled to himself.

Ripper waved a hand over the body, and it just disintegrated into dust, then left without another word. I would thank him, but it was part of the contract. I didn't usually ask, and he wouldn't normally comply, but I did imply a plea. He was still the same guy in death as he was in life, too.

I sat down on the bench and played with a flame until I heard footsteps. There were voices, but no talking. I didn't need to see the future to know that someone had a visitor, and probably me, from the looks of the others. I extinguished the fire, but my cell mates didn't relax. When I heard the door creak open, I looked up to find a man in a costly Armani suit and a body that filled it just right. He had to have his clothes tailor-made too. His skin was a deep brown, and his eyes were amber-colored, almost yellow. He wasn't human, but the others wouldn't notice. His glamour only fooled human eyes.

"Mister Weird, I am Anton Blackwell; I was asked to post bail for you by my client, Miss Key. She said to tell you that you owe her more than one," he said thoughtfully. I couldn't help thinking that if Liz had paid this guy to be her lawyer, she would have never seen him. Not many people trusted the elven kind. Not many elves took jobs that didn't require making something. I looked at the side of his head and noticed that he had tucked the tips of his ears just right in his mass of black curls. I wish I could do that, but my hair is straight, and I don't do perms.

The lawyer moved aside, and I saw another big man behind him; only this one was built like me. He bought his suits at the big and tall store but still looked good. He didn't look as happy to see me as he should have. He looked worried and was flitting nervously, hopping from one foot to the other like a toddler needing the toilet.

"I will thank Liz, when I see her, for sending you. I am sure she will compensate you for your trouble." No matter what type of Fae you dealt with, don't plead and don't thank them. It's not polite to be polite to one of the Fae; it's dangerous.

"Oh, you are a smart one," he said with a wink. Then added, "Detective Kennedy will show you where to go to pick up your belongings. I merely came down here for curiosity's sake. You are getting quite the reputation, Heartbreaker."

He walked away and left me with Brandon and a uniformed cop. Brandon started walking, and I followed. Hey, it had been a while since I had seen his ass. He waited until we were in the elevator to speak.

"Freeze please?" he asked. I froze time, which always felt weird in an elevator. I saw Brandon try to swallow his stomach bile as he continued to move up without the elevator beneath him.

"You asked for it; now, what?"

"Councilman Griffin's body disappeared from the morgue. It was the second time that has happened in recent history. The other was Liz's old boyfriend, Dan Costa."

"Liz didn't do it," I said.

"I know; she was with me at IHOP," he explained. That revelation was interesting. Liz didn't have a lot of friends, and she rarely went out of her way to talk to someone unless she needed information.

"You two aren't comparing notes, are you?" I asked, possibly jumping to a conclusion.

"She says you think about me often," he whispered. He was avoiding eye contact which meant he was afraid of my response. She wasn't wrong, I did think about Brandon often, probably too often.

"I think about many things and people," I mumbled. What could I say, I enjoyed the sex, and his mind was the perfect mix of intelligence and curiosity. I hadn't meant for my words to sting as much as they had. I could feel the tension as he walked beside me down the narrow hallway.

"I wish I could help you, but I can only do so much. The evidence against you...."

"Thanks for reminding me," I said, then I snapped my fingers and allowed time to continue. The fire alarms went off in the whole building, but the fire was small. It would only burn a rope with my blood on it and anything stored nearby. The amulet would survive, but that wasn't my problem.

"Did you just set a fire in a police station?" he hissed.

"How could I do that? I am here with you, walking out of the station. I was thinking of inviting you for a drink after work."

"My shift ended over an hour ago. I was on call thanks to the pandemic," he explained as we neared the end of the hallway.

"I forget that is a thing for your kind," I teased, but the gibe was lost on him.

"Non-magical people?"

"Humans. I was created in a lab, in a way. I can get some diseases but have never had a virus."

"Seriously? So, you are immune to everything?"

"Don't know, don't want to find out. I also don't know if I carry anything that could infect someone like you. I have never worried about that because mages can either heal, make a potion to heal, or find someone who can."

We stopped at a window that had a slight indentation at the bottom. A woman passed a plastic bag to me through the hole without a word. She was wearing a mask and gloves, probably a brilliant idea, though the mandate had been lifted. I put my wallet in my back pocket and my phone in the front. Brandon watched the phone with interest. I walked away from the window and headed for the door. I was going to need a shower soon.

"Those pictures are real? Your parents, your brother? Your–"

"Kids, yes, but their human disguise can become permanent if they stay long enough. It wasn't that way for Alias or me. We lost our color, but not the ears or the eyes. Len kept his color, but he can't disguise now either, since he came into his magic," I explained. I was always oversharing with him, partly to shock but mainly because of that damned curiosity.

"Fuck, I forgot how honest you are and how surreal your world is. You know they will still consider you a suspect in an open investigation, right?"

"No evidence, not a body, and there are things I can do to make people forget me without damaging their minds or forcing potions down their throats."

"You didn't say that the last time."

"Maybe I couldn't do it the last time. It's been months."

We walked through the parking lot in silence. My car was right where I had left it the day before. She's not a magical car, my Tesla, but she's the closest thing to it. Brandon wanted to ask me more questions, and my teacher instincts wanted to answer his questions. I didn't become a teacher for money. I like to educate young minds. I am naturally curious, and I seem attracted to the naturally curious. Detective Brandon Kennedy was an inquisitive man.

"I have a two-hour drive to get to my shower. I swore I would never do this, but would you like to see where I live?"

He walked around to the passenger side and got in. He had his seatbelt buckled before I had settled into the driver's seat.

"I shouldn't do this, I have to work tomorrow, and I didn't even check the board to see if I'm on call," he said nervously. I was already heading down the street when he spoke.

"I can get you back in less than a minute, but if you want, I can turn around."

"That portal thing?"

"Yeah, I prefer to drive, but only because of this baby," I said as I patted the dash affectionately.

We settled into a comfortable silence as I maneuvered through the city streets and onto the interstate. He turned on my Spotify just to fill the silence. It was almost like riding in the car with Liz; I needed it. Griffin's missing body was concerning me. I didn't think Liz or Deathripper would go that far for me. The lawyer was not a surprise to me, except that he was not human. As if reading my thoughts, Brandon asked, "So the Lawyer is like you?"

"No! He's not at all human or alien. You have to watch his kind–all of them. You, humans, think you are at the top of the food chain, but no one ever asks why so many people disappear without a trace. How many missing person cases do you have open with no clue what happened?"

"Not aliens, then, elves?"

"Bingo."

"But he was almost as tall as I am, and I am almost as tall as you are."

"Most elves are tall, other Fae species exist, but Elves and Sidhe are the most human-like. Most of them think human meat is a delicacy, especially children."

"That's sick, man!"

"You eat meat; what makes you think they don't think that is sick?"

"Doesn't help."

I had nothing else to add. I grew up with humans who accused me of being an elf. When I started researching the elves, I learned what an insult that was–at least then. Elves are not the friend of humans, with or without magic. That was why I was pretty sure Liz had never met her lawyer or she owed him a debt. I couldn't imagine her getting caught in a faery trap.

Brandon went silent again. He was thinking, and I wanted to know what was on his mind. Connecting with a person for the first time was not something I knew how to do, but that didn't stop me. He was thinking about sex, of course, and me in his bed. We were both bruised and bleeding, but not from fighting. In his imagination, the rough was in the sex, not the foreplay. I had taken it easy on him the first time, but I might have to rectify that situation. He distracted me driving. I couldn't sever the connection; I had to make him focus.

"Brandon, stop, please?" My telepathic message got through to him quickly.

"What the fuck, Al?" he yelled. If he could have jumped out of his seat, he would have.

"Sorry, your fantasy is a little distracting when I am driving."

"You can just read my mind?"

"I can, apparently, don't ask how. It just happens sometimes; I'll explain more later. At least you won't damage my shower."

"Shower?"

"Long story, and before you think about it, I don't fuck in my home."

"You are inviting me to your house two hours from mine, and we are not fucking?"

"Oh, we can fuck, but not in my house. It's been a rule for a long time that no one sleeps in my bed but me." I didn't need to tell him I had made an exception for one person.

"What's with the shower, then?"

"I need a shower and probably shouldn't tell you this, but running water dampens magic. We can still do it, but it is less potent," I explained.

"Ordinary human here, I don't get it," he said.

"Some things are more show than tell," I added. He was silent at that and thinking, but more about my weirdness than sex. His thoughts were like radio static in my head, and I couldn't block him, maybe because I hadn't slept in days. The silence lasted until we crossed the bridge into Oregon. My building was in an area that had escaped gentrification, which was unusual. The homeless population was an issue throughout Portland. Here, the homeless were not human. They looked, more or less, human to humans. To a troll, anything that looked like a bridge was home. Goblins didn't fare as well near the water.

I pulled around the back of the building to the delivery entrance. The building was nearly a century old, but to the magical eyes, it looked like a modern hotel or office building. Brandon looked confused, and his mind was trying to understand. He thought I was taking him to a magical bar, which I was. An overhead door opened, and I drove inside. The area was too tight for a larger car, but my Tesla Model Three fit well among the boxes of alcohol and other necessities for running a nightclub.

"This is home?"

"This is my club, magical humans only. Don't worry; this time, you won't be harmed."

"Harmed?"

"No one is allowed to do magic in the club."

"No one, including you?"

"There are rooms specifically designed for entertainment, but everyone comes here to escape."

"Escape? Rooms? A brothel?"

"You are out of your jurisdiction, Detective. I own the place; I don't run it."

We walked through a door that opened into the small kitchen. Most people didn't order food, but to some, food and sex went hand in hand. The other end of the kitchen held the door that opened behind the bar. I kept walking until I found Kevin, the host on duty.

"Kevin, I need room thirteen prepared in about two hours," I said to the blonde barkeep. He looked at me, then at Brandon.

"Will we need the cleaners after?"

"Just housekeeping, thanks."

I started walking toward the elevators, but Brandon didn't follow. He was just staring at me with that cop look. He didn't need to open his mouth to tell me what he was thinking.

"Cleaners?" He talked to me in his head. *"Does that mean what I think?"*

"When someone dies or bleeds too much. Don't worry, that rarely happens, and those…people are way out of your jurisdiction, like another world."

"Aliens?"

"Fae, they sometimes come here to die; it's all humane."

"I'm human."

"I make the rules, and it's a special room; he doesn't know a human from a troll."

"Thanks!"

"They throw a mean glamour."

"I figured you all could see each other's real selves."

I wasn't going to answer that question for him. I could see through most glamour but not all. It was better to ease his human mind into the magical world if he was going to be visiting.

"I'm going upstairs to my home, and I am going to take a shower. You are welcome to join me, or I can take you back to the station."

I started walking again, and this time he followed. It was very early in the morning, so not many people of any species were around. I had to stop him before I opened the elevator. I had a card for myself, and the wards were mine so they would recognize me, but the penthouse and the wards would kill Brandon.

"I will have to touch you until you are in my home. I don't hold hands or walk arm-in-arm," I said as I grabbed his arm and twisted it behind his back. I waved the card in front of the laser. The card was coded to my DNA, so no one else could use it without setting off alarms. The only people who know about the keys are those who hold them, although I get them from Svartalves.

When the doors opened, I shoved Brandon in, not letting go of his arm for one second. He would probably have a bruise, but this was just foreplay.

"Please tell me this isn't just for show," he breathed as the elevator door closed.

I leaned all my weight on him, which would have taken the breath of someone smaller. When the elevator doors opened, I shoved him into the penthouse and onto the very hard, uncomfortable sofa. I hadn't gotten around to inviting an interior decorator, so most of the place was still a bit Spartan.

"Welcome to the thirteenth floor of the Mage Tower, or what some refer to as The Sorcerer's Lair."

"It's so…Liz."

"Oh, not nearly enough black for her tastes. Pretty sure her interior decorator was also Dracula's interior decorator."

I could see in his mind that he was wondering if that was where we fucked. Because he could not block me, and I could not forget, he caught a glimpse of what he was wondering about. Liz was on the kitchen counter with her head thrown back, me gripping her ass and pounding myself into her. Worse for him, he got the scene through my eyes, ears, hands, and, thanks to his humanity, my cock. I could see it in his eyes; the look of the mind fucked. Maybe the fault wasn't only his humanity.

"Sorry," I said sincerely.

"My fault?"

"I can't shut you out if there is no door to shut. Your mind was too easy to touch and too hard to shut out."

"This is the first time anyone has been upset by my open mind," he joked.

I started walking toward the bathroom, and he followed. I wasn't communicating; I was doing my best to stay in the moment. I had a lot of practice seeing the present; it wasn't difficult to be right there. It's the future that I had trouble with. I dropped my jeans on the floor, and a black card slid out of the front pocket along with an amulet on a dog-tag-style ball chain.

"Fuck," I said almost too loudly.

"What's wrong?"

I tossed him the card and the amulet, and he looked at them, then at me. You would think I had just proposed.

321

"Those are yours; you will need them soon. The amulet gets you past my wards, and the card gets you in the elevator. Fuck!"

"You give me the key to your place and say fuck like that? I don't know, man."

"This isn't a gift. It's a curse; you will need that sometime in the future to save yourself, probably. I'm still not good at reading the possible futures."

"You see a future where I need a key to a place where I get no sex?"

"I've reserved a room for fun. I need a shower. You joining?"

I didn't wait for him to answer. I continued to undress as I hurried to the shower. He was halfway undressed by the time I managed to get the shower a pleasant human temperature. I tend to take hotter than normal showers. I stepped under the water and let it pour over me from above. The shower was my favorite place in the house. My curse made it difficult to keep time from driving me mad. Inside the shower, I could control the cacophonous voices and sounds of the past and future. I was the first to hold the whole curse without going insane…mostly. Brandon stepped into the shower and closed the glass door. He started toward me, but I stopped him before he got too close.

"Stand there and close your eyes," I said, and when his eyes were closed, I closed mine as well. His eyes didn't need to be closed, but his mind was so open. He was bleeding thoughts even when he was trying not to. I searched his mind for his strongest desires. It wasn't difficult to find. I assume many men have fantasized about me sucking their dicks, but I doubted many imagined a complete set of fangs in their fantasy.

I knew how this felt from the receiving end, but it had been a while since I went down on a man. It wasn't my thing, but this was his fantasy, not mine. I stepped under the water; since this wasn't magic, the water would not be a problem. I stopped time because though this would be like a dream to him, short and sweet, I had to think.

I shoved him against the tile hard enough to crack it. I followed his motion and covered his surprised mouth with my fanged kiss. I kissed him deeply, then moved to his chin and throat, using my fangs to put tiny wounds on his skin at each spot. It was easy to give him the full effect of the fangs since I knew the feeling well. With Liz, I could rely on her carnal knowledge. Brandon was a vampire virgin. I had been easy on him last time.

Continuing the fantasy just as he wanted, I bit tiny holes in his chest and abdomen then wrapped my lips around the end of his cock, and slowly slid him inside my mouth and throat. I could cut off the feelings for myself, but he got the full effect. He could feel the sharp fangs tickle and even cut his cock. In his mind, it went on for several minutes until his orgasm ended the fun. In reality, it was only a few seconds for him. It took me time to create the dream, so I used my power to freeze time. I wouldn't know how to function without that ability now.

He took a few moments to open his eyes, then, he stumbled into the shower door and collapsed to the floor when it opened. He sat there and checked his whole torso for wounds.

"Holy shit! All of that was in my mind? I felt it, and I still feel it!"

"It was in my mind too. And you can do that to me if I don't figure out how to block you."

"Liz?"

"When she is feeling mean. I'm blocking her now. I don't want to have a menage-a-trois in my head."

"She would do that?"

"Have you met Liz? Yes, we fucked, but we are just friends. I can't explain the attraction to you. She knows I'm not straight, but it doesn't stop her from teasing, and I don't mind; I tease back."

I held out a hand to help him stand. He took it and pulled himself up. I turned off the water while he worked on processing the information. His thoughts were slower than Liz's or mine.

I had two big fluffy purple towels hanging on the bar outside the shower door. I usually only had one, but I would have added a towel later, or earlier. I really was enjoying this time travel thing too much. It did mean remembering some minute details, but my memory was sharp as glass. I thought it would be nice to have two robes, and then I noticed two short satin robes on the hooks near the shower.

I reached out and grabbed both towels, throwing one at Brandon. He held it and started drying himself off while watching me curiously. When we both were dry, I stepped out of the shower, grabbed both robes, and tossed him the blue one. He was wondering how I knew blue was his favorite color. He already knew too much about me. If I explained that the robe was from my future self… I slipped into my deep purple robe; it had a golden dragon on it that spanned the entire width of the garment. Brandon's robe bore a silver crane on the back. I had to admit he looked good in blue.

"So, no sex, huh?" He asked as he tied the robe closed.

"That never happened, just a wet dream."

"You could make people believe anything, couldn't you?"

"Do you know that people get abducted by aliens every day? Only one percent remember the ordeal. That one percent is at least half alien themselves."

"Fuck!"

"If only. My mother's people needed fresh DNA; they resorted to cloning a few centuries ago, which made most of the men sterile. Now the men give birth, and the women rule."

I turned to leave the bathroom, but he caught my arm in a firm grip. I turned to look him in the eyes. He sent a vision of himself pulling me in for a kiss. I could feel the kiss, his left hand on the back of my head, yet I still felt the strong grip on my arm. Yeah, I was going to have to learn to block him soon. He let go of my arm and stepped back.

"Sorry, just testing," he whispered as his face bloomed red. He was actually hot when he blushed. I hadn't been with many men who were that innocent.

"I have already broken too many rules for you, Brandon. I won't break this one. Here we are, just two friends hanging out. I will get you home before morning."

"I'm sleeping here?"

"No, I don't sleep with the men I fuck."

"Just the women? Because you have two toothbrushes, two different types of toothpaste, and a plain black robe sitting on top of the hamper. Also, the make-up is not your color."

"The not fucking rule started with Liz, and yes, she sleeps here sometimes. It's the safest place for her to be, but she is a big girl and can take care of herself."

"You worry about her."

"I can't even explain it to myself. She and I have made a lot of enemies."

"One wouldn't be a tall, handsome blonde in a business suit, would it?"

"That describes a lot of people I know. Why?"

"No reason; I saw a guy that looked like he was walking her way. I only paid attention to him in case he came up on a slab in the next few days."

"More like missing persons. Deathripper would clean up the mess. Liz has a safe house of her own. Mine is just safer."

"Yeah, I read about the explosion. Gas main, good thing no one was home."

I knew I shouldn't correct him; it was just another accident, blamed on the gas company. No one thought it was strange that Liz's house was the only house to explode. She cooked and heated with gas, as did I. Sometimes you just need a real flame, and you don't want to make one yourself.

"Liz was home, and a friend of hers named Alma, and there were at least two other people there. One body, but Alma died the first time."

"The first time?"

"I can go back a few days, not many, but that is how you got the card and the amulet. I have them made sometime in the near future."

"So if this isn't an invitation to a relationship, then…."

"It means you will either need to have magical protection, or you will need to identify a body."

"You're kidding about the last part.'"

"Mostly."

I left him and went into the kitchen to grab a couple of beers. The great thing about my place is I didn't have to show anyone around. The view and the open floorplan had them wandering around, staring out every window, and there was more window than wall. Brandon stopped at the archway that led to the library. It was an impressive collection, and I usually welcomed the curious, but Brandon didn't know a magical tome from Harry Potter. Some of them like to bite.

"Look but don't touch; there are books there that could kill or curse you. One or two even scare me a little," I said aloud.

Brandon backed out of the room as if I had told him it was full of venomous snakes. He stopped just before stumbling to the sofa, then gingerly sat and waited for me. I took two Elysian Space Dust bottles from the fridge. It was a decent beer for an American IPA, and it was also a joke from Liz. She liked to tease me about my unearthly origin. I didn't think Brandon would get the joke. I sat next to him and handed him a bottle. I removed the caps with magic and sent them flying to the bar. I put my bare feet on the coffee table. It was one of the new pieces of furniture that I managed to get, handmade from a six-inch slice of wood. It didn't fit with the modern spartan decor, but I liked the wood. Don't worry; the tree had died a natural death.

"You need to talk to a decorator. This place isn't you, except for that table and the library."

"My decorator deals with Liz, a toddler, a high-risk pregnancy, and a Grim Reaper," I explained.

"Reaper?"

"Not as deadly as it sounds. He is technically the father of both children," I said. I knew a lot about Reapers from dealing with the Grim that Liz killed, but I still didn't know everything.

"I thought the Grim Reaper would be like the dead or something supernatural," Brandon said curiously.

"Technically, he was only dead for a few months. Listen, you don't want to know about Grims. Humans can't see them unless they are about to die, and I mean like soon."

"So, I don't want to meet your friend?"

"You've already been in the same room as him. He teased me about your flirting. He took over the territory of the Grim Liz killed."

"Liz killed a Grim? Liz killed death? How?"

"I shouldn't be telling you any of this," I said as I untied my robe and slipped out of it, revealing my tattoos. "This is a contract; I sold my soul to the Grim Liz killed for knowledge and power over death. Liz didn't know she could kill a Grim before she did it. My father told her to do it because he saw her do it. Alton never questioned any of it because he knew everything I knew." I didn't know what else I could say. I was telling him that Liz was responsible for Temp's death, but she had probably already told him. Secrets are a weakness to Liz, but they are armor to me, or they were before I met her.

"I want to say that's so fucking hot, but probably because you just got naked within arm's reach; I want to fuck you, and I want to make it hurt."

"I know, but this is my time. My house, my rules, isn't that how it goes?" I slipped back into the robe and adjusted it to cover the semi he'd given me with his words. The fact that he was the opposite of my type made him dangerous. Joining the dark side made you dampen your emotions, even hate, and rage, jealousy; those were as dangerous as love and compassion. Emotions could fuel magic, but they could also defuse it. Brandon called me a Sith, but the Jedi is truly dark. The Sith feels. Like I said before, nerd, geek, whatever. You may have thought Lucas got it wrong, but I don't think he did. More people loved Darth Vader than Anakin Skywalker. People were addicted to emotion; they needed to feel it and see it in others. Brandon was looking for that in me, but I couldn't give that, not even in his dreams, but damn it, I liked his curiosity.

"You were saying?" he asked, pulling me out of my head. I needed to have that Star Wars marathon with Liz; she'd never seen Lucas' masterpiece, or the other movies, for that matter.

"If it wasn't about Star Wars, then I forgot."

"It wasn't Star Wars, and you weren't reading my thoughts. Does that mean it was temporary?"

"It means I am in my head and thinking to distract. If you want, I can think to you instead of talking. I am just not used to doing that with anyone when I sit with them this close. It comes in handy in a battle but gives me a headache if I stay too long."

"Battle?" he asked nervously.

"It's what I call it when more than one person is involved on either side or both. What do you think I do all day, party and do tricks?" I asked, irritably.

"Battle? With Liz? Against whom? Guys like Griffin? Something worse?"

"Yes," I sighed.

"Yes, to what?" he asked.

"All of it."

"Reapers?"

"Yes."

"Have you killed one?"

"Just one. A black robe; I'm not GrimSlayer or Deathripper. They shared ten between them, but not equally. Liz gets a level up every time she destroys a scythe. Maybe one day she will be better than me. Maybe." I felt a little jealous at that, probably because Liz was already better at magic than I was. Since the first Grim, she'd only killed what Ripper called "Black Robes" but they were still tougher than most mages.

"Reapers are supposed to remove souls from bodies; what happens when you kill too many?"

"Zombie apocalypse?"

"Seriously?"

"The Reaper sends people on their way to wherever they go; If not the souls would leave the body and wander around for a few centuries. I think you call them ghosts."

"Now ghosts are real?"

"You're asking an alien sorcerer and seer, who looks like an elf if ghosts are real?"

"Fair point; I'm new to this sci-fi fantasy meets reality thing you have going on. I said I didn't want to be in your world, but I have been sitting here nursing this beer and listening to every word."

"You're ready to fuck. Your thoughts have been on it since I took off the robe. I wanted to see how long it would take before you found your balls and told me to shut up."

I stood and gestured for him to follow. The elevator was the only way to my home and was close to the other floors. We had to take it down to the lobby, then take another elevator to the twelfth floor. Each floor had four or five rooms, all with three-digit numbers. The twelfth floor had only four, 120, 121, 122, and 113. I didn't design the place; it came this way.

When the doors to my private elevator opened, I grabbed Brandon's arm and twisted it behind his back again. It was a little for show. He needed to be seen as my plaything, not my friend. I held him that way in the elevator to the twelfth floor as well; we weren't riding alone that time. Our elevator companions were regulars in the Tower; Anita Townsend, and Ross Conjure. Yeah, with a name like that, you knew Ross was old blood. He watched every move I made, so I gave him a show. I wrenched Brandon's arm up until he hissed in pain. Nearly having your shoulder dislocated would do that. I almost forgot he was human, with no healing potions in him. All four of us got off on the twelfth floor. It may have been a coincidence, or they may have just wanted to see what I would do. I marched Brandon to the door marked with a 13. The door opened for us, not by magic. Henry, one of the hosts, had been waiting for my arrival. Since I bought the place, I had never used one of the upper rooms. They wanted to make sure the boss was happy, and he probably wanted to see if I did have a human with me. I'm sure the whole building was buzzing with gossip.

Brandon stopped breathing when he saw the inside of room thirteen. It was the BDSM room for those who could take a lot of punishment and survive. There were no leather straps and light bondage. Every whip, every chain, everything in the room was designed to draw pain. My brave detective started fighting to get free as I pushed him inside. Henry smiled knowingly and closed the door behind us. I released Brandon slowly to avoid any more harm. It wasn't my plan to hurt him this time.

"This was your plan? Torture me for fun? It's a little kinky, isn't it?" he asked as he rubbed his sore shoulder. He was in a lot of pain, probably from a previous injury, but he was projecting the pain with his thoughts. It was enough to make me hard, but my plan was never to harm him. I wanted him to do the harming.

"There are potions in the cabinet," I replied, pointing to the small wooden cabinet attached to the wall across from the door. Knives, swords, and various sharp implements of torture surrounded us on the walls. I had heard of this room, but it was my first time in it. Strangely the metal frame that held the shackles was a perfect fit for me. It would be uncomfortable but not overly so. Just enough to make the pain so much more delicious.

Brandon walked over to the cabinet and opened it. He studied the bottles for a moment, then took two out, popped the wax tops, and drank them. He relaxed almost instantly, even though the potions would take time to take effect. He could take the pain; he just needed reassurance that it wouldn't be permanent.

I stepped over and stood in the frame. It was made from steel bars and could be adjusted for smaller people, but Henry had already sized up my companion. It would make him more uncomfortable than me, but only by a couple of inches.

I locked my right ankle, left one, then right wrist into the shackles. The restraints were tight, but that was adjustable, and they could have been tighter. The entire setup was designed especially for magic users. The cuffs wouldn't take my magic away, but the runes on them would make it difficult for me to use it. The precaution was not to make him feel safe; it was to keep him safe. I had been training to control the madness that seeing the future brought, but I still had moments when I would black out, and I had no idea what had happened. Sometimes I would wake covered in blood that was not my own. The only person who knew was Liz. I told her because she wouldn't judge, she wouldn't snoop, and she understood. If I hadn't taken the curse, it would be her with the madness. I was tired of talking; mind communication would give me a migraine eventually, but it was easier to think than talk.

"I can only go so far; you have to lock me in. I can't have my casting hand free."

"You want me to torture you? I'm more into mutual pain, and you worry about that pretty face."

"Don't get too comfortable; I am in charge here. You just get to give back what I gave you. If you want to save me scars, you can give me potions too, as I gave them to you last time."

Brandon locked my free hand into the shackle. He retrieved two vials from the cabinet, poured them into his mouth, then grabbed the back of my neck, and kissed me deeply, shoving his tongue into my throat so that I would be forced to swallow or take the potion into my lungs. He learned quickly.

"So, Alaric, what pleasure do we start with? I can't fuck you like this, and you can't fuck me," he said as he looked around the room.

"I can't grow anything back, so no cutting bits off, but you can do what you want. Beat me, cut me, burn me, whatever you want," I replied. He thought the angle would make sex impossible, but he was wrong. It just wouldn't be pleasant for me.

The descent into darkness doesn't happen quickly, and we still have emotions despite what we want everyone around us to believe. Absorbing Alias and Alton helped me regain control of mine…until the madness. The Weird curse was forever tied with madness. If I were human, I wouldn't be so sane in my insanity. Still, a rational person wouldn't do what I was doing. I handed Brandon, the one person in my life who could kill me, the means to do it. I could taste my fear at the thought of dying by human hands. Sure, Deathripper could bring me back if he wanted, but that bargain was made with his predecessor, not him. I wasn't doing this to feel, though. I was doing this to gain Brandon's trust. I liked this human. He was curious, good and had a dark streak that he denied He reminded me of myself before I became me.

Brandon took a Scottish Dirk from the shelf on the wall. It reminded me of the knife I had given Liz. He'd seen one nearly identical in my penthouse, but mine had my family crest carved into its hilt. The dirk in Brandon's hands had a thistle engraved, whereas mine had the three spirals of fate. He held the knife at my Adam's apple, and I could see the desire in his eyes. He didn't want to kill me; he wanted to make me feel. Every lover, every family member, all had the same desire to see love or hate, jealousy, passion, anything, in my eyes. I couldn't give anyone those, but I had one emotion that drove me to embrace the darkness. It was Vader's weakness, too; I couldn't completely control my fear.

No one feared Brandon Kennedy. If they had a Policeman centerfold calendar, they would want him on every page. He was hot, he was brave, he was sweet, and he was good. If found standing over a corpse, covered in blood, with the murder weapon in hand, it would be assumed he was there to help the victim, and they would probably be right. He was a thrill seeker, with just a touch of danger that he hid from the rest of the world. But he couldn't hide it from me. I'd seen that look in the mirror one too many times while I tried to deny my true nature.

He slowly slid the razor-sharp blade down my neck and chest as he lowered himself to his knees. The cut stung because it was superficial. The potion would heal it in minutes, but that didn't matter. He got my attention, which was what he wanted. He practically swallowed my engorged cock. The knife stayed on my abdomen, just below my diaphragm. With every deep breath, I could feel the trickle of blood as the blade cut. He teased my cock with his tongue, but his rhythm wasn't meant to give me a quick release. It was just getting interesting when a shadowy figure materialized behind him.

"Oh, for fuck sakes, Weird! This is just…this is too weird, even for you," Deathripper commented. He had to know I wasn't alone.

"Jesus Christ!" Brandon yelled. He dropped the knife and crab-crawled away from the Reaper until he found the wall. He used it to help him stand as he stared at the Grim. Deathripper had shown up in full gear, at least his version, which meant looking like a cross between a biker and a goth. Oh, and he'd brought the scythe. The fact that Brandon had seen him wasn't lost on me. I knew that humans could only see Reapers if their lives ended soon.

"Brandon, this is Deathripper, my Reaper…friend. I need you to unshackle me now," I hissed through clenched teeth. Friend Deathripper may be, but I wasn't going to allow him to take Brandon, not now. I couldn't freeze the Reaper, but I could go back and stop this from happening. It wasn't a heart attack; I could hear Brandon's heart racing, but that was just a healthy fear, nothing dangerous.

"Relax, both of you. I am not here on business. Well, not that business," Deathripper remarked as he sent his scythe away to the void. He walked over and carefully unshackled me before Brandon could get the courage to move. I had told him he wouldn't see the Reaper before his time.

"How long does he have?"

"To tell the truth, I didn't know he had a time limit until he saw me. Sorry about the timing, but Soph insisted I ask you if you know where Liz is."

He unshackled my hands but left my feet to me. I closed my robe and tied it before unlocking my feet. Brandon had gotten the courage to step away from the wall, but he was still keeping his distance from the Reaper.

"Liz blocked me, or at least I haven't seen or heard from her."

"Soph was hoping you would use your other…the curse."

I didn't do this often. Liz and I relied on the alien connection to see each other and communicate. If we wanted privacy, we used the phone because the connection ran both ways. She could see the present but hadn't learned to control it. I thought about her and what she was doing and got nothing. The harder I tried to see her present self, the more my head ached. Something was blocking my sight, and her wards weren't strong enough.

"You can't just pop in on her?"

"She's not called Grimslayer for nothing. And no, I don't feel her either. If she were dead, I would know. I think."

"She's not dead; I would know. Hold on," I said, then gave Brandon a stern look to get him to focus on me. He was in my head again, and the realization that he would die soon had settled in his mind. He may be a daredevil, but he didn't want to end any more than I did.

"Brandon, I need you to think about Liz or nothing. I need to see if I can contact her, and you are creating noise. You aren't dying today, and maybe not at all. If anyone can cheat death, it's me," I said more calmly than I felt. Liz was important to me; she was the only person I truly trusted. I didn't love her, but I would go through hell to keep her safe because she would do the same for me. Brandon nodded and closed his eyes. His thoughts were on Liz in IHOP, flirting with him. It was less distracting than his death panic. I left him with his memory and concentrated on Liz. I felt something, but I couldn't see or hear it. It wasn't a mental block. That would give me nothing. She was feeling…cold. I tried to reach out, but something was wrong in her mind; then I heard it. *"No, no, no, no!"* Her voice was inside my head, but I couldn't see her. I only felt a chill that ran through my bones.

"I can't see her, but I feel something. She is alive, but beyond that, she– She's not blocking me; she is just not there." My mind went to her vision. She had seen her death, or she thought she had. She gave me glimpses of it; until that moment, I had never really put all the pieces together.

337

Someone had her, and they had the book I was sure was still in my library.

"What do you mean, not there? Weird?"

"Like I'm not all there sometimes, dude!"

"You mean batshit crazy?"

"They have her warded, and the only way they could ward against the curse would be for them to know I have it. At least the present." I explained. Someone had been spilling my family secrets, and whoever it was knew as much as I did, or more.

"No one can ward against me, not with her. I could still translocate to her position, even in another realm," Ripper explained.

"Especially in another realm," I replied. Grims all had a territory, but the people who lived there were their jurisdiction, as Brandon would say. Liz was more than just a person; she brought Deathripper to life. He could have found her anywhere and any when…dead or alive. The only thing that could cut a Reaper off from one of his own was another Reaper.

"Death. Dan, have you felt any new activity with your cohorts?"

"What are you thinking?"

I looked at Brandon; he told me two things I had dismissed. A body went missing; the last time that happened, Deathripper was born. He got his moniker by killing other Reapers. I knew eventually that they would have to replace their own. They liked to pick souls who were dark and powerful. Dan had been a human with a curse, but as a human, he had tasted darkness and had been very strong in character and body. His was the first body to disappear from that same morgue.

"Brandon, you knew what Councilman Griffin looked like, right?"

"Yes, why?"

"The man who followed Liz, could he have resembled the Councilman?" I got my answer in the form of memory. Brandon had seen the man, not his face, but I would recognize him without seeing his face. Brandon shouldn't have seen him either; Tempest Griffin was now a Reaper.

"It's Temp; he has her, somehow," I whispered almost to myself.

"Merda! Foda-se! Fuck! Temp? You sure, Weird?" Deathripper's emotions brought his scythe back to his hands. "I'll owe that fucker a death. I'll find him and–" His face went blank as if searching his mind for a word, but I knew he was searching for a fellow Reaper.

"You can't. Can you?" I asked.

"Not her, not him. Foda-se! He can't hide her anywhere that I couldn't find her."

"She's alive, and she's cold…and I think she is not in her right mind, and I can only think of one thing that could cause that."

"That damned book is in your penthouse. She told me it was safe there, that even a Reaper couldn't get it."

"It's in her vision. If this is her vision, not the other…the time I changed the timeline, then this is her end," I sighed. My father warned me about messing with the future, but not the past.

"No!" Ripper yelled. "They can hide her, but they can't take that from me! She is mine for the Reaping, and it's not her time yet!"

"But soon?" I asked. Liz seemed to think her time was close, but I wasn't prepared to give her up for dead.

"You know I can't tell you, and you should know. You're the one who can see the future. Have you told him everything?" he asked, pointing at Brandon, who had been inching closer to us.

"He told me that you own his soul," Brandon said accusingly.

"I'm not the devil; I don't collect souls. I Reap, it's my job, thanks to Liz."

"But could you not reap me? I will do anything to help," Brandon offered.

"If I hadn't been human only a few months ago, I would ask what you could do, but I know there isn't always a magic solution. Your lover boy here taught me that," Reaper said, pointing at me.

"What can a human do that we can't?" I asked.

"He's human and an investigator. He's a cop, and there is a missing body. Cops try to find those, or so they tell Soph."

"I have no idea about your world–worlds, but I know mine. Have you ever overlooked something that was right under your nose? My mother always misplaces her glasses–on her head. What if she is not somewhere else?"

"Detective Kennedy, if you can find her alive, you and I will have a contract, but not before! That asshole, Reaper wannabe, will not take Lizzie from me!" At that, he disappeared, leaving us alone again. Brandon stifled a shiver as he watched the Reaper vanish.

"That dampened my mood a little," Brandon commented.

"I've met a lot of Grims, but none like him. You don't have a lot of time if you want to avoid death," I replied.

I opened a portal into Brandon's home. He stepped toward it, but I stopped him with a hand on his chest. When he looked at me, I gathered the robe in my fist and pulled him in for a kiss that sent my teeth vibrating. It was a goodbye kiss and something I never did. If Deathripper didn't save him, I would, but I knew it would cost me. I shoved him through the portal and onto his sofa before he got too comfy massaging my tonsils with his tongue. I closed the portal quickly before he could say anything. I didn't want to hear it. I didn't want him to live if he didn't find Liz. If he didn't find Liz, I didn't want any of them to live!

Liz

"Hello, lover," I heard a familiar male voice say, and I felt my whole body freeze like I was submerged in iced water.

Tempest Griffin, who I had seen burn to a crisp months before, was smirking at me in the dark alley I found to conjure my portal home. He was dead. I killed him. He was dead. I made sure of it. This is not possible, yet here he was. His ice-colored eyes looked at me like I was prey. His blonde hair was in the same man bun he wore when I had met him.

"Temp, you look great for a walking corpse," I teased, recovering from the surprise. He took a step forward, giving the nod, and I instantly took a step back, bumping into something that was not there seconds before. The tall black figure grabbed my arms from behind, and I felt a pinch in the neck. As I tried to summon fire with my right hand, I saw the second figure show off a syringe.

Are you kidding me? Not again! As the flame I started to create vanishes, my legs give out, and my vision went black. The last thing I saw was Temp closing in.

* * *

I need a new mattress; I thought as I woke up feeling very uncomfortable. But then it hit me; I was not at home or in bed. Temp!

I forced my eyes open, and I saw him. Temp was pretty much the same, wearing a formal black suit; he was still fit; a little more dead, but we all changed with time. I smiled to myself at this thought. A regular rope restrained my hands and feet; I felt no magic. He was feeling cocky if he thought he could hold me like this. I would kill him, again. I heard him stand from the chair in front of me, and he walk over. Struggling, I got to my knees. *My clothes. I was wearing a damn rag! Where were my clothes? Who had dared to touch–* But my breathing stopped when I looked at my hand. They not only took my necklace, the one I use every day to distract a possible enemy from the ring, they'd taken my ring. I was losing consciousness again when he squatted beside me.

"Welcome back, sleeping beauty." He spat the words at me while gripping my jaw painfully. "Everyone kept saying I needed to give you this treat while you slept, but I wanted you awake. I need to thank you for killing me, Lizzie."

"You are very welc–" But my sentence cut short because of a burning, lacerating pain through my chest where his hand touched me. I screamed and fell back to the ground, landing hard.

It took a few agonizing minutes to regain my breath and steady the bile rising from my stomach. I tried to invoke my magic, but the drugs and pain make it impossible. He was laughing when he left my side.

"You son-of—" I manage to yell through the pain before at least six black figures appear behind him. Some were tall, some were thinner, but all wore black robes. I couldn't hold back my shiver.

Death, I thought, using all my strength to get on my knees again. I forced my magic; I tried to connect to it. A flame. Come on, just a little flame to burn the rope.

Temp was amused watching me try to get up, and he came closer again. His cold hand on my chin tilted my head to look him in the eyes. I still felt my chest burning from whatever he had done to me. His lips were also cold when they touched mine in a quick kiss. It hurt, but what hurt more was the feeling of emptiness where my magic had flowed not too long ago. He'd done something to me. My limbs were heavy, and my body was heavy like I was drowning in hot cement.

My head fell to my chest the moment he let me go. Time to be wise here; I could not win this alone. I needed Al. Tempest killed his father; he should want a fun time kicking his ass. I hoped. I tried to open a connection with Al; it was always easy to connect to him, even without trying. The connection would allow him to see where I was, with whom I was, and what was happening. Because he was more intelligent than me; he planned. He would need –not need- he would want the information before he acted. Again, I hoped.

Nothing happened. Maybe he had me blocked, it was rare, but… '*Al, do not make me go there,*' I thought. I would have to try Deathripper, which alwa̐ys ended up in a lecture. I tried the connection again. Nothing.

It was hard to breathe; it was hard to stand, so I summon Deathripper. Or I thought I had, but there was nothing. Nothing happened, no connection was made, magic tingling, or shiver from calling Death.

My vision. That is how I am going to die.

Looking up at Temp, I saw his wicked smile. I desperately tried to feel Sophie. Not to ask for help but to test something. I didn't want them to know I could contact her, the angel they sought. I reached out for her mind, but I did not feel.

"Nothing?" Tempest asked his wicked smile now almost a sneer. "You found out you are out of magic already, baby? Seeing you so weak made me think it would take more. You always were…special. But this. The famous Key the legends talked about for centuries. You have very precious blood, Sorceress Elizabeth Key."

I tried not to, but I trembled when he grabbed my waist with both hands and pulled me close to his face. He smelled like an old grave, ash, and death. "Do not worry; I will give you pleasure if you are a good girl after every ritual. You always were a good fuck," he added, getting closer. "But you were also too smart for your good."

"Temp, honey, I think you went a little too far on foreplay, but I can work with that," I teased, trying to get my thoughts in survival mode and not panic.

"Liz, Liz. I cannot say I do not admire you. That made our fucks so much more pleasurable," he said. I stopped trying to invoke the fire that should have been burning the ropes already. "I will see your fear, Lizzie. I will break you. Those guys over there will use you, your blood, over and over again, and I will be here, watching."

I did not know why I could not use my magic at that moment, but I dated an Army Officer, and I was friends with a Sorcerer that liked to get physical, so I had learned a few things. In anger, I headbutted Temp with all my strength. He stumbled backward and put his hand on his now bloody nose. That was not smart; it hurt like hell and made me dizzy, but I was not looking for smart. No one, not a single being in any world, would touch me without my permission. Not to take my blood, and especially not in bed!

His bloody hand, which he'd used to stop his nose from bleeding, grabbed my throat in a painful grip. "I am not allowed to kill you, but I am allowed to hurt you. And baby, I have wanted to for such a long time." His eyes showed his hate, his darkness. The darkness, which was so similar to…Deathripper.

"You are- a Reaper." I said, trying to breathe and talk, but his grip was too firm.

"I am a Grim Reaper and will make you wish for death."

"Fuck- you!" My vision was fading, and I could not feel my legs or hands anymore by that moment. Temp's grip loosened, and I dropped to the ground. He took a silk handkerchief from his pocket and held it to his nose.

"Gather her blood! I want that curse cast before dawn! She will lose that smart mouth and her mind," he said, disappearing from the dark room.

I was still recovering from the lack of oxygen when two dark figures grabbed me hard enough to bruise my armpits and threw me to the back of the room. They cut the rope; by instinct alone, I hit one of them in the throat. The other did not take any time responding to my action, launching a magical force that felt like my skin was on fire and my insides were liquified. The pain took me to my knees, but I did not give him the pleasure of hearing me scream because of it.

"Touch me, and you will die! Take my blood, and you will die!" I said to everyone and no one at the same time.

"I will burn all of you, you piece of rotting meat!!" That only made him throw an energy blast that hit my right shoulder, resulting in another burn. "Nice foreplay, but I will still not fuck you," I said as they forced me to stand. I fought them as they tried to restrain me with the iron chains on the wall. "Seriously, you need to get to a sex shop; this is so old-fashioned." My strength was draining, and my vision darkening. I fought them, but they fought back. One brought a ceremonial knife and a beautiful silver bowl. He caressed my jaw when he was close enough. It burned like it was in flames as I breathed through the pain. His hand moved to my upper arm, and I felt the same sensation of my skin on fire. His touch made my bile rise, and I fought the chains to keep him away.

"Do not touch me, your piece of—" I felt little cuts, here and there, until he reached the scar I let no one near–my lower belly.

"You should have died years ago. You belong to us. You may have cheated death. But you deserve everything that comes to you in the near future." His voice was empty and cold, something anyone would fear.

Burned, battered, and in pain, I almost did not see the Key grimoire open nearby or him preparing the bowl, but I felt the knife slicing my wrist open and the warm liquid pouring…My blood.

I remembered what Al told me the day we tried one curse from that; "*I will not take more than I am willing to give.*" Something told me these people would.

I had no idea how much time had passed since the first cut that made me feel like I was a pig brought to slaughter. But not for one second did he take his disgusting hand from my body; he burned me until he stopped thinking it was amusing.

Temp entered the room, all cleaned up and with a victorious smile. But I had no strength. Not anymore. I let my head fall, feeling drained. How much blood did they need? He drew closer to admiring the work of his friend.

"Put something on her wrist. We do not want her to die yet," he said, touching my face surprisingly softly. "What an angelic face that covers so much ugliness."

He sat on the floor before me, crossed his legs, and put the book close enough to touch me. The exact words I heard in the magic tower, so beautifully spoken by Al that day, were now being butchered by Temp while he used my blood; only my blood this time.

"No," I manage to whimper. "You have no idea what you are doing!"

Temp ignored my words and kept reading from the book, as I felt a terrible aura around us. I was a dark sorceress, and this was dark and aimed at me, and I had no magic or amulet. Something that felt like a storm formed around us as the book sang loudly in my ears, almost deafening, my skull almost exploding.

The curse hit full force, and I could have sworn my head was cracking as a thunderstorm hit me—tainted magic all around me, buzzing most uncomfortably. Pain, dizziness, and sudden nausea came first, making me throw up and cough. My body had nothing left to defend me from the curse, my magic… was gone. "Burn…In…Hell…Temp," I murmured, feeling myself lose conscienceless. The curse Al did, did not feel anything like this. The blood loss, whatever they were doing to me, I could not fight it. *Al, find me.* I tried with a connection that was not there anymore.

Temp said something; I heard it like I was underwater. In my head, I heard screams, felt pain besides my own, and images passed before my eyes too fast to understand. The pitch of the screams became so high. "Stop!" I tried to yell louder than the voices. "Stop!"

Tempest Griffin had cursed me and used the same curse my ancestors used on Al's family. How ironic. The only difference was I had no drop of alien blood to help me fight the madness. With this thought, I felt my body give up, and all went black.

Brandon

hat would you do if someone told you that you would be dead by the end of the week? Most people would talk about sex, drugs, and booze. The sex was out because the only one I wanted to do that with had given me a goodbye kiss. I'm not talking about a see you later kind of kiss. I'm talking about the kiss that said, "I will never see you again." I didn't know how much time I had, it could have been an hour or could have been the week. I had seen two Grim Reapers within forty hours of each other.

All I had to do to avoid death was find a needle in a needle stack. Elizabeth Key was a sorceress, rival, sort of, and somehow more important to Al than anyone else…including me. Yeah, so technically, we only fucked once, and they fucked twice, but I should get points for being the correct gender, right? I knew I sounded jealous. I couldn't use the word love for many reasons, mainly the one-time sex, but I wanted to listen to him talk. The sex was indescribable, but his world fascinated me more. I wanted to live long enough to learn all about it. Most people would probably talk about finding a vampire or werewolf, but I didn't want to be the walking dead or furry, and as far as I knew, they could be killed too.

I had one way out of this; find Liz before she died at the hands of a Grim Reaper, who I assumed was souped up on magic. When I thought about what I would do in the last days of my life, it was more like coming out to the family and getting my affairs in order.

I could hop onto the laptop and start searching the police database. My hacking skills could be better, and my password only gave me my schedule and a portal to my benefits. Work email was restricted to the computers at work because no one should take their work home, especially the cops. Also, sensitive stuff could get leaked if everyone could do everything from any computer.

My first act was to take a shower and get dressed. I was reasonably clean, but I'd gotten some alien blood on me. I chuckled while imagining Al with black blood or as an alien from the movie. I stopped imagining when I got an image of Alien ripping my head off while Al ripped my still-beating heart out of my chest and ate it. Okay, I needed to figure out how to block this two-way video conference before I was the one going crazy.

The one thing I could look up was the property holdings in the area owned by Griffin INC. I'd once dreamed of being a Private Investigator until I talked to one. He said the job was mostly taking pictures of cheating spouses. It didn't take long before I realized that I needed more information. If I was right, he was hiding Liz in Deathripper's territory. I didn't know how magic worked, but Deathripper thought he would know if Liz left his territory. I needed to know how big that territory was. How did you ask a Reaper where he reaps?

I sent Al a text asking that very question. I knew he would answer even if he had given me the kiss of death. He needed her safe, his friend, his…whatever she was to him. His reply was for me to 'wait for information.' It seemed cold, but we didn't text; we only talked in long, information-filled chats. My problem wasn't Liz; my problem was that Al was giving me mixed signals.

Getting my answer didn't take long, but it was disheartening. Deathripper's territory spanned the Rocky Mountains to the Pacific Ocean in the North American continent. I wondered if he dressed differently for the Canadians, but probably not. He didn't seem like a dress-to-fit-in kind of guy.

The information did limit my search to fourteen still operating businesses and about twenty-one that had been shut down. The chance that she was being held in an operating company was slim. Al had mentioned that she was cold, and since it was a stifling hot summer, she was probably underground. Most buildings were having trouble keeping the air conditioning running. I needed more information before searching; at least seven buildings were in the greater Seattle area. I wish I knew how much time I had to explore, and I wish there was an easier way.

I was going to text Al to tell him what I had found, but I wanted to test this connection. Maybe I wouldn't die alone if he couldn't shut me out. I closed my eyes and thought of him, of the softness of his lips and the sandpaper texture of his unshaven face. His hair was fine, but it looked thick. It was an illusion of ginger hair. I imagined the smell of him—expensive cologne mixed with an ozone smell, like a lightning storm. His hands were rough, not soft like you would imagine. He was a field archeologist and used to work hard. His chest showed the layers of muscle he used to dig with a pickaxe, and his legs told a story of him carrying heavy weights. He didn't get that body in the gym; it was years of back-breaking work…for a human. His skin was free of scars, but he had freckles, even between his toes.

I could stare into his purple eyes for days while I ran my finger along the rim of his pointed ears. When I had the picture in my head, I pictured myself grabbing the back of his head with both hands and kissing him. I wasn't going for the deep-throat kiss. Instead, I wanted to taste his mouth, tongue, and lips. I wanted him to remember that I made him feel something, even if it was just arousal. He grabbed the back of my neck with his left hand and my ass with his right, pulling me close. I realized we were both naked when I felt his silky hair touch my skin. I wondered how far this would go, and he replied to my unasked question with, *"As far as you want, Brand."* He didn't call me Brand, and I thought it was my fantasy for a moment. I didn't care; I wanted to feel him inside of me. He spun me around and pushed me onto the bar counter in his penthouse. I could feel the cold granite countertop. I could hear him spitting into his hand. Spit isn't the best lube, but this wasn't real. It might look, sound, smell, taste, and feel natural, but it was all in our heads. I had never had a vivid wet dream, but the feel of him pounding his cock into my ass made me cum hard. I woke from the dream, if you could call it that, with my jeans soaked. I could still feel him in my head.

"Was it good for you?" I could hear the teasing from his voice in my head. The telepathy was cool, but it felt a little invasive. Unfortunately, I was going to have to ask for more.

"I have to change, and then I want you to try and contact Liz again. I need to know if you can see anything or hear

anything that would give me a clue. There are too many possibilities."

"And I always thought it would be Liz who would initiate a three-way."

"You can do that? Pull me in so I can see and hear?"

"I may be able to do one better if I can get in her head. I don't know what is wrong, but they must have her drugged with something strong. She blew up her house the last time someone tried to capture her."

"She did that herself? Alone?"

"She had a charge a little before. You don't want me to go there again."

"If you can do it as you do with me, if you can show me what she sees and hears, maybe even smells."

Everything went dark in my head. I realized it was dark because I was seeing what she was seeing, what Liz was seeing. In my mind, I was both standing next to Al and hanging by my wrists by shackles. They weren't your medieval-style cuffs, but some padded suede style you would get at the sex shop. They didn't choose them for comfort because they had her shackled with her arms above her head. She was already numb wherever her muscles weren't straining. She had her bare toes touching the ground but couldn't put her whole foot down. Her ankles were also shackled, probably to keep her from struggling too much. There was a needle in her left thigh, possibly in the femoral artery. They were collecting blood. I couldn't see anything, but I could hear the squeaks of mice or rats.

"Liz, open your eyes." Al's voice was loud inside my head. Liz stirred a little and opened one eye. I couldn't see anything but darkness. It was early morning in the whole

of Deathripper's territory. If there was no light outside, there was no traffic.

"It's gone," Liz whispered. It wasn't a voice inside her head; she was speaking.

"We will get your book back, Liz. We need to find you. Where are you, Sorceress Key?"

"Lizzie, I'm Lizzie; where is Dan? I don't want them to find me! Alma, please? I don't want to be like them. I don't want to be them!" Her whispers were cut off because her mouth was dry. Her throat was dry. Her eyes and face were dry too, but I had a feeling that was more Liz than Lizzie. She wouldn't let them see her cry. Al could feel her pain, and so could I.

The vision cut off quickly, and I felt a weight like my heart was turning to lead. I saw glimpses of another vision as Al tried to block my connection. He'd seen the vision before; only he was outside of Liz watching. The vision was more medieval and less medical, but the results were the same. They were taking her blood and doing some sort of magic with it. I didn't see the results because a wall came between us, and Al blocked me. I heard the notification on my phone a moment later.

Al: That is how she dies; she's seen it. Anything?

Brandon: Nothing

It wasn't entirely true, but he didn't want to know what I did learn. She was cold, numb, and dehydrated. There were rodents near, and they would be attracted to the blood. The air was cool and damp, so she was underground. I wasn't on the board to work, but since Covid, they could use all the hands they could get. I needed to work this through another angle or something. I was restless and feeling anxious. I hadn't had anxiety since I first realized I was gay and crushing on Father Jack. He was a new priest in his mid-twenties, and I was a confused fourteen-year-old trying my best not to confess that I wanted him to kiss me.

The drive to the station made me nearly panic, wondering if this was me. Could Al care enough about Liz to feel this way, or was I projecting my human emotions? If it was me, was I causing him to feel? This connection could be bad for him and me because I didn't know how I felt about him. He was my new Father Jack, and I was that fourteen-year-old boy trying to separate my emotions from my sex drive.

There were only a few people in the station when I arrived. Patrols would be out, but it was barely three in the morning. I had the day off, but it wouldn't hurt to look over-eager as a new Detective. I nodded at the officer on duty at the desk. She was looking at a video on her phone. It might be a city full of crime, but sometimes you just need to watch a silly cat video. The job could drive you insane faster than a black curse. Yeah, I was thinking like them now.

I made it to my cubical without seeing another soul. Soon the station would be buzzing with the morning shift. I needed to narrow the search for Liz, which meant I had to think like a Grim Reaper who used to be a powerful wizard. My life had turned into a fantasy story. I would laugh, but the timer was running, and I didn't know when my ticket would be punched. It was weird because I always thought I would die protecting the innocent. I wasn't sure I knew anyone innocent anymore. Maybe I would die saving a kid from being hit by a bus. That would be a good death and quick. I was hoping for a painless death, but I never really feared pain…not until I felt Liz's pain. I knew from Al that they could take more pain than humans. Maybe he could take more than her, but no one could survive that for long. If I wanted to live, I now had a deadline, which wasn't an attempt at a pun.

I sat at my desk and turned on the computer. I had a list of several places they could be holding Liz. I had a feeling, though, that it was close. To catch a criminal, sometimes, you have to think like a criminal. To capture this one, I had to think like a wizard turned Reaper who would have a hard-on for the woman who killed him. I searched for activity around the seven buildings I had found in the greater Seattle area. I added a couple in Tacoma to be safe. I was pretty sure she was in an underground parking garage. I hadn't seen anything, but there was an echo to her voice and even to the rat's squeak. The homeless would have moved in if the parking garage were both in an abandoned building and had little or no security. I couldn't smell anything but rodent piss and blood. That worried me even more than the cold and numbness. Al was immune to viruses. so he said, but he wasn't sure about other infections. Humans are worried more about the viruses like HIV. Liz was magical, but he never said she was anything but human. If they planned to keep her alive and her blood pure, there would be the smell of disinfectant and rubbing alcohol. I tried to close my eyes and think of anything else I had missed. There was a smell like beeswax and incense or burnt leaves. It was faint, but somehow, I knew that it meant spells. I tried looking at DMV records for cars or vans registered to the Councilman himself. It was a long shot, but he had been living as a human. He had one listed,

357

a 69 Corvette Stingray. It was currently in our impound lot, having been found abandoned on a seedier side of town shortly after his body was found. The car was intact, with no signs of disturbance. That would have been interesting if any of the buildings I looked at were nearby. They weren't. In life, he could probably make a portal and travel that way. He wouldn't have abandoned his car without protection. Al had given me a pretty cool amulet. It had the Elder Futhark Runes carved in silver around an obsidian cabochon. I had no idea what the runes meant, but I knew it was intended for me to get past his magical wards and security without being harmed. I had the key but not the codes to disarm the alarm. I assumed Councilman Griffin would have warded his car; I know Al would. The car was a dead end, but his main office had a handful of cars and vans registered to his place of business. I couldn't just check the activity of every vehicle, it would take too long, and they had magic; they didn't need to use a van. I was thinking too human…or was I?

I searched for the DMV and got three license plate numbers for the vans. I then searched the traffic cameras around the seven buildings in the Greater Seattle area. I was right, too much human in my thinking. Not one van had been picked up near any of the buildings. Another dead end that made me think of my upcoming dead end. It had been nearly forty-eight hours since I saw Liz and the Reaper. She might have another forty-eight to live, but I didn't know if I had that much time.

I started thinking of criminals again. Wards would harm humans, and both Al and Deathripper mentioned strong wards. I started searching for cases of homeless death. That was more fruitful than the van. There had been a death near all seven buildings in my narrowed search. They thought that someone magical was looking, so they warded all seven. That was interesting because they couldn't possibly know about me. Al wouldn't go to the police; he would search independently. If his actions said anything, he didn't have faith that I would find Liz. He was being too familiar with me and too friendly. He was feeling things that I didn't know he could handle. I couldn't say he was in love because I didn't know what that was like.

I love my family and friends, but I've never looked at someone and thought about burning the world to save them. I wouldn't give up my sanity to save theirs; not even my own kin would get that kind of loyalty from me. I might die for a stranger, but I didn't think I would kill for anyone. I was beginning to rethink some of my moral code, though. I had been issued a gun to protect myself and my partner. Criminals had them, and they weren't afraid to use them. I wasn't afraid to kill someone to save my life, my partner's life, or the life of an innocent, but I didn't want to. I didn't want to kill, but I also didn't want to die.

There were seven buildings, all abandoned, all warded, and all patrolled by the same security company. I had been looking at Griffin INC, but not at Sound Security. There had been an S.S. Van in every traffic cam area I had searched. It would seem like a dead end again.

My thoughts were interrupted by someone clearing their throat behind me. I turned to see an Adonis in a dark blue suit standing behind me. His hair was so dark brown it was almost black, and his eyes were a deep blue. He had a visitor badge on his lapel, but I could see his gun, and I wasn't talking about the one in his pants. He looked down at where I was looking, and I saw the glint of metal from his badge. Tacoma Police Department.

"Eyes up here, man. I may be your new partner soon, but not in that way." He said while pointing two fingers at his eyes. He sat in the empty chair that belonged to my current, temporary partner. He held his hand out for a handshake. I resisted the urge to squeeze hard. Al would have crushed his hand for the comment.

"Brandon or Bran," I said, then I released his hand without causing him pain. I was still under the influence of the potions, and though they didn't make me stronger, they did make me more careless.

"My parents named me Zachary, but please call me Zack. Zack Daniels. Are you on the missing body case?"

"Why would you say that?" He pointed at the computer monitor. I had the closest traffic cam feed for all seven buildings. In each one, there had been a van for Sound Security.

"You seem to be searching the holdings of Griffin Corp in the area. Am I wrong?"

"Yes, and no. I am looking for something else," I said. I couldn't keep the emotion out of my tone. I kept imagining Liz in the dark.

"Your tone says that it's something personal and a little desperate. Can I help?"

"It is a little personal. A friend may have been taken against her will by an old boyfriend.

"Gone less than seventy-two hours? Has it been reported?"

"Yes, and technically no, and I know I am not supposed to be doing this. "

"Hey, partner. I am with you on this. If she was my friend…"

"She wouldn't be your friend."

"Lesbian? Not saying anything negative; I just give off straight, white, male vibes."

"I think she's bi, but it's not that. She's different…and you are a straight white, male."

"I like different. I would ask if she's hot, but you're gay."

"Do I have rainbows painted on my face?"

"Lisa told me when I put in for the transfer. She thought I might be too, at first."

"Lisa, huh? When she discovered I'm gay, she suddenly became Captain Moss."

"That's…yeah… Captain Moss it is."

"She's not that bad; she just likes hot men. She won't sexually harass you, but she gets more personal."

"You are excusing some discrimination against you. You know that, right?"

"She and I dated once. She was a senior at Stanford University, and it was my first day."

"You went to Stanford?"

"My dad's choice. Stanford Law. I was supposed to be a lawyer."

"So, you were questioning or…?"

"I've always known. She asked me out, and my dad was right there. I couldn't say no."

"You can; I would have. She's nice-looking, but she's four years older than you."

"Five, I graduated high school a year early."

"So, you were not a legal adult? Did she know?"

"She does now. Hey, I just came out recently, my family doesn't know, and my old partner asked for a transfer just to get away from me. He was denied, but then I made detective."

"No worries; sorry about the comment. I didn't know. I figured we were in the twenty-first century, and it's Washington, not Tennessee."

"My family is Irish Catholic, and my father moved us here from New York when I was a baby. If my mother even thought that I–"

"Enough of that; you have a missing person case to solve. When and where was she last seen?"

I was just about to answer when I saw a woman marching through the station without glancing at the desk. It was not office hours anyway. Civilian people just don't voluntarily show up at five A.M. at a police station. She locked eyes with me, and her pace quickened. I had no idea why she was looking for me until Deathripper appeared behind her, holding a toddler. I gasped and rolled my chair into the cubicle wall. Sophie Smith looked at me with a sad and frightened expression. She said, "Oh no!" and then quickly covered her mouth.

"It's okay, Miss Smith, I know."

"Shit, sorry, man. Soph, it's okay; he is helping us."

"Okay, you idiot! You almost gave him a heart attack!" She hissed without turning to look at the Reaper. She kept her eyes on mine as if she was reading my mind. I didn't think she could do that, but I didn't know much about her other than she was with Deathripper or he was with her. "You're Detective Hottie? You know why I'm here?"

"I'm on it, but it's not official for another twenty-four hours."

Everyone looked at Zack like he was the elephant in the room. He couldn't see Deathripper, and Sophie had just scolded him while looking at me. He probably thought we were both batshit crazy.

"Hey, you two seem to need some privacy. I have to report to the captain in a couple of hours. I wanted to get some breakfast anyway; it's good to meet you, Bran. Miss Smith," he said, then he pushed out of the chair and headed for the door. I indicated the newly vacated chair, and Sophie sat down in it. She reached into her jacket pocket and pulled out a pacifier and a piece of paper from a lined notebook. She handed me the paper and returned the pacifier to her pocket.

"Sorry, I always carry a spare. She gets fussy unless he is right there," she said, then pointed her thumb at the Reaper behind her. He wasn't carrying the scythe, but I would know he was Death even without all of the tell-tale signs.

I unfolded the paper and stared at the symbol on it. It was a gang tag, but most people wouldn't know that. It was a small gang of kids who didn't know what gangs were. Most of the gangs came from California, the Midwest, or the East Coast.

"Where did you see this?" I asked. I didn't know how magic worked with anyone but Al. I had no idea Sophie Smith was magical, but she seemed to have Death in tow. That counts as magic to me.

"In my dream, that symbol and your face. She can't…I don't know what is wrong, but I had that dream, and it was like I was with her. I don't know if you understand or believe me," she whined.

"I understand more than you know. She knew I would recognize it." I took off my jacket and rolled up my right sleeve. The scaring from the laser was faint, almost gone.

I had the tattoo removed when I turned eighteen because I couldn't disappoint my dying father. Liz had seen pictures of me at the beach as a teen. My juvenile records were sealed, so sealed they probably didn't exist anymore.

"I used to have the tattoo here. I was in a gang, not like you think. We did illegal things; drugs, drank and got into fights, but I know now that we were just playing at being tough. Some around still use that tag, but it's very territorial."

"Will it help you find her? She's not doing well, and I can't contact her."

"I've felt her. Sorry, she isn't doing well."

Deathripper disappeared, giving me another start for him just to vanish. Sophie didn't seem to be phased by it. It must be challenging to have a relationship with someone who was basically on call all the time. Death never sleeps.

"You felt her? Al?"

"It seems you know more about me than I do about you."

"Sometimes she talks about him. She has been reticent since she chose the darkness. She's not the best friend she was in high school, but she is still there for me."

"I'm getting that…they have loyalty and trust for each other."

"She talked about you too; she thinks you are good for him. He is too alone and too secretive. She says secrets are weaknesses. She's dying, isn't she? Just like in her vision?"

"I have only seen little glimpses of both, but your…Grim has given me a chance to help. I'm only human, but I will do whatever is humanly possible. This mark helps me narrow from seven places to two."

"She trusts that you will help, she believes in you…and so does he; I can feel it."

"Al?"

"No, my Grim, Deathripper."

She patted me on the shoulder, then stood precariously. It was then that I realized that she was pregnant. I had learned enough from what was said and what wasn't that her Grim was her one-time fiancé, Daniel Costa.

"Will you get home alright?"

"I'm pregnant, not helpless, and I have him watching me. He's not the same anymore, not all the time. But sometimes…sometimes my Daniel is there."

I watched her walk out the door. I resisted the urge to follow her and watch over her. She was Liz's friend, she had magic, and she had a Reaper at her beck and call. She didn't need a vanilla human to watch over her. I texted Al as soon as she left, telling him to meet me at the station. The duty roster had me off today, probably because I had been putting in extra hours. My new partner would be working on transfer papers and orientation. I returned to my desk and shut down my computer. I didn't need to see anymore. I knew the two buildings that were in the gang territory. Griffin Corp hadn't directly owned either, but they were in my hood. The bad guys had thought about someone smart, someone powerful, someone Grim. But they hadn't thought about someone human…or had they?

Al was standing outside the precinct door when I walked out. He didn't have the Tesla with him, but he looked dressed for a fight. He wore loose khaki cargo pants with full pockets and a black T-shirt. He also had a knit cap covering his ears and sunglasses on his face. He wasn't using glamour to disguise himself. He just stood there waiting like a robot waiting for commands.

"Do you have a coin?" I asked. I was half afraid he would pull out some cursed Spanish doubloon or something similar. He stuck a hand in his left front pocket and pulled out a quarter. He tossed me the coin, and I caught it with my right hand. It was an old coin with no mark of copper running through the middle of it. I couldn't read the date, but it had to be older than the sixties.

"You want to toss a coin with someone who can see the future?" he asked.

"Two buildings, I assume, with magical wards or shields…whatever. They will know we are coming if we get it wrong the first time."

"Wrong, they already know we are coming. I can't let that book, or its key, remain in their hands."

"You talk about Liz like she's a thing, not your friend."

"Liz is more than a friend; she is an ally and an asset. If there were any way for her to get through, she would let us know where she is."

"She did, or at least she narrowed it down. Sophie Smith just left here ten minutes ago. She gave me a clue."

"So, flip your coin, and let's go."

I pictured the two buildings in my head and marked one with a head and the other with a tail of the coin. I tossed the coin, caught it, and slapped it onto my left palm. When my right hand moved away, the head of the coin was revealed. We would go to the closest of the buildings and hope it was the right one. I was afraid Al's lack of emotion meant he was shutting Liz out as he had me. He wasn't sure she would make it….and he could see the future.

I pictured the building in my mind and the address. I had closed my eyes to concentrate, so Al pulling me through a portal was jarring enough to give me motion sickness. I puked when I stepped foot on the other side of the portal. Al patted me on the back and seriously asked if I was okay inside my mind. I was beginning to worry about the total seriousness he was projecting. This was more important than any other task, but nothing to get too emotional about. It didn't help matters much that I could feel a buzz coming from the building in front of us. It was like standing under one of those huge power lines that ran through the country. I wondered what Al sensed if it felt like that for me. His actions would say that it wasn't bothering him at all, but I could hear the vibrations of the ward in my head, loudly. I wanted to say something, but we both heard the noise when he reached out to touch the wards. I tried to talk to Al, but he held up a hand to stop me.

"Don't freak. I'm calling for help." He closed his eyes and said something that could have been an incantation or hello in a foreign language. Deathripper popped in front of us before Al was done speaking.

"She's in there?" Deathripper asked. He didn't wait for Al to answer. Instead, he took out his scythe and slammed it into the invisible wall. Al joined him in the destruction with a lightning bolt from his left hand. There were sparks and a sound that I could only describe as a giant screaming; then there was silence. Not one of us hesitated. The two of them had the advantage over me, but I was a sprinter in high school track. I still ran for fun and to keep in shape for the job.

The garage wasn't blocked for foot traffic. The security patrol was the only thing keeping the building free of the homeless population. Well, and that ward. I found them all quickly enough, mostly because Liz was screaming at the sight of Deathripper. *And Al thought I would freak.*

"Stay away! Don't touch me. Just kill me, please? You're a Reaper, reap, please? I don't want to live like this! Why can't you all just let me die?"

Deathripper was trying to calm her down, and Al was trying to get close enough to get to the shackles without hurting her. I ran over and did my best to get between the Reaper and Liz.

"Liz, it's me, Hottie; it's okay, he's not one of them. Shhh," I hushed, trying to calm her. Al managed to grab her, but she was still struggling too much.

"No, no, no, no, not you! Go away! Tell him I'm sorry; it's my fault, mine, not hers!" She was talking to me, and I knew who she wanted me to tell. Or I should say Al knew. He blocked me before I could ask what it all meant.

Al grabbed a shackle, then hissed as the flesh on his palms sizzled. Deathripper stepped up and grabbed the shackles only to get the same. He acted like it didn't hurt, but I could smell burning flesh. I found it interesting that death could be hurt.

Liz kept struggling to get away from Deathripper while she whimpered pitifully. I couldn't tell if her eyes were dry from dehydration or just Liz's non-emotional self. They were wide with terror, though, and she was doing everything she could to move away from Deathripper.

"You're making it worse, buddy. They did this to her; she isn't seeing Dan," Al explained.

"I'll go, Al, but I'll be back…with a few scythes to drop at her feet! I'll kill everyone; then I'll give him a taste of my fists before I end him too!" He disappeared, leaving us alone and Liz still hanging. She was quiet, almost too quiet. She was staring into the space Deathripper vacated.

"I think I need your help, Brand; I can't use magic on them, and I can't touch them."

"Does that mean a human did this? A human locked her in there?"

He grabbed Liz around the waist and lifted her to give the cuffs some slack.

"It doesn't matter who or what did this. They will be extremely sorry," he hissed. His hands had to be hurting, and as much as he liked pain, the palms of your hands are not something you want to burn. I was shaking as I grabbed the shackles, but they were just cold steel and leather in my hands. A latch was holding the sides together, and they easily slid open. I caught Liz's arms and lowered them slowly to her middle. Al lowered her to the floor and held her in his lap.

"Shhh, Liz, it's Al; I'm right here," he whispered. He brushed her hair out of her face and looked into her frightened eyes. I could feel his rage and his despair. He felt more than he said he could, making my heart heavy with grief. I had fulfilled my bargain with Deathripper, but Liz…Liz was almost gone.

"We must get her to a hospital, Al; she needs fluid, blood, and antibiotics!"

"She's not safe at a human hospital. They would lock her up; she is dangerous this way."

"You said you couldn't feel her magic."

"Not dangerous that way; she could tell someone their future or past; she is cursed and insane. Humans would want to lock her up and give her medication. None of that will cure this madness; it would only make it all worse for her."

"You know, that is the most you've said to me since you discovered I was dying."

Liz coughed, then looked at me like she knew me, or at least knew that I wouldn't hurt her now.

"He's a demon, Ma said so, he will take you away and cut you open. He will plant a seed inside you, and you will give birth to a demon. Demons use people; they make clones. He made a clone. He will devour your heart and drink your blood!"

She coughed again, then continued louder, "Don't let them take me, Al, please? They are all around; they stink of death in their black robes. Don't let them take me!"

"Demons?" I asked Al. I was raised Catholic; we had an image of demons that Al didn't fit into.

"It's what they called my mother's people. It's probably where the idea of angels and demons came to the religious. If you met someone who could do magic or science centuries ago, you would feel the same."

"Centuries?"

"My people have been breeding with yours for a very long time. It may be why human magic is dying."

Al stood with Liz in his arms. I rose and stood next to him, just in time for him to push Liz into my arms. I understood; he couldn't do magic while holding her. She seemed unconscious, but she whispered something in a language I didn't understand. Al walked over to the table that was set up as an altar. The silver bowl there held remnants of Liz's blood. Al was only interested in the knife, covered in blood and a small ring. He slipped both into a pocket, then made a portal and gestured for me to go first.

I didn't want to stay in that place anyway. It felt evil, like nothing I had ever felt. If Al was a demon, who were the angels, and were they the good guys or the bad guys?

I stepped through the portal and turned to wait. Al made a hand gesture. The parking garage was swallowed by purple flames and then turned to ashes within seconds. He turned and stepped through the portal before the flames died. He took Liz from me and moved her quickly to the bed. He laid her down gently and propped her head with a pillow. I went into the kitchen and grabbed a glass. Al had one of those refrigerators with a water and ice dispenser in the door. I filled a glass with cool water, then walked over and handed it to Al. Liz grabbed the glass when it touched her lips and gulped the water down. It wasn't good for her to drink that fast, but her zeal was encouraging.

"Brand, medicine cabinet over the sink. I need the purple and the green potions."

I didn't question; I nearly ran into the bathroom and grabbed two potion bottles. I ran back out and handed them to Al. He popped one of each color with his teeth and tried to get Liz to drink them. She fought him like a cat getting a pill. The potions ended up all over the bed. I started to hand him the next ones, but he stopped me with a palm facing me. He flicked his wrist around, and a portal appeared.

"Knock on the door and tell her that Liz needs her at the tower. She can't come in through the portal; it's one way for anyone but me. You'll have to stay with her and touch her when she enters the elevator."

He sent a picture of an older woman. She was probably in her fourties or fifties, but she was perhaps older. I was making assumptions based on the fact that no magical people looked their age. The portals weren't my thing, but I wanted to ensure I got my get-out-of-death-free card before getting my ticket punched by some thug. It would probably take me hours to drive to the woman's home.

The house was a modest-looking post-war ranch-style home. I didn't know anything about the owner other than she had a connection to Liz. Al thought she could somehow help Liz. There was a doorbell, but Al said to knock. I thought that might be important, so I knocked.

The door was opened by the lady Al had sent me to find. I instinctively flashed her my police badge. I figured it would serve as an introduction.

"Can I help you, Officer?"

"Detective Kennedy, mam…. Sorry, I don't know your name. I just came to deliver a message."

"Message?"

"Al Weird said to say Liz needs you in the tower."

"What did that demon do to my Liz!" She marched into the house and started gathering items into a bag. There was a younger woman there holding a toddler. She didn't seem to care about what was going on. I waved at her and the baby as I tried to follow the woman through her house. Once she had what she wanted, she marched to the door, threw it open, and said, "Where is your car?"

"Portal, but I can get an Uber."

She reached into her bag and grabbed some keys. She pushed a button on the key fob, and a car's lights flashed.

"You drive, Detective, I can't see that well without my glasses, and we don't have time to search for them."

I opened the door of the little Subaru Impreza and automatically moved the seat back so that I could get into the car. It still felt like a tight squeeze, but I got the seatbelt on. My companion was already belted in and anxious for us to get going. I wanted to ask many questions, but she looked straight ahead.

"My name is Alma; that is all you need to know about me. You're human; I suppose he has you under some compulsion spell. You probably won't remember any of this, but I don't want to be rude," she said. I guess she noticed my curiosity.

"No spell, potions, or curse; I am just a human who stepped into your world, and you are wrong about Al."

"He is no angel; he is a demon with magic, a dark sorcerer, and he has my Lizzie; I'm not the wrong one, Detective Kennedy. You are in more danger than you know."

I returned my attention to the road. I've met a few religious zealots who talked about angels and demons like that. I didn't think Alma was that religious. I drove the rest of the way in silence. I was curious, but I've learned to temper curiosity with caution.

AI

I sent Brandon to find Alma. I should have sent him to Sophie, but I wasn't thinking straight. I searched Liz's mind for anything I could use to bring her out of the madness. She was reviewing every past trauma. She was also reliving her death, which hadn't happened yet. I wanted to go back and change the past, but my interference in the previous attempt was why they had the book. If I hadn't saved Alma, Liz would be okay. That's not true; no one would be okay if I hadn't saved Alma. Liz would burn the world to avenge her death, and I would be right there with her.

I wrapped the blanket around Liz and held her close because she was shivering. Her wrists were burned and bleeding; her body and face were bruised. I was taking an inventory of every injury. It wasn't just for my sake. Deathripper would want to know every detail. I didn't connect with him as with Liz and Brand, but I could give him a vivid picture. Her toes bothered me the most. They were scraped and torn from her trying to stand…from trying to breathe. She was still having trouble breathing, and the shivering didn't help. She wasn't cold, but her dehydration was severe. Without Brandon to do the leg work, I had to refill the glass with magic. You're probably picturing the glass going back and forth to the refrigerator, but it was easier to materialize the water inside the glass. She had no problem with me touching her, which seemed to me a sign that she wasn't raped. They did that to my ancestor, raped her, got her pregnant, and had regretted it since those three girls were born—the first true Wyrd Sisters. The madness passed only to the daughters who saw the past and future, but by the time my father was born, even that caused very little madness.

I searched Liz's mind for something that said, "Sorceress Key lives here." I didn't need to talk to Lizzie, Elizabeth, or even Liz. They were all there running through scenarios that were relevant to their timeline. The present Liz was the person I wanted to find. She would be sane in all of that insanity. I gave her the tool to ground herself the first time she was cursed, by me. I wasn't sure her human mind would recover as mine had, but if any human could, it would be Liz. In the few months we had been friends, I had visited her mind many times, sometimes against my will. The fact that her will was often stronger than mine said to me that I could bring her out.

I had to because I needed her. That Grimoire wasn't just dangerous to her; those curses couldn't end up in the hands of our enemies. Liz's sanity was vital for the search. I needed her to fight with me. Sorceress Elizabeth Key was my friend. I finally found her, but she wasn't exactly the Liz I had been searching for. She was in my bed, broken, bleeding…dying. I didn't need to see this picture in my head; I could just open my eyes. This wasn't mad Liz. This was what was left after the torture and abuse. No tears, no fear; she was just Liz.

She didn't notice me; she was staring at the ceiling. She wasn't completely lucid, but I could tell she was thinking. I had never gone further than the first layer of consciousness. The deeper you go, the more emotion you encounter. I didn't need to know what Liz was feeling. I didn't want to, but I did have to know what she was thinking. Her inner thoughts were her own, and they were personal; they were Liz.

Liz

Suddenly, I knew exactly who was in front of me; I knew exactly where I was and in whose bed I was lying. He was just there.

"*Save me…Kill me.*" I managed to push my thoughts to him Looking at his lavender eyes, I meant every word. Those words made me cough dryly. I felt like I had swallowed a desert full of sand. I didn't need a voice to talk to him, not him.

"*Kill me, Al. Do not make me pretend I love you, so you have to do it.*"

Anything would beat dying alone, bleeding in a dark alley. I lifted my slightly burnt hand to his face, my fingertips traced his jaw, feeling his facial hair, his warm lips. Yes, the madness is here; otherwise, who would think of sex at a time like this? The madness is coming back, drowning my mind in images of things that never happened, in pains that were not mine alone, in feelings I long ago locked, in screams.

I almost saw him weighing his options in his eyes; that was Al. Genius, powerful, practical.

"*I have no more magic. I can feel the madness crawling back, winning. I want you to do it, Al. It has to be you.*"

My hand slid to the nape of his neck, pulling my weight on my elbow and getting my hair away from my neck with a head shake. The scar Temp left on my chest burned deep, making me wince every time I move. *"But this time, do not make it hurt!"* I smirk at him one last time. *"It was fun working with you, Sorcerer."*

Al

I had to get out of her thoughts quickly, not because I was feeling her pain, but because I felt something else. You probably think that I meant love, but it didn't. She was awakening something in me that I kept buried…him. Alias was gone, or at least I couldn't feel him inside me, but he left me with cravings that were not human or alien. I wasn't talking about blood; it was much more than that. It was a death that I was craving, and Liz pushed the buttons. I opened my eyes to the same scene, but my thoughts were my own this time. I wasn't seeing this through her eyes. It wasn't any better. She was lucid and determined.

"They took everything from me, Al. They took my magic, my ring, my dignity. What use am I to you, to anyone? Without me, they can only do so much damage before the book goes dormant," she shared in my mind.

She sat up and scooted closer to me, just like in her mind. This was her conscious mind; anything that happened here would stay here. She wanted to die, and I could do that…I could give her that. I couldn't feel her magic; it wasn't there anymore. If I were in her place, I would want to die. I was born with magic, and it's all I had known since my first accidental spell as a child.

I could give Liz her death and keep her breathing. it would just be like a dream; on waking, she would find she was still alive. I could give her everything she wanted, but first, I would make her show me what they did. I didn't know if I could reverse what they did to her, but I knew I needed to find out. The only way to do that was for her to show me.

"I'll do it, Liz, but first, you will show me what they did to you. I want to burn every face in my memory so we can make them pay for this. I will end every Grim, and Dan will be beside me, clearing my path with his scythe!"

I saw that even in her mind, she didn't want to relive the last three days. I didn't want to put her through that, but I needed to know if what was done to her could be undone before granting her the death she was pleading for. I couldn't count the times I had wanted to kill Liz; I needed to, sometimes. I'm not talking about the short bursts of "I could kill you!"; I'm talking about the fantasies of choking her until she stops breathing or draining her of every last drop of blood, which was what she was asking for. She wanted death, and I wanted to know why. I gave her a little mental push, I could break into her memories, but if I did, I would lose the present and deal with the past Liz. She was fighting even a gentle nudge, and she was slipping away.

"No, please? Don't make me do it. Don't make me go there again."

It was too late for her protests; I was in her memories. She was drugged, and most of the time, it was dark. I saw the robed Grims, some had faces, and others were just shadows. They could choose their form; they weren't bound to a living being like Deathripper was. Most would not even have solid bodies without expending magic to form one. Those were the wraiths in the background. I tried to use Liz's eyes to count them, but I lost track around thirty…thirty, and that was just the Grims. Temp was there; he was taunting. She wasn't letting me hear his words, but I could lip-read well enough to know he threatened to rape her. Her chest burned where he marked her, but I couldn't see the mark. This was no tattoo, he had branded her, and her skin was on fire; her arms were already burning from hanging there. This was before he broke her, I knew because I watched through her eyes as she head-butted Temp in the nose. I could hear the delicate nose bones break. He was probably regretting the fact that he was in his body. The most powerful Grims, those who wielded the sapient scythes, had to have a body. I never learned why, but it didn't always have to be their own body. Temp backed away before she could strike again.

There was a little fear in his eyes, and Liz could see it. She was afraid, but he wanted to see her fear, and she refused to give it. She could see her ring and the Dagger I gave her, sitting next to the book. Temp went to the book and the bowl of blood. He opened the book to the page with the Wyrd curse. I don't know if it was because that was the curse we used or if the grimoire wanted him to complete it. It would only complete what I started…and refused to finish. Liz protested when she heard the words; she knew what they meant.

The spell was created to cause madness in the cursed. The fact that the person would see all time, was in there, but I wasn't sure that was what the original. Temp knew what the words read as well as I, but he didn't live this curse; I did. The madness could be overcome, even for someone born from earthly parents. He didn't know, but giving Liz this curse was his biggest mistake. I'd seen all I needed to see. I learned about the needle and the bags of blood they were taking from her. They watched as she slowly bled to death in anguish, and I memorized every face I could see, Grim, Mage, and human. Brandon was right; they had a human, a male, in his early thirties. His red hair reminded me of someone. He was mildly handsome, but that was my opinion. Liz was trying to change him into a toad, and his image kept wavering between human and amphibian. Liz closed her eyes and shoved us both out of that memory. We were back on my bed, just as we were in reality. I held her in my lap with her back against my chest. Her skin was going cold in her mind and in fact.

"Make them burn, Al, please? Make them all burn," she whispered. She had shown me what I had asked, and I could give her what she asked for inside her head. I could give her the pleasure of a painless death. It would only be a dream, and when she woke, she would probably ask it of me again, but I had time. I had all the time in the world, and I could keep sleeping beauty in her dream for months, maybe even years.

I gently turned Liz on my lap and kissed her lips and then her neck. I knew the secret of making the bite pleasurable. It was all in the venom. It's easier to drain a victim who wanted to be drained. Biting a taught neck is not the easiest way to drain a person of their blood, but Liz was already running on empty in reality. It would make the dream feel real.

I matched my heart rate to hers and slowly pierced her skin while licking the tiny pinholes to make the blood flow. This was in her mind, so I could give her even more than a vampire could. I knew what gave her pleasure. I could taste her blood, which was a little unusual, but I was trying to make this feel real for her, so I pulled myself along with her. I could taste the magic in her blood; it was there, faintly. It was like someone put a kink in the hose, but a little trickle still drained out the nozzle. There was something else there, too, like the taste of death. It was intoxicating, and I couldn't get enough. I bit harder, trying to get the blood to flow from her fluttering heart into my mouth. I'd never tasted blood like this before. Her blood was usually hot and spicy; this was cool like mint…like death. Maybe it was my ties to the reaper, but I found myself gulping it down like a cool glass of water on a hot day. Her heart was beating like a hummingbird's wings. I felt drunk and almost didn't notice Brandon screaming at me to stop.

"Al, stop; you're killing her!" he screamed in my mind.

"It's what she asked for, Brand. It's okay," I thought to him in my head. He had to be close to break into this dream.

"Al, No. Don't!" I heard him scream, he said my name, but it didn't sound like he was talking to me. I didn't realize what was happening until I saw the blood blossoming from his chest. I'd heard a gunshot. How? I opened my eyes to see Alma holding a smoking gun. Rage burned through my head when I saw Brandon fall to the floor. He was gasping for air like a dying fish on the riverbank. Alma was still pointing the gun at me. She had the nerve to kill what was mine in my home, and now she would kill me? I reached out and wrapped an invisible hand around her rapidly beating heart. She gasped in pain and dropped the gun. I squeezed steadily; I wanted her to die slowly for this. I wanted–

I could feel the knife slide between my ribs and into my heart. There was a sharp burning pain, and blood filled my lungs. Everything went numb but my head. Liz fell back, and her hands dropped from the knife in my chest. I saw myself collapse on her, but I couldn't feel it. I could only think. This must be what it was like to get your head chopped off by a guillotine; then everything went black…

Deathripper

They called me Deathripper because I killed reapers. It was not my job…more like a hobby. My job was to show up and pull souls out of dead bodies to keep them from becoming lost spirits. I was allowed to collect those that I thought would make good reapers. I didn't do that. You had to die to become Death, and I was supposed to be Management in this shit show. These freaks in their bathrobes didn't make me a reaper, and they couldn't tell us what to do…sorry, couldn't tell me. Sometimes the scythe talked to me. I'm not crazy; the scythe and I got along pretty well. We both had the same goal, do the job, and kill the Grims.

I was just starting to enjoy the hunt when I got the pull to the mage tower.

Shit, I never got to have any fun since those two met each other!

The scythe disagreed with me. He thought we had a lot of fun since the day it helped Liz kill its master. Killing a reaper or two could be fun when you are stuck with someone that dull. The scythe liked Liz and Al; they had fed it reaper blood. Sometimes I felt like the thing was cheating on me, but that was ridiculous. He wasn't jealous of Soph; he was strangely protective of her. Maybe I should be jealous…

The thing about being a reaper is that you always arrive late to the party; I managed to arrive just before the last person died. She had already cheated death once or twice. Technically, Al cheated death for her. She was outside her timeline too. It was my job and my right to take her soul, but this was Alma; she used to bake cookies for us. She had a daughter and a granddaughter. I put a hand on her chest and willed her heart to beat. She gasped and grasped at the amulet around her neck. Her color returned to her face as she held it. Alma was the only person I knew who Liz considered family.

I turned from Alma and walked over to the bed. I kicked the dead human to the side to get closer to the bed's occupants. The purple sheets were soaked with blood. I knew they had been intimate, but for some reason, it bothered me to see her in his bed with him on top of her. I rolled him off her and onto his back. He had a dagger sticking out of his chest. It had slipped between two ribs, not an easy way to stab someone. That was my Lizzie; she never really liked to take the easy road, even when trying to live as a human. She had to be head cheerleader, valedictorian of our senior class, and student body president. She was always on top. I didn't know what that 'conas' of a reaper did to her, but I would make him pay for every injury. The scythe in my hand vibrated in agreement; it wanted to taste Temp's blood.

I pulled the knife from Al's chest. It was too ornate for Liz. It must have been a gift from him. He had swords and daggers all over the wall that looked nearly identical. It was that stupid thistle motif that you see at any Scottish festival. It was probably the purple jewel at the top, more than ancestry, that made Weird like them. The blade had more than just his alien blood on it. I tasted it just to be sure, and the moment my tongue touched the blood, I knew it was hers, tainted with death. I wiped the rest of the blood onto Al's sheets; it was not like he could complain about the mess. He needed Soph to renovate the place. The place screamed robot or vampire. It wasn't as dark as Liz's home. But that was Liz. She always preferred black even when she was human-humanlike.

I placed a hand over each of their hearts. My contract was with Al, not Liz, but I would not let Liz pay for what was done to her. She'd owe me one; maybe I would ask her to babysit…or not. She would never be Auntie Liz, and that was fine with me. I didn't want her around Soph and Violet; they were off-limits. Both Liz and Al caught their breath and gasped at the same time. They moved away from each other quickly. I placed a healing potion in their hands, and they popped the top and drank without thinking. No one wants to die, and second chances are rarely unwanted.

Speaking of second chances, I had another contract to sign. This one would be different than the one Al had. The detective would get a limited offer. I wasn't going to be his path to immortality, but as long as he played with us, he would probably die several times. I didn't sit around thinking about who would die and when. It was too much trouble and too dull. I would instead just take a walk and stumble across a body. I like surprises.

I placed a hand on Brandon's chest and willed the tattoo into being. It was a simple one that Al wore when I first met him. The circle of runes with the raven in the center was the seal of my position. Everyone had their mark, they probably got to choose, but I stole the job. It's not like they handed me the company handbook when I took over.

Brandon sputtered and gasped as he struggled with the idea that he was not dead. I knew it was harder for humans; I used to be one. He put his hand on his chest to check his heart, and it came away sticky with his blood. That carpet was ruined. I also handed him one of Soph's healing concoctions; she had improved at making potions and keeping herself safe. I was so proud of her, but it was hard to tell her. Sometimes I was Dan to her; sometimes, I was the reaper who looked like Dan. It didn't matter to me; I would be anything she needed or wanted. Soph was why I was here, not the stupid scythe or the job. I came back for her and her alone. I promised never to leave her; even death wouldn't make me break that promise. I held a hand to the Detective and pulled him to his feet when he grabbed it. Everyone was looking at me like I had grown another head.

"Party is over, folks," I said. Then I looked at Al and Liz specifically and said, "I always knew it would end up like this between you two. You're like fire and gasoline together. We have to fix all the shit we stirred up."

"We, buddy?" Al asked. He looked a little lost, but since he'd cursed himself, he often does.

"Thanks to all of you, I'm an outlaw. I hunt Grims for sport now, and if I have my way, they will all be gone."

Liz shivered when I mentioned Grims, and that made my blood boil. I would hunt down every one of them as soon as I ensured everyone was done killing each other here. Alma was still staring daggers at Al. Liz was still looking like someone had torn her soul from her body. No one in the room had the right mind to heal anyone…so I popped Soph into the middle of the living area. She was bouncing Violet, who was crying…my bad.

"I had just gotten her to sleep. Idiot!" she hissed, then she looked around the room and ran to me, shoving Violet into my arms. My girl stopped crying the moment she set eyes on her daddy. She didn't care if I was death incarnate; I was "dada" to her.

Soph went to Liz first and hugged her. Liz did not react to the hug. Usually, she would push Soph away both physically and verbally. The potion was in her, but Liz wasn't healing as she should. Al was already sitting up, and the Detective was on his feet, even if he was swaying like a tree in a windstorm. Soph put her hands on Liz's stomach, and they lit up with white light. She'd been doing that for a while now that she had her magic under control. Liz was visibly better when Soph was done. The detective was next for Soph's attention. I would have told her to slow down, but lately, she'd just call me an idiot whenever I tried to get her to take it easy. It was okay; I kind of liked it. It was better than calling me Reaper, Grim, or Deathripper. I dared not tell her she could call me Dan; it was too soon.

Alma was next on the triage list. You might assume that Soph was trying to avoid Al, but she knew what I knew; he was the strongest physically of all of them–he was not human. When Soph turned to Al, he shook his head. He would be alright without risking my girl or my baby. We had both agreed upon it one late night or early morning, while imbibing the poison that passes for alcohol now. It takes a lot to get a dead man drunk unless you add a little depth to the mix.

Al grabbed Brandon by the front of his bloody shirt and half dragged him toward the bathroom. I didn't even want to know what he had planned, hopefully just a shower. That left me with the women and the overwhelming smell of blood. Soph's thoughts told me this was no place for a baby. She still didn't know that I could see into her mind. I didn't know why, but her subconscious kept pulling me to her. It's not like I could ask another Grim unless torture worked. It might be fun to find out if you could make a Reaper talk before you kill them.

Dan

I died less than a year ago. I wasn't surprised by my death, just by the method. My fiancé had been slowly dying from a bloodline curse that had awakened when her magic was unlocked. I had asked every expert I could find in magic and curses. I even asked Liz to help, though I vowed I wouldn't allow her to taint Soph with her dark magic. In the end, I was desperate. I asked the other dark sorcerer I knew. He was my neighbor on an island of fewer than thirty families. I still don't remember why we moved there. Some people would use words like 'fate', but I've never been much of a believer. The Weird house was the closest to ours. I knew they were magic users, and I knew that they were aliens. My former job was in Army Intelligence; I know that sounds like an oxymoron. I knew things your average person didn't. Aliens have been around for a long time, and I found it strange that most people lived their whole lives thinking we are alone in the universe.

They, the Weirds, caused my death, but not on purpose. I'd met Alaric Weird in the local pub, but unlike the rest of his family, he had never given me the alien vibes. He was like Liz. Those two got along like a house on fire…one that they set ablaze. He offered me something that no other magic user could, a scientific way around a magical curse. All it took was tricking a bloodline curse into thinking I was Soph. I don't know the science of it, but after a fun night, I was dying, and she cared for me. In case you're wondering, that wasn't what ended me. I was killed by a warlock searching for the curse or the witch who was cursed.

It should have been the end of my story. Maybe it would pan out into a military funeral with Soph all in black with my baby balanced on her hip. Instead, I woke dressed all in black, holding a scythe in my hands. I should have been in my dress uniform, but the dead aren't too picky. Besides, I looked excellent for a dead man. I only knew two things the day I was raised from the dead. First, I was a Grim Reaper, a taker of souls. The second was that I owed my afterlife to Sorceress Elizabeth Key, also known as Grimslayer.

So much has happened since that night. I remembered who I was and what I had been in life. I remembered my promise to Soph when I asked her to marry me. It seemed easy at the time; just never leave her. No problem, right? I was only gone a few months, but those months crushed Soph's soul. It was even worse when I first came back because I couldn't remember who she was to me or who I was to her. I knew she was my tie to life and the world. She made me real, and she made me whole.

Just when things were starting to go okay for me, some asshole Liz used to date, the guy who killed me, decided to kidnap her to make recipes from a stolen magic book. I'd better tell you that Liz and I were a thing in high school. I knew her as Lizzie back then, the hottest cheerleader on the squad and the second friendliest girl in our school. I loved her violet eyes and her sweet smile. She'd been the girl every guy wanted, but she was mine. If someone had given me a choice between Liz and Soph back then, I was young and stupid, and I probably would have chosen Liz. Given a choice today, it wouldn't even be an option. Liz didn't love me. She didn't hate my guts, but if she was given a choice today, it wouldn't be me, either. She brought me back for the same reason she left me with Soph in the first place. She had a choice to live with magic or die with me. She chose to live that day; I don't blame her. I blame her for choosing to die in his arms. Alaric Weird, the sorcerer's sorcerer… If anyone had a love for Liz Key, it was him. He was the reason the Grims had caught, tortured, bled, and left her for dead. He was the reason, but she cared for him; Soph cared for him, and that Cop cared for him. Hey, he was just a valuable tool to me, and one day I might just see if he knew how to take orders. No, he would make a terrible Grim. I don't understand why my predecessor marked him as a candidate.

I was holding this scythe, standing outside what looked like a giant mausoleum in a dark, foggy cemetery. I wasn't in the real world; this was what they called the Shadow Lands. It's where Grims existed, and the souls of those chosen to become Reapers dwelled until they were called. The mausoleum was the headquarters; I'd only been there once, and that was by summons, which was very unpleasant. They all had a stick up their ass and thought they could do whatever they wanted in the living world. Ripper, my scythe, intended to start new. He wanted to burn the shadow realm, and I planned to be there. Maybe he would hold the marshmallows over the flames for me.

The last time I was here, they sent a bunch of recruits at me to get my scythe away from me. You can see how well that worked. I have another scythe sitting at home, or at least my house, on this side of the Vale. When Al and his Detective friend found Liz hanging from shackles, nearly dead, I vowed to kill them all. I was hunting because I was alone. It was me against every other dude with a scythe, and all of them had one thing I didn't. They all had some form of magic held over from their previous life. I was on a reconnaissance mission. They were gathering together regularly now. The ones who should have been reporting to me were reporting to someone else. They probably thought it was funny to leave me doing the job alone instead of taking my place in upper management. The Army taught me to respect the chain of command, it had been broken long before I showed up to shake their cages.

My scythe had an excellent idea of how to take out a few hundred recruits. He transformed into a thin wire, nearly invisible in the foggy night air. I was the distraction for the evening. One thing I learned about the shadow realm was that if it worked in the real world, it worked here. The mausoleum was made of what looked like carved wood. In the real world, wood was flammable; if you had enough gasoline, it was here too. Do you want to know the hilarious thing in all of this? They had wards protecting them from magical flames. They thought denying me access to the rules meant I wouldn't break them. That's the thing they didn't understand, the thing that would be their downfall. *If you want me to follow the rules, I must know them first.*

I used a match to light the flame, mostly because I didn't have a lighter at home. I mean the home here, not the one Soph and I shared. I had a fireplace in my library that looked like it needed a fire. That was how I figured all of this out. I asked Al, too, because he spent some time here. He was pretty smart for a magic dude.

The flames licked their way up the back of the building. The shadow wood burned like old timber. I didn't stick around in the back there. I popped back to the only entrance to watch the show. It didn't take long for a bunch of the bathrobe crew to stampede out the door. They were new and still had some fear of fire. I left them to Ripper. He only took out about thirty of them before they realized the fire wasn't the real danger. The smarter ones simply popped out of the building and tried to suppress the fire. None of the soldiers noticed me, but he did.

His name was Tempest Griffin, but he was calling himself, Ash. The scythe he carried was called Asher because it preferred wielders who died from a fire. Our Liz turned him into a charcoal briquette to avenge my death. Okay, so she'd done it for herself too.

Temp was twirling his scythe in the air like he was leading a marching band. It was so awesome when I did that; he was unremarkable. I made a show of calling Ripper to my hand; then I made him disappear. I was going to teach this asshole how to fight like a human man.

He came at me swinging his scythe over his shoulders like nunchucks. He was trying to intimidate me. I cracked my knuckles and glanced at my hands. I had a pair of black brass knuckles on my fists, but these had little spikes running along the tops of the weapons. Ripper knew just what I wanted to do to this asshole. I preferred bare fists, but he was a reaper like me. I couldn't kill him while he had his scythe, but I could hurt him. I was looking forward to putting the hurt on Tempest Griffin!

I ducked under his swings and hit him in the jaw with a right cross. I followed with my left into his right eye. Blood sprayed from the cuts, and his eye began swelling immediately. Other reapers gathered to watch the fight but stayed far from me. Temp cheated by teleporting behind me, so I twisted and hit him in the head with a roundhouse kick. He wavered, but he didn't go down. Instead, he tried to fry me with fire. Oops, he forgot the rules. He got blasted with his flames when the wards kicked in. He was a little crispy when his fire died, but it did not hurt too badly. His scythe would protect him from the worst of it.

Temp was starting to waver, and he was becoming more cautious. In its natural form, the scythe was unwieldy, making the fighter clumsy. I guess they didn't let Temp read the handbook, either. I could see that he was trying to figure out how I managed to change my scythe, but he couldn't do it. It wasn't me changing Ripper; it was the scythe itself. That meant he possessed the scythe, but his scythe didn't choose him. I could feel the tension between Temp and his weapon.

I didn't dwell on that because Temp kept coming after me. That was fine; I wasn't even close to being done with him. He tried hitting me with magic but forgot the area's rules. His firebolt fizzled out before it reached me. He went back to scythe twirling, and I let him close in. He took one good swing at me, but I just discorporated. His swing never touched me, not that he could kill me while I held my scythe. The establishment wouldn't let me into the secret society so I could read the bylaws, but I didn't need a manual to know what Reapers do. I moved in and punched Temp in his pretty face. I knocked a tooth or two loose when Ripper contacted his jaw. He spat blood onto the ground, but he wasn't down yet. I didn't want him down yet. We were just starting to have some fun with this dance. Unfortunately, duty called me away. I had killed one too many bathrobes, and the Reaping was falling into my hands. I could usually ignore the pull, but this one was strong.

"Just give up the scythe, Costa; I will let you live just like I let Liz live," Temp said as he noticed my distraction.

"You call that living, cabrão? I'm going to kill you for that, Griffin," I replied, taking another swing at him.

One of the capos thought he could pop in behind me and take me out while Temp had my attention. Ripper changed into a short sword. I slid the blade close to my left side, slipping into the Reaper's abdomen like a hot knife in warm butter. The Reaper's scythe clattered to the ground, and I picked it up. It coiled around my arm like a snake and settled on my bicep. It looked like one of those armbands the Vikings wore with runes stamped into it. I didn't have a chance to finish my fun with Temp Griffin. The urge to take a soul was too strong. I was pulled from the shadowlands to the mortal world. I usually arrive just as a person dies, and I take their soul and send it on its merry way. This time was different. We were in the forest somewhere in Washington. The sandy blond hair and light brown eyes on the dead guy were familiar, except the last time I saw Otto, he didn't have a hole where his face should be. His jeans and T-shirt were soaked with blood. He'd been murdered with a shotgun at close range. My heart sank knowing my buddy would never invite me for drinks again. That thought alone fueled my rage. I wasn't a Grim Reaper for nothing, and one thing I knew I could do was raise the dead; I'd done it enough lately.

When Liz did this to me, she was mumbling some words, but I didn't need words; I just had to think Otto was alive and well. It was easier than taking souls from bodies and

395

more fun. I took Otto's hands and pulled him to his feet. As he stood, the scythe on my arm slithered over to his wrist and crawled its way up the sleeve of his denim jacket. His brown eyes went black for a moment as the scythe changed him. I didn't mean to make him a Reaper. It's not a bad gig, considering the alternative, but it wasn't for everyone. Otto's face returned to normal as the black faded from his eyes. His first reaction was to salute me.

"Easy, Sergeant, you've been permanently retired from the army."

"Old habits die hard, Major."

"Tell me about it. I've been trying to get the instruction manuals for the scythe for months. Assholes have me locked out of headquarters."

"I went to your memorial service. I guess this is why they didn't ever find your body."

"Were there many people there? I didn't know I was me at the time. I think it is about how long I was dead."

"Your fiancé?"

"We are about to have a baby. She's still getting used to the Reaper thing; I'm patient."

"Wow, the Grim Reaper will be a daddy again?"

Otto glanced at the pool of blood on the ground. There was no gun, no objective evidence of a crime other than the blood. He would be listed as a missing person, not dead like me. No one would seek vengeance for his murder—but me, The Grim Reaper.

"Sorry about this, man. I didn't realize the scythe would choose you."

"You bring me back from the dead, give me an incredible job, and apologize? I was career military and burned out."

"It's an eternity of monotony. Humans can't see you, and freaking cats will follow you around. Sucks if you are a dog person because they bark at you."

"Cindy got the dog and the house in the divorce. I have been living in base housing. I didn't even unpack my five boxes."

"Well, you won't need that. This job comes with a place, but no Wi-Fi or electricity."

"Ex took the computer, and the assholes that robbed me took my phone, wallet, and gun after they shot me with it."

I put a hand on his shoulder and thought about the place I call my 'man cave.' We both appeared between the desk and the fireplace. The fire I had built earlier was gone, but the place was warm and cozy. I grabbed the whiskey from the drawer and two glasses from the bookshelf. The glasses were new, but the place had a way of knowing what I needed, just like my scythe did. I poured three fingers of the amber liquid into the glasses and passed one to Otto. He was studying the books on the shelf. He always was more of a reader than me. We'd served two tours in Afghanistan together before I was shipped state-side. After Soph and I finally got together, I didn't want to leave her for long periods. We talked about moving closer to the base in Washington, closer to Liz too. My death spoiled that plan and others, but I had things back on track. Liz was rebuilding her house, and the same builders worked on a beach house not far from the Key mansion. I promised myself I would never take Soph away from the ocean, but the island was too dangerous for her and the babies.

"Nice place! Is this where you sleep?"

"You don't need to sleep, eat, or drink anymore," I said as I held the glass up in a mock salute.

397

"We are drinking, but this has the same kick as water," he replied.

"I'll take you somewhere soon where you can get a drink that would kill a raging bear."

"Not our usual dive bars, I imagine."

"It's a club owned by a friend."

"Reapers have friends?"

"Friends, allies, pains in the ass. Whatever you want to call them, I have them."

"I assume there are others like us."

"Nope, none like us. The bathrobe group will want to kill you so they can level up, the capos will want to kill you because you are human, and the big wigs will want to kill you because you are with me."

"Oh, just like old times then, Major," he said, gingerly finishing his drink and setting the glass on the desk.

"Call me Dan, Otto; we are not in the army anymore."

"Funny, it feels like the army," Otto replied.

I finished my drink and slammed the glass on the desk. It was more fun at the bar, but I wanted to keep Otto a secret for now. I still had a lot to learn about being a Grim Reaper, and now I had a student. More important, though, I had an ally with a scythe. It might be two against two thousand, but it was better odds than I had yesterday.

"Maybe it will be an army; we will need one. These fuckers pissed me off."

Otto leaned a hip against the desk, almost knocking the little velvet covered box onto the floor. I grabbed it quickly and slid it into a desk drawer. It was too precious to lose.

"So, how do I get a crib like this?" Otto asked as he watched me closely.

"Just tell your scythe to take you home," I explained.

"Is that what you did?" he asked as he eyed the weapon he still held in one hand.

"This isn't home for me, Buddy; this is the office," I said with a grin.

"Ah, your home is with the raven hair beauty. Sophie, right?"

"She makes me real. I feel alive when I'm with her."

"Strange words, coming from a reaper."

"Well, they keep telling me I am not the type of person they want for a Reaper."

"So, when will you put that ring on Sophie's finger?"

"She already has an engagement ring; this one is for the big day."

"What will that make her? Queen of the dead? Empress of death?"

"Empress of Death, I like how that sounds," I said. I stood to shake Otto's hand. It felt good not to be alone anymore. My friends were cool, but they were alive, and if I had anything to do with it, they would stay that way for a long time.

Otto disappeared, leaving me alone. Ripper, my scythe, teleported himself to his hangout to sleep. It seems weird to even think that a tool slept, but not as odd as him saying goodnight to me. Weirder still, because it was always night in the Shadow Realm.

I would have to reboot my war against the Grims, but this time I had more than fire to surprise them. The next time I saw Temp Griffin, I would show him what I thought of his treatment of Liz. She might be my ex, but she also made me who I am today. I owed her so much more than just my life.

Al

Liz's magic was gone. I could taste something, a remnant of something, like filling your juice glass with water. There would be a hint of juice, but all you were drinking was water. Whatever that mark was made her soul burn. I had to do something; I had to help, not just for her but for all of us. If they could do this to the strongest of us (and I am sure she was though I would never admit it), then what of the others? They would have already killed Alma had I not interfered.

Alma and Sophie took Liz into the bathroom for a shower. Cleaning spells would work well on the mess, but it was easier to open a portal above an active volcano and just levitate any traces of blood through the portal. A waterproof mattress cover saved the bed (don't ask) and the floor made it because of the many rugs. I lost the couch, but I hated it anyway. When the women returned with Liz, the bed had fresh deep purple satin sheets and a new matching duvet. Liz crawled under the covers without a word, which said more than anything how badly she felt. She was still high on vampire venom, which was probably why she slipped into an easy sleep. Sophie slipped into the bed with her, worry clouded her face, but Liz was oblivious. Sophie watched Liz in her fitful sleep. She had tried unsuccessfully to heal Liz and remove the mark no one had seen. Our only proof was the burn marks on Sophie's right hand where she touched Liz's chest.

Alma was tidying up the place like someone who needed something to do. She was also staring daggers at me. I killed Liz in front of her eyes and nearly killed her. If I had been sane, I wouldn't have even tried, it was Brandon's time to die. No one trusted me alone with Liz, but they couldn't take her; they couldn't leave without Brandon, Deathripper, or myself with them. I wasn't even sure that Liz could leave alone without her magic. My wards recognized her because she had made them do it. Breaking through each other's wards was our little game and kept us safe from others. Liz was the only person there who trusted me, and she was the last person who should. I'm not saying that out of guilt. Tasting Liz's blood woke Alias. Whatever spell Liz accidentally cast on me gave me a reprieve from my other personalities, but that was gone, and with that break came more madness. They say only the sane think that they are insane, but only the insane know how to act sane. I was getting good at acting sane. Or at least we thought so. If you were wondering why I was trying to act rational in my own home, you try acting crazy with someone in the room who wanted to kill you hours earlier for acting crazy.

My penthouse was an open room with nooks for sleeping or reading. The only place for privacy was the large bathroom. I couldn't get them all to stop staring at me, even Brand. Maybe it was just my paranoia getting to me. I felt like I needed to get out of there, but I couldn't trust Alma either. It wasn't because she tried to kill me; it was because she might try to take Liz away. Brand broke through the cacophony of my thoughts with a whisper inside my head.

"Time is going by so slowly, it's almost as if it should just stop...maybe we could talk."

I froze Liz and Soph in a small bubble. I couldn't bring Soph in with us without touching her, and she wasn't the one I needed to talk to. I turned to Alma, who had frozen herself, not from my magic, but because she noticed that time had stopped around her. Only two living people knew that I could freeze time…until Alma. I hoped that my trust wasn't a mistake.

"How–" she began.

"The curse that Liz now carries, the one causing insanity, is how; I can freeze time and travel into the past, but not too far back. That is how I saved you from your death."

"You see the future like your father?"

"Not many people had that knowledge, and the rest are dead," I said, sounding more accusatory than I meant it to be.

"I had nothing to do with that; he was a good man. It wasn't his fault he got mixed up with demons," she replied. I had no idea that she knew my father, but she had been around long before I was born. She might look like a woman in her mid-forties, but we don't age like other humans. We are magical people. Brandon tapped his left wrist, indicating that I was wasting time. He had no idea how much time I could waste here. We could talk for days, and it wouldn't even be a heartbeat to them. I hadn't tested to see how far I could save the time bubble. I didn't presume to think that I could freeze the entire world, and I had never thought of the ramifications of altering time…until that moment.

"She's in pain, and it's getting worse," Brandon said, surprising us both. I had been blocking him since we found Liz…or I thought I was.

"The mark? I cannot see anything there, but I feel something. Sophie, poor girl, her hand is healing slowly," Alma murmured so quietly that Brandon hadn't heard her. She knew I would; she knew more about demons than she was letting on.

"I won't apologize for doing what she asked. I wanted to ease her suffering, and I still do. I never meant to kill her, only give her the relief she needed to find her sanity. Do you know about my people? The aliens? Do you know what we can do?"

"Mind manipulation, you can plant memories that aren't real. It is why most don't believe you exist," she replied. She slid onto a chair at the small dining table that served as my second desk. I rarely ate at home unless Liz was there. I like to cook, but cleaning has never been my thing. I think Alma noticed.

"She can do that to me, and so can he," I said, pointing to Brandon.

"I can?" Brandon gulped. He had no idea how easily his human mind could break into my thoughts. I was beginning to think that my alien mind was weaker than the human mind…magic or not.

"You are saying that you are innocent?" Alma scoffed. She folded her arms over her chest in a way that reminded me of Alena when Alias and I had been caught doing something terrible.

"Never! I am saying that Liz was not innocent," I replied defensively.

Brandon sat at the table, leaving me standing and everyone looking up at me. I was back in the classroom with all eyes on me again. I was going to take a chair myself, but Liz's voice broke through the silence.

"I asked him to kill me, Ma. I made it real, and it's rude to talk about someone when they are in the room," Liz commented as she sat up in bed. All eyes turned to Liz and away from me. It didn't make me feel any better because she shouldn't have been able to break through my time bubble.

"Oh, Lizzie! Why?" Alma asked with a tone of motherly concern.

"I was already dead. It was my fate. It was your fate, Brand's fate, and Al's fate. We didn't cheat death; death cheated us," she said, then she laid back down and closed her eyes. Her mind was on a dream of the past, not us. Her moment of clarity was gone. Soph hadn't stirred, so my time bubble was still intact.

"Is she…" Brandon began to ask if Liz was still listening.

"She's lost in the past again," I answered his unasked question. She was gone, frozen in time again. Speaking of Soph, I released the time flow and walked over to place a hand on Soph's shoulder. She had fallen asleep but needed to be part of this discussion. I saw Alma tense when I touched Sophie. I wanted Alma to at least believe that I wouldn't harm anyone in the room. Brand's voice broke through the moment of tension.

"Alma, may I call you Alma? Al is a dark sorcerer, a confessed murderer, a narcissist, and an alien whom you call a demon, but I trust him. I am not under the influence of any spell, potion, or drug, so when I say this, it's as Detective Kennedy. I trust him completely."

"I do too!" Sophie declared as she stood and walked over to the table to join the others. I stayed close to the bed for a moment, watching Liz. I was going to freeze her in time again, but she was truly lost in a dream from the past. It wasn't a good dream, but I've had worse. I turned to address Alma since she was the one who needed reassurance. Sophie had already been through hell with me, and Brandon had died for me. I didn't need any assurance of their loyalty.

"If it makes you feel any better, I don't trust me either, but I promise I won't harm anyone in this room. I am as mad as Liz, maybe more, but my demon brain keeps me from doing anything too crazy. I am going to apologize for trying to kill you; don't get used to it."

"The word is sorry, Alaric," Alma said with a slight smile. She reminded me of Alena, my other mother.

"Sorry, Alma," I said with a respectful bow. Some habits are hard to break, and that was one. Women on Proxima were the rulers, and the leaders and the men were lesser. They'd even found a way for the men to bear and raise the children. It wasn't as sexist as human culture, but men showed respect by bowing. I would never have given my mother that honor, but Alma deserved it. If she understood, she didn't show any sign.

"She's in pain from the mark; it burns her, and I can't heal it. Dan-. Deathripper makes it burn more; that is why he is staying away until I call him," Sophie said. She was rubbing her hand where the burn mark was earlier. If her hands were any larger, we might have been able to look at the mark in mirror form. It was true that Deathripper was staying away because his presence seemed to make Liz uncomfortable…at least that was his take on it. I knew the mark would flair when he was near; I could feel it. Maybe he could too. We already knew the sigil was given to her by a Reaper, so it made sense that a Reaper's presence would cause her pain. It took a lot of searching to find her in her madness. Sometimes I am unsure if I have seen her sanity or if my madness just has a tea party with hers. She gets lost in the past; that is where I've found her most often. The future for her is still vague. That first night, after we died, I wasn't sure I would reach her.

"I can make a potion that might help her. It's not exactly white magic," Alma said, looking at me. "She slept well at first, but I need vampire venom and a lot."

"The vampire in me is a reflection of my brother's soul. I have no venom sack for you to extract. Therefore, your potion would be gray at worst," I explained. We wouldn't have to torture some monster, but I would even do that for Liz. If Alias were alive, I would rip the venom sacks out of his throat, and he knew it. He wasn't the only one holding grudges.

"I need my spelling room, my Ley line, my tools, Sophie and Liz," she said.

"And I need sleep," Brandon replied.

"Liz stays here, I don't want them finding her; only one Reaper can get into this penthouse uninvited. I'll get you your venom, Soph will call your transportation, and we all will get some sleep."

"I won't sleep until I know my Lizzie is normal. They did this to her, her family, her parents, and people like you, Alaric Weird."

"Your Lizzie has been gone since she accepted the darkness; Liz is who she is because it's her nature. Nothing will change that, not this mark, not the curse, not losing her magic. We shape the darkness, but it shapes us too, and you need the dark to appreciate the light, according to my father," I said.

"Your father was not one of them. He was like me, with just a little magic but a lot of knowledge. Your family didn't deserve to die, not all of them. I mourn the passing of the Weird family line," she sighed.

I nodded to her. I understood more than she knew I could. I didn't need a connection to understand that she meant the Weirds were gone in her eyes because those of us descended from them were demons, not pure blood. She wasn't being racist or bigoted; it was just a fact. It had been why I wanted the curse. The curse made us who we are and could make us again, but I knew now, looking at Liz, that the price for that was too high. Maybe it was a good thing for the curse to die in demon blood. No one should have to live in madness. I needed that book, the Key Grimoire. If I could use it to curse, maybe we could find a cure for Liz. If not, I needed it to keep her safe. They were draining her after they took her magic. That meant what they needed was in her DNA, not magic. That was why I wouldn't let Alma take her, not because I thought she was safer with me.

"I know that you don't trust Al, Alma, so trust me," Brandon said. He stood, kicked off his shoes, and walked over to the bed, then sat and put a hand on Liz's shoulder. She stirred, then moved to the edge of the bed, away from Brandon. It was probably her actions, more than anything, that made Alma relax a little. Liz was getting more accustomed to sleeping in my bed.

"Why don't you get cleaned up, and I'll drive you home, Ma," Sophie commented.

"I suppose it would be better not to go home in the same clothes I left in," Alma replied. I had completely forgotten that Brandon had driven her here the day before. She gathered her bag and headed for the bathroom. Sophie had been the last to arrive, but she looked weary too. Before I could comment, she said, "I'm fine, Al, just very pregnant."

"Now, who is mind reading?"

"More like face reading, and no, I am not hungry. Just tired. He will make me eat when I get home, hungry or not."

She stood and walked over to the library. It had glass walls and an archway for a door and was the only penthouse room with no windows. The books inside were too precious to be exposed to direct sunlight. The desk sat close to the interior glass wall making it very visible. It had been my mistake to leave the Key Grimoire there for anyone to see. I had reason to mistrust Alma, but I didn't have to read her mind to know that she thought the same thing. None of this would have happened if she hadn't taken the book.

Sophie sat at the desk and opened the book on angels and demons I had left on the desk. Brandon had dozed off seated against the headboard. Liz was tossing and turning in her sleep. The stress of the last few days had even made me tired. I crawled between my two friends and pulled Liz close. She laid her head on my arm and relaxed in her sleep. She was dreaming of the past again, her childhood. My nightmares were of the future, but my past had been easier than hers. As soon as I settled on my back, Brand rolled over and snuggled close. Neither of them woke, though their heads were nearly touching. I hadn't slept like this since my two older children were young. I managed to doze off after a while. I woke to find Alma looking at me quizzically.

"Do you have children?" she asked.

"I do. Four of my own, three from my magical clone, and three stepchildren. I also have a grandson," I whispered. She looked surprised at that but shrugged it off. She knew the secrets of staying young as well as I did. She also knew that I was not human.

"Good! I am ready to go home," she said with a nod, "I will need the venom as soon as possible." She was determined to leave, and I wouldn't stop her.

"It will be waiting for you when you get home. Don't ask," I replied. I made a portal to the parking garage. Sophie closed her book, and the two women entered the open doorway. I closed my eyes for some much-needed rest. I had seen a little of what we faced in the future. The magical community wanted Liz for some evil curse; the Grims wanted her gone. We needed that book and what they had done to take her magic. I drifted off to a fitful dream with those thoughts in my mind.

Stay tuned for **DEATH MARK**, Book Two of the Grim Sorcery Series releasing in 2024.

DEADLY CONNECTIONS

Acknowledgments

This book would not have been possible were it not for Daniel B., our Grim Reaper and best friend. He believed in us when everyone else tried to tear us down. Daniel has valiantly defended and protected our characters and ourselves from those who wanted to ruin everything we worked so hard for. He sacrificed his time, effort, and even, at times, his health to make sure our dream could become a reality. Daniel was the one who introduced us to each other, and we are both grateful. We started this journey together in December of 2021, and it has been a very rough year, especially for our Deathripper. Daniel tirelessly encouraged us and sat with us through long nights. He read every word of English, though he is not a reader or a native English speaker. He supported us through all of it, even from a hospital bed. I hope you can get a sense of Daniel through his character, but if not, just know that he is one of the best. You won't find many men so honest, caring, and generous.

They say that good men are hard to find, but Sofia and I have found two. My husband, Jim Jones, has gone to bed many nights alone because I couldn't stop writing. He has encouraged me since the beginning. He helped me come up with a few plot points and helped me through some rough spots. He helped me create the character of Alias and even helped me name Al. Our thanks go to these two men who stuck by us through the good and worst times.

About the Authors

B.J. is a proud member of the LGBTQIA+ community living in the scenic Pacific Northwest, USA, with their husband, Jim, and two cats, Dex and Jax. They have been an avid reader since early childhood. This year will mark the 20th year of love for B.J. and Jim and the 20th year of Al Weird's existence. B.J. has been writing stories and fanfiction for most of their life. They graduated from business school in 2001 and work in retail when not writing fantasy.

Sofia is a reader, gamer, and photography enthusiast living in Northern Portugal with her mother, MR, nephew, R, and cat, Kika. When she was little, her sister introduced her to fantasy, and ever since, Sofia has carried fiction worlds and characters in her heart hoping one day she would be able to create her own. Writing is therapeutic for her; her first attempt to write a book was at age 14. When she is not caring for her family, you can find her on her computer playing/writing/rendering and listening to music or snuggling in bed with a good book (usually in English even though her native language is Portuguese).

Though he would swear he is not a writer, Daniel B. has written some of the words in this book. He won't take credit because we took his words and made them part of the story. Neither of us could have done this without him, and though we thank him in the acknowledgments, he has his place here, too. Dan also lives in Northern Portugal.

DEADLY CONNECTIONS

About the Book

This book is a collaboration of two stories written we wrote separately before we met. Al Weird has been around for a few decades; I have written blogs and short stories about him and the Weird family for many years. If you are wondering, his name pays homage to Weird Al, an incredible musician and artist. All the Weirds in Al's family are named "Al Weird," whether male or female. There is quite a backstory on the Weird family that will be unveiled to you should you wish to continue your journey with us. No spoilers!

Sophie and Dan have been in blogs and online stories for a few years. Sofia's writing style was so similar to mine that I knew our stories could blend like pancake ingredients. Dan first introduced me to Sofia in December of 2021. She and I had both been bullied and harassed due to the content of our stories. Daniel involved me in helping him find a cure for Sophie's curse that didn't involve magic. He was the genius that brought us together, introduced us, and began our journey. Dan truly gets the credit for the existence of this book. He is our inspiration, our biggest fan, and our Alpha reader. We hope to keep him reading for many years. This first story has been over a year in the making and has caused us some tears of sorrow and joy. We've collected our share of haters as we tried to protect our characters and our work from copying and downright theft.

There are words in here that your average English speaker won't understand. Dan, the person is Portuguese and our Grim is also of Portuguese descent, so he occasionally swears in Portuguese.

413